A year of wonder ...
A year of change ...
A year of conjecture ...

And a year of science fiction in books and magazines, in short stories and novelettes, in new magazines and in old ones.

How did those in whose eyes the future is always reflected see the year?

In this long-established anthology series of the best of the year, you can see for yourself.

This is one science fiction collection no one can afford to miss.

Anthologies from DAW

THE 1977 ANNUAL WORLD'S BEST SF
THE 1978 ANNUAL WORLD'S BEST SF
THE 1979 ANNUAL WORLD'S BEST SF
THE 1980 ANNUAL WORLD'S BEST SF
THE 1981 ANNUAL WORLD'S BEST SF

WOLLHEIM'S WORLD'S BEST SF: Vol. 1
WOLLHEIM'S WORLD'S BEST SF: Vol. 2
WOLLHEIM'S WORLD'S BEST SF: Vol. 3
WOLLHEIM'S WORLD'S BEST SF: Vol. 4
WOLLHEIM'S WORLD'S BEST SF: Vol. 5

THE BEST FROM THE REST OF THE WORLD

ASIMOV PRESENTS THE GREAT SF STORIES: 1
ASIMOV PRESENTS THE GREAT SF STORIES: 2
ASIMOV PRESENTS THE GREAT SF STORIES: 3
ASIMOV PRESENTS THE GREAT SF STORIES: 4
ASIMOV PRESENTS THE GREAT SF STORIES: 5
ASIMOV PRESENTS THE GREAT SF STORIES: 6

TERRA SF

THE 1982 ANNUAL
WORLD'S BEST SF

Edited by

DONALD A. WOLLHEIM

with Arthur W. Saha

DAW BOOKS, INC.

DONALD A. WOLLHEIM, PUBLISHER

1633 Broadway, New York, NY 10019

FIRST PRINTING, MAY 1982

1 2 3 4 5 6 7 8 9

DAW TRADEMARK REGISTERED
REGISTRADA. HECHO EN U.S.A.
U.S. PAT. OFF. MARCA

PRINTED IN U.S.A.

Table of Contents

INTRODUCTION *The Editor*   vii

BLIND SPOT *by Jayge Carr*   11
Copyright © 1981 by Omni Publications International, Ltd.; reprinted by permission of the author and her agent, Valerie Smith.

HIGHLINER *by C. J. Cherryh*   31
Copyright © 1981 by C. J. Cherryh, from the book *Sunfall.* By permission of the author.

THE PUSHER *by John Varley*   59
Copyright © 1981 by Mercury Press, Inc. By permission of the author's agent, Kirby McCauley.

POLYPHEMUS *by Michael Shea*   76
Copyright © 1981 by Mercury Press, Inc. By permission of the author.

ABSENT THEE FROM FELICITY
       AWHILE . . . *by Somtow Sucharitkul* 129
Copyright © 1981 by Davis Publications, Inc. By permission of the author.

OUT OF THE EVERYWHERE
       by James Tiptree, Jr. 143
Copyright © 1981 by James Tiptree, Jr. By arrangement with the author and with Ballantine Books, Inc.

SLAC// *by Michael P. Kube-McDowell* 181
Copyright © 1981 by Davis Publications, Inc. By permission of the author.

THE CYPHERTONE *by S. C. Sykes* 207
Copyright © 1981 by Davis Publications, Inc. By permission of the author.

THROUGH ALL YOUR HOUSES
       WANDERING *by Ted Reynolds* 222
Copyright © 1981 by Davis Publications, Inc. By permission of the author.

THE LAST DAY OF CHRISTMAS
       by David J. Lake 276
Copyright © 1981 by Paul Collins for *Distant Worlds*. By permission of the author's agent, Valerie Smith.

INTRODUCTION

"It was the best of times; it was the worst of times." That was Dickens' comment on the crisis of the 18th Century. It could apply now to the outlook for many periods of the 20th. There were the times just before the great wars—and just after. There were the times before the economic crises that have racked this century . . . the times of ideological debate, of fog and confusion . . . times confronting the advent of surprising new scientific achievements.

It applies to this year, when various problems are coming to a head simultaneously. These are problems concerning the livelihood of millions and yet also involving the possibility of great events in the years to come that could dwarf all that had gone before. We think of space stations and orbital shuttles, and then we think of nuclear warheads and unemployment. We think of the right to speak freely and then of the necessity of curbing incendiaries. We talk of democracy, then of military dictators who talk of democracy.

Science fiction is accepted as the medium of prognostication. It tells of times to come when today's crises will have faded and tomorrow's strange new crises will be at the fore. It tells of an infinite universe full of infinite wonders—and sometimes, all too often today, it tells of devastation and the Earth returned five thousand years to primitive ways and a bare hunter-gatherer existence.

Science fiction is, like all literature, a form of escape reading. More so than most because it requires a farther-out imagination and because it depends on readers who are already aware of the potentials of things to come—and things that have been or might have been.

This year has been a year of uncertainty in the realm of science fiction/fantasy writings. Reflecting, as SF does in its subtle way, the time in which it is written, this year's batch of imaginative constructions seems to lack the exuberant high spots of some past years. Instead there are two tendencies we detect. One such is a pondering of the inner problems of the day, the meaning of man in a confused and shifting world. The other is more escapist and more like the great SF of the

past—it has to do with aliens, inhabitants of other worlds, beings of other intelligent species.

The big feature of the past year was Carl Sagan's remarkable television series and accompanying book, *Cosmos*. In
this, which held the attention of millions, was embodied exactly the real problem of our time. Can our planet, our species, overcome the problem of controlling atomic energy and
our own dissentions of politics—and survive? Can we, as it
were, graduate from the cruel school of learning how to be
the dominant species of a life-bearing planet and thereby enjoy the fruits of a thousand generations of struggling ancestors? Or shall we go out to extinction like a million minor
species before us? Or, as Sagan put it, like a myriad other
worlds' would-be star conquerors?

The message of *Cosmos* struck me as being simpler and yet
greater than all the slogans of patriotism and jingoism. It was
simply this—grow up! Put away the overkill weapons you
dare not use. Face up to the facts of living together in peace
and progress—or die.

That this thought is becoming more and more part of the
consciousness of all mankind—working its way against the
tide of emotion-charged political sloganeering—is evident if
you seek out the signs. This is the undercurrent which dis-
plays itself occasionally in science fiction and even in fantasy
—and which we hope will someday dominate the world's
thinking.

In the realm of literature, fantasy is taking more and more
of a role. Not surprising since writers themselves do not know
how to answer the questions of today and so resort pure
imagination, to the spinning of adult fairy tales. To take the
mind off unpleasant reality, spin a tale of wonders in lands
without locataion.

Fantasy in another form has achieved a new high in general
paperback publishing—the "sweet romance" novel is in its
cyclic rise—and millions of women are burying themselves in
these fantasies of young love and chivalric romance. Yet this
category of book is as much fantasy as any science fiction.
The dreams they spin are far from the realism of today's life,
of real love and marriage today. But here again, fantasy is
an elixir that restores minds and helps them face up to day
by day realities.

We mentioned aliens in the science fiction of the past year.
Without deliberately thinking about it, in the course of select-

ing stories for this anthology, seeking tales of special interest, with qualities of the unusual and those extra perks of the imagination, we notice that a high percentage of what we deemed best dealt in one way or another with aliens and their impact on Earthly humanity. But these stories even so confront the times in which they were written and published.

Lest this introduction seem to be gloomy, let me assure you that such is not my intention. I speak of light in darkness. Where there is imagination and faith in the universe, faith in the stubborn life-force of humanity, there is always a spark of light and always a way.

You will find these stories on a par with some of the best of previous years. They will give you enjoyment, they will perk the mind, they uphold the best traditions and meaning of science fiction.

—DONALD A. WOLLHEIM

BLIND SPOT

by Jayge Carr

Although the human being is the most vicious predatory beast on the planet, art and music have always been a contrary and redeeming characteristic throughout existence. The contradiction between the "animal" side of our nature and what must be called the "divine" side is precisely that drive for the appreciation of beauty in sight and sound. These cross-currents in the substance of high intelligent life are the basis of this moving tale.

Some of a doctors duties are hard—and some even harder.

"You're blind." Lip unconsciously caught between his teeth, he faced the mirror. "You're blind. Totally, incurably, and permanently blind." His holo image stared back at him; hairless, pale skin over neatly muscled bones, a sensitive mouth, cruelly jutting cheekbones, and E-norm ears flat to the narrow skull. And the eyes: jewel-faceted like an insect's, glittering silver. The prosthetic eyes that could see macroscopic or microscopic, in a range of wavelengths much broader than human norm, in a full three-hundred-sixty-degree scan, as if his head and body weren't there or were transparent.

He ordered the holo mirror to show him in the latest fashion in reflective body paint: a splashy chrome- and vermilion-distorted houndstooth check.

"You're blind, and there's nothing medical science can do."

He replaced the houndstooth with an intricate pattern of paisley tears in gold/orange/turquoise/scarlet, his own natural skin color, a shadowy blue-gray, showing between.

"There's nothing medical science can do, but there are prosthetics that we can use."

He ordered his eyes to "see" in infrared, decided he didn't like the pattern in that mode, and replaced two of the colors with heat paints. To normal vision, heat paints were merely a subtle, haze; in infrared a transparent color unlike anything "seen" in normal range. He made a few minor adjustments to the pattern and shut his eyes. Holding his breath, he ordered the autovalet to spray, and he felt the warmth envelop him. Very good! The pattern had been faithfully transferred. Only . . . it looked a little . . . incomplete.

"Prosthetics," he repeated aloud, his mind still with his Very Important Patient.

At his mental command, the holo image added a long scarf in a complementary color. He experimented with various drapes, added a few hundred angstroms to the shade and nodded to himself. The autovalet obediently dispensed a long strip of cloth. He held it up against himself, approved the shade, and arranged it carefully with the neat movements of a man who splices living nerves. Some preferred to have the autovalet do it all, but he felt the results, when it came to actual synthetic materials, were a little artificial.

He ordered true image again and stiffened his spine. He was ready.

The patient was sitting in the solarium, as she always was when she was free of testing or therapy, her face turned toward the sun she could no longer see except as the palest blur—and not even that for much longer.

She turned toward him as he approached, the rippling floor carrying him along with a barely perceptible hum. And despite the fine, downy white hair that covered her face (and her body, too) he knew that she knew what he was going to say. Her soft "Well, Doctor," was anticlimactic.

He ordered a seat, and the floor formed one. He sat down before answering. "I have the results of the latest test."

"How much longer?"

"Before the deterioration of the optic nerve is complete and total? Between twenty and thirty days."

"Ah!" A deep, shuddering sigh. She took the blow well; he had to admire her gallant spirit. He wondered whether she looked as ugly to her own people as she did to him, or was her ugliness merely the product of a different world, a different culture? She was short and round, totally covered with the velvety, milk-white fur. She never used any kind of body paint. Her nose was broad, lying against her flat cheeks; the inside of her nostrils, the lips, and the naked tips of the huge furred ears were black like an animal's.

"And the other possibilities?" she asked.

"We'll try autotransplants first," he told her patiently, as if she hadn't heard it all a dozen times before. "We'll control-clone new nerves and try to graft them in. It's a tricky procedure all around. It can succeed. I've used it successfully myself many times." *You're the problem*, he was thinking. Many high-T worlds had low-T enclaves, peopled with those who rejected the technology for religious or other reasons or who had been isolated and had never developed it. And the records showed in an amazing number of cases that when those low-T people were exposed to high-T procedures, especially delicate medical procedures, those procedures failed. The mind rejected or disbelieved, and the body followed. Her preliminary tests had not been promising. But he was the best; he'd never failed a patient before. And he wouldn't fail this supremely important one.

"What if the grafts fail to—take?" she asked, her ugly face, with the visual augmenters that made it even uglier, turned toward him.

"We've discussed that," he replied. "We'll have to go to the prosthetics, with a direct mind interface."

Her hands clenched. He saw the effort she needed to unclench them. "Yes." Her voice was calm, but it was the calmness of a thin net holding back an avalanche. "We've discussed it. Do you really think your artificial eyes will be usable? Do you imagine that I will be able to continue my work, using dead . . .?" She left the sentence unfinished.

She was ugly, but she was a genius—a genius whose works were revered, almost worshiped, throughout the inhabited galaxy. It was his responsibility to restore that genius so that it could continue those deathless creations of sublime art. He gritted his teeth. "I assure you, if it comes to that, you won't even be able to tell the difference."

"I will." That utter assurance that geniuses need to have now turned against him—and her own future. "I will."

"Treat the patient as well as the problem," one of his professors had been fond of saying. But how was he to treat this strange off-worlder whose precious eyes were deteriorating daily? This primitive from a culture so degenerate that, had it not been for luck and some determined missionaries, she would have spent her entire life in the wild, grubbing for roots, speaking in grunts, fighting with every other member of her species she met except, of course, during the rutting season.

Now—a genius. Unique. Honored and adored. And facing the worst of all fates, the loss of what made her what she was.

"I have a reproduction of one of your works. Did I tell you that?"

"Yes," she said, nodding. "You mentioned it. *Mayflight in the Morning.* One of my earliest and best. What size is it?"

"I hold it in my hand."

He remembered his surromother bringing in the program, crooning. She had said that the artist would be recognized as a genius, and she had been right. He remembered her inserting the program, waiting that fraction of a second while the machine constructed the artifact. The children had surged forward, irresistibly drawn toward the strange concatenations of subtle curves and infinite interplays of color and texture. But the first child to touch it had jerked back as the piece sang with the gentlest tinkling voice.

"It's a multisense piece." the surromother had told them. "You feel it, you look at it, and when you touch it, it sings. Here—" She programmed for two more copies and passed them around so that there was a chorus of fairy voices. "I understand the original had scent and taste, too. You could lick it, but since it was made by an off-worlder, whose sensory judgments might be different from ours, those have been suppressed."

"An off-worlder?" he had asked, reluctantly passing the piece along (share-and-share) to his neighbor. One day, he had promised himself, he would have one of those for his very own. And he had kept that promise.

"Yes, the artist was discovered by a group of missionaries and was brought here, to be properly trained and to have her works disseminated through our simultaneity projector. And quite right, too. Such talent belongs to all worlds. Ironically, though, thanks to the relativistic effects on the voyage—you do know about relativistic time effects at almost the speed of light, don't you, children?—while she was traveling from her world to ours, her own world was able to acquire both a simultaneity projector of its own and technicians to service it. But their loss is our gain."

"It sings soprano in that size," the genius who created it told him, as if he hadn't heard the song a thousand times. "And do you like what it sings?"

"Yes . . . no," he admitted. "It makes me sad sometimes. I don't know why, and yet I can't keep my fingers off it, even though I know its song is likely to make me sad."

She smiled, and her almost blind eyes looked at him and saw something else. "When you understand the song, you'll understand what the difference is, and why it's so important."

"We'll try the grafts first," he said firmly.

Three times he painstakingly inserted and spliced the fragile nerves, then supervised the slow recovery. And three times something in her rejected them. A normal person would be satisfied with the sight they gave her. But she was not normal. She was a genius. She demanded perfection, or perhaps something beyond, something that made her subtle creations possible. She would not be satisfied with anything less, and three times the implanted nerves withered and died.

They tried the prosthetics next. He did the delicate work, the implanting of the organically neutral interfaces, the almost unnoticeable (because he was sure that this was what she wanted) exterior scanners. And though it wasn't his personal responsibility, he watched over her therapy, his face twisted into a frown as again and again she lurched through the obstacle course. A genuinely blind subject would have done better. And this from a mind that could curve shapes together into the subtlest of relationships, an artist whose works were balanced to within a microgram, a millimeter.

"It's not seeing. I can't *see*," she insisted over and over. Often her control would fail, and she would pound on the nearest objects with her hard, bony fists, bruising those fingers that had worked miracles.

He had carefully adjusted her prosthetics to normal vision. He tested them repeatedly, showing her how the graphs matched up, how the prosthetics were well within the tolerances.

And still she fought—or wept. "I can't see."

He tried to comfort her, but she only turned away. No one else in the giant hospital complex had any better luck. He thought of getting her foster parents to help, but they were missionaries of a rootless sect on whose homeworld religion had died centuries before, and they had already moved on, not wanting to linger in a world that denied the need for what they offered. Now they were on another endless voyage to another primitive world, riding one of the giant wombships, hollowed-out asteroids that carried the necessities of life from world to world. Wombships traveled more slowly than light, but they were fast enough that their voyages involved relativistic time contraction. People aboard the ships lived months while decades passed on the worlds they visited. Only simultaneity projectors could exceed the speed of light, and they were limited to transmitting knowledge, programs, and nonmaterial information.

"Don't keep showing me your machine-made charts. They're wrong, they're all wrong. I can't *see!*"

He searched for others on this world who might help—teachers, lovers, friends. But she had so surpassed her teachers, and so quickly, that she had formed no lasting relationships with any of them. As for lovers or friends, she was an alien, an off-worlder, obsessed with her work. She had none. Her life had been her art, and her art her life, and now she had lost it.

There were a dozen rehabilitation centers in the giant medical complex. Physical therapy, occupational therapy (the cruelest failure of all), many varieties of mental gymnastics—and she tried every one of them unsuccessfully.

"I can't see."

Failure. *His* failure. His *first* failure.

He should have been glad when she announced, "I'm going home."

But in his own way he was as fanatical about his work as she was about hers. First he ordered no, as her doctor. When she laughed in his face, he threatened, cajoled, begged, tried to have her declared mentally incompetent, sulked when that failed, and always, always argued. Usually she ignored him Once, when he accused her of deliberately denying her art to the worlds, she answered wearily, "My world has simultaneity projectors now, like any *civilized* world. Or at least the cresters do." It was the first time he realized that her world was populated by two separate races.

"I'm a trog," she asserted matter-of-factly. "But the cresters aren't fools. They've enjoyed the prestige of my work for years, simply because I come from their world. If I ever manage to work again, they'll trip over themselves rushing to program duplicates through the simultaneity projectors for other worlds to admire."

"I'm going with you," he declared.

"What?" She was incredulous. Then, "Why? Love? It's physically impossible, you know."

"I'm a doctor," he reminded her.

"Then you'd know better than I. But it hasn't stopped—the infatuates, the worshipers, those who tried to translate artistic admiration into something more physical."

"I'm a doctor," he repeated stubbornly. "You're my patient."

She shook her head. "You don't know the 'floor.' You can't imagine . . . believe me, there's nothing, *nothing* you can do."

For once immovable object met irresistible force. "Your world is primitive, except for a few high-T enclaves. I know that. All right. I'll just have to be careful to bring everything I might need with me, that's all."

"Doctor—" She took a deep breath, for the first time moving those unseeing eyes away from him. "It isn't just the primitiveness. My world is far away. We couldn't get a direct route. We'll be lucky if we have to change wombships only once. In real time that's fifty years, a hundred, or more, for the trip. If you ever returned here, all your friends, children, family—all will be dead or changed almost beyond recognition. And your profession—"

"If I ever return, I'll catch up, professionally and personally. But if it's such a bad trip, why are you taking it?"

"I'm going home," she muttered. And he told himself he didn't hear two more unsaid words: to die.

He consulted a reference library about her world and found out why she didn't want him to go. Her world was even more primitive than he had thought. The trogs lived on the forest floor, in an eternal night produced by the shadows of the giant leaves in the crests of immense trees, animals among animals, without language, clothing, tools, or society.

The cresters were a different race entirely; they lived in the sunlight, in the tops of the huge trees. Not much was known about them except that they were bioengineers with the highest skills. Crester plants, for food or cloth or simply exotic beauty, were valuable exports that had paid for the simultaneity projector that was installed and for the technicians willing to exile themselves from their homeworlds to keep the device running.

Some of the other information about them was confusing or simply unbelievable. (Cultivating on giant leaves? Irrigating *leaves*?) Most physical trading was done through the wombships. And the simultaneity projector disseminated all kinds of art and information, but the cresters were not so foolish as to pass on the secrets of their skills.

The doctor absorbed all the information he could, and when his patient boarded the wombship, he was right behind her.

The wombers refused payment. (They revered the artist and her work.) And the doctor agreed to spend time and skills on patients aboard the ship. He even trained as many healers as possible in whatever skills he could pass on.

He never asked what the wombshippers thought of her, as a person, or what they thought of him for that matter, but he was fascinated by them.

For thousands of years wombshippers had been pariahs. But they were also the only thread that held the human worlds together, that is, the worlds colonized by humans, or what had been humans before they adapted to their new environments. Each isolated world thought of itself as the norm, its people as human, and anyone different—and the wombship pariahs were invariably different—as not human.

Then the simultaneity projector was developed, linking the worlds together with pictures. World after world realized that *all* of their thousands of brother and sister worlds held intelligent beings who were different yet "human."

Some worlds reacted by raising their barriers higher, rejecting projectors and wombships alike.

Some rejected only the projectors, grudgingly allowing the alien pariah wombshippers to trade.

And some transcended their insularity, their prejudices, and recognized that it was the soul, not the body or the culture, that was important.

And the pariahs, too, were a culture—a culture formed by countless years of rejection and by the radiation they couldn't shield against entirely, that killed many of them in their physiological teens and twenties. It was a cosmic irony that one of the reasons why they were rejected was that they seemed immortal, possessing the immortality that relativistic time contraction at almost light velocities gave them so that they would return after fifty planetary years and seem only a few months older. The truth was that their actual life spans were much shorter than those of most planet-bounds.

The wombship itself was a spaghetti tangle of corridors and living spaces. The doctor's guide was a tall, thin, but prepubescent female, bald and radiation scarred, whose vocabulary consisted of "Essr" and "Nossr" and whose jaw continually worked on something. He preferred not to speculate on what it was. The first time she took his hand and they were, with no transition he could detect, someplace else, he nearly had a heart attack. Eventually he learned to appreciate the speed of travel and to be thankful that his hosts had assigned him a guide capable of taking him as well as herself "through." He did what research he could on psionics, another gift of radiation, but his results were contradictory, and with a sigh he simply accepted.

There were plenty of medical problems to occupy his time, and doing what he could for the wombers helped keep his mind off the continued deterioration of his prime patient. Over the months he became friendly with many of the wombers, mostly the medical staff, and especially their chief, a wizened gremlin of a woman with the unlikely sobriquet of Camel. But when he told her his pet theory regarding his patient, she only threw back her head and laughed.

"This is the wrong place to talk about back to the womb, you know." She sobered. "But it's certainly one of our major problems. If that's her trouble, you needn't worry. She'll decide to stay here, and we've developed a few"—a toothless grin—"techniques that might prove effective. Anyway, once a diagnosis is confirmed, you're more than halfway to a cure. But I think you're off the mark. Way off. I've talked to her myself, and I think she's just following instinct. Sometimes following one's instinct is the smartest thing to do."

"Even if it means going back to a primitive, scratch-for-a-living world?"

Camel shrugged. "You see it that way. But she wants to go *home*"—all the longing of a people denied a permanent home for generations contained in that one word. "Sometimes that's the best—and only—medicine."

He grew to like the wombshippers, to find in their company a relief from the continual frustration of his primary task. He was almost sorry when the voyage ended.

But nothing on the tapes had prepared him for the frantic vitality of the world called (not by its own people) Sequoia Upper.

It was hard to remember he was in the crest of a giant tree. He seemed to be walking on a thick, resilient carpet, muddy aqua (the basic plant color here). The gently moving, ever-changing "walls" were like a halo abstract; actually they were leaves, vines, stalks, growths, saprophytes, tendrils, some close, some far away, the whole blurring into a panorama of relentless growth.

"It's as if the very air were alive and growing," he told his guide, a short, prehensile-tailed male whose costume revealed no fewer than six apparently functional nipples as well as indisputable evidence of masculinity. (The doctor learned later that the costumes—all the "clothes" in fact—were plants, stem and hair roots concealed somewhere in the fur or manes, the rest growing in a controlled pattern around the sequoian wearing them.)

"Rainforest, I believe it's called," the guide commented, politely. "Though I understand on other worlds what they call rainforest would be a strand of sprouts not yet ready to be transplanted here. Now this tree, called baldcypress"—he waved his hand, and the doctor, who hadn't seen any trace of structure or point of division, wondered whether everything he saw wasn't part of a single organism—"has sprouted an ancient and honorable family; I myself"—a deprecating gesture, but a smug grin over it—"am proud to be an acknowledged branch of the hundred ninety-seventh generation nurtured within its leaves." He obviously expected a reaction. When it didn't come, he made a disappointed moue and went on, "So this entire tree is quite well cultivated and most tame. If you wish to visit one of the wilder trees, it can be arranged."

The doctor heard his patient mutter something under her breath.

"And of course"—the guide was obviously working up to an oration—"if there's anything you need, for any reason, we'll be pleased, and proud, and honored, to be allowed to serve, in however minor a fashion—"

The doctor tuned out the rest; he'd sat through banquets before.

It was then that a fluff of silver tendrils drifted against his patient's cheek. Automatically he reached over to pluck it off, but her hand was quicker. With a facile gesture that spoke of long habit, she grasped it, slid it into her mouth, and sucked on the arsenic-green roundness below the pale parachute.

He opened his mouth to protest, but she had already spit the thing out, not a gesture of distaste, but rather an absent-minded expulsion of something sucked dry of interest. It tumbled along the surface until he couldn't see it any longer.

She didn't drop dead, and before he could lick his dry lips and *ask*, his guide interrupted his monologue long enough to repeat the gesture, this time with a thing like two gray wings run together but no bigger than his finger.

This time he did ask, and the guide laughed and caught something from the air and put it to his lips. Five minutes later the doctor was still mulling over the multiple subtleties of his first taste of sequoia.

There was so much to assimilate, so many flavors and smells and customs and whatnot, that adapting to life on the wombship had been like preform play, while this was final specialization residency. But he was enjoying it—part of him even wallowed in the VIP treatment—until his patient told him the truth.

"We're both pariahs, you know."

He didn't believe her. He'd been escorted through some of their finest research strands of planting (though he still wasn't sure whether the sprouts were merely being nurtured on their leaf fields or whether they were products of the leaves themselves), wined and dined and deferred to and flattered and listened to and even entertained in an ancient but still appreciated fashion.

She interrupted his protests by reaching over and tapping the wall of the room they were in, one of several that was "theirs" for the duration. "Dead," she said simply "Dead wood." She tapped again, and it was a dull sound. "The ultimate insult in their language is 'Go live in deadwood.' " She spat, and he watched the green-tinged liquid disappear into the floor. "Or is it merely the penultimate insult?" she mused aloud. "Go live with the trogs. Yes, I think that is the ultimate. And I wonder which of us they despise more, me, the trog, or you, the trog lover." A breath. "Doctor."

"Yes?" He wondered about something himself: what the penalty was here for a doctor strangling his patient?

"Take my advice. Take the next wombship away from here, no matter where it's going. Just *go*. Get away. This isn't your world, and ultimately it will reject you."

"You're my patient, and I'm going to cure you. I promise."

"Blind, blind," she murmured. "But which of us is it that will not see?"

Three days later she was gone.

"Once a trog, always a trog," said the incredibly old woman coldly.

"And that's it. Throw her and her potential away." He had bulled his way up to this Sequoian Ultimate Authority in a barely controlled rage.

"She's a trog," the woman muttered. Something fluttered through the air and landed against her cheek. Her fingers went up in a caressing gesture, and—he blinked—had those fingers somehow flicked the airborne wisp away, or had it been absorbed into the crepey, powdery old skin?

"And that covers it," he heard himself snarling. Some of the leaves from the plant he'd been forced to wear fluttered away from his mouth, and he saw her flinch. That plant had driven home his patient's point, about his being a pariah. It clung to and covered every inch of skin and gave off a rank odor. Even the windbornes kept away from him, and he knew it for what it was: this world's equivalent of a contamination suit. Nothing of him must infect their happy lives. "Just throw her away. She's a trog, a worthless, useless animal of a trog. All right, all right then. But don't be surprised at how other worlds react to what you've done. Other worlds have values different from yours. They might see your actions in an unflattering light. On other worlds racial prejudice is considered—"

"Prejudice!" She was slight and slender, antique and fragile. "Off-worlder, you came here, *knowing* you knew all there was to know about us. You look and you do not see. You are a—a dissonance, a flaw in our lives, a wrongness we cannot right. Yet we have made you welcome. And in return you would tell other worlds about the sins that we committed only in your mind." She stood, one hand against a leaf that formed the "wall" of this cozy nook, and tiny tendrils twined around her arm. He had a sudden vision of woman and tree, unity, a single living organism.

"Your prejudice," he said, but more calmly, "drove her off this world in the first place. And now it has driven her down to her death."

"*Our* prejudice? Prejudice means prejudging, doesn't it? Were we given a chance, or were we prejudged, off-worlder? Some people see only what they want to see, and perhaps the motives of those so-called selfless missionaries ought to be examined more closely." He caught his lip, remembering a news holo of an awards ceremony; there had been several off-worlders with the artist then, all of them radiating a complacent, almost arrogant pride. "The trog was spirited away from here. Did you know that? Because my predecessors protested at the very thought. And after, when we warned that she would be damaged away from her home, when we asked that she be returned, we were sneered at, accused of wanting to keep her treasures selfishly to ourselves, accused—it was sickening. And no one believed us, as you don't believe us now." She shrugged. "We could prove all we have said, but you, outlander, with your closed mind, have already determined our guilt. Would you believe the truth if it were right in front of you?"

"Try me."

"It will be dangerous."

"For you or for me?" He couldn't help sneering.

"So be it." Her pale lips were tight, and the very wall of living plant seemed to shudder with her restrained anger.

The only way down, short of the dangerous climb down the clifflike trunk, was by being lowered, at dizzying speed on immensely long vines.

The others were armed with a variety of weapons, only some of them recognizable. His companions were all grim, their prehensile tails stiffly erect, and he knew that if looks could kill, he wouldn't survive to reach the floor.

The floor. It wasn't as totally dark as he'd imagined, because many of the plants—and animals, too—phosphoresced. A phrase he'd heard once long ago kept echoing through his head. The caves of night. He was wandering lost through the caves of night. Above was a leafy canopy of solid darkness. And beneath . . .

The trunks of the giant trees were tens, some even

hundreds, of meters in diameter, and girding their lower reaches were living buttresses, great knees of wood larger than most of the trees he was accustomed to. And in and around and on and under and through was all living forest, a veritable ocean solid with life, competing, eating, growing, dying, layer on layer, predator on predator. A normal rainforest (he had consulted the records he had brought) was actually scant of life on its floor, because the canopy above shut out too much light. But here, even without light, there was enough organic material raining down from the giants above to provide the basis for an ecology. And what an ecology! What a competitive, fetid, voracious ecology! And so complex!

He saw vines climbing up a treeling a mere ten meters or so high. He blinked, and the vines swarmed upward and spread out, sending in tendrils to tap the tree's life fluids, round and round, leaves unfurling and sending spines into the treeling until between one breath and the next what had been a tree was a mound of pulsing leaves.

"Stranglervine," one of the guides (guards) answered to his stammered question. "By tomorrow it'll have sucked the infant dead and dry. Then it'll curl up in a ball and tumble away, until leaf-breath wind brings it to another vine."

"Will it . . ."

She snorted, her swishing tail imperiously contemptuous.

"You wouldn't taste right. But there are threats here, plant and animal, that make the stranglervine seem like Anna Sweet-teat."

He glared. But in minutes he knew she had spoken the simple truth. The floor was a pesthole, a hothouse and breeding ground for desperate appetites. Animal, plant—and trog.

Two strong cresters were at point, hacking with off-world metal machetes at the living mass. Hacked and headless corpses of small animals were trampled underfoot along with the severed plants. The cresters' progress was measured in meters. He could still see the doomed tree under its mound of strangler vine when a shapeless, many-legged horror dropped onto the shoulder of a crester walking not two paces in front of him. The victim dropped without as much as a gasp, but another guide reached over and touched the wetly glistening horror with a vine wrapped around her wrist, and, with a teeth-tearing keen, legs convulsing, the horror shriveled and fell off, to be kicked away into the dimness. Its victim was loaded onto a sling and carried by his fellows.

The attacks were almost continuous. From above, behind, the side, the front. Things even slithered up out of the crushed-down matter they were walking on. Big things, little things, all bristling with every natural weapon he'd ever heard of, and a few he wouldn't have dreamed existed. Things crisped by lasers, hacked by machetes, destroyed by the symbiotic plants. Still, dying, they came on, claws grasping, tendrils reaching, teeth slavering, spitting acids, dribbling caustics, limbs flailing, tentacles reaching—reaching—reaching—

Despite all their efforts, there was soon a second casualty and, even before that victim could be settled in a sling to be carried, a third one.

The trogs, his guide informed him between attacks, are among the most dangerous of the floor dwellers, thanks to their claws and teeth, their cunning and ferocity; they glide through the growth like sunbeams through broken clouds. They kill and eat and breed prolifically, a dozen or more to the litter, and so survive. They're marsupial, and if the mother's killed, the tough pouch convulses shut, protecting the litter against all but the worst of tooth and claw and acid. The newborn are tiny, and the pouch is small, often the killer swallows it whole. But inside the stomach, the dissolvents act on the pouch in a curious way. The pouch has a simple nervous system of its own; it attaches itself to the stomach wall and absorbs nutrients from its surroundings to feed the litter. The litter grows until it completely blocks off the stomach, and the killer starves. Then the litter eats its way out of the pouch, fast, before the floor dwellers can devour corpse, pouch, litter, and all.

"But would you have believed this?" she finished with a grim nod to the voracity around them. "Any of this if you hadn't seen it with your own eyes, actually experienced—the floor?"

Around him birth and death alike exploded in the green-white light.

"How long do you think a blind trog would survive?"

"Seconds," he admitted, "minutes, no more. But can't *you* understand? I have to *try*!" Despite the protective clothing he'd been given, things had burrowed under it. He could feel the skittering legs—or were they tendrils?—in a dozen places.

He jumped abruptly as a white-hot needle bored in just below the point of his left shoulderblade.

And then a trog attacked. It had the cunning to go for one of the back points, but the troops were all watching one another, and a loud voice gave the alarm before the victim hit the ground. The trog tore off a great chunk of its victim with its teeth and ran, the bleeding strip dangling from its mouth. One of the guards made a throwing motion with her arm, and the trog went down, its booty still clamped tightly between its teeth. By the time they ran up to it, both the trog and is gruesome treasure were being swarmed over by hundreds of tiny crawling and flying things.

He watched, gulping and unable to speak. Dead eyes, yellow-green like hers, stared up at him; the white fur was slimed with dark blood, the teeth glistened with it. As he watched, the body disintegrated, and the swarm ate it, bite by bite. It was no longer a body; it had become nothing but a heap of crawling, fighting—

Fascinated, he continued to watch until he was staring at a scatter of yellow bones, polished, gleaming, clean. Something no bigger than his hand, a cuddly gray ball of living velvet, ambled over, snapped off a rib, and chewed it with gusto. The rib went down in seconds, and the ball cracked off a second and began chewing, but an odd, growled rumble made it freeze and then scurry hastily away.

The "dead" guard was being attended to by one of the troops. The doctor was embarrassed, professionally shamed. It was his duty, after all, to tend the wounded. He had seen the bright arterial blood spurting from the torn throat, but the trog had been the greater compulsion. Even so, he told himself, what could he have done with the few supplies he'd brought with him? He was about to ask why the corpse hadn't been attacked by the crawling things when the "corpse" fluttered her eyelids.

"An even chance for her, if we turn back now," the chief of the guard said.

"But how? It would have taken a high-T machine to have stopped the bleeding in time. I don't understand."

She shrugged. "What you do with machines, we do with life." Impatiently, "How many of us must die before you are convinced?"

His head flicked back the way they'd come, then again forward, drawn by the inexorable compulsion, drawn to the floor, the hotbed of life, knowing he was a fool, knowing it was failure. His failure he couldn't face, and yet—He licked his lips and said, "As long as there's a chance, any chance that—"

He didn't see the chief make a gesture to a guard standing directly behind him; he didn't see that guard move. Then he didn't see anything at all, not even the guard's rueful mixture of regret and admiration as she gazed down at his limp body.

He opened his eyes to an almost perfect replica of his room back at Continental General. It wasn't until he reached out his hand to the intercom that he realized it was a clever fake. Everything was plant growth. But even as intellect recognized falsity, his instincts were relaxing, so that he was already smiling muzzily when the crester bustled in, "clothed" in the traditional blue of surgery service.

"Don't tell me, plants," he murmured, a man purged temporarily at least of every emotion but a sort of languid curiosity. "But how did you get them the right shade of blue?"

She twinkled at him, her tail curling and uncurling joyously. "Oh, you're feeling better at last. Wouldn't a little sun be nice, eh? Easy over now—"

He had a lot of time to think, sitting in the warm sunlight, shaded by a friendly leaf. "I can teach you as much as you can teach me," he told them. And it was true. He never found their secret, how they grew the plants they did, but he isolated a dozen useful ones and helped them develop a dozen more, from the little saprophyte that could be clamped on an open wound and would seal in seconds, reducing blood loss immeasurably, to a seed that when swallowed went directly to an ulcer and grew over it, protecting all the delicate tissues. He taught them new medical techniques: how to set a bone pin, how to treat the stump of a limb so that when it healed, it could be fitted with a (hand-carved) prosthetic, how to transplant organs, and how to do a bypass.

And then the wombship came. When it left, he went with it, taking supplies of all the plants he thought would be useful on other primitive worlds, as well as the Agrippa seeds he had learned to love chewing.

His patient had been right; as much as he loved his work, this wasn't his world, and it was better that he leave it.

He knew that he could never go back to his own world.

Too many years, too many changes, had alienated him as
much as any of the wombers.

And the years passed. Few for him, many for the worlds
spinning warm and smug around their suns, and he discovered that, thanks to relativistic time contraction and the simultaneity projector (were *people* really going through the
projector now?), he was becoming a legend. Whole worlds
were grateful to Johnny Healerseed.

Even the wombers took to calling him that, at first in
gentle derision, later just from habit, and he gradually forgot
he had once been called by any other name.

It was on a world called Getchergoat that he found the last
piece of his personal puzzle. Getchergoat had projectors, and
a fairly high level of technology, so that he was learning as
well as teaching. When he learned and taught as much as he
could, and knew that his ship would be orbiting for several
standard weeks yet, he asked, as he had on many other
worlds, what sights his colleagues recommended he see.

Everyone agreed that the one thing he mustn't miss was
the Pan-Art Exhibition in the Septmillennial Memorial Audisseum. The Audisseum was multilevel, a freeform hugeness in
transparent weather sheathing. He hesitated in the dilating
entrance, a radiation-scarred old man, and an ovoid shimmer
materialized at his elbow. "May I direct you to any specific
exhibit?" the ovoid inquired.

"Have you anything here by the Sequoian troglodyte
Inanna Kantanitanki?"

"A man of taste," the ovoid purred. "Do you prefer Early,
Mature, or Final period?"

"All three," he said.

In the Early display, he was pleased to see a copy of
Mayflight in the Morning, enlarged so that it sang baritone
instead of soprano. When he tried to arrange some sort of
credit, so he could have another copy to replace the one left
behind somewhere long ago, he was embarrassed because
they refused any exchange. A middle-aged man, attired only
in Mercury's winged shoes, came sailing out on a striped
orange-and-lime flying disc. He was holding a large-sized
copy in his arms, and he refused to take anything. The artwork would be the smallest possible appreciation to Johnny
Healerseed from the grateful world of Getchergoat.

It was this man—"My current label is Drifting-through-

Anomie," he said—who insisted on guiding him through the rest of the display, which ended in a series of untitled pieces. "Why untitled?" he wondered aloud, his hands caressing a piece that curved subtly around and through itself.

His guide shrugged. "It's the custom here, with pieces untitled by the artist, or where the title is unknown or has been lost."

"Solipsism," he said, still playing with the piece.

"Good, good, very good." Drifting-through-Anomie beamed. "Should I add it to the list of suggested titles?"

"No." He continued to turn the piece, shaking his head. "So many pieces I don't recognize, and I thought I knew most of her work. I must be getting senile."

"Idegosuper forfend!" Drifting-through-Anomie was appalled. "No, these would be the pieces discovered on Sequoia after you left there to begin your pilgrimage, I'm sure!"

"Discovered *after*—" His mouth dropped open. "You mean, she was alive after all! *She was alive, and I left her!*"

"I'm sure not." Drifting-through-Anomie cocked his head to one side, as if listening to unheard silent voices, as he undoubtedly was. "No, the first work of her final period was discovered in Stanyear 809, at least two hundred years after she returned to her native world. The next three—"

"Two hundred!"

"Oh dear! How mannerless of me! You'd like to see it *in situ*, wouldn't you?" Between them a tiny sphere appeared, and the doctor realized it was a holo, taken from the crests. "It was a womber who spotted it—" The view descended, hovered over the treetops, and focused on the oddly convoluted crest of one particular tree.

"*Aesculapius!*"

"The style is unmistakable, of course. The original is about seventy meters high and about twenty-five meters in diameter, and its song has been recorded"—a deep rumble of triumph filled the air around them—"though how that great genius managed to shape the growth of the trees, we don't know—"

The doctor thought of a hand putting a seed into a mouth, the mouth spitting it out again—of chemical signals of amazing complexity that make a body grow and change—of a world where plants and animals had grown so interrelated that he had often thought of it as one, immense, complex, single living organism, a living world that isolated outside contaminants in deadness—and he knew how his once-hosts grew their medical and other miracles and why the trog had *had* to return. He smiled gently at Drifting-through-Anomie.

"They ate her soul with her bones," he said.

HIGHLINER

by C. J. Cherryh

*In this, the Age of Steel, the world's population
has grown far beyond the boundaries of forest edge
and river bank. While the original habitant of humanity was the green world of open nature, the city
has become the home of more and more of the expanding horde. The towers that are springing up all
over the world, the shielding of men from the vicis-
situdes of nature, show the direction of the future.
Here is a picture of the far end of that change—
here is New York after the millennia. . . .*

The city soared, a single spire aimed at the clouds, con-
cave-curved from sprawling base to needle heights. It had
gone through many phases in its long history. Wars had come
and gone. Hammered into ruin, it rebuilt on that ruin, stubbornly rising as if up were the only direction it knew. How it
had begun to build after that fashion no one remembered,
only that it grew, and in the sun's old age, when the days of
Earth turned strange, it grew into its last madness, becoming
a windowed mountain, a tower, a latter-day Babel aimed at
the sullen heavens. Its expanse at the base was enormous, and
it crumbled continually under its own weight, but its growth
outpaced that ruin, growing broader and broader below and
more and more solid at its base and core, with walls crazily
angled to absorb the stresses.

Climate had changed many times over the course of its

31

life. Ice came now and froze on its crest, and even in sum-
mers, evening mists iced on the windward side, crumbling it
more; but still it grew, constantly webbed with scaffolding at
one point or the other, even at the extreme heights; and the
smaller towers of its suburbs followed its example, so that on
its peripheries, bases touching and joining its base, strange
concave cones lifted against the sky, a circle of spires around
the greater and impossible spire of the City itself, on all sides
but the sea.

At night the City and its smaller companions gleamed with
lighted wndows, a spectacle the occupants of the outlying
city-mountains could see from their uppermost windows,
looking out with awe on the greatest and tallest structure man
had ever built on Earth . . . or ever would. And from the
much higher windows of the City itself, the occupants might
look out on a perspective to take the senses away, towering
over all the world. Even with windows tinted and shielded
against the dying sun's radiations, the reflections off the surface of the land and the windows of other buildings flared
and glared with disturbing brightness; and by night the cities
rose like jeweled spires of the crown of the world, towering
mounds which one day might be absorbed as their bases had
already been.

It was alone, the City and its surrounding companions, on
a land grown wild between; on an Earth severed from the
younger inhabited worlds, with its aged and untrustworthy
star.

The tower was for the elite, the artists, the analysts, the
corporate directors and governors; the makers and builders
and laborers lived at the sprawling, labyrinthine base, and
worked there, in the filling of the core, or outward, in the
quarrying of still more and more stone which came up the
passages, from sources ever farther away; and some worked
the outer shell, adding to it. It was mountain and city at
once; and powerful yet. It had pride, in the hands of its
workers and the soaring height of it.

And the highliners walked with a special share of that
pride, proud in their trade and in the badges of it, among
which were a smallish size and a unique courage.

Johnny and Sarah Tallfeather were such, brother and sister; and Polly Din and Sam Kenny were two others. They
were of the East Face, of the 48th sector (only they worked

everywhere) and when they were at the Bottom, in the
domain of the Builders, they walked with that special arro-
gance of their breed, which could hang suspended on a
thread in the great cold winds of Outside, and look down on
the city-mountains, and wield a torch or manage the erection
of the cranes, which had to be hoisted up from the smallest
web of beginning lines and winches, which, assembled, hoisted up more scaffolding and stone and mortar. They could
handle vast weights in the winds by patience and skill, but
most of all, they could dare the heights and the ledges.

Others might follow them, in the platforms they made,
creep about on those platforms anchored by their lines, Builders brave enough compared to others, who found it all their
hearts could bear just to go up above the two hundreds and
look down from the outershell windows; but those who
worked the high open face on lines alone were a special
breed, the few who could bear that fearful fascination, who
could work between the dying sun and the lesser cities, who
could step out on nothing and swing spiderwise in the howl-
ing winds and freezing mists; and rarer still, those with the
nerve and with the skill of engineers as well. They were the
first teams on any site, the elite of a special breed.

That was the 48th.

The order was out: the city would grow eastward, toward
the Queens Tower; the work was well under way, the Bottom
skylights covered on that side, because the high work required it. There was a burst of prosperity in the eastside Bottom, establishments which fed and housed the Builders who
were being shifted there.

"It's going to *change*," some higher up muttered, less
happy, for it meant that favorite and favored real estate
would lose its view, and accesses, pass into the core, ultimately to be filled, and their windows would be taken out
and carefully, lovingly transferred to the Outside as the build
ing progressed: the computers ruled, dictated the cost-effec-
tive procedures; and the highliners moved in.

They began by walking the lower levels, work which made
them impatient, mostly leaving that to Builders, who were
skilled enough; then their real work began, mounting the East
Face itself, floor by floor, swinging out in the winds and seeking with their eyes for any weaknesses in structure or stone
which deviated from what the computers predicted. Small

cracks were abundant and ordinary; they noted them on charts and the regular liner crews would fill them.

The liners worked higher and higher; came to the Bottom each night in increasing numbers, for the scaffolding had begun now, far across the Bottom, and new joy dens and sleeps had opened up to accommodate them in the sprawl of the base.

There were of course deeper levels than the liners ever saw: and they too were worked by a special breed that was doing its own job, men who probed the foundations which were going to bear that new weight, who crawled the narrow tunnels still left deep in the stonework heart of the base. Rivers, it was rumored, still flowed down there, but long ago the City had enclosed them, channeled them, dug down to rock beneath and settled her broad bottomside against the deep rocks, perched there for the ages to come. That great weight cracked supports from time to time, and precious conduits of power and water had to be adjusted against the sideways slippage which did happen, fractional inches year by year, or sometimes more, when the earth protested the enormous weight it had to bear. The sea was down there on one side, but those edges were filled and braced; the dead were down there, the ashes of all the ordinary dead, and many a Builder too, who had not gotten out of the way of a collapsing passage . . . but the dead served like other dust, to fill the cracks, so it was true that the living built upon the dead.

So the city grew.

"Go up to the nineties tomorrow," the liner boss said, and the four other members of 48 East, tired from the day and bone-chilled from the mist and anxious to head for the Bottom and its dens, took Jino Brown's instructions and handed in their charts. "So where were you, bossman?" Sam Kenny asked. Sometimes Jino went out with them and sometimes not; and it was a cold, bone-freezing day out there.

"Yeah," said Johnny. "The wind starts up, Jino, and where were you?"

"Meeting," Jino said; fill-in for their retired boss, he took such jokes with a sour frown, not the good humor they tried with him. "You worry too much," Johnny said, and unbelted the harness about his hips, last in, still shivering and bouncing to warm his muscles. He started peeling out of the black rubber suit, hung up his gear beside the others in the narrow Access Room, with the big hatch to Outside firmly and safely sealed at the end; they had a shower there: Sarah and Poll had first use of it. They came out looking happier and Johnny peeled out of the last of his rig, grabbed a towel and headed in with Sam, howled for the temperature the women had left it, which on their chilled bodies felt scalding. Sam dialed it down, and they lathered and soused themselves and came out again, rubbing down.

The women were dressed already, waiting. "Where's Jino gone now?" Sam asked. The women shrugged.

"Got to be careful of him," Sarah said. "Think we hurt his feelings."

"Ah," Johnny said, which was what that deserved. He grabbed his clothes and pulled them on; and Sam did, while the women waited. Then, "Going Down," Sarah sang, linking her arm in his, linking left arm to Sam's and laughing; he snagged Polly and they snaked their way out and down the hall, laughing for the deviltry of it, here in this carpeted, fine place of the tower, quiet, expensive apartments of the Residents. They used the service lift, their privilege . . . better, because *it* stopped very seldom, and not at all this time, shot them down and down while they leaned against the walls and grinned at each other in anticipation.

"Worm," Sarah proposed, a favorite haunt.

"Pillar," Poll said.

"Go your way; we'll go ours."

"Right," Sam said; and that was well enough: Sam and Sarah had business; and he and Poll did, and he was already thinking on it with a warm glow . . . on that and dinner, both of which seemed at the moment equally desirable. The lift slammed to its hard-braking halt on second and the door opened, let them out into the narrow maze, the windowless windings of stairs and passages, granite which seeped water squeezed out of the stones by the vast mass above their heads.

And music—music played here constantly, echoing madly through the deep stone halls. There was other music too, conduits, which came up from the rivers, and these sang softly when the hand touched them, with the force of the water surging in them up or down. There were power conduits, shielded and painted; there were areas posted with yellow signs and DANGER and KEEP OUT, subterranean mysteries which were the business of the Deep Builders, and not for liners, and never for the soft-handed Residents of the high tower who came slumming here, thrill-seeking.

"Going my way?" Sarah asked of Sam, and off they went, by the stairs to the next level down, to the ancient Worm; but Johnny hugged Poll against him and took the corridor that snaked its way with one of the waterpipes, toward the core of second level; the Pillar was liner even to its decor, which was old tackle and scrawled signatures . . . they walked in through an arch that distinguished itself only by louder music—one had to know where one was down at the Bottom, or have a guide, and pay; and no Residents got shown to the Pillar, or to the Worm, not on the guides' lives. He found his favored table; next the big support that gave the place its name, around which the tables wound, a curve which gave privacy, and, within the heartbeat throb of the music, calm and warmth after the shrieking winds.

He and Poll ordered dinner from the boy who did the waiting; a tiny-"tiny," he said, measuring a span with his fingers—glass of brew, because they were going out on the lines again tomorrow, and they needed their heads unswollen.

They had of course other pleasures in mind, because there was more to the Pillar than this smoky, music-pulsing den, and the food and drink; there were the rooms below, down the stairs beyond, for such rest as they had deserved.

He finished his good meal, and Poll did, and they sat there sipping their brew and eyeing one another with the anticipation of long acquaintance, but the brew was good too, and what they had been waiting for all day, with the world swinging under their feet and exertion sucking the juices out of them. They were that, old friends, and it could wait on the drink, slow love, and slow quiet sleep in the Bottom, with all the comforting weight of the City on their backs, where the world was solid and warm.

"Tallfeather."

He looked about, in the music and the smoke. No one used his last name, not among the highliners; but it was not a voice he knew . . . a thin man in Builders' blue coveralls and without a Builders' drawling accent either.

"Tallfeather, I'd like to talk with you. Privately."

He frowned, looked at Poll, who looked worried, tilted his head to one side. "Rude man, that."

"Mr. Tallfeather."

No one said Mister in the Bottom. That intrigued him. "Poll, you mind? This man doesn't get much of my time."

"I'll leave," Poll said. There was a shadow in Poll's eyes, the least hint of fear, he would have said, but there was no cause of it that he could reckon.

"No matter," the man said, hooking his arm to pull him up. "We've a place to go."

"No." He rose to his feet all right, and planted them, glared up at the man's face. Shook his arm free. "You're begging trouble. What's your name? Let me see your card."

The man reached for his pocket and took one out. *Manley,* it said, *Joseph,* and identified him as an East Face Builder, and that was a lie, with that accent. Company number 687. Private employ.

So money was behind this, that could get false cards. He looked for Poll's opinion, but she had slipped away, and he was alone with this man. He sat down at the table again, pointed to the other chair. "I'd be crazy to walk out of here with you. You sit down there and talk sense or I do some talking to security, and I don't think you'd like that, would you?"

Manley sat down, held out his hand for the card. Johnny gave it to him. "So who are you?" Johnny prodded.

There was no one, at the moment, near them. The huge pillar cut them off from sight and sound of others, and the serving boy was gone into the kitchen or round the bend.

"You're of the 48 East," Manley said, "and this project you're on . . . you know what kind of money that throws around. You want to stay on the lines all your life, Tallfeather, or do you think about old age?"

"I don't mind the lines," he said. "That's what I do."

"It's worth your while to come with me. Not far. No tricks. I have a friend of yours will confirm what I say. You'll trust him."

"What friend?"

"Jino Brown."

That disturbed him. Jino. Jino involved with something that had to sneak about like this. Jino had money troubles. Gambled. This was something else again. "Got a witness of my own, remember? My teammate's going to know who you are, just in case you have ideas."

"Oh, she does know me, Mr. Tallfeather."

That shook his confidence further, because he had known
Poll all his life, and Poll was honest.

And scared.

"All right. Suppose we take that walk."

"Good," Manley said, and got to his feet. Johnny rose and
walked with him to the door, caught the young waiter before
he went out it. "Tommy, lad, I'm going with Mr. Manley
here." He took the order sheet from the boy's pocket and
wrote the name down and the company number, probably
false. "And you comp my bill and put your tip on it, and you
remember who I left with, all right?"

"Right," the boy said. Builder by birth, Tommy Pratt, but
small and unhealthy and sadly pale. "You in some kind of
trouble, Johnny?"

"Just remember the name and drop it in the liners' ears if I
don't come back before morning; otherwise forget it."

"Yes, sir."

Manley was not pleased. Johnny smiled a taut, hard smile
and walked with him then, out the winding ways where the
man wanted to lead him. In fact it was curiosity and nerves
that brought him with Manley, an ugly kind of curiosity. He
was no Resident to go rubber-kneed at the sight of the lines,
but this had something to do with those he was going out
there with, and where their minds were, and this he wanted
to know.

There was another dive a good distance beyond, down a
series of windings and up and down stairs, on the very mar-
gin of the territory he knew in the Bottom; and being that
close to lost made him nervous too.

But Jino was there, at the table nearest the door, stood up
to meet him, but did not take him back to the table; walked
him with his hand on his shoulder, back into one of the
rooms most of these places had, where the pounding music
and the maze gave privacy for anything.

"What is this?" Johnny asked, trusting no one now; but
Jino urged him toward a chair at the round table that occupied this place, that was likely for gambling—Jino *would*
know such places. Manley had sat down there as if he owned
the place, and stared at both of them as they sat down. "I'll
tell you what it is," Manley said. "There's a flaw on the East
Face 90th, you understand?"

"There's not a flaw."

"Big one," said Manley. "Going to deviate the whole project a degree over."

"Going to miss some important property," Jino said, "whatever the computers projected. *We're* the ones go out there; the computers don't. We say."

He looked at Jino, getting the whole drift of it and not at all liking it.

"Mr. Tallfeather," Manley said. "Property rides on this. *Big* money. And it gets spread around. There is, you see, a company that needs some help; that's going to be hurt bad by things the way they're going; and maybe some other companies have an in with the comp operators, eh? Maybe this just balances the books. You understand that?"

"What company? That ATELCORP thing that made the fuss?"

"You don't need to know names, Mr. Tallfeather. Just play along with the rest of your team. They'll all be in on it. All. And all it takes is your cooperative—silence."

"Sure, and maybe you're telling that to all of them, that I went with it."

Manley frowned deeply. "You're the last holdout, Tallfeather, you and your sister. You two are the sticking point, the ones we knew would have been hard to convince. But it's a team play. You respect that. You don't want to cut your three partners out of that company's gratitude. Think of your old age, Tallfeather. Think how it is when you stop being young, when you still have to go out there. And this company's gratitude—can go a long way."

"Money," Jino said. "Enough to set us up. Influence. We're set, you understand that, Johnny? It's not crooked; just what he said, balancing the influence the others have on the computer input. So both sides are bought. This goes *high*, Johnny; the Council, the companies they run . . . this is a power grab."

"Mr. Brown," Manley cautioned.

"Johnny's reasonable. It's a matter of explaining."

"I think I see it," Johnny said in a flat voice.

"Trust the company," Manley said. "Someone's talking to your sister too."

Panic settled over him. He settled back in his chair. He went out on the lines with these people. Had to. It was all he had. "Sarah will go with it if I do. Who's financing this? What company? If we're in it, I figure we should know."

"Never mind that."

"Just shut up and take it," Jino said. "And agree with the charts. I do that part of it. You just keep your mouth shut and take your cut."

"All right," he said. "All right. No problem from me." He pushed back from the table. "I'd better get back, you mind? I left some instructions if I didn't get back quick."

Jino frowned and motioned him gone. He gathered himself up, walked out, through the main room and down the corridors, with an increasingly leaden feeling at his gut.

Tommy's face lit with relief to see him; he clapped the boy on the shoulder. "Poll?" he asked, and Tommy blinked and looked about.

"I think she left," Tommy said.

He checked. She was not in the room they had rented. Not upstairs. He frowned and left, hunting Sarah, down in the Worm.

She was gone too. So was Sam Kenny.

He sat down, ordered a drink to occupy a table by the door of the Worm, a den as dark and loud and smoky as the Pillar, but smaller and older; and he asked a few questions, but not too many, not enough to raise brows either among the liners there or with the management. The drink gradually disappeared. He sat with a sick feeling at his stomach and ordered another.

Finally she came in. He restrained himself from jumping up, sat cool and silent while Sarah spotted him and walked over with a distressed look that told where she had been. She pulled up another chair and sat down.

"I know," he said. "They got to you and Sam?"

"What do we do, Johnny?"

"What did you tell them we'd do?"

"I told them we'd think about it."

"I told them we'd go with it," he said. "What do you think we are, Sarah?"

Her shoulders fell and she sat and looked morose. His drink came and he pushed it over to her, ordered one for himself. "I don't think," she said when they were alone, "I don't think they trust us, Johnny, whatever they promise."

He thought about that, and it frightened him, agreeing with his own thought. "We go along with it. It's all we can do. Report it . . . we don't know what it would stir up, or how high; or what enemies we'd have."

She nodded.

They took rooms in the Worm. He took a bottle with him, and Sarah did, and he at least slept. Sam never did come back, to his knowledge.

And came late morning, he and Sarah walked together to the service lift, got on it with two other liners not of their team who were making the ride up to tenth; they exchanged no words. The other liners got off, and they said nothing to each other, the whole long ride to the ninetieth.

Down the carpeted hall to the access hall: they were first to arrive. They stripped and put on the suits, waited around with hoods back and gloves off. Sam showed up, and Poll, avoiding their eyes. There was poison in the air. There had never been that, quarrels yes, but not this. Jino showed, clipboard in hand, and the silence continued. "Blast you," Jino said. "Look up, look alive. Get your minds on it. Who's been talking?"

Johnny shook his head. Jino looked from one to the other of them. "What's wrong?" Johnny asked. "Jino, maybe we and you better get this all straight. Or maybe we don't go out there today."

"Questions, that's all." Jino took his suit and harness off the hook and started stripping like the rest of them. "Had the man back, you understand me? Stopped me, asking . . . asking whether any of the team might have had second thoughts. Any of you been talking?"

Heads shook, one by one.

"Right then." Jino climbed into the suit, zipped up, and the rest of them starting getting hoods up and masks hung in place. "It's all right," Jino said. He belted the harness about his chest and up through his legs, took the clipboard and hung it from his belt. "It's started, anyway. I've got the figures. All we have to do is keep developing this data; and it's all figured; they gave it to me the way we have to turn it in. Is that hard?"

They shook their heads again. There was a bitter taste in Johnny's mouth. He shrugged into his own harness, pulled it up, hooked it, checked the precious line, coiled in its case, to be sure it rolled and that the brake held as it should.

"So get moving," Jino said. "Go, get out there."

They moved. Sam opened the access door, a round hatch; and wind howled in, nothing to what it would do if the back door were open. Poll swore and bounced slightly, nervousness; it was always this way, going out. Sam went first, hooked his first line to the access eye, eased out of sight, bowed in the wind, facing outward for a moment and then turning to face the building. Sarah moved up next, as soon as that eye was free.

His turn. He hooked on, looked out into the blasting wind, at the view Residents never saw unshielded. He pulled his tinted mask down, and the sunglare resolved itself into the far dizzying horizon. He stepped to the ledge, jerked to be sure the brake was holding on his line before he trusted his weight to it. This was the part the groundlings could never take, that first trusting move in which he swung out with all the dizzy curve of the city-mountain at his feet, windows and ledges . . . shielded ledges below, as the curve increased, and finally mere glass tiles, thick and solid, the windows of the Bottom, which were skylights, thick because there was always the chance of getting something dropped through one . . . winter ice, which built up and crashed like spears weighing hundreds of pounds; or the falling body of a liner, which had happened; or something a liner dropped, which was enough to send a man to the Bottom for a month: even a bolt dropped from these heights became a deadly missile.

Ninety floors down.

The insulated suits protected from the cold, barely. The masks did, or the windchill would have frozen their eyes and membranes and robbed them of breath; every inch of their bodies was covered. He clipped his line to another bolt and let the last retract, dropping and traversing in a wide arc that made all the stones blur past, caught the most convenient ledge with a practiced reach that disdained the novice's straightline drop and laborious climb back; he had his line of ascent above him now, the number ten; Sarah had the eleventh; Sam the twelfth; Poll, coming after him, number nine; Jino number eight, near the access. Climb and map and watch for cracks, real ones, which was their proper job; and swear to a lie. He tried not to think of that. They still had a job to do, the routine that kept the building in repair; and out here at least, the air was clean and minds had one steady job to occupy all their attention—one small move after another, eyes straight ahead and wits about them.

They checked and climbed, steady work now, feet braced, backs leaning against the harness. They had come out after the sun was well up; paused often for rests. He felt the day's heat increasing on his back, felt the trickle of sweat down his sides. The ice was burned off, at least. None of that to make feet slip and line slip its brake in slides that could stop even a liner's heart. His mask kept the air warm and defogged itself immaculately, a breathing that those who spent their lives in the City never experienced, sharp and cold and cleansing. He got near the windows as the day wore on toward afternoon. He could see his own monstrous reflection in the tinted glass he passed, like some black spider with a blank, reflective face; and dimly, dimly, the interiors of the offices of ATEL-CORP: he recognized the logo.

He was out of love with them. But a woman had the desk nearest the glass, looked up at him with bright innocent eyes. She smiled; he smiled, uselessly, behind his mask—freed a hand and waved, and watched her reaction, which looked like a gasp. He grinned, let go the other and then, businesslike, reached for the next clip and edged higher, to spider over a bit onto the blank wall. But the woman mouthed him something. He motioned with his hand and she said it again. He lipread, like many a liner, used to the high winds, the same as they used handsigns. He mimed a laugh, slapped his hand on his gut. Her half-mirrored face took on a little shock. She laughed then. The invitation had been coarse.

He let go again, mimed writing with his hand, teasing her for her number. She laughed and shook her head, and he reckoned it time to move on.

He had fallen behind. Poll and Sam and Sarah were ahead, two floors above, Jino about even with him. He made a little haste on the blank wall, like them, where there were no windows to be careful of, reach and clip, adjust the feet, reach and clip, never quite loose. They reached the ledge of the hundred, and stopped for a breather, eyed the clouds that had come in on the east, beyond the ringlet of other towers. "Going to have to call it soon," Sam said.

"We just move it over," Jino said. "Traverse five over, work it down, come back to the 90 access."

They nodded. That was what they wanted, no long one with that moving in. It boded ice.

And when they had worked the kinks from backs and shoulders and legs, they lined along the ledge, the easy way, and dropped into their new tracks, a windowless area and quick going. Johnny leaned over and bounced as he hit the wall, started working downward with enthusiasm. It faded.

Muscles tired. He looked up, where Sam and Sarah seemed occupied about some charting; so maybe they had found something, or they were doing a little of the minor repair they could do on the spot.

It was a good route up; the computers were right, and it was the best place. He looked down between his feet at the hazy Bottom, where the ground prep had already been done with so much labor, tried not to let his mind dwell on the lie. It was getting toward the hour they should come in anyway, and the wind was picking up, shadows going the other way now, making the tower a little treacherous if he kept looking down, a dizzying prospect even to one accustomed to it.

Wind hit; he felt the cold and the lift carried him almost loose from his footing.

Suddenly something dark plummeted past. He flinched and fell inward against the stone, instinct. Something dropped—but big; it had been. . . . He looked up in the shadow, squinted against the flaring sky, saw the channel next to him vacant; Sarah's channel, a broken line flying.

He flung himself outward with his legs, looked down, but she had fallen all the way by now, spun down the long slow fall.

Sarah.

It hit him then, the grief, the loss. He hung there against the harness. By now the rest of the team had stopped, frozen in their places. He stayed put, in the windy silence, and the belt cutting into his back and hips, his legs numb and braced.

His hands were on his lines. He caressed the clip that was between him and such a fall, and was aware of a shadow, of someone traversing over to him.

Poll. She hung there on her lines' extension, touched his shoulder, shook at him and pointed up and over. Shouted in the wind and the muffling of the mask. *Access,* he lipread. *Get to the access.*

He began, the automatic series of moves that were so easy, so thoughtless, because the equipment held, but Sarah's had not. Sarah was down there, his own flesh and bone spattered over all the protected skylights on the mountain's long, slow curve.

He began shaking. He hung there against the flat stone, out in the wind, and his legs started shaking so that he could not make the next step, and hands froze so that he could not make the next release, could not make the swing across to the next track, suspended over that.

Another came. Sam, and Poll. He felt them more than saw, bodies hurtling near him on their lines, and he hung there, clinging with his fingers, flinched, shuddering as a third plummeted and came against him from the back, spider fashion.

They lined to him. He knew what they were doing and would do, but he was frozen, teeth chattering. The cold had gotten to him, and he clung desperately to the wall, trying to see nothing else, felt them hooking to him, felt them release his lines.

He screamed, hurled free by the wind, swung down and stopped against the lines as they jerked taut against his body harness. He hung there, swinging free in the wind gusts, while the twilit city spun and flared in streaks and spirals before his blurring eyes. He heard a scream, a chorus of them, and there was another body plummeting past him, an impact that hit his shoulder and spun him. He tried to catch it, but the body got past him as he spun, and he watched, watched downward as it spread itself like a star on the winds and whirled away, in slow, terrible falling. Vanished in perspective. He never saw it hit. Tried to convince his mind to see it soar away, safe, unharmed; but it had hit; and it was a terrible way to die. Like Sarah.

His stomach heaved. He swayed in the buffets of the wind. Two of their team fallen. *Two.* He hung there, thinking of the line, that never gave, never; it was beyond thought that it should give. But two had, and he hung there with his body flying loose from the building in the gusts.

He twisted his head, tried to help himself, but his arms were too chilled to move accurately and his hands fumbled in trying to turn himself against the stone. He managed to look up, saw the two other survivors of the team working at the latch of the access three stories above. They would winch him in, once safe themselves. But it was not opening.

Jammed. Locked. Someone had locked them out here.

And two of their lines had broken.

He moved again as a gust of wind caught him, slammed him against the building. The impact numbed that arm. He manipulated the extension hook with the right arm, shot it out, and even when the wind swayed him farthest that way, it was short of the next hook. He retracted it finally, let it swing

from its cord again and his aching arm fall as he sank in his
harness. He struggled to lift his head finally, saw his team-
mates likewise still. Their lines had tangled. They were in
trouble, twisted in the wind, exhausted. Now and again when
he would look up one of them would be striking at the hatch,
but there was no sound; the wind swallowed it. There were
no windows where they were, in this blind recess. No one
saw; no one heard.

The light waned, wrapped in advancing cloud in a stream-
ing of last colors. The wind kept blowing, and mist began to
spit at them, icing lines, icing the suits, chilling to the bone.
He watched the lights come on in the far, far tower of
Queens, thinking that perhaps someone might be looking out,
that someone might see a skein of figures, that someone
might grow curious, make a call.

No. There was no way they could see so far. He could un-
clip, die early. That was all.

He did not. He hung there with his body growing number,
and the chill working into his bones. How many hours until
someone missed them? Until the other liners started asking
questions?

He looked up, immense effort, saw what looked like the lift
of an arm to the hatch in the dusk. They were still trying.
"Who fell?" he tried to ask. He could not; waved a feeble
hand to let them know he was alive. In the masks, in the
dark suits, there was no seeing who it was in that tangle of
line and bodies.

It darkened further into night, and he felt ice building up
on his right side, flexed and cracked it off his suit. The
harness about his chest and waist and groin was stressed at
an angle, gravity and the buffeting of the wind cutting off the
blood to one side. He struggled, and began, when the wind
would sway him far out and then slam him back against the
building, to think of the thin line fraying with every move. It
was not supposed to.

Was not supposed to. They had been murdered.

Were dying out here because of it.

Out and back. He moaned from the pain, a numb whim-
per, having had enough, and having no one to tell it to.
Again . . . out and against the wall.

It went on and on, and the clouds cut off even the stars
from view, leaving just the city lights, that streaked and spun
and danced like jewels. He got a sliver of ice in his fingers,

slipped it under his mask and into his mouth to relieve the thirst that tormented him; his arm dropped like lead. He stopped moving, aware only of the shriek of the wind, of battering like being taken up by a giant and slammed down again.

Release the catch, a tiny voice whispered to him. *Give up. Let go.*

Someone did. A body hurtled past, a thin, protesting cry— mind changed, perhaps? Grief? Outrage?

He could not see it fall. It went into the dark and the distance, a shadow for a moment against the light below, and then gone, kited on the winds.

Don't they find us down there? he wondered. *Don't they know?* But all the Bottom down there was shielded over for construction. No one would know, unless someone looked out at the moment of falling, unless someone just chanced to see.

There was one of his team left up there. One companion in the dark. "Who are you?" he cried. "Who?"

His voice was lost. No answer came to him.

He sank against the harness, let his head fall, exhausted, senses ebbing.

Came to again at the apex of a swing, screamed as he hung free a moment; but he was still lined. The jerk came, and he slammed against the stone, sobbed with the battering. The night was black, and the corner where they were was black. He dangled and twisted, his lines long since fouled, saw the whole world black, just a few lights showing in the Bottom, the tower of Queens a black, upsweeping point of darkness.

Early morning? How many hours until daylight?

"Who's still up there?" he called in a lull in the wind.

No answer. He dropped his head to his chest, tautened his muscles as a random gust got between him and the building, flying him almost at a right angle to the building, so that the city and the sky spun dizzyingly. The gust stopped. He swung back, hit, went limp, knowing the next such might break his back.

Let it go, the inner voice urged him. *Stop the pain.*

The line might break soon. Might save him the effort. Surely his harness had been tampered with like all the others, while it hung there in the access room.

Jino, he thought, Jino, who had stayed nearest the access. But the door had jammed.

Get rid of this team, get another one assigned more compatible with someone's interests.

He thought about that. Thought about it while the wind slammed and spun at him and the cold sank deeper.

Light flared above. He tried to look up, saw the hatch open, black figures in it against the light. A beam played down, caught him in the face.

The line slipped. He went hot and cold all over at that sickening drop. He twisted, tried to lift an arm, raised it a little. The light centered on him. The wind caught him, a brutal slam out and across the beam. And then the light moved off him. He shouted, hoarse and helpless. Then he felt one of the lines begin to shorten, pulling him in. The winch inside the access; they had that on it, a steady pull, dragging the line over the stone, one line, up and up. He hung still, hardly daring breathe, more frightened now than before . . . to live through this, and to have the line break at the last moment. . . . The wind kept catching him and swinging him far out so that he could see the lights below him.

Almost there. He twisted to see. Hands plucked at the taut line, seized his collar, his shoulders, his chest harness, dragged him backward over the sill of the access. One last sinking into human hands, an embrace which let his cold body to the floor, faces which ringed about him. Someone pulled his mask off, and he flinched at the white light.

"Alive," that one said. Liners. The hatchway was still open. He tried to move, rolled over, looked and saw his teammate, first recovered on the tangled lines, lying on the floor by him, open-eyed and dead.

Jino. It was Jino. He lay there, staring at the dead face. Jino tampered with the harness . . . maybe; or someone else—who locked the door and left them all out there . . . to die.

"There's no more," he heard someone shout; and the hatch boomed shut, mercifully cutting off the wind. His rescuers lifted his head, unzipped the tight suit. "Harness," he said. "Someone tampered with the lines." They were brothers. They had to know.

"Lock that door," one of them said. He let his breath go then, and let them strip the suit off him, winced as one of them brought wet towels that were probably only cold water; it felt scalding. He lived. He lay and shivered, with the floor under him and not the empty air and the dark. Someone seized his face between burning hands while continuing to soak the rest of his body. Dan Hardesty: he knew the team, four men and a woman; the 50 East. "What do you mean, tampered? What happened?"

"Tried to fake the reports," he said. "Someone wanted the reports doctored, and didn't trust us. They killed us. They— or the other side. Tampered with the harness. Lines broke. *Two lines broke out there.*"

They hovered about him, listening, grim-faced. His mind began to work with horrid clarity, two and two together; it took more than one team bought off. Took buying all that worked this section; them too. The 50th. He lay there, shivering as the water started to cool, thinking ugly thoughts, how easy it was to drop a body back out there.

"Someone," he said, "jammed the latch. Locked us out there."

Dan Hardesty stared at him. Finally scowled, looked above him at one of his own, looked down again. "Bring that water up to warm," he said. "Move it. We've got to get him out of here."

He shivered convulsively, stomach knotting up, limbs jerking; they set him up. They got the warmer clothes on him and he flinched, tried to control his limbs. His left leg and his right were blackening on the sides; his left arm already black. "Look at his back," the woman Maggie said, and he reckoned it was good he could not see it. They sponged at it, trying to get him back to room temperature.

"Tommy Pratt got worried," Dan said. "Started asking questions—where were you, what was going on—other questions got asked. So we figured to come up to your site and check. Wish we'd come sooner, Johnny. Wish we had."

He nodded, squeezed his eyes shut, remembering his friends. Sarah. Part of him. It was not grief, for Sarah. It was being cut in half.

Someone pounded at the door. "Security," someone called from outside.

"Hang Tommy," Dan said.

"They were unlocking the door. "Help me up," he begged of them; and they did, held him on his feet, wrapped one of the towels about him. The door opened, and security was there, with drawn guns.

"Got an accident," Dan said. "Team went out, lines fouled,

wind broke them. We got two in; one live, one dead; the others dropped."

"Call the meds," the officer in charge said. Johnny shook his head, panicked; the hospital—corporation-financed. He did not want to put himself in their hands.

"I'm not going," he said, while the call went out. "Going to the Bottom. Get myself a drink. That's what I want. That's all I want."

The officer pulled out a recorder. "You up to making a statement, Mr.—"

"Tallfeather. Johnny." His voice broke, abused by the cold, by fright. He leaned against the men holding him up. "I'll make your statement. We were out on the 90s, going down. My sister Sarah . . . her line broke. The others tried to spider me down, to come back, and the lines fouled. Hours out there. Lines broke, or maybe one suicided. The wind—"

"Man would," Dan said. "You ever been Outside, officer?"

"Names. ID's."

Dan handed his over. Another searched Johnny's out of his coveralls, turned everyone's over, dead and living. The officer read them off into the recorder. Returned them, to the living. "Dead man here?"

"Team boss," Johnny said, moistening his lips. "Jino Brown. The others dropped."

The officer looked at Dan Hardesty and his team. "Your part in this?"

"Friends. They didn't show and we came checking. Boy named Tommy Pratt in the Pillar, he put us onto it. Let the man go, Mister. He's had enough."

The officer bent down and checked Jino's corpse, touched the skin, flexed the fingers.

"Frosted," Dan said. "Pulled his mask off, you understand? No mask out there, you die quick. Painless, for those afraid of falling."

"Thought liners weren't afraid of falling."

"Lot of us are," Dan said levelly. "Come on, officer, this man's *sister* died out there."

"Think he'd be more upset about it, wouldn't you?"

Johnny swung; they stopped him, and the officer stepped back a pace.

"All right," the officer said carefully. "All right, all right. Easy."

Johnny sucked air, leaned there, glaring at the officer, cooled his mind slowly, thinking of what he wanted—to be out, down, away from them—alive.

The officer thumbed his mike. "Got an accident here," he said. "Liners fouled, one survivor, Tallfeather, John Ames, city employee."

Noise came back. The officer touched the plug in his ear and his eyes flickered, looking at them. The door opened, the rest of the security officers showing two meds in. "Get him out," the officer said with a gesture at Jino's body. "The other one says he's walking."

The meds ignored the body, turned on him. Johnny shook them off, shook his head while one of them told him about massive contusions and blood clots and his brain. "Get me my clothes," he told the liners. One did.

"Somebody," Dan was saying, "needs to go out there and get those bodies in off the Bottom."

He heard. Maybe he should protest, give way to grief, insist to be one to go even if there was no chance of his walking that far. He had no interest in finding Sarah's body, or Poll's, or Sam's. He had only one interest, and that was to get his clothes on, to get out of here. He managed it, wincing, while the meds conferred with the police and wondered if there were not some way to arrest him to get him to the hospital.

"Get out of here," Dan warned them, There was sullen silence.

"Mr. Tallfeather," one of the medics appealed to him.

He shook his head. It hurt. He stared hatefully at them, and they devoted their attention to Jino, who was beyond protest.

"Free to go?" Dan asked the police.

"We've got your numbers," the officer said.

Dan said nothing. Johnny walked for the door between two of them, trying not to let his knees give under him.

They got him to the service lift, got a better grip on him once inside, because he gave way when the car dropped, and he came near to fainting. They went down, down as far as they would go, got out in the passages, walked the way to the Worm.

He fainted. He woke up in a bed with no recollection of how he had gotten there; and then he did remember, and lay staring at the ceiling. An old woman waited on him, fed him;

labored over him. Others came in to look at him, liners and
Builders both. When he was conscious and could get his legs
under him he tottered out into the Worm itself and sat down
and had the drink he had promised himself, remembering
Sarah, who had sat with him—over there. And the word
whispered through the Worm that there was a strike on, that
none of the liners were going out; that there was a Builder
slowdown, and the name of Manley and ATELCORP was mentioned.

There was a quiet about the place, that day, the next.
There were police, who came and took photographs inside
the Worm and read a court order in dead silence, ordering
the Builders back to work. But the silence hung there, and
the police were very quiet and left, because no one wanted to
go Outside but liners and the whole City would die if the
Builders shut things down. Up in the towers they knew their
computers. A lot was automated; a lot was not. The computers were all their knowledge.

There was talk of an investigation. The Mayor came on
vid and appealed for calm; said there was an investigation
proceeding about gang activity, about bribes; about corrup-
tion in certain echelons far down the corporation lists. There
was a lot of talk. It all moved very quickly.

"We'll get something," Dan Hardesty told him. "We got
the one that went by Manley. Fellow named George Bettin.
ATELCORP'S man. Flunky; but we got him."

"They'll hang him out," he said quietly, hollowly. "So
much for Manley. Yes. We got him."

And that day the Bettin trial started he rode the lift up to
the hundredth, and walked to one of the observation windows, but when he got close to it, with the far blue distance
and the Newark spire rising in his view, he stopped.

It was a long time before a passerby happened to see him
there, against the wall; before a woman took him by the arm
and coaxed him away from the wall, down the corridor. They
called the meds; and they offered him sedatives.

He took them. Rode the lift down. That itself was terror.
He had had dreams at night; wakened with the world hang-
ing under him and the sky above and screamed until the
Worm echoed with it.

The drugs stopped that. But he stayed below, refused to go
near the windows. Three, four days, while the Manley/Bettin

trial dragged on. They never called him to testify; never called any of the liners.

But a message came to the Worm, signed with big names in ATELCORP; and that failed to surprise him. He went, up the far, far distance to the nineties.

He walked in, looked about him, flinched from the windows, a mere turning of his head. They wanted him to go into an office with windows. Paul Mason, the door said, President.

"Mr. Tallfeather," someone said, trying to coax him. He turned his back to the windows.

"He comes out here," he said, staring at the blank wall in front of him, the fancy wallpaper, the civic contribution citations. "He comes out to *me*."

He stood there. Eventually someone came, and a hand rested on his shoulder. "The windows. I understand, Mr. Tallfeather. I'm terribly sorry. Paul Mason. I called you here. You want to walk back this way, please?"

He walked, trembling, until they were in the hallway, in the safe, stone-veneer hall, and Mason drew him into a small windowless office, a desk, a few bookshelves, some chairs, immaculate, expensive. "Sit down," Mason urged him. "Sit down, Mr. Tallfeather."

He did so, sank into a chair. A secretary scurried in with an offer of hot tea.

"No," Johnny said quietly.

"Please," Mason said. "Something else."

"Tea," he said. The secretary left in haste. Mason sat in another chair, staring at him . . . a thin man, white-haired, with hard lines.

"Mr. Tallfeather," Mason said. "I've been briefed on your case. My staff came across with it. I've heard what happened."

"Heard," he echoed. Maybe there was still a craziness in his eyes. Mason looked uneasy.

"It was a man of ours, George Bettin. That's as far as it went; you've followed the trial."

He nodded, staring at Mason all the while.

"ATELCORP has no legal liability—certainly no criminal fault—but we want to make amends for this. To do right by you."

"To get the liners working again," he said bitterly.

"That, too, Mr. Tallfeather. I think your case, more than

the end of the trial—I think justice done on this level may do more to heal the breach. We want to offer you a position. This office. A job."

"Only I stop talking. I stop saying what happened."

"Mr. Tallfeather, the public welfare is at stake. You understand that; it's more than the project. The strike . . . is illegal. We can't have that."

He sat still a moment. "Yes, sir," he said, very, very softly. Wiped at his face. He looked about him. "Thoughtful of you. No windows."

"We're terribly sorry, Mr. Tallfeather. Our extreme condolences. Sincerely."

"Yes, sir."

"You just come to the office when you like. The door . . . doesn't go past the windows out there. You come when you like."

"Doing what, Mr. Mason?"

"We'll develop that."

"And I don't talk about my sister; about my team."

"We'd prefer not."

"You're scared," he said.

Mason's face went hard.

"I'll take the job," he said. The tea had just arrived. Mason put on a smile and rose, offered him a hand and clapped him on a still-bruised shoulder. "Your own secretary, you choose from the pool. Anything you want in the way of decor . . ."

"Yes, sir."

Mason smiled, which was not a smile. The secretary stood there with the tea, and stepped aside as Mason left. Johnny walked over and took the tray, set it down himself. "That's enough," he said. "Go away."

And that afternoon the press came, escorted by Mason.

"What do you think of the investigation, Mr. Tallfeather?"

"What was it like, Mr. Tallfeather?"

He gave it to them, all the titillation the vid addicts could ask for, how it felt, dangling in air like that, watching the others die. He was steady; he was heroic, quiet, tragic; appealed for the liners to go to work, for an end to the civic agony.

They left, satisfied; Mason was satisfied, smiled at him. Clapped him on the shoulder and offered him a drink. He took it, and sat while Mason tried to be affable. He was pleasant in turn. "Yes, Mr. Mason. Yes, sir."

He went back to his office, which had no work, and no duties.

He was back in the morning. Sat in his office and stared at the walls.

Listened to vid. The liners went back to work. The strike was over. The whole City complex breathed easier.

He stayed all the day, and left by his own door, when Mason left; used a liner's key to prep the service elevator; waited in the hall outside.

"Mr. Mason."

"Hello, Johnny."

He smiled, walked to join Mason, and Mason looked uncomfortable there in the hall, the quite lonely hall, in front of ATELCORP's big soundproof doors.

"Want you to come with me," he said to Mason.

"I'm sorry—" Mason started to say, headed for the doors.

Johnny whipped the hand and the razor from his pocket, encircled his neck, let it prick just a little. "Just want you to come with me," he said. "Don't yell."

Mason started to. The razor bit, Mason stopped, and yielded backward when he pulled him, down the hall, which at this time just before quitting time, with the Man in the hall—was very quiet.

"You're crazy," Mason said.

"Move." He jerked Mason backward, to the service elevator. Someone *had* come out. Saw. Darted back into the office. Mason started resisting and stopped at another nick.

"Look here," Mason gasped. "You're sick. It won't go bad for you; a hospital stay, a little rest . . . the company won't hold grudges; I won't. I understand—"

He dragged Mason backward into the lift; pushed TOP; and PRIORITY, with the key in. The door closed. The car shot up with a solid lift, that long, impossible climb. He let Mason loose, while he stood by the lift controls.

Mason stood against the wall and stared at him.

"I just want you," Johnny said ever so softly, "to go *with* me."

Mason's lips were trembling. He screamed aloud for help. It echoed in the small car.

"We have a head start," Johnny said. "Of course they'll come. But it takes the computers to override a service key. It'll take them a moment to realize that."

Mason stood and shivered. The car rose higher and higher,

lurched at last to a stomach-wrenching stop. The door opened on a concrete room, and he took Mason by the arm and walked him outside the car. It left again. "I think they've called it," he said calmly. Used his left hand to pull the hatch lever.

The door slammed open, echoing; the wind hit them like a hammer blow, and Mason flinched. There was a wide balcony outside, heavy pipe from which lines were strung. Mason clung to the door and Johnny dragged him forward by the arm. All the world stretched about them in the twilight, and there was ice underfoot, a fine mist blowing, bitter cold, making muscles shake. Mason slipped, and Johnny caught his elbow, walked a step farther.

"I can't go out on the lines," Johnny said. "Can't look out the windows. But company helps. Doesn't it?" He walked him far out across the paving, his eyes on the horizon haze, and Mason came, shivering convulsively within the circle of his left arm. The wind hit them hard, staggered them both, made them slip a little on the ice. His right side was numb. He kept his arm about Mason, walked to the very railing. "No view like it, Mr. Mason. I dream of it. It's cold. And it's far. Look *down*, Mr. Mason."

Mason clutched at the railing, white-knuckled. Johnny let him go, moved back from him, turned and walked back toward the lift doors.

The hatch opened. Police were there, with guns drawn. And they stayed within the doorway, leaned there, sickness in their eyes, hands clenched together on the levelled guns.

He laughed, noiseless in the wind, motioned toward the edge, toward Mason. None of the police moved. The world was naked about them. The soaring height of the other towers was nothing to this, to the City itself, the great Manhattan tower. He grinned at them, while the wind leached warmth from him.

"Go get him," he shouted at the police. "Go out and get him."

One tried, got a step out, froze and fell.

And slowly, carefully, holding up hands they could see as empty, he walked back to Mason, took his right hand and pried it from the icy rail; took the other, stared almost compassionately into a face which had become a frozen mask of horror, mouth wide and dried, eyes stark and wild. He put his arm about Mason like a brother, and slowly walked with him back to the police. "Mr. Mason," he said to them, "seems to have gotten himself out where he can't get back. But he'll be all right now." Mason's hands clung to him, and would not let go. He walked into the housing and into the lift with the police, still with his arm about Mason, and Mason clutched at him as the lift shot down. He smoothed Mason's hair as he had once smoothed Sarah's. "I had a sister," he said in Mason's ear. "But someone shut a door. On all of us. They'll convict Bettin, of course. And it'll all be forgotten. Won't it?"

The lift stopped at a lower floor. The police pushed him out, carefully because of Mason; and there were windows there, wide windows, and the twilight gleaming on the other buildings on the horizon. Mason sobbed and turned his face away, holding to him, but the police pulled them apart; and Mason held to the wall, clung there, his face averted from the glass.

"I don't think I want your job, Mr. Mason," Johnny said. "I'm going back out on the lines. I don't think I belong in your offices."

He started to leave. The police stopped him, twisted his arm.

"Do you really want *me* on trial?" he asked Mason. "Does the Mayor, or the Council?"

"Let him go," Mason said hoarsely. The police hesitated. "*Let him go.*" They did. Johnny smiled.

"My lines won't break," he said. "There won't be any misunderstandings. No more jammed doors. I'll go back to the Bottom now. I'll talk where I choose. I'll talk to whom I choose. Or have me killed. And then be ready to go on killing. Dan Hardesty and the 50 East know where I am; and why; and you kill them and there'll be more and more to kill. And it'll all come apart, Mr. Mason, all the tower will come apart, the liners on strike; the Builders . . . no more cooling, no more water, no more power. Just dark. And no peace at all."

He turned. He walked back into the lift.

No one stopped him. He rode down through all the levels of the City, to the Bottom itself, and walked out into its crooked ways. Men and women stopped, turned curious eyes on him.

"That's Johnny Tallfeather," they whispered. "That's *him.*"

He walked where he chose.

There was peace, thin-stretched as a wire. The liners walked where they chose too; and the Builders; and the Residents stayed out of the lower levels. There was from all the upper floors a fearful hush.

So the city grew.

THE PUSHER

by John Varley

*Travel between the stars is often stereotyped by
writers as if it were not much different than flying
across the ocean. But there are laws of space and
time that will come into play which cannot be overlooked when such flights become reality, whatever
the methods involved. John Varley tackles one such
problem—the time lag between the men who fly to
the stars and the folks who stay at home.*

Things change. Ian Haise expected that. Yet there are certain constants, dictated by function and use. Ian looked for
those and he seldom went wrong.

The playground was not much like the ones he had known
as a child. But playgrounds are built to entertain children.
They will always have something to swing on, something to
slide down, something to climb. This one had all those things,
and more. Part of it was thickly wooded. There was a swimming hole. The stationary apparatus was combined with dazzling light sculptures that darted in and out of reality. There
were animals, too: pygmy rhinoceros and elegant gazelles no
taller than your knee. They seemed unnaturally gentle and
unafraid.

But most of all, the playground had children.

Ian liked children.

He sat on a wooden park bench at the edge of the trees, in

the shadows, and watched them. They came in all colors and all sizes, in both sexes. There were black ones like animated licorice jellybeans and white ones like bunny rabbits, and brown ones with curly hair and more brown ones with slanted eyes and straight black hair and some who had been white but were not toasted browner than some of the brown ones.

Ian concentrated on the girls. He had tried with boys before, long ago, but it had not worked out.

He watched one black child for a time, trying to estimate her age. He thought it was around eight or nine. Too young. Another one was more like thirteen, judging from her shirt. A possibility, but he'd prefer something younger. Somebody less sophisticated, less suspicious.

Finally he found a girl he liked. She was brown, but with startling blonde hair. Ten? Possibly eleven. Young enough, at any rate.

He concentrated on her and did the strange thing he did when he had selected the right one. He didn't know what it was, but it usually worked. Mostly it was just a matter of looking at her, keeping his eyes fixed on her no matter where she went or what she did, not allowing himself to be distracted by anything. And sure enough, in a few minutes she looked up, looked around, and her eyes locked with his. She held his gaze for a moment, then went back to her play.

He relaxed. Possibly what he did was nothing at all. He had noticed, with adult women, that if one really caught his eye so he found himself staring at her she would usually look up from what she was doing and catch him. It never seemed to fail. Talking to other men, he had found it to be a common experience. It was almost as if they could feel his gaze. Women had told him it was nonsense, or if not, it was just reaction to things seen peripherally by people trained to alertness for sexual signals. Merely an unconscious observation penetrating to the awareness; nothing mysterious, like ESP.

Perhaps. Still, Ian was very good at this sort of eye contact. Several times he had noticed the girls rubbing the backs of their necks while he observed them, or hunching their shoulders. Maybe they'd developed some kind of ESP and just didn't recognize it as such.

Now he merely watched her. He was smiling, so that every time she looked up to see him—which she did with increasing frequency—she saw a friendly, slightly graying man with a broken nose and powerful shoulders. His hands were strong, too. He kept them clasped in his lap.

Presently she began to wander in his direction.

No one watching her would have thought she was coming toward him. She probably didn't know it herself. On her way, she found reasons to stop and tumble, jump on the soft rubber mats, or chase a flock of noisy geese. But she was coming toward him, and she would end up on the park bench beside him.

He glanced around quickly. As before, there were few adults in this playground. It had surprised him when he arrived. Apparently the new conditioning techniques had reduced the numbers of the violent and twisted to the point that parents felt it safe to allow their children to run without supervision. The adults present were involved with each other. No one had given him a second glance when he arrived.

That was fine with Ian. It made what he planned to do much easier. He had his excuses ready, of course, but it could be embarrassing to be confronted with the questions representatives of the law ask single, middle-aged men who hang around playgrounds.

For a moment he considered with real concern, how the parents of these children could feel so confident, even with mental conditioning. After all, no one was conditioned until he had first done something. New maniacs were presumably being produced every day. Typically, they looked just like everyone else until they proved their difference by some demented act.

Somebody ought to give those parents a stern lecture, he thought.

"Who are you?"

Ian frowned. Not eleven, surely, not seen up this close. Maybe not even ten. She might be as young as eight.

Would eight be all right? He tasted the idea with his usual caution, looked around again for curious eyes. He saw none.

"My name is Ian. What's yours?"

"*No*. Not your *name*. Who are *you*?"

"You mean what do I do?"

"Yes."

"I'm a pusher."

She thought that over, then smiled. She had her permanent teeth, crowded into a small jaw.

"You give away pills?"

He laughed. "Very good," he said. "You must do a lot of reading." She said nothing, but her manner indicated she was pleased.

"No," he said. "That's an old kind of pusher. I'm the other kind. But you knew that, didn't you?" When he smiled she broke into giggles. She was doing the pointless things with her hands that little girls do. He thought she had a pretty good idea of how cute she was, but no inkling of her forbidden eroticism. She was a ripe seed with sexuality ready to burst to the surface. Her body was a bony sketch, a framework on which to build a woman.

"How old are you?" he asked.

"That's a secret. What happened to your nose?"

"I broke it a long time ago. I'll bet you're twelve."

She giggled, then nodded. Eleven, then. And just barely.

"Do you want some candy?" He reached into his pocket and pulled out the pink and white striped paper bag.

She shook her head solemnly. "My mother says not to take candy from strangers."

"But we're not strangers. I'm Ian, the pusher."

She thought that over. While she hesitated he reached into the bag and picked out a chocolate thing so thick and gooey it was almost obscene. He bit into it, forcing himself to chew. He hated sweets.

"Okay," she said, and reached toward the bag. He pulled it away. She looked at him in innocent surprise.

"I just thought of something," he said. "I don't know your name. So I guess we *are* strangers."

She caught on to the game when she saw the twinkle in his eye. He'd practiced that. It was a good twinkle.

"My name is Radiant. Radiant Shiningstar Smith."

"A very fancy name," he said, thinking how names had changed. "For a very pretty girl." He paused, and cocked his head. "No. I don't think so. You're Radiant . . . Starr. With two *r's*. . . . *Captain* Radiant Starr, of the Star Patrol."

She was dubious for a moment. He wondered if he'd judged her wrong. Perhaps she was really Mizz Radiant

Faintingheart Belle, or Mrs. Radiant Motherhood. But her fingernails were a bit dirty for that.

She pointed a finger at him and made a Donald Duck sound as her thumb worked back and forth. He put his hand to his heart and fell over sideways, and she dissolved in laughter. She was careful, however, to keep her weapon firmly trained on him.

"And you'd better give me that candy or I'll shoot you again."

The playground was darker now, and not so crowded. She sat beside him on the bench, swinging her legs. Her bare feet did not quite touch the dirt.

She was going to be quite beautiful. He could see it clearly in her face. As for the body . . . who could tell?

Not that he really gave a damn.

She was dressed in a little of this and a little of that, worn here and there without much regard for his concepts of modesty. Many of the children wore nothing. It had been something of a shock when he arrived. Now he was almost used to it, but he still thought it incautious on the part of her parents. Did they really think the world was that safe, to let an eleven-year-old girl go practically naked in a public place?

He sat there listening to her prattle about her friends—the ones she hated and the one or two she simply adored—with only part of his attention.

He inserted um's and uh-huh's in the right places.

She was cute, there was no denying it. She seemed as sweet as a child that age ever gets, which can be very sweet and as poisonous as a rattlesnake, almost at the same moment. She had the capacity to be warm, but it was on the surface. Underneath, she cared mostly about herself. Her loyalty would be a transitory thing, bestowed easily, just as easily forgotten.

And why not? She was young. It was perfectly healthy for her to be that way.

But did he dare try to touch her?

It was crazy. It was as insane as they all told him it was. It worked so seldom. Why would it work with her? He felt a weight of defeat.

"Are you okay?"

"Huh? Me? Oh, sure, I'm all right. Isn't your mother going to be worried about you?"

"I don't have to be in for hours and hours yet." For a moment she looked so grown up he almost believed the lie.

"Well, I'm getting tired of sitting here. And the candy's all gone." He looked at her face. Most of the chocolate had ended up in a big circle around her mouth, except where she had wiped it daintily on her shoulder or forearm. "What's back there?"

She turned.

"That? That's the swimming hole."

"Why don't we go over there? I'll tell you a story."

The promise of a story was not enough to keep her out of the water. He didn't know if that was good or bad. He knew she was smart, a reader, and she had an imagination. But she was also active. That pull was too strong for him. He sat far from the water, under some bushes, and watched her swim with the three other children still in the park this late in the evening.

Maybe she would come back to him, and maybe she wouldn't. It wouldn't change his life either way, but it might change hers.

She emerged dripping and infinitely cleaner from the murky water. She dressed again in her random scraps, for whatever good it did her, and came to him, shivering.

"I'm cold," she said.

"Here." He took off his jacket. She looked at his hands as he wrapped it around her, and she reached out and touched the hardness of his shoulder.

"You sure must be strong," she commented.

"Pretty strong. I work hard, being a pusher."

"Just what *is* a pusher?" she said, and stifled a yawn.

"Come sit on my lap, and I'll tell you."

He did tell her, and it was a very good story that no adventurous child could resist. He had practiced that story, refined it, told it many times into a recorder until he had the rhythms and cadences just right, until he found just the right words—not too difficult words, but words with some fire and juice in them.

And once more he grew encouraged. She had been tired when he started, but gradually caught her attention. It was possible no one had ever told her a story in quite that way.

She was used to sitting before the screen and having a story shoved into her eyes and ears. It was something new to be able to interrupt with questions and get answers. Even reading was not like that. It was the oral tradition of storytelling, and it could still mesmerize the nth generation of the electronic age.

"That sounds great," she said, when she was sure he was through.

"You liked it?"

"I really truly did. I think I want to be a pusher when I grow up. That was a really neat story."

"Well, that's not actually the story I was going to tell you. That's just what it's like to be a pusher."

"You mean you have another story?"

"Sure." He looked at his watch. "But I'm afraid it's getting late. It's almost dark, and everybody's gone home. You'd probably better go, too."

She was in agony, torn between what she was supposed to do and what she wanted. It really should be no contest, if she was who he thought she was.

"Well . . . but —but I'll come back here tomorrow and you—"

He was shaking his head.

"My ship leaves in the morning," he said. "There's no time."

"Then tell me now! I can stay out. Tell me now. Please please please?"

He coyly resisted, harrumphed, protested, but in the end allowed himself to be seduced. He felt very good. He had her like a five-pound trout on a twenty-pound line. It wasn't sporting. But, then, he wasn't playing a game.

So at last he got to his specialty.

He sometimes wished he could claim the story for his own, but the fact was he could not make up stories. He no longer tried to. Instead, he cribbed from every fairy tale and fantasy story he could find. If he had a genius, it was in adapting some of the elements to fit the world she knew—while keeping it strange enough to enthrall her—and in ad-libbing the end to personalize it.

It was a wonderful tale he told. It had enchanted castles sitting on mountains of glass, moist caverns beneath the sea, fleets of starships and shining riders astride horses that flew the galaxy. There were evil alien creatures, and others with much good in them. There were drugged potions. Scaled beasts roared out of hyperspace to devour planets.

Amid all the turmoil strode the Prince and Princess. They got into frightful jams and helped each other out of them.

The story was never quite the same. He watched her eyes. When they wandered, he threw away whole chunks of story. When they widened, he knew what parts to plug in later. He tailored it to her reactions.

The child was sleepy. Sooner or later she would surrender. He needed her in a trance state, neither awake nor asleep. That is when the story would end.

". . . and though the healers labored long and hard, they could not save the Princess. She died that night, far from her Prince."

Her mouth was a little round *o*. Stories were not supposed to end that way.

"Is that *all?* She died, and she never saw the Prince again?"

"Well, not quite all. But the rest of it probably isn't true, and I shouldn't tell it to you." Ian felt pleasantly tired. His throat was a little raw, making him hoarse. Radiant was a warm weight on his lap.

"You *have* to tell me, you know," she said, reasonably. He supposed she was right. He took a deep breath.

"All right. At the funeral, all the greatest people from that part of the galaxy were in attendance. Among them was the greatest Sorcerer who ever lived. His name . . . but I really shouldn't tell you his name. I'm sure he'd be very cross if I did.

"This Sorcerer passed by the Princess's bier . . . that's a—"

"I know, I *know,* Ian. Go on!"

"Suddenly he frowned and leaned over her pale form. 'What is this?' he thundered. 'Why was I not told?' Everyone was very concerned. This Sorcerer was a dangerous man. One time when someone insulted him he made a spell that turned everyone's heads backwards so they had to walk around with rear-view mirrors. No one knew what he would do if he got really angry.

" 'This Princess is wearing the Starstone,' he said, and drew himself up and frowned all around as if he were surrounded by idiots. I'm sure he thought he was, and maybe he was right. Because he went on to tell them just what the Starstone was, and what it did, something no one there had ever heard before. And this is the part I'm not sure of. Because, though everyone knew the Sorcerer was a wise and powerful man, he was also known as a great liar.

"He said that the Starstone was capable of capturing the essence of a person at the moment of her death. All her wisdom, all her power, all her knowledge and beauty and strength would flow into the stone and be held there, timelessly."

"In suspended animation," Radiant breathed.

"Precisely. When they heard this, the people were amazed. They buffeted the Sorcerer with questions, to which he gave few answers, and those only grudgingly. Finally he left in a huff. When he was gone everyone talked long into the night about the things he had said. Some felt the Sorcerer had held out hope that the Princess might yet live on. That if her body were frozen, the Prince, upon his return, might somehow infuse her essence back within her. Others thought the Sorcerer had said that was impossible, that the Princess was doomed to a half-life, locked in the stone.

"But the opinion that prevailed was this:

"The Princess would probably never come fully back to life. But her essence might flow from the Starstone and into another, if the right person could be found. All agreed this person must be a young maiden. She must be beautiful, very smart, swift of foot, loving, kind . . . oh, my, the list was very long. Everyone doubted such a person could be found. Many did not even want to try.

"But at last it was decided the Starstone should be given to a faithful friend of the Prince. He would search the galaxy for this maiden. If she existed, he would find her.

"So he departed with the blessings of many worlds behind him, vowing to find the maiden and give her the Starstone."

He stopped again, cleared his throat, and let the silence grow.

"Is that all?" she said, at last, in a whisper.

"Not quite all," he admitted. "I'm afraid I tricked you."

"Tricked me?"

He opened the front of his coat, which was still draped around her shoulders. He reached in past her bony chest and down into an inner pocket of the coat. He came up with the crystal. It was oval, with one side flat. It pulsed ruby light as it sat in the palm of his hand.

"It shines," she said, looking at it wide-eyed and open-mouthed.

"Yes, it does. And that means you're the one."

"Me?"

"Yes. Take it." He handed it to her, and as he did so, he nicked it with his thumbnail. Red light spilled into her hands, flowed between her fingers, seemed to soak into her skin. When it was over, the crystal still pulsed, but dimmed. Her hands were trembling.

"It felt very, very hot," she said.

"That was the essence of the Princess."

"And the Prince? Is he still looking for her?"

"No one knows. I think he's still out there, and some day he will come back for her."

"And what then?"

He looked away from her. "I can't say. I think, even though you are lovely, and even though you have the Starstone, that he will just pine away. He loved her very much."

"I'd take care of him," she promised.

"Maybe that would help. But I have a problem now. I don't have the heart to tell the Prince that she is dead. Yet I feel that the Starstone will draw him to it one day. If he comes and finds you, I fear for him. I think perhaps I should take the stone to a far part of the galaxy, some place he could never find it. Then at least he would never know. It might be better that way."

"But I'd help him," she said, earnestly. "I promise. I'd wait for him, and when he came, I'd take her place. You'll see."

He studied her. Perhaps she would. He looked into her eyes for a long time, and at last let her see his satisfaction.

"Very well. You can keep it then."

"I'll wait for him," she said. "You'll see."

She was very tired, almost asleep.

"You should go home now," he suggested.

"Maybe I could just lie down for a moment," she said.

"All right." He lifted her gently and placed her prone on

the ground. He stood looking at her, then knelt beside her and began to gently stroke her forehead. She opened her eyes with no alarm, then closed them again. He continued to stroke her.

Twenty minutes later he left the playground, alone.

He was always depressed afterwards. It was worse than usual this time. She had been much nicer than he had imagined at first. Who could have guessed such a romantic heart beat beneath all that dirt?

He found a phone booth several blocks away. Punching her name into information yielded a fifteen-digit number, which he called. He held his hand over the camera eye.

A woman's face appeared on his screen.

"Your daughter is in the playground, at the south end by the pool, under the bushes," he said. He gave the address of the playground.

"We were so worried! What . . . is she . . . who is—"

He hung up and hurried away.

Most of the other pushers thought he was sick. Not that it mattered. Pushers were a tolerant group when it came to other pushers, and especially when it came to anything a pusher might care to do to a puller. He wished he had never told anyone how he spent his leave time, but he had, and now he had to live with it.

So, while they didn't care if he amused himself by pulling the legs and arms off infant puller pups, they were all just back from ground leave and couldn't pass up an opportunity to get on each other's nerves. They ragged him mercilessly.

"How were the swing-sets this trip, Ian?"

"Did you bring me those dirty knickers I asked for?"

"Was it good for you, honey? Did she pant and slobber?"

"*My ten-year-old baby, she's a-pullin' me back home. . . .*"

Ian bore it stoically. It was in extremely bad taste, and he was the brunt of it, but it really didn't matter. It would end as soon as they lifted again. They would never understand what he sought, but he felt he understood them. They hated coming to Earth. There was nothing for them there, and perhaps they wished there was.

And he was a pusher himself. He didn't care for pullers.

He agreed with the sentiment expressed by Marian, shortly after lift-off. Marian had just finished her first ground leave after her first voyage. So naturally she was the drunkest of them all.

"Gravity sucks," she said, and threw up.

It was three months to Amity, and three months back. He hadn't the foggiest idea of how far it was in miles; after the tenth or eleventh zero his mind clicked off.

Amity. Shit City. He didn't even get off the ship. Why bother? The planet was peopled with things that looked a little like ten-ton caterpillars and a little like sentient green turds. Toilets were a revolutionary idea to the Amiti; so were ice cream bars, sherbets, sugar donuts, and peppermint. Plumbing had never caught on, but sweets had, and fancy desserts from every nation on Earth. In addition, there was a pouch of reassuring mail for the forlorn human embassy. The cargo for the return trip was some grayish sludge that Ian supposed someone on Earth found tremendously valuable, and a packet of desperate mail for the folks back home. Ian didn't need to read the letters to know what was in them. They could all be summed up as "Get me *out* of here!"

He sat at the viewport and watched an Amiti family lumbering and farting its way down the spaceport road. They paused every so often to do something that looked like an alien cluster-fuck. The road was brown. The land around it was brown, and in the distance were brown, unremarkable hills. There was a brown haze in the air, and the sun was yellow-brown.

He thought of castles perched on mountains of glass, of Princes and Princesses, of shining white horses galloping among the stars.

He spent the return trip just as he had on the way out: sweating down in the gargantuan pipes of the stardrive. Just beyond the metal walls unimaginable energies pulsed. And on the walls themselves, tiny plasmoids grew into bigger plasmoids. The process was too slow to see, but if left unchecked the encrustations would soon impair the engines. His job was to scrape them off.

Not everyone was cut out to be an astrogator.

And what of it? It was honest work. He had made his

choices long ago. You spent your life either pulling gees or pushing *c*. And when you got tired, you grabbed some *z*'s. If there was a pushers' code, that was it.

The plasmoids were red and crystalline, teardrop-shaped. When he broke them free of the walls, they had one flat side. They were full of a liquid light that felt as hot as the center of the sun.

It was always hard to get off the ship. A lot of pushers never did. One day, he wouldn't either.

He stood for a few moments looking at it all. It was necessary to soak it in passively at first, get used to the changes. Big changes didn't bother him. Buildings were just the world's furniture, and he didn't care how it was arranged. Small changes worried the shit out of him. Ears, for instance. Very few of the people he saw had earlobes. Each time he returned he felt a little more like an ape who has fallen from his tree. One day he'd return to find everybody had three eyes or six fingers, or that little girls no longer cared to hear stories of adventure.

He stood there, dithering, getting used to the way people were painting their faces, listening to what sounded like Spanish being spoken all around him. Occasional English or Arabic words seasoned it. He grabbed a crewmate's arm and asked him where they were. The man didn't know. So he asked the captain, and she said it was Argentina, or it had been when they left.

The phone booths were smaller. He wondered why.

There were four names in his book. He sat there facing the phone, wondering which name to call first. His eyes were drawn to Radiant Shiningstar Smith, so he punched that name into the phone. He got a number and an address in Novosibirsk.

Checking the timetable he had picked—putting off making the call—he found the antipodean shuttle left on the hour. Then he wiped his hands on his pants and took a deep breath and looked up to see her standing outside the phone booth. They regarded each other silently for a moment. She saw a man much shorter than she remembered, but powerfully built, with big hands and shoulders and a pitted face that would have been forbidding but for the gentle eyes. He saw a tall woman around forty years old who was fully as beautiful as he had expected she would be. The hand of age had just begun to touch her. He thought she was fighting that waistline and fretting about those wrinkles, but none of that mattered to him. Only one thing mattered, and he would know it soon enough.

"You *are* Ian Haise, aren't you?" she said, at last.

"It was sheer luck I remembered you again," she was saying. He noted the choice of words. She could have said coincidence.

"It was two years ago. We were moving again and I was sorting through some things and I came across that plasmoid. I hadn't thought about you in . . . oh, it must have been fifteen years."

He said something noncommittal. They were in a restaurant, away from most of the other patrons, at a booth near a glass wall beyond which spaceships were being trundled to and from the blast pits.

"I hope I didn't get you into trouble," he said.

She shrugged it away.

"You did, some, but that was so long ago. I certainly wouldn't bear a grudge that long. And the fact is, I thought it was all worth it at the time."

She went on to tell him of the uproar he had caused in her family, of the visits by the police, the interrogation, puzzlement, and final helplessness. No one knew quite what to make of her story. They had identified him quickly enough, only to find he had left Earth, not to return for a long, long time.

"I didn't break any laws," he pointed out.

"That's what no one could understand. I told them you had talked to me and told me a long story, and then I went to sleep. None of them seemed interested in what the story was about. So I didn't tell them. And I didn't tell them about the . . . the Starstone." She smiled. "Actually, I was relieved they hadn't asked. I was determined not to tell them, but I was a little afraid of holding it all back. I thought they were agents of the . . . who were the villains in your story? I've forgotten."

"It's not important."

"I guess not. But something is."

"Yes."

"Maybe you should tell me what it is. Maybe you can answer the question that's been in the back of my mind for twenty-five years, ever since I found out that thing you gave me was just the scrapings from a starship engine."

"Was it?" he said, looking into her eyes. "Don't get me wrong. I'm not saying it *was* more than that. I'm asking *you* if it wasn't more."

"Yes, I guess it was more," she said, at last.

"I'm glad."

"I believed in that story passionately for . . . oh, years and years. Then I stopped believing it."

"All at once?"

"No. Gradually. It didn't hurt much. Part of growing up, I guess."

"And you remembered me."

"Well, that took some work. I went to a hypnotist when I was twenty-five and recovered your name and the name of your ship. Did you know—"

"Yes. I mentioned them on purpose."

She nodded, and they fell silent again. When she looked at him now, he saw more sympathy, less defensiveness. But there was still a question.

"Why?" she said.

He nodded, then looked away from her, out to the starships. He wished he was on one of them, pushing *c*. It wasn't working. He knew it wasn't. He was a weird problem to her, something to get straightened out, a loose end in her life that would irritate until it was made to fit in, then be forgotten.

To hell with it.

"Hoping to get laid," he said. When he looked up she was slowly shaking her head back and forth.

"Don't trifle with me, Haise. You're not as stupid as you look. You knew I'd be married, leading my own life. You knew I wouldn't drop it all because of some half-remembered fairy tale thirty years ago. *Why?*"

And how could he explain the strangeness of it all to her?"

"What do you do?" He recalled something, and rephrased it. "Who *are* you?"

She looked startled. "I'm a mysteliologist."

He spread his hands. "I don't even know what that is."

"Come to think of it, there was no such thing when you left."

"That's it, in a way," he said. He felt helpless again. "Obvi-

ously, I had no way of knowing what you'd do, what you'd
become, what would happen to you that you had no control
over. All I was gambling on was that you'd remember me.
Because that way . . ." He saw the planet Earth looming
once more out the viewport. So many, many years and only
six months later. A planet full of strangers. It didn't matter
that Amity was full of strangers. But Earth was home, if that
word still had any meaning for him.

"I wanted somebody my own age I could talk to," he said.
"That's all. All I want is a friend."

He could see her trying to understand what it was like. She
wouldn't, but maybe she'd come close enough to think she
did.

"Maybe you've found one," she said, and smiled. "At least
I'm willing to get to know you, considering the effort you've
put into this."

"It wasn't much effort. It seems so long-term to you, but it
wasn't to me. I held you on my lap six months ago."

"How long is your leave?" she asked.

"Two months."

"Would you like to come stay with us for a while? We
have room in our house."

"Will your husband mind?"

"Neither my husband nor my wife. That's them sitting over
there, pretending to ignore us." Ian looked, caught the eye of
a woman in her late twenties. She was sitting across from a
man Ian's age, who now turned and looked at Ian with some
suspicion but no active animosity. The woman smiled; the
man reserved judgment.

Radiant had a wife. Well, times change.

"Those two in the red skirts are police," Radiant was saying. "So is that man over by the wall, and the one at the end
of the bar."

"I spotted two of them," Ian said. When she looked surprised, he said, "Cops always have a look about them. That's
one of the things that don't change."

"You go back quite a ways, don't you? I'll bet you have
some good stories."

Ian thought about it, and nodded. "Some, I suppose."

"I should tell the police they can go home. I hope you
don't mind that we brought them in."

"Of course not."

"I'll do that, and then we can go. Oh, and I guess I should

call the children and tell them we'll be home soon." She laughed, reached across the table and touched his hand. "See what can happen in six months? I have three children, and Gillian has two."

He looked up, interested.

"Are any of them girls?"

POLYPHEMUS

by Michael Shea

*An extraordinary eye for anatomical detail and
the forms which living matter may take has become
the hallmark of this astonishing new writer. But by
a handful of stories, readers already know that
when they see his name they will be encountering
something vivid and unforgettable. In this novella,
Shea shows us what might be as life develops on a
planet not dissimilar to our own.*

The sunlight falls bright and strong on the wastes of Firebairn at noon, but the wind is fresh, and cuts through the
warmth of it. Consequently, murmions usually sun themselves
in the lee of the buttes and the eroded volcanic cones that
stud those plains. In the lee of one such cone—more like a
ragged ring-wall really, no higher on the average than a
hundred meters, but more than four kilometers in the diameter of its enclosure—a murmion luxuriated on a patch of red
sand.

The creatures are rather like baby seals in shape, though a
bit smaller, which still makes them among the largest of Firebairn's sparse terrestrial fauna. The lakes, such as the one in
the crater behind this murmion, and the sea contain the overwhelming majority of the planet's animal life, and all its most
impressive forms. Indeed, the colonists there had recently established that the murmion evolved from an aquatic line, the
same order to which the economically important and much

larger delphs belonged. Members of this order were sometimes called 'mammalian analogues', based on their reproductive systems, lungs, and vascular organization, but there was something of the arthropod in all of them, perhaps most noticeably in this little pioneer of the dry land. It had a smooth, chitinous hide and primitive eyes—ommatidia, really—like small, black knobs, while its 'flippers', fore and aft, were rigid and three-jointed, though of an oar-like flatness that proclaimed their ancestral function.

This murmion had chosen an unfortunate spot for its nap. It was dark blue in color, and the sand's red put it in sharp relief. This had not gone unnoticed by a second organism which now crouched up on the crater's rim, still dripping from the lake within, whence it had just emerged. This, known colloquially by the colonists as a 'gabble' (*sturtis atrox thomsonia*) was batrachian in form, though morphologically a far simpler organism than any frog, being in fact more analogous to an immense rotifer or roundworm in its internal structure. It moved on four pseudopodia: a green, viscid mass with a vast slot for a mouth and, above the mouth, a freckling of rudimentary eyes reminiscent of a spider's. It found prey by a subtle discrimination of color contrasts, and since it frequently left the water to forage along the land-fringes, one could not help feeling the murmion's sunbathing habits were singularly maladaptive. The gabble was easily four times the size of the murmion, and swift and silent as liquid—properties it now demonstrated as it leapt and flowed down the side of the crater towards the sleeper. Its final lunge came from so high that the force with which it smacked down on the murmion imparted a paralyzing shock to the prey. The gabble stepped daintily back from the stunned creature, bobbed and weaved, seemed to shudder with delicate anticipation, and swallowed the murmion whole.

It crouched there, settling down for its digestive stasis on the warm red sand. Had it possessed more highly evolved eyes, it might have been alarmed, for something of immense size was already quite near, grinding its slow way across the desert towards the crater. Perhaps not. The gabble had no natural land-dwelling predators larger than itself.

The wastelands of Firebairn would have moved any viewer susceptible to nature's grandeur. The genesis of this, and of the planet's other, quite similar continent, were not well understood. They were immense tables of volcanic outflow, produced by several primary magma-vents in the sea floor, and both ruptured and augmented by a multitude of lesser vents. The period of active vulcanism was a hundred-million years past. For the latter half of this period an oceanic weather-cycle had been established which seasonally scoured the land with hurricane winds and hammering rains, burnishing the glassy buttes and cones, scouring the obsidian fangs and claws off them, till now they shone like glazed ceramics in the sun. Only the stumps of the once-vertiginous volcanoes remained, twisted pots and cauldron-rims, loaf-shaped nubs of mountains—all red, black, green and ochre. Between these ruined works of the planet-furnace were the glorious, level wastes of wind-rounded gravel and sand in patches, stripes and tangled ribbons of the same colors, or in eerie melds of all four where the weather patterns had mingled them. And bejewelling this already jewelled terrain, the numberless lakes—most of them in the craters, but many on the flats where their stark, cruel blue shown impossibly intense within their shores of polychrome detritus. It was a world of inexorable beauty, through which a man might go in rapture, but only if borne in steel, only in a juggernaut harder than the harshness of that stern paradise.

The sand-hog was such a craft, a great tractor-transport, tank-treaded, that chewed across the gravel, gnawing it with a continuous, fifty-ton bite. It bore three boats in its undercarriage, nine men and women in its upper decks. In its middle was a holding tank, a belly that whole schools of delphs could be swallowed into and carried off to sate the hunger of the growing colony. It was now farther from the colony than it had ever gone, not due to any shortage of delphs in the colony's immediate vicinity, but in order to combine forage with exploration and mapping of the continent. As the vehicle drew near the landmark its captain had selected for inspection, Penny Lopez, watching from one of the ports, said:

"Look. There's a gabble."

Several of the others joined her at adjacent ports. Aside from indicating that the crater indeed contained a lake, the presence of a gabble was a good sign that the lake would contain delphs, for the creatures were typically ecological associates. Both inhabited 'ocean rooted' lakes, those whose containing craters possessed open vent systems that connected their waters with subcontinental marine influxes.

"Why is it wobbling like that?" asked Japhet Sparks, the cartographer. Nemo Jones, one of the armorers, smiled within his ragged beard.

"Maybe he ate something nasty." Penny looked at him sharply. Nemo's ability to irritate her, by even the most innocent-seeming remarks, was a source of open humor among the colonists. But Orson Waverly, who was the expedition's biologist, glanced at Nemo and shared his smile.

Indeed, the gabble did not look well. Pseudopodia spread, it seemed to be trying to brace itself, while spasms and tremors made it quake like a shaken plate of jelly. One of its sides bulged. From the bulge, something sprouted that looked like a blue, crooked knife blade, and even as it did so, a second, identical one erupted from the creature's opposite side. With a synchronized, sweeping motion, like oars plied by a boatman, these blades began to cut two jagged incisions through the flanks of the gabble.

"Captain Helion," said Waverly, "would you go at one-third for a moment for a field observation?"

The formality of the request was necessary, for the Captain, a tall and statuesquely handsome man, disliked modification of any of his procedures. He arched an eyebrow, nodded cooly, and cut speed.

The observation required little time, for as the gabble ceased its impotent quiverings of resistance, a second pair of angled blades thrust from its sides. With an undulating, swimming motion (not unlike a baby seal's) these four trenchant protrusions completed a circuit of the froglike belly. Head and forelegs flabbily collapsed, and from the bloody-edged barrel of the gabble's hindquarters, the bright, eye-knobbed snout of a murmion poked into the sunlight. It was a brief, exulting gesture, as a dolphin might make, breaking the surface out of sheer exuberance to dive again—and this the murmion did, greedily, into the nourishing pot of its prey's stomach.

Penny scowled at Nemo Jones, who smiled again, more broadly this time. She marched to the piloting module, where Helion was already gearing up again, and guiding the sandhog into a course around the crater's base, to begin the search for an access to its interior negotiable by the fishing boats' tractor treads.

"What are the chances of finding a break?"

Captain Helion's normal manner of stalwart composure

was always faintly heightened in Penny Lopez's neighborhood. He cocked an eye at the crater wall and murmured a judicious reply. Nemo Jones turned to Waverly, who was making a journal entry, and said:

"You won't see that happen on dark sand. Murm's always lie up on red or yellow, to show up better for the gabbles."

"Don't tell me," put in Jax Giggans from where he stood by the armory, readying the rifles. "You hunted murmions on Katermand. Katermandian murmions. And you know all their tricks. And when they can't find sand the right color to lie on, they make use of special polychromatic piss-glands they have to dye it red."

Nemo laughed—a single bark of pleasure only, practically a cachinnation from this rather solemn man. From another he would have greeted the remark—a typical colony joke on his origin and his seemingly endless repertory of woodsman's tricks and lore—with a courteous look of attention, and perhaps a blink of bafflement. That the Katermandian showed what for him amounted to an outright fondness for his burly fellow-armorer was doubly puzzling to the other colonists.

The men had been enemies—or rather, Jax had been Nemo's insistent antagonist, during the Katermandian's first year on Firebairn. Nemo was taciturn, stoically compliant with orders, most of the time. Periodically he volunteered an observation or a suggestion. This usually derailed whatever train of thought the others were pursuing, and not uncommonly led to a solution of the problem at hand. To this subtly irritating pattern, he added a disposition towards rare fits of stubbornness, when he immovably refused to execute some order. He had spent a number of weeks in the detention cubicle as a result.

Senior staff balanced his recalcitrance against his usefulness, and soon realized that a tolerance must be developed for his occasional infractions. This had triggered Jax's enmity. Jax was a first-rate weapons man, but one of those whose strictness with himself extended to a jealous watchfulness of others' discipline. On a quarrying expedition just before the last rains, Nemo had gone sullen over something, and refused an order. Jax had bellowed "Enough!", and stood to confront him. The Katermandian was informed that he would get cracking, or have his head cracked.

Jax was bull-bodied, over six feet tall. He shaved his scalp, and his head looked like a battering-ram. Nemo Jones was a handsbreadth shorter, and lighter by fifteen kilos. He was not unimpressive—a lean, wideshouldered man with knot-muscled arms and legs, roped with sinew and vein, and hairy as a goat.

But still the smaller man by far. Deep in the grotto of his shaggy beard and vine-thick hair, his black eyes had looked gravely out at Jax. Captain Helion, secretly pleased, turned to direct another matter, but—sidelong—watched, as everyone did. Nemo stood up and made a simple beckoning gesture to Jax.

It was an eventful fight, though not a long one. In it, Jax lost an upper canine tooth, had his nose broken, a rib cracked, his left shoulder dislocated, and received a multitude of astonishingly large and vivid bruises on face, throat, chest and arms. He was a man of courage, and picked himself up no less than four times, but he fell five. Afterwards he harbored no bitterness, and would unabashedly describe the fight and his role in it to anyone who asked. He told Nemo that anyone who could fight as he did had to have good reasons for whatever course of action he chose. It was perhaps this magnanimity in defeat on Jax's part that had won Nemo's particular regard. Not only did he laugh aloud now—he riposted:

"No. They always piss green. Diet of gabbles."

"A joke! First a smile, then a laugh, and now Nemo Jones has made a joke! Check the ports. The sky may be falling."

It was Sarissa Wayne, one of the pilot-gunners, who said this. In doing it, she drew more surprise on herself than Nemo's sally had roused. It was customary for all of them to mock his sober formality, but not with the sneer she put into it, nor with the attentive eye to the details of his behaviour that her words betrayed. Sarissa was a small, wiry woman, blackhaired. Tart and unequivocal speech was more her style than taunts, and it took Jones aback. She joined Angela Rackham, her fellow pilot, at a port on the opposite side of the cabin. The Katermandian, impassive though his face usually was, could be seen for an instant to wonder if there was something about him that made women mad.

Angela put her arm across her smaller friend's shoulders and made talk about the view. She dearly loved Sarissa's pride, but knew that in recent months it had often brought her where she now was—very close to crying with frustration. And she knew that this particular occasion's cause—surely humiliatingly pathetic to Sarissa herself—was jealousy that it was Jax who had had this opening-up from Nemo, and not Sarissa.

Angela had given up offering any direct counsel on the matter. The ardor that so mortified Sarissa it prevented her from making any but the most understated bids for Nemo's attention also made the topic too hot for even the most compassionate handling. Angela would have liked to point out to her friend that the Katermandian's background was such that he had yet to be taught the kind of easy intimacy that Sarissa craved from him. Even to Penny Lopez, whom Nemo was ceremoniously (and without the slightest success) courting—even to her he showed no such openness.

"We are approaching a likely entry point. Pilots below-decks, please." Helion used the intercom, though he might have spoken over his shoulder and been heard by all. Angela and Sarissa were joined by the mechanic, Norrin. They went below, to check the chemical balance of the quarry tanks between decks, and then to start the motors of their boats warming. Orson Waverly and Japhet Sparks went to the lockers to start laying out the field gear, while Jax and Nemo got out rifles for themselves and the captain, and stood ready behind him, watching the scene from the pilot's port.

Erosion had broadened a crack in the cone wall, creating a gravel-floored defile that could be reached by a few meters' climb from the desert floor. Helion stopped the sand-hog below the defile. "Reconnaisance party stand by to disembark," he said, again through the intercom. He thumbed a switch. The door coughed open and the gang ramp creaked outwards, downwards to the bright sand. He gave the controls to Penny, took his rifle from Jax, and preceded Jax and Nemo down the ramp.

The defile appeared more than adequate for the boats. Before they were halfway through it they saw the lake: a vast, brilliant arena of water, steep-shored save for a small beach at the defile's foot. Near the water's center, perhaps two kilometers off shore, was a small, craggy island.

"There's delph here. No doubt of it," Nemo muttered. As was often his way on unknown ground, he moved tautly, "ready to drop to all fours" as Sarissa had once expressed it. Helion disregarded him, but Jax looked at his friend with an air of inquiry, not so much for the remark as for an undertone of unease he had heard in it.

The boats' access assured, they climbed to the crown of the rim and moved along it. The island seemed to be a volcanic plug, an upwelling of magma that had succeeded the cone's formation by a long time, for it was far less eroded than the wall they stood on, to a degree for which the wall's shelter could not account. They had gone less than a mile when a deep cove in the island's flank was revealed.

"Shit," Jax growled in awe. The cove teemed with delphs, by far the biggest school the men had ever seen. Even at that distance, they didn't need the glasses to see the beasts—scores of them sunning in the shallows, their backs bulging above the water looking like a nestful of silver eggs, and scores more where the cove deepened, playing the leaping game of tag characteristic of the younger members of the species. Helion gazed in silent satisfaction. Nemo Jones said:

"There's something wrong with the way the water moves. Have you noticed it?"

The captain's face changed as if a sourness had touched his palate. Jax asked, "How do you mean? Where?"

"Out in midwater, this side of the island. Twice now it's looked jittery in a way the winds don't account for."

Helion sighed. "For God's sake Jones. *Jittery?* There's some wind-chop, a little swell, the sun-dazzle . . . Just what kind of ominous subtleties do you think you're seeing?"

"It *is* subtle, Captain, and it's not happening right now. But I've seen it twice since we've been up on the ridge here. Subtle but definite. At the least it means some kind of deep current."

"Jones, you may be sincere, but you are also compelled to concoct frontiersman's intuitions about even the most straightforward good luck. I've been watching the lake and I saw nothing. What about you, Jax?"

"I can't say I did, but I don't make light of Nemo's eye for things."

"Nor do I make light of it, Jones. It'll go in the log if you wish. Meanwhile our job here seems strikingly clear to me, and I think we'd better get to it."

The Katermandian shrugged, staring not at the captain, but at the lake. "Maybe it's meaningless—how can I say? But it wasn't intuition. It's something I *saw*."

He didn't immediately follow the other two back towards the sand-hog. He watched the water a few minutes more, then tensed.

"Again," he murmured. "Yes, I see you. A convective eccentricity, from some magmal vent? I think you're too erratic for that. . . ."

He spat on the ground for luck, and hurried to catch up to the others.

The boats, moored at the little beach, rode the soft heave of the waters, their armor-glass cockpit bubbles flashing in the sun. The expeditioners stood on the shingle. Nemo squatted a bit apart from the group, watching the lake, meditatively grinding his rifle-butt against the gravel. Captain Helion stood facing the other seven. His stance was more erect than usual, truculent one might almost have said.

"Captain, I have to question this," Orson Waverly was saying. "If you make a special Command Override of it, naturally I'll obey, but it seems needlessly—"

"Needless, Waverly? We don't need delph roe? We don't need fresh breeding stock for the pens at base? Maybe we should radio home and have our surpluses destroyed. Perhaps we should just relax, have a swim, and go back."

"But Captain," Jax said, "two boats or three—what's the differential?"

"You tell me the differential, Giggans. With three boats out there we can dye the cove and drive damn near the whole school to shore in one sweep. With two we might get a third at the first sweep, and then we could go back cruising and gunning all day and not get more than another third from the scatterers."

"But that's just it," Waverly said. "More than two-thirds of a school that size would put the hog near overload. With the tanks that full, half the live take could die on the ride home. It's roe we need more than meat."

Helion's proposal was a distinct departure from his normal style, undeniably unorthodox. Colony procedure was quite explicitly prescribed on this point: one fishing craft was to remain on shore at standby during any maneuver in unexplored environments. The captain's numerical assessment of the situation was not wrong. For a few minutes after a school had been blinded by a dye grenade, it was panicked enough to be moved en masse if the boats' ultrasonic pulsars could effectively bracket it with their crossfire. Here, three boats might handle it, but two could not. Meanwhile, blinded delphs rapidly reoriented to a sightless defensive pattern—sounded shallowly and dispersed—and individuals that eluded a first sweep would have to be painstakingly stalked and harpooned one by one.

But considering the probable yield of even the two-boat deployment, Helion's insistence on the three-boat plan was unreasonable—gluttonous. Waverly saw that his objection hadn't moved the captain, and he added:

"Listen, sir. I respectfully suggest that you're excited by the size of the find. You want to make a record catch. You're letting pride bend your judgment. I'm not rebuking—it's normal, healthy ambition, but—"

"Thank you, Waverly. Now that you've spit out your bit of malice, we'll proceed. We'll start in Formation Delta, assignments as follows. . . ."

When the briefing was done and the group dispersed to their boats, Angela Rackham detained Sarissa to give her a kiss on the cheek. Sarissa did not like the captain, but she had not added her voice to those of Jax and Waverly, and her friend had been able to read from her glances that anger at Nemo Jones in some way caused her silence. Angela hesitated, then decided to break her own rule in this matter. "Talk to Nemo, Sari," she whispered. "Get it out. What can you lose?"

She didn't wait to be answered, and Sarissa didn't try to. They went to their boats. Nemo was assigned to Sarissa's, and before she got in she watched for a moment his slow approach to it. She almost smiled when she noticed that Helion was watching him too. Nemo's glum silence had contradicted him more painfully than all of Jax's and Orson's words.

In fact, Jones had spoken only once since returning to the sand-hog. He had gone up to Penny Lopez and said:

"Listen, Penny, I think this lake is dangerous. It . . . smells wrong. I'm going to watch out for you, but be alert."

Penny had turned to Helion and said, "Captain, Armorer Jones reports a negative olfactory observation on reconnaissance. Should it be entered in the log?"

There was a faint shade of dubiety underlying her sarcasm that caused Helion's jaw to tighten, and made him ignore the joke. Her tone betrayed that it was impossible to dismiss absolutely even Jones' most enigmatic misgivings. The captain had directed the disembarkation curtly. When the boats had been driven through the defile, and it was clear the terrain offered their treads enough traction to haul the quarry cages out again, he had the cages taken out and assembled on the beach, and then announced the plan he had not known, till that moment, he meant to propose. Only when he saw Sarissa close her cockpit bubble, securely locking the Katermandian into his place in the expeditionary order, did Helion join Penny and Jax in his own boat.

And presently the triangle of domed ellipsoids slid out onto the breathing blue serenity. Their wakes were so slight they scarcely marred the waters, wherein the colossal wall containing them, all glossy carmine marbled with jet black, was repeated.

Japhet Sparks sat amidships, between Sarissa and Nemo. He had a true cartographer's love for physical creation, and he turned his bony face greedily upon the scene surrounding them.

"By God, look at it! I've never seen such a gorgeous lake. A marine vent for sure—probably along the magma vent at the root of that island. And talk about recent vulcanism—if that island's a day over ten million, I'll eat it. Oh, for a week to check it out with a lung!"

Without turning, Sarissa asked, "How does the water smell to you?"

Sparks grasped the allusion, but only granted the gibe an irritated shrug. Nemo stared at the back of their pilot's head. "I didn't say it in jest, Sarissa. What it is I don't know, but—"

"You gave Penny Lopez a special warning. You didn't give me one." She said it flatly, foreknowing the humiliation it would cause her. Her eyes filled with tears, though she did not cry, and in a burst of anger she violently cut a veering loop out from their wing position in the triangle. Both men nearly lost their seats with the fierceness of the turn.

By the time Helion's corrective bark issued from the intercom she had already begun pulling them back into the formation, and the captain's order had the effect of aggravating her insubordinate impulse. She pulled back out of position and threw a wide, dreamy parabola across the water.

The bulk of the island lay between them and their quarry, and Sarissa gave herself the luxury of bearding Helion more thoroughly, since it could not jeopardize the success of the hunt. She meandered insolently far afield, enjoying Helion's outrage crackling from the speaker. Then she began a leisurely return, half a mile astern of the other two boats. Both she and Sparks jumped with the shock of Nemo's movement.

He sprang from the stern seat and dove for the communicator, whose reply-switch he threw repeatedly, signalling the captain that he wished to cut in.

Helion was ordering Sarissa to dock at the nearest shelving of the island's shore, toward which he already had the other two boats putting in, and there to yield her helm to Japhet. Nemo's signals, far from inducing him to open the line, made him flood it even more furiously.

But in Sarissa's boat he now went unregarded. Both she and Japhet had just seen what Nemo had seen. With a moan of horror she accelerated to catch up, zig-zagging wildly as she did so, trying to set up a watery commotion that would draw the eyes of their friends behind them. The other two boats were at half engine as they approached the island. Just astern of them, a huge shape bulged beneath the surface of the lake.

It was not a turbulence, but a coherent, pallid mass that glided after the boats perhaps a fathom down in the water. Subtler, but as horrific, was the wake it left—a greasy surface-boil hundreds of meters broad, bespeaking a bulk far vaster than was visible, though that blurred globe was many times the size of all three boats combined.

The two advance craft were scarcely a hundred meters from the island, and their pursuer half as far behind them, when Helion's boat accelerated explosively, a full-drive leap that should have run it straight up onto the shoal. Instead, its thrust snagged and slowed to the leaden crawl that shackles flight in nightmares. Black grass sprouted from the water, engulfing both the boats.

Grass that writhed like snakes as it grew, meters high and dense as on the lushest prairie—a medusa grass, dark as space, its every fibril clutching and raking the air with a blind and busy greed. Angela's boat was completely enmeshed, its stern cocked high above the water, turned weightlessly in the shuddering weave as a bug is turned by the spider wrapping it. Helion's boat, however, was gradually tearing shorewards from the net, whose grip its burst of speed had half-foiled.

And now Sarissa had reached them. At ninety knots she swerved obliquely to the uncanny meadow and plowed across its fringe. A shockwave, as of pain, rolled through the field. Helion's boat lurched free, roared through the shallows and plunged, spraying sparks, up onto the island. Sarissa's drive had slowed to fifteen knots before she herself fought

free into the shoals that fringed the isle, and which the monstrous growth had not invaded. She swung parallel to the
shore and tucked the boat into an inlet.

The colonists jumped from their vessels and gathered on
the shore. Jax and Nemo broke out the rifles, but those they
gave them to held them helplessly, standing in a rapture of
horror, watching the struggle. Then, near the meadow's center, the pale bulb rose and swelled up from the water.

It was a titanic eye—a transparent orb of gold, intricately
veined within, the pupil a scarlet rhomboid into which five
sand-hogs could have driven abreast. Deep in the yellow
ichor, black shapes moved, whole constellations of them
swarming through the kelp-like jungle of veins, while outside
the globe, round its base, a collar of huge, tongue-like tentacles stirred, stretched, and licked the air. With cyclopean
sloth the whole orb rolled within this tentacular calyx and
aimed the red vent of its pupil upon the captured boat.

And now a dreadful purpose entered the action of the fibrils. Variously, testingly, they turned and tilted the craft,
probing and caressing it in every orientation. There was a
grinding noise. As a man might open a jar, the creature
twisted off the boat's cockpit bubble, inverted and shook its
hull. Norrin and, a moment later, Angela Rackham tumbled
down into the black seethe. The fibrils heaved, and catapault-
ed the boat away. It crashed on the island's shore.

All that the watchers did was as a dream. Jax and Nemo
pumped explosive shot against every part of the eye and its
corolla. The grenade slugs produced only negligible tatterings
of its gelatinous substance. Sarissa struggled to free a coil of
harpoon line from the wrecked boat's equipment locker,
while Helion and Penny helped Sparks lift Orson Waverly
from the space beneath the control panel where he had
wedged himself, and where he now lay bleeding and coma-
tose. But these were ghostly acts, performed in stupefaction,
while every man and woman did but one thing—watch Norrin and Angela and the thing that had them.

The black meadow undulated still, but less chaotically,
with an insistent, peristaltic surge that brought the victims
towards the eye. Like castaways caught in a hideous, slow
surf they struggled in the snakish, multibrachiate grip—
clutched, stroked, raised and dipped, but always eased inexorably nearer the eye. The colonists saw now Florrin's arm
clawing sunwards, festooned with serpents, now Angela's

back and shoulders, bucking to wrench her head free of the nauseous swell.

The tentacles nearest the victims began an obscene elongation, till finally two of them plunged down and plucked the captives free. Swinging them high, the tentacles brought the women inwards and poised them above the alien pupil, which moved below, as with a savoring gaze. The tentacles uncoiled. The women plunged into the red vent, and sank kicking down within the golden ichor.

In the eye-blink of their vanishing through that red chasm, they entered another world, and were transformed to different beings. Drifting down they came within the eye, dancing the drowning agony in a tempo surreally slow, an almost comic pantomime of life's wrenching-free from its frame. Their faces and limbs were bloated, corrupt of color in the amber light. Angela's hair bannered wantonly, slow-motion, while those on the island could see her eyes—black holes in a gape-jawed mask—aimed downward on the swarming deep she sank to. Webbed veins, huge, crooked roots now partly screened their fall, which showed in glimpses as the over-all organic movement within the eye began to boil with a new energy.

Those on the island watched what followed with an amazement so complete it looked like rapture. At one point, responding no doubt to some impulse to avert his own eyes (though he never did so) Nemo Jones cried out:

"Don't look away. Remember details. We've got to know it to kill it."

His companions needed these exhortations as little as Nemo himself did. Forgetting even to attend to Waverly's serious head injury, they watched as if the universe and all time contained no other thing to see. And there were many details to be remembered.

Firebairn's moonrise is two-phased. The first one to rise is so small it looks like a huge, slightly blurred yellow star. The second follows in about three hours, and at full is a large silver disk. Colonists had come to speak of the 'pendulum' rising rather than the 'moons', because three bright stars, forming a neat perpendicular to the horizon, connect the moons for the first two hours after the second one's appearance, and the latter, especially when it is in a crescent phase, seems a weight depending from the golden pivot of its higher, smaller sister.

The pendulum was just up, and it was cold. The group sat in a circle around the camp's field stove. Helion sat closest to its light, more visible, more erect than the others. But there was less pride of rank in his posture than an air of pained self-presentation, as if in response to a tacit charge lodged against him by the others slouched tiredly in the shadows. He had been arguing with Nemo for the last five minutes. Throughout, his normal inflexibility had been accompanied by an uncharacteristic calm. Now he shook his head definitively, rejecting in the gesture not only all the Katermandian had said, but all that he might say. When he spoke, it was formally, his eyes sweeping the whole group by way of preface.

"You will all, as a body, formally depose me and place me under arrest, to which I willingly accede, or you will do this as I prescribe, and with the personnel I have designated. There is no more to say, Jones. Take it or leave it."

The Katermandian squatted on his hams. The light escaping the shadow-pools over his eyes was baleful, and this the captain saw; but it was also—and this Helion did not see—compassionate. He set his words out carefully:

"Listen, I beseech you Captain. You have all the good of pride, as well as the bad of it. You want to atone for our danger, but you've done no real wrong. If you've been foolish, why, everyone's a fool! I've been one thousands of times—it's a wonder I'm alive! It's my plan. Do you want to throw on me the guilt of having someone else take the risk of it? You *know* that Jax and I are our best swimmers. . . ." He gestured awkwardly, breaking off. He read his failure in the captain's sour smile before he heard the man's answer.

"The plan was yours. The log already so witnesses. Our need for it, our predicament here, is wholly my doing, and the log testifies this as well. My decision is as before."

Nemo stood up. He nodded and stepped out of the circle. The wind was freshening, but he left the shelter of the hollow they had camped in and climbed up to the island's saw-toothed crest and found himself a seat overlooking the delph cove, some hundred meters below. He had not been there long when his fellow armorer joined him. They sat in silence for a while, watching the pendulum and, alternately, its image in the molten black mirror of the lake.

"That time we fought," Jax said. "I truly deserved the beating I got. I told myself it was your contempt of duty that enraged me. In fact I knew you were guilty of no such thing. It was simply that I envied your freedom."

The way Nemo jumped on these words revealed that his silence had masked a purpose. "You feel trapped now Jax, right? You're as much as saying goodbye with that speech. You *are* trapped in this plan. It will fail. With Helion leading it, without me along, it's doomed. He's brave but he has no style, no hunch-nerves. Please. Refuse your post. *Force* him to use me. Your dissension will have more weight with him than anyone's."

"What a storm of words! You've put more of your voice in my ears in the last two hours than in all the year I've known you. No. Sorry. And it's not necessarily because I don't believe you."

"Shit." Nemo said this mournfully, looking now more directly below their perch to the cove. Only eyes which had watched the school at dusk, when the beasts found berths in the fissures of the shore and emptied their flotation sacs to sink to their rest, could have found them now in the moonlight—vague torpedoes of silver just under the heave of the black water.

He scowled at them. The austere disapproval of his expression might have been that of some creating deity gravely displeased with what he had wrought. It was Firebairn and its unique bio-generative forces that had made the delphs, of course; Nemo had made only an escape plan which enlisted them. He looked again at Jax, his eyes bitter, refusing to speak his request again, but also refusing to withdraw it. For answer, his brawny friend turned his face, wryly, to the island's northern quarter, where all explanation of the morrow's insanity lay.

It looked like an immense planktonic toadstool now, the pale orb still exposed, though half sunk from its former elevation. The field of cilia was similarly contracted. Only the tips of the tendrils showed, bristling the moon-polished waters, a field of thorns. The two men stared at the thing for a long time.

"It *is* watching us," Jax said, speaking his decision in the debate that both had pursued internally. All useful speculations had long ago been traded, mutual conjecture exhausted. "So huge it is, and so sharply *aware. . . .*"

"It had to be Orson blinded," Nemo raged. He spat towards their enemy. "Something that big's got to be marine, up that vent, and that's the maddening thing. Orson's been sidelining in marine studies all this last half year, always going out to Base Two to talk to their biomaths. And if we just knew how it worked, maybe there'd be. . . ."

"Be what?"

"Maybe there'd be some way *into* it. I'm sorry I ever spoke this plan. The more I think the more I feel it—there's no sneaking past that thing, it's got to be killed. Gotten into."

"Who's that?"

"It's Sarissa."

The pilot-gunner was climbing towards them, choosing her handholds from the crag-face as easy and sure as a woman gathering shells from a level beach.

"Orson's completely conscious now. He took some broth."

"Thinking straight?" Jax's eyes winced slightly at the brutality of his own question.

"Yes. He's not lost to us—we both think he can help, and he wants to talk to the two of you right now."

The men got up, but Sarissa did not move yet. "The captain's asleep," she said. Nemo heard the shade of pity in this—Sarissa usually called him 'Helion'. "We're all agreed he's to be left out till we work out what we want to do. Penny didn't want it that way, but she gave in to the rest of us." Her eyes flashed briefly to Nemo's here. The three started down.

It was past midnight when Captain Helion was wakened. Jax and Japhet told him the group's proposal. Any innovative consensus among his subordinates could now only strike the exhausted man as veiled mutiny. He gave Jax an *et tu, Brute* look, and stared disgustedly into the glowing coils of the camp stove.

"It's clear you'll all do what you want. Kindly trouble me with no further parades of obedience. Spend the time any way you please between now and tomorrow."

"No! Someone bring me out to him. Captain!"

As surprised as Helion, Jax turned to help Sarissa and Nemo carry Orson Waverly's camp chair into the center of the circle. The biologist's eyes were bandaged. Some few tears of blood had escaped the bandages and tracked his cheeks.

"Captain?" The face scanned, hunting a voice-fix on Helion.

"I'm here Waverly."

"Listen, Captain. Don't slacken now. Give us strictness here, where we need it. This will have to be a systematic information-pooling, using the log. Make it official to make it strict. This thing is epochs ahead of us in its adaptation to this world. We had better evolve a very sharp and efficient group mind to fight it with, and do it pretty damn fast, or else we're all going to die, and you've seen how we're going to die."

The captain rose to the occasion, but only just. He nodded. "Wake me when it's my turn." He went back to his bed.

The second moon's setting came three hours before dawn that morning. Nemo and Orson Waverly sat by the stove. Everyone else was asleep. Waverly had just turned off the log, which he'd had on playback, and now he sighed. The two men's ears still rang with all the perplexities the tape had woven round their weary minds.

"Two distinct groups of carnivores inside the sphere," Waverly said monotonously. "The members of both working in subgroups. Packs. The individuals in both groups anchored by slender umbilici to the base of the sphere. In both cases— Shit! Shit shit shit! My brain is a knot. There isn't a nerve in me that's not twisted into a rock-hard knot. If I could just have a look, the faintest, five-second *glimpse* of it! Words! Dear God, for an image—a true, solid, detailed, polychromatic *image*. Grotesque caricatures is all I get out of this, meaningless exaggerations of the chance suggestions sparked by all these endless *words!*"

Silence followed. Listlessly, Nemo asked, "Caricatures? Like what?"

"Fat-headed, taper-tailed, saw-mouthed fish. Sharks. Sharks and squids, swimming in segregated schools in a spherical tank full of kelp."

"Kelp? Sharks?"

"Kelp is a terrene marine vegetable, grows in long stalks. Sharks are marine carnivores. So are squids, invertebrates with beaks centered inside bouquets of tentacles—like those other things you described, except squids have fewer tentacles and most of them are the same size. . . . You know, I find myself wondering about those tethers. You said that both the squids and sharks patrolled everywhere, but the two kinds of school never intermingled, correct?"

"Yes. They always dodged each other very smoothly."

"But both groups had the same kind of caudal umbilicus, of a pale, almost translucent material, very slender, tough and flexible. Now what about the anchorages of those umbilici to that—basal muck that everything in the globe was rooted in? Was there any kind of pattern to their attachment down there? Did they attach just anywhere, or in clusters? If the latter, were the clusters segregated as the organisms themselves were?"

Nemo considered for perhaps half a minute. "I just can't be sure. With the prowlers' anchor lines all criss-crossing higher up, and with all those big kelp stalks—down at that bottom level my eyes just couldn't unweave it all. But you've reminded me of something else about those lines anyway. The squids fed second, milled around very excited all the time the sharks were feeding. Then, when the sharks finished, a lot of them sounded for the bottom of the eye—I didn't see even as much as Japhet did about why they did that—and the squids moved in for their turn. When they did that, I saw one of them get its tether snagged on a kelp stalk. I think it sensed it and tried to double back, but the others were crowding it along, and the tether broke."

"And what was the effect of the tether breaking?"

"It forgot about feeding. It swam a corkscrew pattern for a minute and then, like it had suddenly got a fix, sounded straight for the bottom. I lost it in the kelp, but when it came back up about a minute later, it was trailing a new tether."

Waverly said nothing for a long time and Nemo became immobile, like a pair of hands intently cupping an embryonic flame, cherishing it to life within their stillness. But at length the biologist sighed again.

"I was guessing the tethers were some sort of alimentary connection with the larger organism. But how could such a pipeline be so relatively delicate, and so quickly repairable? We'll have to set it aside. I want to hear Japhet again. There's some suggestive things in his description of the feeding process."

Orson felt for the rewind button on the log and punched it. Nemo checked a notebook for the calibrations of Japhet's report and hit the replay switch when it appeared on the gauge. Orson Waverly's voice came from the speaker.

"OK Japhet. Now lets move to what happened on the inside. What did they do to them?" 'Them' meant Angela and

Norrin, well loved by all, not least by Japhet. There was a silence in which the cartographer worked to find a steady voice.

"They were alive. I think that fluid in there half-paralyzed them somehow. . . . Their bodies were swelling too, very noticeably after the first few seconds, and they sank slower than—than you would have expected. There wasn't much fight in their movements, but they were struggling some. Just about when they'd sunk to the top of all that. . . . seaweed, all those long purple stalks—just about then those first things hit them, the big, saw-toothed ones with the black studs all over their—their brows, I guess you'd say. Little knobs set in stripe patterns. They reminded me of delph eyes. Anyway they hit them first. Started tearing chunks out of them, out of every part of their bodies, swarmed on them like ants so that both their bodies just looked like two wriggling clusters of those things. Their blood—Angela and Norrin's blood—" Japhet stopped, then resumed, talking faster. "Their blood came out in clouds and the swarms of the things were pretty much hidden in the . . . the smokiness of it. But I think there was a high turnover, no one of them fed long, and it looked like most of them got their . . . turn."

"Yes. I'm very sorry about having to do this, Japhet. Did they keep sinking as they were being fed on?"

"Very little. The feeding swarms kept them up in the upper levels of that seaweed tangle. And it was pretty abrupt when the last of them all broke away, a couple seconds when the two of them, their remains, just hung there, started sinking again. . . ."

"Yes Japhet. I'm sorry, but the remains. I need everything."

"All the flesh gouged off!" It was a shout, a burst of rage evading intolerable pain.

"Please Japhet."

"Most of the skin and muscle bitten out. Skeletons still held . . . held together by scraps of tendon. Maybe half the entrails still hang—hanging from the body cavities. Skulls intact. The parts inside the ribcages too. Then the others converged all at once. They seemed to concentrate on the upper parts of the bodies. It was like with the others. If not all of them took their turn, most did."

"Listen Japhet. Helion and Penny and Nemo all thought that the squid-like things were feeding, like the saw-toothed

ones, and they also agreed that there were close to a hundred
of them. Now it seemed to me, given the number of them,
and how little was left of their prey . . . forgive me, but it
didn't seem to me that there was . . . enough to go around.
Would you say you were sure these tentacled things were
feeding, devouring lung and brain tissue?"

"A good place to feel a doubt." Japhet's voice warmed a
little. He sounded grateful for the balm of reportorial objectivity. "It was clear that they gnawed through the bone in
both places. But my feeling was that after they had gnawed
through, they discharged something *into* them. They would
hug tight with their tentacles and give a kind of shudder, and
it didn't seem to me they were taking something out so much
as pumping something *into* the chests and skulls. . . ." His
voice died again as the frail defense against pain crumbled.
Waverly said quickly:

"Thank you, Japhet. That's very vivid. Just two other
points now. First, is it correct that once these second attack-
ers dispersed, the remains of our friends suffered no further
assault, and were left to drift down to the basal muck?"

"That's right. They sank down and I lost sight of them."

"Fine. Now most of the others agree that these squid-like
things, after feeding or whatever they were doing, returned
immediately to their circulation within the globe—went back
to cruising around, and, as Penny put it, tickling the walls of
the globe with their tentacles. And in fact, most of them were
back patrolling before the shark-like things were. These had
fed first, but after feeding, had sounded to the bottom, and
took longer to get back to their patrolling pattern than the
second group did. Tell me if you agree with this, and if so,
tell me anything you can about what they were doing down
at the bottom during that time."

"You've got it right. And I think I can tell you something.
I had just one clear glimpse of one of them while they were
down there, through a gap in the stalks. It was a quick look.
But I got the impression it was half burrowed, head first, into
that spongy layer everything was rooted in. Stuck halfway in
with its tethered end clear and kind of vibrating or trembling.
That's all I can be sure of. After a few seconds the whole eye
shifted slightly and I lost sight of the thing."

"Remarkable. No one else saw that. Maybe it'll help.
Thank you Japhet. Thank you very much."

Waverly felt for the switch and turned off the log. "Christ!

My poor, aching head. It doesn't help. So far it doesn't help at all. I feel like a god damned square wheel. I can't get any kind of interpretation *moving*. It's stupefying, this bizarre complexity. The field of prey-snaring cilia, the central, mouthed dome of intestinal structures, surrounded by a calyx of major cilia—there are pseudo-coelenterates they've found over at Base Two that have these features. They're littoral benthic zone dwellers—one meter across at the biggest, god damn it, and with nothing like this kind of endosomatic complexity. There might be bathic varieties that are bigger, but the things are sensorially impoverished, slow, groping, tactile hunters. You say this thing tracked out boats towards the island and is now hemming us in, dodging laterally to catch any move we try to make from shore. This thing sees or smells or hears or all three. Monstrous. Incomprehensible. I need more medicine. I need some sleep. Maybe the answer will come in a dream. But I'll give you one thing to dream on, Nemo. If this thing does in some way follow the model of those little pseudo-coelenterates they've found—if it hangs proportionally deep in the water, and is able to expand as broadly in the lateral dimension, then its tail end hangs down into this lake for at least half a kilometer, and its field of cilia is able to hug this island's whole perimeter, or damn near it, in its loving embrace.

"Take me to my cot, Nemo, and God help us all. Helion and Jax are going to die tomorrow. I'm sorry, but this seems to me a simple fact. I've told them what I'm telling you, but I couldn't change their minds. So I say to you now, brutal though it is—choose vantage points from which you can see down into this thing from all possible angles. Have the log microphone run out on an extension, and issue field glasses. When our friends die I want it to pay off with every scrap of sight and sound that can be gotten out of it. If Polyphemus takes their lives, it's going to betray itself to us in the process. Wake me an hour after dawn, and don't fail me. By the time they set out, I'll have a list of specific questions I want answered, and some final arrangements I want made."

Just after dawn, Sarissa Wayne climbed to the ridgetop where Jax and Nemo had sat the night before. She settled down and watched the preparations, already well along, being made in the delph cove below. She and Penny had begun them. The roll of metallic net that each craft carried had been taken from its spool in the stern of Sarissa's boat and brought over to the cove. One end of it was anchored to the cove's southern spur, and then she and Penny had swum it across the cove-mouth.

They had made marvellously silent work of it, and only partly for fear of waking the delphs, which Jax and Helion were already edging up on with the tranquillizer guns. Polyphemus—this was what Waverly, without explanation, had bitterly dubbed their persecutor the night before—Polyphemus had already demonstrated how swiftly it could pour itself around the island's perimeter. The previous afternoon the colonists had done some experimenting. They had driven Helion's boat—only slightly damaged—to the opposite side of the island, choosing a launching spot more than four hundred meters upshore from Polyphemus' visible limit of extension. They detached its harpoon winch, anchored this ashore, and tethered the boat to its cable. They set it on auto-pilot with just enough fuel in the tanks for a few hundred meters' run. It was making thirty-five knots within the first four seconds of its launching, and was snared by the giant's sudden-sprouting tendrils less than seventy meters offshore.

The capture was not resisted—cable was paid out as the titan wrestled its prey towards its central orb. But the craft never reached that organ. Well before the cilia had brought it within the grasp of the larger feeding-tentacles they froze, still gripping it. A few seconds later they flung it into the air, and by the time it had struck the water, had vanished from beneath it. The colonists hauled the boat ashore, feeling themselves, if potentially wiser, no less baffled and terrified.

Swimming in the black, pre-dawn waters with this recollection of the giant's speed, its inscrutable responsiveness, had been the closest thing to lived nightmare in Sarissa's experience. Her legs could still feel that ticklish expectancy of Polyphemus' caustic, sticky first touch. Her heart still remembered its terrifying, clamouring power, and her shoulder muscles their spring-steel readiness through every second it had taken to string the barricade.

But her mind was now wholly detached from these bodily memories. It was not the scene below her that so distracted her. The tranquillizer darts used on captured delphs to prevent their panicking and crushing one another during their transport in cages to the sand-hog had paralyzed six of the creatures in the cove. The men had collared them with cable in two trios, staggered so that the middle delph of each trio was positioned half a length in advance of its flanking fellows. The trios had been tethered to shore, and though the beasts were just waking, and getting restive, Jax and Helion were able to slip into the under-carriages they had rigged and test their fit. Their boot-heels were just visible through the water, kicking for purchase under the tails of the delphs. Their recirculating respiration packs made no more than a faint boil in the water and this the delphs' motion, once they were goaded forward, should obliterate.

Sarissa's own life, and those of all the others, depended on this grotesque rehearsal, which did not alter her staring inattention. Her preoccupation was elsewhere, its focus revealed when her eyes narrowed at Nemo Jones' reappearance in the cove. He came down from the knoll that flanked it, where he had been helping Japhet make the two harpoon-gun emplacements she had requested the evening before. He went straight to Penny Lopez, who was working on a release mechanism for rolling back a segment of the cove-barrier when it was time for Jax and Helion to make their sortie. Whatever Nemo said to Penny made her straighten and face him.

He talked to her for perhaps a minute, and when, with a queer, formal bow, he left her, Sarissa's eyes didn't merely fail to follow him—they refused to. Thereafter, she didn't watch anything in particular so much as she avoided watching that sector of the crag that lay between herself and the point from which Nemo had left her view.

"Sarissa. Sarissa. I have something important to say. Will you talk with me?" The question seemed necessary to Nemo, as she had not looked up when he saluted her. Still not looking, she said:

"Whether or not I'll talk to you depends on what you have to tell me."

Nemo nodded at this, and sat down at a discreet distance from her so she would not have to strain to keep him out of her field of vision. He looked at the sky a minute before saying, "I've just given Penny Lopez my apologies, and told her I was withdrawing my suit for her. To disappoint a woman is always grave, so no lying should go with it. I confessed to her—"

Sarissa snorted, shook her head and, visibly in spite of herself, began to laugh. Nemo looked at his knees and waited

humbly. Sarissa had to make several attempts before she
could speak her retort:

"'To disappoint a woman is always grave.' Nemo, I swear
to you. I was watching your exchange with her. After you
walked away from her, that poor woman literally jumped
into the air and clicked her heels together. If she doesn't live
another day, if none of us do, she'll at least have that last day
in peace. She's *never* wanted you."

"I agree her feelings are mixed. But I have never entirely
displeased her. Once I had stated my case to her, last summer, she became sarcastic and piquish to me. Some of this is
a kind of coquetry, for which a woman must be forgiven, as
it is a natural defense against capture. But she started out—"

"What did you confess to her?"

"She started out not entirely disliking me. I confessed to
her that the woman I first chose, first desired—that I did not
lay suit to this woman only because she *did* entirely dislike
me, and though I am not faint-hearted, it's a fool that sets
out hunting impossible quarry."

Sarissa looked at him now. She studied him with wrath,
perplexity, relish. "What was this woman's name, this first
choice of yours? This select soul, this feminine paragon, this
august personage who merited Nemo Jones' initial desig-
nation as his mate? Bless my ears with this pearl's name."

"Sarissa Wayne."

"Horseshit."

"Horseshit?"

"Yes. The shit of a terrestrial quadruped. Invoked by some
terrestrials to denote absolute disbelief." Her fine-honed little
body fairly danced on its seat with contained kinetic im-
pulses, making Nemo think of the way a candleflame sits on
its wick.

"You were caustic and curt to me from the very first, Sarissa. Mocked every advance I made to you. At least Penny
started out being nice."

"To make Helion jealous, you backwoods dolt. And you
never made *any*, not the *slightest* advance to me!"

"Horseshit."

New movement down in the cove distracted them momentarily. Helion and Jax had begun to goad their 'mounts'
through some elementary paces. They did not use the sonic
pulsars designed for delph herding—all too probably detectable by Polyphemus—but small electric prods that Jax had

improvised. The method seemed to be working, though it produced an uncharacteristically jerky movement in the beasts. The sun's edge kindled on the eastern crater rim. Sarissa and Nemo faced each other again.

"Name one advance Jones. Just one, in explicit, unmistakable detail."

"Our very first expedition together. When you harpooned that hydra—"

"That! Huh! You did all you could to steal my thunder and show off your swimming, and then tossed me a compliment like a meatless bone, that I was a good shot."

"I dove in to cut you the trophy from your kill—the gravest gesture of honor among my people! I brought you back the major tentacle and I said you were a *master* shot, not just a *good* shot. You wouldn't even meet my eyes. You could have read how I meant it *there*."

"Hogwash! You—"

"Hogwash?"

"Shut up! You made that showy twenty meter dive from the crater wall and had butchered the prime cut from my kill before I could get it even half reeled in! You—"

"Where else could I have dived from? That's where I was. *standing*. The gesture has to be immediate. It's a huntsman's acclamation for a great hit! You don't say excuse me and climb down to a more seemly—"

"What *other* advance did you ever make to me? Hey? Name one other."

"Two days later. I went up to you to explain after the council meeting. I brought you—"

"You walked up dragging the god damned trophy you'd cut off *my kill*! You had *tanned* it. I was with the other gunners and just then they were congratulating me on that shot, and just then you walk up to me grinning like a fool dragging that suckered *hose* after you. . . ."

Her indignation lost steam, punctured by remembered regret. She hadn't needed reminding of this scene. At the time, seeing the uncouth Katermandian approaching her with his four-meter, snakelike token of esteem, Sarissa had marvelled to herself that pleasure and mortifying embarrassment could ever be so compounded as they were in her own mind then. She did something she had never done before. She fled. Croaked some excuse to her friends about checking her gear, turned, and ran. Even so, she didn't manage to flee an excruciating awareness of the scene. She saw her hapless suitor, nonplussed, speed up to pursue her and ensnare the ankles of two of her colleagues in the trailing tentacle so that one of them—it had been Angela—was toppled from her feet. Later Angela had laughed about it and, after feeling out her friend's emotions in the matter, had said to her:

"Listen Sari. Nemo is a wonderful man. There's no petty pride in him. He took that dive out of pure joy in your shooting. He's a Katermandian, sweetheart! Naturally he's going to embarrass you. He's *courting* you, girl! You're going to let embarrassment stand in your way? Toughen up. Take him for a walk out where there's no one around, tell him you want him, and explain to him how to avoid embarrassing you. He'd jump at the chance to please you. He's only lived a mere thirty-six years in deep rainforest. You want urbane manners and conceited reserve? You want Helion?"

The advice came too late. Sarissa could not immediately conquer her reserve towards Nemo, and soon the Katermandian had retreated to a melancholy, unvarying courtesy with her. He began his formal courtship of Penny a few weeks later. Now, renewed grief for Angela filled Sarissa's eyes.

"Forget what I just said. I know how you meant it all. Angela made me see it. She was always telling me you were a wonder . . . a wonderful—"

She stopped when she realized her voice was going to break. She turned her face away—sensed rather than saw Nemo's sudden move to comfort her, and prevented it with a violent straightarm. A long silence followed. They both watched the cove. Jax and Helion had their teams fairly well under control now, and were maneuvering them around with such energy that every delph in the cove was wakened and the water seethed. In spite of this Penny was running tests on the barrier-opening arrangement and managing not to lose a single delph in the process. At length, Sarissa took a deep breath, and stood up determinedly. She turned to face Nemo.

"Jones, you miserable idiot, I, Sarissa Wayne, want you. I want you to pay suit to me, to love me, and to make love to me, and not ever, at all, to anyone else. That's how it is. So answer me now, once and for all. Let's face this and have it done, one way or the other."

Nemo nodded energetically, but though his mouth opened, nothing came out of it. Apparently, this ardent inarticulacy conveyed an answer to Sarissa that she found satisfactory.

She wrapped her arms around his waist, and pressed her face against his chest. He held her, looking over her head towards the sunrise, and clearer than the happiness his face showed was his amazement. All in his world had been craft, the stalking, second-guessing, and teasing-out of quarry from the hostile complexities of its habitat. To have Sarissa, whom he had thought irreversibly inimical to him, holding him with such single-mindedness, was to him in the nature of a prodigy. It was as if, in his native rainforest, an archidand—that wily, toothsome biped, splendid-winged and brazen-taloned—had leapt from its cover in the dense warp-vine and sparx and—far from dodging away with invisible speed—had ambled up to the astonished hunter and dipped its head to nuzzle at his hand. The pair did not notice the two figures approaching them until they were in speaking distance and one of them, Japhet Sparks, hailed them.

Sparks was leading Orson Waverly. The lovers broke their embrace—not out of shame, but from a chilling of their hearts. They knew Waverly's errand. Sarissa helped him to a seat. She, Nemo and Japhet—all those who must be Waverly's eyes—now looked only at him, not down towards the cove, not at each other.

"I've already briefed Penny. I wanted to do it while they were still in the water. They know what I'm doing and approve but its pointless to sicken them with the sight of my actually doing it. So let's be quick. The Captain will be assembling us for his own briefing in a little while, as soon as he and Jax make some last adjustments to their undercarriages. Sarissa?"

"Here Orson."

"The guns from Helion's and Angela's boats are set up. Japhet's wound double cable on the winches and got the guns anchored where you wanted them. Give them both the fieldglasses, Japhet. Hang these around your necks now. Get them focussed for Polyphemus immediately you take up your positions. I want you on the knoll across the beach from Sarissa's, Nemo—Japhet has it worked out. You'll be on the other side of the thing from her and almost as high above it. Penny and Japhet will be shoreside, watching it from different angles. They'll both have mikes we've rigged to the log. I want to get any sound any of us makes correlated with a running account of its moves. We want all its behaviour, and every possible synchronicity of that behaviour with what happens around it.

"Because of course we can't assume it sees, just because it looks to us like an eye. It twisted our boat open like—someone unstoppering a specimen bottle. But it could have felt organic presences inside vibrationally, electrochemically—we just don't know. I'd been jammed in under the panel and it missed me. It makes me think the thing does see, and my invisibility to it saved me. If it does, I don't think Jax and Helion have a prayer.

"Here are my specific questions. First and foremost, how precisely does it track us? Every detail of its behaviour that we can correlate with any detail of its *prey's* behaviour—" Waverly's mouth moved speechlessly a few times. He resumed more quietly. "If we can relate these two spheres of activity in any new way, we may get a key to how to dodge it. Killing it seems to me as good as impossible. Nevertheless, it *has* occurred to me that if we understood its feeding mechanism, we could conceivably poison it. Its whole alimentary set-up is one of the things that confuses me most. These quasi-independent packs. By the time they're through with the prey, it's just a carcass, seventy per cent reduced in volume, that drifts down to the base of the orb. If they are highly articulated organelles, if they are the digestive apparatus itself, how are they transmitting the nutrients they absorb to the macro-organism? These threadlike, breakable tethers seem ludicrously unlikely as transport ducts for nutrients of such bulk. If they are not transferring the nourishment, then Polyphemus itself must be a kind of huge detritivore, nourished by the sharks' and squids' carrion leavings. But then why the gross volumetric disproportion? Why does Polyphemus get forty per cent, at most, of every kill, and these. . . . predacious saprophytes sixty or more? What service to the whole rates that big a part of the take?

"But to test this, study the basal areas all you can—Sarissa and Nemo especially. That's why I've got you high. Look for . . . feeding debris, its relation to the inner landscape of Polyphemus. What's the structure down there? If motile, how does it behave? Japhet and Penny will be studying the packs more particularly, but I want all of you to be constantly checking the whole, trying to catch over-all gestalts of movement, responsiveness and what stimulates it.

"With the squids and sharks, two specific things interest

me. Watch for waste excretion in any form. They could be using a selective fraction of their intake and be producing useable wastes that Polyphemus absorbs. Second. You all seemed to be in agreement that the squids didn't appear to consume nearly as much as the sharks, if indeed they actually *fed* at all. Precisely what were they doing? Study that closely.

"That's it. As far as productive guesses go, I've got next to nothing to offer at this point. This thing is completely incredible. God help us to think effectively together, because so far, I am truly in the dark."

Midmorning on Firebairn is, next to sunset, its most golden hour. The jumbled colors of the igneous wastes blaze, melt, smoulder under the sky's brilliance as if the land were still in its molten nativity. And in this particular place the young sun kindled a special jewel even more dazzling than the vast ring-wall, or the waters contained by it. As Nemo climbed the knoll assigned him, he looked upon that jewel with loathing and wonder. Within the sphere of lustrous amber, the patrolling packs wove their own distinct colors through the black and purple jungle. Those that Waverly called 'sharks' were especially striking. Their torpedo bodies had streaks of pigmentation that flashed iridescent as the things cruised through the filtered sunlight. Nemo thought of the cove—invisible to him now beyond the ridge Sarissa stood on—from which he had just come. Helion, mute and businesslike, had turned directly from the briefing to the water, and slipped under, snuggling himself out of sight beneath his harnessed beasts. But Jax had paused by the brink so that Nemo could take his hand. Nemo had said:

"Lucky fellow. In an hour you'll be in the sand-hog, radioing air rescue."

The big man had smiled, glanced at the binoculars hanging against the fur on the Katermandian's chest, drawing their owner's eyes upon them, filling his heart with wretchedness. But Jax had grinned:

"That's right. Use these, and when I climb ashore you can see me waving to you."

Nemo had reached his position, but before he signalled to Sarissa he looked down on their enemy. He pressed his clenched fist against his chest, which is the way the hunters of Katermand take oaths, and he said:

"Hear me, Polyphemus. My name is Nemo. Nemo Jones.

And I am going to rip the life right out of you. We together will find the way, but it's me that's going to do it to you."

He raised his arm, and signalled to the short, slight figure manning the guns on the next knoll over. Even as he had turned his eyes away, a detail had snagged at their periphery. He caught up his glasses, and trained them on the orb, at a point deep within the anchorings of the kelp.

Sarissa hesitated. Japhet, Penny, Nemo—all were stationed now, but for a moment she found herself unable to pass on the go-ahead to the cove. She checked the welded cable moorings Japhet had rigged for the guns, and for the third time reassured herself that the crag she stood on would break before they did. She looked down into the cove, where Orson waited for her word, the barrier-gate's pull-cord in one hand. Jax and Helion held their beasts ready—not near the gate, but by the shore of the inlet, for before they emerged themselves they would drive out a large part of the school ahead of them, and thereafter keep as many of these as possible around them as they penetrated the dangerous waters off-shore.

The delphs had swum unmolested past Polyphemus; some of them had even cruised through its peripheral field of cilia. It was one of the first observations they had made the previous afternoon, once some measure of organization had succeeded their initial trance of horror. The plan had seemed good. Now, without any of Waverly's biological training to reinforce her pessimism, she felt a gloom as deep as his. It was not going to work. It would fail because Sarissa now had everything to lose—not just her life, but Nemo as well. Whenever the heart prayed entirely for luck, that was when luck failed. She cupped her hands by her mouth and, in a tone scarcely louder than conversational, said:

"Now."

Orson, seventy meters below, pulled the cord. When Jax and Helion saw the opening, they launched prearranged, converging drives on the gate that cut out about two thirds of the school and herded it before them. "Close it," Sarissa said. Orson relaxed his grip on the cord and let the gate spring back. If the sortie failed, its survivors would need food.

The shepherding of a protective screen of free-swimming delphs did not start well. The trios were bulky enough to exert a local dominance on their unharnessed fellows, but too awkward of movement to work the group as a whole into any formation. As the teams edged past the sheltering horn of the cove, the school began to dissolve before them, individuals and couples—gamesome with the unpent tensions of their confinement—dispersing swiftly. Sarissa watched the two men's cover bleeding away, branching out into the lake in quick, silvery trickles. She ground her teeth and looked to Polyphemus.

The giant was half the island away—the knoll she stood on walled off the cove from its vision, if vision it had. And with the captain and Jax angling sharply away from the giant as they penetrated the open waters, they would be three quarters of the island's length distant from it before the shoreline ceased to mask them. It was not conceivable that two men, the subtlest shadows of men, really, clinging to the undersides of living screens twice their size, could be detected at such a range. And still Sarissa groaned at the steady shrinkage of the school. As the lure of open water grew stronger, the clumsy goading of the two trios came to seem itself a force of dispersal, an irritation even the nearer delphs began to flee.

And then it seemed the two men abandoned the attempt to herd the rest of the school and began to make smoother progress outwards. They were already a hundred meters offshore, and she watched them make the next fifty as quickly as they had that first stage. As if in illustration of her thoughts about luck, a fair-sized cluster of delphs, uncoerced now, cohered, and stayed just ahead of the escapees.

Sarissa realized that for perhaps the last full minute, the men had been out in the zone of Polyphemus' unimpeded survey. Her head snapped round towards the colossus. The swarming globe was as before—though perhaps a shade farther out from its sector of the shore? She looked back to the trios, but even as she turned to do so, something about the lake-surface between her two foci of concern disturbed her, and brought her eyes back to itself.

There, some hundred and fifty meters straight off of her promontory, a narrow boil of movement scarred the waters—the surface track of a subaqueous motion whose rate was perhaps thirty knots. It was moving on a course that would intercept that of the delph school.

Sarissa stepped over to the gun whose emplacement commanded the coveward sector of the water, kicked up the muzzle for a long shot and trained it on the spot where the surface scar and the delph trios would impact. Touching the

gun, which always calmed her, helped little—her heart was
all hollowness and terror. The two men must have seen what
was approaching them. The trios veered sharply about three
seconds before it struck, and the water all around them
sprouted Polyphemus' viperous cilia. Within another two seconds, she had already fired her first shot.

It was well over two hundred meters, at the very limit of
the harpoon's effective striking power. Only her elevation
made it even feasible. The line's silver arc sang out and
down. She held her breath, as she always unconsciously did
when she feared to disturb the plunge of a long shot that she
already knew, as soon as it had left the cannon, was good.
The medusa-tangle had already gripped the lead trio, and
propped the silver beasts upwards, like three bright tomb-
stones against the sun, while other cilia worked for what was
under them. It was the delicate, descriminating motion of a
man lifting a trapdoor to pluck something out from beneath
it. The line's arc crumpled, shuddered through its two-
hundred and twenty meter length as the spear impacted,
transfixing the lead delph of the trio. With one hand Sarissa
flicked on the automatic winch and the line pulled straight—
one puny machine engaging Polyphemus in a tug-of-war. Her
other hand had already re-aimed the gun.

The second trio, while equally entangled, was not held so
clear as the first. She fired, and knew in the instant of doing
it the shot was bad. She writhed through the seconds' wait before she could fire again. From under the trio she had hit, a
struggling weave of cilia and human limbs fought its way
round to the backs of the beasts. A snake-wrapped arm
sought and seized the shaft of the harpoon.

"Yes!" Sarissa screamed. "That's it! Climb the line!" Her
second shot dove short of its mark. The instant the cable had
ceased to pay out, and cleared the feed-out spools, she fired
again, and again, knew she had it. A tremendous expectancy
filled her. To beat this titanic enemy, rob it—never had she
felt that the delicate geometry, the fleet calculus of her art,
an art of parabolas and pin-sharp steel points, could achieve
so much. Far away, a tiny Laocöon, the man wrestled half
his body onto his trio's backs, having to fight the panicked
heave of the beasts as well as the great leeches woven round
his frame. It was Jax. His shaven head, stripped of its respiration helmet, fought clear. Now he had the shaft by both
hands.

Her third shot struck, and she geared the line taut. The speared trio came easily out of the cilia. She sickened, watched the field for what, an instant later, she saw: Helion, making the now-familiar, storm-heaved progress through the field, whose acreage had now sprouted in a long swath leading back to the orb.

Sarissa howled with rage, and concentrated furiously on the one she might save. Switching to her magazine of untethered harpoons, she began to pump them down upon the zone surrounding Jax, hoping to scythe down just enough cilia to give him a fighting chance.

And the armorer fought indeed against the giant—himself a giant of relentless will, his big muscles sharp-cut in the morning light with the strain. His struggle had tilted the trio toward him and he had worked his grip up to the harpoon line itself. Sarissa's shots rained around him, as close as she dared put them, and suddenly it seemed he had several fewer cilia round his chest. He surged up, working two handspans higher up the line—but the cilia had not withdrawn, merely shifted their grip to his shoulders. They bowed him backwards, folded him impossibly. Sarissa saw his hands let go before the sharp sound of his breaking back reached her. He collapsed back into the meadow, like a wearied man throwing himself back on the grass for a rest. His trio was now also winched easily shorewards. The swath that bore Jax and, farther along, Helion, now began a swift contraction, without submerging. Round the island's shore the two were swept, while the huge orb rolled langorously, and turned what she could not help but feel was a lusting gaze upon them as they drew near, the red, rhomboidal pupil/mouth contracting and dilating in anticipation.

"When is she coming down?" Orson Waverly asked. "I need everyone's report. It just doesn't cohere yet. What's she doing?"

The other three traded looks.

"She's crying, Orson," Nemo Jones said. "Let her be, just a while yet. She thought for a minute she had saved them."

The biologist sighed. "All right. Let's rake through it again. Penny and Japhet agree they saw both squids and sharks excrete—eject large clouds of fine sediment, of considerable volume, that drifted down to the base of the orb. Meanwhile, early on, Nemo caught sight of some kind of large carcass, a

cetaceanoid he thinks, being actively swallowed down, by
minute movements, into the basal stratum. Cetaceanoids are
bathic lake dwellers and Polyphemus hasn't left the surface
for the last two days. Conclusions: first, it *is* a giant detritivore; second, it's hunting and feeding from deep down even
as it sits here, my guess being that it hunts with structures
similar to those it uses up here, and probably engulfed the cetaceanoid last night. Fine. At this point, I see no way those
things help us.

"Now to the packs. Very little that's new, essentially. Both
Japhet and Penny now agree that when the squids fasten to
their prey they show a shuddering movement that might be
the reverse of peristaltic. But as to what they might be
pumping into the bodies, you caught no clues. What would it
be?" Waverly sounded petulant, exhorting his own imagination rather than the others. "Digestive fluids? Then what
feeds the squids themselves if they just soften up the prey for
Polyphemus—and if nourishment flows from it to them, how
does it do so? And this about the sharks. You all three now
say you saw them dive to the bottom even when their tethers
had not been broken—saw more than one of them worming
themselves belly-down against the basal stratum and then re-
joining their packs above. Were they grazing on some of the
detritus there? No one saw them using their jaws down
there?"

All shook their heads and Nemo answered for them: "No."

"Shit! It's too much to cope with! Was there nothing else
new, no change in the pattern of the packs' collective behaviour, for instance? In the way each group acted together, or
the way the two groups interacted?"

"Well . . ." All faces, including the blind one, turned
towards Penny. "Look. This is nothing certain, but I had the
feeling, at least, that the packs, both kinds, were concentrated
a little more heavily at one side of the globe just before. . . .
just before Sarissa started firing." She had started weeping,
though she struggled stubbornly against letting her voice
break. Nemo laid a hand on her forearm and she clutched it.
She let herself go then, cried in slow, quiet gasps, which Waverly didn't seem to notice. His mind had snagged on something.

"They concentrated on the side nearest the prey? Penny?
On the side nearest the prey?"

"Yes. They . . . always kept *circ*ulating . . . circulating so much it was hard to say. But yes. I think so."

Waverly nodded. His face had tightened. His teeth ground slightly, busily, behind his closed lips, a sign of thought in him. The faded blood-tracks on his cheeks ceased to resemble tears, looked more like warpaint now.

"Japhet. Tell me again about the movement of the squids' tentacles—not while they were on the prey, but well before that."

"But what can I say that I haven't already—"

"Try this on. You've all reported that their tentacles show size differential—some quite short and fine, others thicker and considerably longer. All, you've more or less agreed, 'vibrated all the time.' But are you sure? Absolutely? Did anyone notice, for instance, that sometimes it was the smaller, finer tentacles doing most of the vibrating, sometimes almost exclusively the larger ones, and only sometimes all of them together?"

Nemo's eyes immediately came up, to meet Japhet's. These were similarly kindled. Japhet said:

"Yes. That's precisely right. Nemo saw it too."

Waverly's back straightened, and his palms rested carefully on his thighs. "And the sharks' eyes. Someone on the log, Jax I think, said they were reddish black, in three triangular clusters that tapered back to sharp points on the dorsum. And you, Japhet, said they reminded you of delph eyes. There are three clusters instead of two, but what would you others—"

"Look," Nemo said. "Sarissa. She's seen something."

Even Waverly turned his futile gaze towards the knoll where the gunner stood. Her body was taut, and she had her glasses trained on Polyphemus. She lowered them, raised them again. Then she let them drop to her chest, spun around, and rushed to her as yet unused gun, the one trained on Polyphemus' sector of the lake.

Sarissa sighed, and wiped her eyes. She had cried this way once before, at the training camp on Cygnus IV. She had been just seventeen, and had failed her first gunnery finals. Failed. She had placed third in the class (of over a hundred)—not first. She had gone into the sand dunes fringing the lake where the finals were given each year and thrown herself down like a piece of trash discarded in the wasteland. Then she had mourned her shipwrecked pride, and mourned two target floats, grazed but unpunctured, that had bobbed back up to mock her after she had fired on them. Now, two faces grieved her, and these would *not* bob back up from the water they had slipped into an hour and a half before. She faced Polyphemus and spat towards it, feeling hate enough to make her spittle caustic, to make her eyes spout laser beams. She saw what looked like a deep crease forming down in the muddy floor of the giant's interior.

She trained her glasses on it. It was not a stable feature of the stratum. It had not been there before, and now she could see it deepen, as if the whole layer were contorting for some unguessable effort. A few seconds more, and a shudder passed through the titan that made the crystalline walls through which she spied blur in the magnified field of her vision. The puckered place at once began to smooth out again.

Perplexed, she took the glasses from her eyes and it was then, viewing Polyphemus as a whole, that she saw a boil of motion to one side of the globe, halfway out amid the circumambient field of cilia. She brought up the glasses again.

As she focussed on the turbulence, its cause popped to the surface: a glassy, opaque ellipsoid, perhaps half the size of one of the fishing boats. One end was more tapered than the other, and at this end, two flagella, perhaps three meters long, were attached. With a slow, labored thrashing, they drove the organism out of the black meadow.

Once the thing had been a few moments in progress, it seemed that it hugged, preferentially, the shallows fringing the isle, for it began to make its way round towards a point just off the knoll Sarissa stood on. The perception and the reaction came in the same instant. She rushed to the nearer gun, swept its muzzle downwards, and waited. It was already within range, but she waited for the shot to become absolutely sure, waiting meanwhile for the slightest sign of divergence from its course as her signal to fire. She heard the others hailing her, but spared no fraction of her attention for a response. This little piece of her enemy she could take from it, and she meant to do so.

It was within a hundred meters when she saw bubbles appearing around its flanks, and realized that it had begun to sink even as it thrashed onward. She fired. The line hissed vindictively, the barb plunged to the little orb's center, fierce as a viper. The flagella continued to thrash, impotently but not, it seemed, particularly excitedly. She noted that the main part of the orb was tough only in its sheath, and that its contents were gelatinous. So she set the winch going on the first line, and planted her second shot at the base of the flagella, where she reasoned a greater muscular rigidity should give her barb a firmer bite. Her aim was surreally true—she saw where the lance would lodge well before it did so, and almost set the winch on the line before it had even struck. She was already hauling her catch along the surface of the lake by the time the others reached her.

"Polyphemus ejected it—its basal stratum seamed up and squeezed it out somewhere on that side, just below the water level."

The winches had dragged it directly below them now, and began to lift it from the water. The flagella, with a brainless mechanicity, did not cease to flail as the blubbery mass floundered up the rock wall. Out of the group's watchful silence, Nemo muttered:

"Polyphemus can see it—if it sees. Can hear it—if it hears. But it's not interfering."

"Polyphemus sees and hears," Orson Waverly said. "But it doesn't think. That thing isn't prey if it came out of the giant's body. And what isn't prey our greedy, mindless friend doesn't bother with."

The five people stood around the thing, watching its flagella's movement weakening gradually. Their knolltop group might have been a scene of ancient sacrifice. The things Waverly had called for when the organism had first been lashed to the rock promoted the illusion. Japhet, Nemo, Penny and Sarissa all held flensing knives, and Japhet had used the little industrial lasers the boats carried to good effect on the plastic oars their emergency rafts contained. A large scoop, fork, and oversized pair of tongs had been fashioned, and a large sifting screen improvised from cable. The log was set up on a rock near the blunt prow of the sacrificial beast. The recorder's console might have been the abstracted face of the deity this druidic cult had gathered to appease: the Group Mind's memory-amplifier. Into this, the blindfolded priest meant to feed each scrap and nuance of the offering he could not see, hoping to purchase with this rite the greater insight that he and his fellow supplicants sorely needed.

The warm wind washed over the sacrifice, and the propul-

sive energy slowly metronomed out of its black stern-whips.
Its smooth envelope had been faintly translucent, but now
had grown waxier, and begun to wrinkle. Out of the silence
Sarissa said:

"I think it's weak enough to cut. Let's open it."

"Remember," said Waverly. "First the integument. If it has
a distinct structure, flense me out sections and separate it as
neatly as possible from what's under it."

At first, once their giant scalpels had been at work a few
minutes, everyone was reporting that no clearly defined integument existed, but this proved an error. A distinct outermost
layer did exist, but it was more than two feet thick. It was a
gelatino-fibrous material. Its fibrosity was attenuated at the
outer levels, but the deeper into the stratum one went, the
more sharply articulated, and more darkly pigmented these
fibre-bundles became until, at the stratum's interface with the
subincumbent tissues, it looked like a tightly packed surface
of black-tentacled sea anemones. An embryonic Meadow of
Medusa—all question of the thing's identity was settled here.

Within the *cavernum* lined with this dark pile of fibril-tips
was a smooth, elongate capsule perhaps twice the size of a
man. Its surface was of a thin, tough material of linked,
hoop-shaped plates, so that the whole suggested a giant pupal
case. The celebrants of the rite exhumed the whole upper surface of this sarcophagus shape. They worked with gusto,
scattering the black, blubbery rugs of tissue about them on
the sunlit stone, until the core of this biological torpedo lay
upon a supporting remnant of the integument—lay on a
crude-cut altar hewn from its own protective material.

Waverly, considering a moment, decided, "Cut in thirds,
carefully and gradually, along seams in the plating. Be looking for clear structures, and also be checking with each other
as you cut to see how far along the length of the thing those
structures run. Then, when you've cut halfway down through
it, open it lengthwise, along a lengthwise seam if you can find
one."

His vatic crew raised their drenched blades and returned
eagerly to work. Their concentration was complete. Their victim could have been as huge as its parent—their every move
expressed an unconditional will to sift its secrets out of it. But
revelation was quick to come. The pupal case proved thin,
easily cut, and all reported that a dense, very delicately fi-
brous grey tissue underlay the sheath. It was macroscopically

featureless, and after they had gone some thirty centimeters down, it began to look like the sheath's sole content. Then Sarissa's blade scraped on something hard.

Japhet and Penny joined her with knives. They scooped a hollow round the object, shaved it free from webs of tissue, pried it out. It was a human skull, which the tissue packed within as densely as it had without, filling its orbits with grey, gelatinous pseudo-eyes. Sarissa held it up in the light of the noon sun. Her eyes stared into its jellied gaze, and her face worked as if she was struggling to read a message in its masklike expression. She said:

"It's . . . fresh. There's still some cartilage in the . . . nose-hole."

Nemo had come up behind her. He reached around, took it gently from her hand, gave it to Japhet, and gripped her shoulders. His hands strained, as if by the firmness of their grip he could throttle—as with a tourniquet—the grief and horror rising in her. Face blank, she let Nemo steer her to a seat on the rock. She watched the lake.

Waverly was deeply excited by the find, and made them bring him to the site of discovery. His hands, tremulous and lustful as a gloating miser's, caressed the socket the skull had lain in, palped the surrounding tissue. A blind augur, he did a thorough divination from the alien entrails.

"Its deep inside a highly specialized structure. It didn't just wander in. Saw it open. Comb out the tissues packed inside it."

The skull had hardly been opened before something was found: thumb-sized white ovoids, nearly a score of them, embedded in the tissue. Penny helping him, Waverly cut one open, fingered its contents with exquisite thoroughness. "Listen," he said. "Improvise a large comb, fine toothed as possible. Start with the fork we made while Japhet makes something finer. Anywhere in this tissue, whether it's encased in fragments of prey or not, look for anything that might be an egg—smaller than these, larger, I don't know—but probably on a similar scale and, hopefully, of a recognizably different form. Nemo and Penny on that. I'm going to open a few more of these. Sarissa, I want you to help me with knife and tweezers, but first help me rig a little table. Sarissa?"

Not speaking, she came up, touched him. The augurers went to work.

A bit later, they all sat together on the knoll. Waverly sat

at his little bench, where he and Sarissa had unravelled the
innards of three more of the objects found in the skull. On
the same bench were four black pellets, half the size of those
from the skull, which Japhet had just combed from the tissue
of the sarcophagus. He had cried, "Orson! I found some.
They're black. They're a little like delph roe. Smaller, harder,
separate, but shaped like roe." Waverly had straightened
then. He had called them all around him, but once they had
gathered, had sat quiet a long time.

They waited, the bright, bulky tatters of their butchery
scattered all around them. Waverly's face came up, and he
smiled slightly, as if with pleasure at the flood of sunlight that
bathed him. His mouth groped for speech, but luxuriatingly,
as if his mind were rummaging through a wealth of ut-
terances.

"Delph eyes have the incredible motion-detective power of
a jumping spider's, and we've recently confirmed to our satisfaction that their resolution of image and detail—of the very
subtlest gestalts—that it probably surpasses our own. Polyphemus doesn't eat delphs."

This might have been the gloating introduction of a very
hot paper read at an academy meeting. Waverly paused, visibly trying to sober himself. "I think the reason is that inde-
pendent organisms, evolved more or less directly from the
delphinid order, have become functioning saprophytes in the
systems of Polyphemus' kind. These delphinids have first
crack at their host's prey, and they function as their host's
eyes." He talked faster now, rushing to include his fellows in
his new overview. "My guess is that the sharks' ancestors
were engulfed by polyphemids as food, enjoyed some natural
resistance to their digestive enzymes, and learned to thrive on
their captors' meals. If polyphemids resembled the smaller littoral analogues I mentioned, they had only tactile sensibili-
ties, with perhaps some primitive olfactory discrimination.
Any one of them whose saprophytes could start cueing it to
their visual recognitions of prey would surely eat better than
its blind fellow hunters. And the saprophytes, evolutionarily
speaking, would feel a great stimulus to providing such cues.

"And I'm convinced the squids are similar in their history.
Their tentacle activity is discriminative in just the way the
cilia of our own organs of Corti are. When the smaller tentacles vibrate, higher frequency sounds are being registered,
and when the larger, the lower frequencies, while all are usu-

ally in some kind of motion, as would be expected from the mixture of frequencies in most environmental noise. The squids are the giant's ears—grotesque though it sounds, I have no doubt of it. Both these captured species have evolved a caudal nerve-link with the giant's own major ganglia, which I am certain are in that basal stratum. The kelp is part of its own neural system, and perhaps respiratory and alimentary as well. If what's in this egg's yolk is at all analogous, and I think it is, then the giant's basal stratum is a dense neural tangle, the plane of intersection for Polyphemus and its two breeds of saprophyte, as well as being its zone of absorption for nutrients. And when those sensory cooperatives breed, their reproductive packets are planted in that same stratum. The squids embed their eggs in the carrion before it is absorbed there. Quite possibly, they don't feed at all as adults, and take in their life's nourishment during some kind of larval phase. The sharks go down and lay their eggs directly in the stratum. These genetic packages are then apparently well located to be included in that of the host itself, and the tidy partnership is perpetuated, while those that are not entrapped in the material of Polyphemus' spores no doubt hatch endosomatically to replenish the adult host's sensory packs. And as for the nutritive disproportionality between host and saprophytes, it's even less than I thought, for as the individual adult sensories die, they surely fall to the basal stratum and feed their master with their own corpses."

Waverly stopped, but with an air of cutting himself short. He sat, a small, canny smile on his face, as if challenging his friends to see what he did. Nemo said:

"Then if those sharks are still close enough to being delphs—if their eyes are built the same—our dyes could blind them."

Waverly cackled—it was the most blatant hilarity that any of his fellows had ever heard from him. Then all five of them were talking at once. But when the first gusts of jubilation and (often fantastic) strategy had subsided, the biologist said:

"Listen. I think we can do it. And if it works, it's surely a start, a great satisfaction if nothing else. But it may not be enough. Because if blinding fails to drive it away, its auditory mechanism may be all it needs to kill us. I've got one or two specific suggestions to add to all you've said. Let's get down to the beach, finalize our plan, and get to work."

The second moon was half sunk below the crater's western
rim before the island grew as dark as the waters encircling it.
Until that time, a few hours before dawn, the island wore an
unsteady constellation of lights, flaring and guttering stars:
Japhet welding harpoon line into three-strand cables, Nemo
and Sarissa working by a lantern, modifying rifle ammuni-
tion, Penny and Orson working together with the lasers to
melt the tough hides of three freshly slaughtered delphs into a
hundred meters of tubing, Orson scrolling the material and
holding it for Penny to fuse with the bright, needle-fine beam.

Just after sunrise, the boat that Polyphemus had rejected
once already set out from the island's shore. It was, as before,
tethered to a rock, though even more strongly than before.
But this time it had passengers: two rather rigid figures with
heads of stuffed cloth, painted features, and stuffed wet-suits
for bodies. A system of wires, guyed to one of the boat-en-
gine's flywheels, imparted a jerky agitation to the lifeless
shapes.

Polyphemus reached for the craft the moment it was off-
shore. As soon as the creature took hold, Japhet stepped up
the winch paying out the cable, to facilitate the giant's speedy
taking-in of the prey. A quarter of the island's circumference
away, Polyphemus' mouth opened.

And when that red-rimmed trapezoid dilated, there came a
series of twelve explosive barks. They sounded from the knoll
Sarissa had been stationed on the day before. Their noise, ee-
rily gradual, travelled out to cross and fill the lake's whole,
vast arena, and before the second had sounded, their effects
began to appear: a series of twelve splashes in the lake of
ichor bordered by the mouth's rim. Violently expanding
clouds of yellow smoke began to bloom within the orb, some
near its surface, others deeper down. The coalescence of
these roiling masses had stained the contents of the entire
globe within a minute and a half. Sarissa and Nemo, whose
rifles had launched the missles, stood with field glasses trained
on Polyphemus.

The giant's overall movement had suffered a marked
change. The steady, peristaltic surge of the cilia faltered—the
entangled boat ceased to flow so smoothly towards the orb. It
paused, was joggled as by choppy seas. Then the fibres en-

meshing it grew more active, but frenetically so, and somewhat less purposive.

"It's groping the boat," Penny shouted up to the two on the knoll. She stood on the beach, the nearest of them all to the captive bait. "It's not pulling it in nearly so fast!"

Nemo and Sarissa probed the thinning mists of dye for clues to the fate of the giant's eyes. The pigment was dispersing according to its normal behaviour in lake and sea water, the bulk of it settling out in a harmless precipitate within three minutes of going into solution. The orb's inner jungle melted back into visibility. Sarissa said, thick-voiced as with desire:

"They're scrambling. Panicking."

"Yes. It's their normal patrolling motion, speeded up. Can you make out the eye color?"

"Yes! Red! Check that pack to the lower left." In both delphs and Polyphemus' visual sensories, the eyes' normal color was blackish red in most light. And now the eyes on the 'eyes' of Polyphemus flashed deep ruby as they boiled in their kinetically heated-up patrol movements. This was the color of dye-blinded delph-eyes, once the chemical had converted their chromatophore molecules to an isomer that the impingement of photons could not reconvert—that is, once the eyes' retinal substances had been permanently bleached.

"But they're not colliding," Sarissa said. The joy in her voice had diminished several degrees. "Getting snarled more often, but still coordinated. I think they can still hunt and kill. . . ." Nemo knew that the foreboding in her tone related not to this part of their assault, but to a secondary phase of their plan that everyone hoped would not need implementation, but he pretended not to understand this.

"So what? They can't show it the way to its food, that's all we care about."

"The boat!" Penny called. "It's started bringing it in again!"

The action of the cilia, though different in quality, more searching and gradual, was smooth again. The craft wallowed and toppled onwards.

And it was, some moments later, consumed by the giant. There was no opening of it, no shaking out of the tasty nutmeat and discarding of the husk. The cilia brought it to the feeder-tentacles, which plucked it up, crushed it like a large shellfish, and hurled it whole into the mouth. As it sank the sharks, clearly endowed with fine directional control and some form of sensitivity to mechanical vibration, swarmed on it. All took their turns, assaulting hungrily, retiring unsatisfied from the metallic morsel. The squids too took their futile turns, and at length the craft settled to the basal murk, with Japhet still paying out cable to allow its sinking.

The day's agenda was completed a short while later, executed by five rather taut, silent people. A respirator, rigged to a float so that it rode some six feet under water, was set adrift from the cove. A hundred meters of improvised airhose linked it to the shore, where Nemo and Japhet worked a crude bellows of delph hide to produce continuous aspiration in the device. Polyphemus struck it with violent accuracy a short distance offshore.

Sarissa Wayne tilted the muzzle of the harpoon gun a little higher. This brought the grappling hook strapped to the underside of the harpoon up to her eye level. She reached out and touched one of its needle-sharp points looked at the hook with distaste and unease.

"It's ludicrous," she said. "The more I think about it. How did we ever convince ourselves that it was rational? All of Orson's god-damned *inferences*. . . ."

These words were addressed to no human shape, but to a grotesque mannikin, half beast, half machine, that stood beside her on the flank of the knoll. The body was a squamous hulk, ensheathed in overlapping plates, shingles and greaves of a dark, leathery substance. The head that crowned it was a metal-and-glass bulb with insectoid mechanical mouthparts, while on its back something like an engine was mounted on a shoulder frame. This Caliban replied in an eerie remnant of a voice, filtered by the respirator mask?

"Don't start doubting it now, Sarissa—you won't function as effectively if you do."

"Horseshit! I'm getting you out of there if I have to spear you and fish you out. Function effectively! You think I'm going to let you down, Jones? All this shit about trusting me, everything you said to me in bed last night, all lies, right?"

Nemo knew she was not really concerned with his words, that essentially she needed to hold him again before he went down. He shook his head, shifted his feet wretchedly in their delph-skin boots, his queer expeditionary armor a torment bottling up his answering need to hold her.

"Dearest love. I'm going in, and I'm coming out."

"Coming out," she said quietly. "That's just it. You won't have any trouble getting *in*. . . ."

They looked at the cable that belted the entire hummock they stood on. From a point just under their feet it dove in a shallow arc to Polyphemus' mouth-corner. Within the orb the cable dangled through the kelp. Down on the neural mulch their eyes could just pick out the wreck of their decoy boat. Sarissa stepped over to the second gun and checked its angle, speaking in a tone so carefully constrained it sounded absent. "If this thing wants to pull away, submerge, all our lines together won't hold it. If it's aroused while you're . . . *deafening* it—if it reacts, it will take you down."

"Listen, sweetness, if we let ourselves go over it all again, we only lose what time we have to talk about our love."

"Talk about our love!" She whirled on him. "I don't want to talk about our love, I want to *have* it."

Japhet Sparks called from the beach: "It's ready!" He and Orson had slipped their bait into the water. It was the engine of their most seriously damaged boat, mounted on a cut-down raft and anchored to the rock by a length of tripled cable. Sarissa went round the knoll-top and called to Penny down in the cove. She sat the helm of their escape craft—their own good boat, driven in the shallows around the island, and hooked to a trailer-raft for the two riders who would not fit inside.

"Penny! Bait's up! Here we go!"

"Hit it! I'm standing by!"

Nemo raised his gloved hand to Sarissa. She stood still and nodded, staring him straight in the eyes through his faceplate. Nemo took from the ground a large, heavy hook with a handle-gripped bar attached. He eased down to the lower ledge cut for him to stand on, just under the cable where it began its plunge to the giant's mouth. He checked the weaponry in the side racks of his back-frame. The motor the frame supported was one of the small ones with which each boat's emergency raft was supplied. Nemo switched it on briefly for a final assurance of its stability on its improvised mount, and switched it off. Then he hung the hook on the cable above his head and gripped the bar with both hands.

"OK Sarissa."

She called down to Japhet: "Now!" The noisy little bait-raft fired on, and chugged out towards the black meadow.

It was seized by the fibrils and tumbled orb-wards. Poly-phemus' mouth began to open—and then the raft hit the limit of its tether. The cilia began to toil, frustrated, roused. The mouth, as if impatient, gaped fully open. Nemo jumped from the ledge.

As he dove, he felt metamorphosed into a kind of bomb. He wore two wet-suits, and to the outer one his delph-hide armor was sewn with steel wire. A padded, capsuled thing, his body felt strangely snug and remote from the dreadful vision into which he plunged. The veined opacity of the orb's wall loomed into sharper focus, and the teeming am-ber lake in the giant's lips rushed to him. Nemo brought his feet up and locked his knees. With the sense of exaggerated mass his gear gave him, it seemed to him when his heels im-pacted that he struck a titanic hammer-blow on the bell of his own doom. The true proportionality of the matter was that he was like a sparrow touching down on the flank of a large hill. Even so, when he freed his hook and hacked it for purchase into the orb wall, the suicidal blatancy of the act horrified him. The material was tough, pierceable only with fierce blows. He worked his way up from the mouth-corner along the giant's lip, a swollen, scalloped border of tissues shot with purple fibrosities. He gained his feet and began to stalk along the border of the golden tarn.

From his rack he took a crooked scythe welded from the blades of three flensing-knives. He stuck its razor tip into the ichor and vigorously slashed up its surface. Sharks, fast as rockets, rose and converged on the spot, mouths foremost. Nemo saw that their ragged fangs moved independently in addition to the jaws' movement of them—mouths that worked more like shredders than scissors. They milled there persistently, their red, poisoned eye-clusters flashing with their sharp, snakish turns. Nemo racked the scythe and took down one of his three rifles. He began to pump explosive shot into the haggle-toothed mouths. Outside the orb, at the fringe of its dome just behind where he stood, something huge moved. It was a trio of Polyphemus' feeder-tentacles, beginning to elongate yearningly outwards, towards the stubborn bait-raft. Nemo kept firing.

When he had killed perhaps a dozen, he found he was kin-dling unhoped-for havoc among these blinded sensories. Each one hit, as its head ruptured, went into spasms that snarled the coordination of its pack. Each, as it thrashed, scribbled the ichor with ribbons and wraiths of its blood, waking the appetites of the squadron it jostled. The cannibal frenzy spread as the blood got thicker and made every beast smell like food to its fellows. It was, apparently, some visual cue that normally inhibited this kind of accident—the taste of cannibal food itself certainly did not.

Two other of Polyphemus' feeder tentacles had gone out towards its recalcitrant prey. So far none had reached it, but all showed a slow, inexorable extensibility that was not yet exhausted. Nemo scanned the red uproar beneath his feet. His goal was now the basal stratum, and he sought a window to it through the fanged turmoil. He saw one down along a major strand of the kelp, turned the ignition of the motor on his back, and dove in, rifle first.

They had seen Helion's still masked face remain unaffected after his engulfment, while Jax's hand soon begun to bloat and corrode, but curiously, it was in his face that Nemo dreaded first feeling some caustic leakage, rather than his hands which, for his manipulation of his weapons, had been left fairly thinly gloved. The stalk he followed was as thick as his body, and he kept it just above his back, to force any attacker into a frontal approach.

Down where the stalks coalesced towards their common rootage, while there was still room to navigate between them, he branched off to his first task, where the wreck lay.

The hulk's cable had supported it against complete subsidence. It was sunk in a turgid, half-liquid zone just above a more solid neural mulch. Its fractured hull offered many places where the coils of cable he had brought could be threaded through its chassis. Firmly and intricately, he wove the wreck to several major kelp-stalks. Yesterday's bait had now set its hook in the prey that had swallowed it. Yesterday's bad luck—that Polyphemus should not flee in panic at its blinding, but feed regardless and wait to feed again—was today's good luck. "Take me down now if you want to," Nemo hissed in the smothered silence of his helmet.

Now came the task that probed luck's spider web. They had observed three distinct basal zones in which the sensories' neuro-umbilici attached. Now Nemo sped to the nearest of these, and, trying to stay ahead of his fear, charged into it, scything through tethers in broad sweeps. He found a lateral branching of kelp to stand on and cut his motor.

As the squids came down, he shot them. They rained

towards him with the erratic, dodging movement of moths or snowflakes, and he shot them as they applied their caudal tips to the mulch to regenerate their tethers. The inner explosions tended to split them lengthwise, and several, in dying, vomited upwards from their beaks little clouds of eggs like those found in the skull.

Nemo scythed the remaining tethers. Overhead, the silvery interface of ichor with open sky was visible in patches through the churned gore of the sharks, and Nemo saw it shattered by the impact of one of Sarissa's grappling hooks. The bait raft's tether must be near breaking. He worked faster, darting upwards from his ambush now to meet and kill those that were slow in descending. At least half of the tethers he cut must have been those of sharks, but few of these came down except in bleeding tatters, more mulch for the undiscriminating titan, which now dined upon its own senses.

And then Nemo was on to the second zone. Here he swept zig-zag through the field and mowed it all at once. Panic was big in him, trying to split from within the shell of his self-command. His compromise was to push the very limit of recklessness. He stood in the center of the mown patch and fired directly overhead, accelerating his motor periodically against the muddy tug of Polyphemus' appetite at his feet. The sensories came dodging down through the veiny gloom, while from the smoky plane of the higher turmoil sharkmeat drizzled ever more continually, trailing wisps of torn tissue. He saw Sarissa's second hook hit the interface and glide towards its purchase in the giant's mouth-corner.

The rent and ragged molluscoidal shapes piled in little drifts around him. When the weapon's fifty-shot magazine gave out he dropped it and snatched down another rifle. And then no others descended. He waited two seconds, five, then launched himself towards the third attachment zone.

In the same instant that he did so, the floor of his little ocean tore itself from under his feet. In the inertial shock that followed, Nemo sprawled helpless in the turbid boil. He collided with a stalk and hugged it, and then the giant was still. A moment later, the silver ceiling of this living cosmos exploded a third time. The bait raft, its snapped cable fluttering behind it, dug an effervescent shaft down towards him. Nemo accelerated towards the last of the sensories' anchorages.

Those on shore saw him raise his scythe, dart forward—

but then check his swing, and pull up just short of the unbilical thicket. There, at the edge of the webwork, the scaly little man-shape paused and, from his place in the orb's deepest murk, seemed to guage how far the thicket towered over him.

"What's he doing?" Japhet called to Sarissa from the beach. She didn't take her eyes from Nemo, and her answer to Japhet was spoken only to herself, almost whispered:

"He's thinking how to kill them from higher up. *Yes*. Get near the exit before you do it—get near as you can!"

The scaly shape probed the kelp adjoining the thicket, and separated out from it a slender side-stalk perhaps fifty meters long. Nemo grasped this by the tip and began to drag it in a gradually rising spiral round the thicket's perimeter. He tightened the spiral as he rose, gathering the lower parts of the neural tethers into a sheaf. When the stalk ran out he tied it to a more massive growth and found another, higher-branching one.

Orson Waverly had extrapolated rather extensively from what the previous day's test had shown them: "I think it fell back immediately on a more primitive feeding taxon, probably geared for motile but armored or shelled prey. Maybe it feeds on some of the pseudo-brachiopoda—there's some big bathic ones just been found.

"But it's the implications of this behaviour that are most significant to us. Totally blinded, and no panic reaction. I think these saprophytes, during their evolution, have maintained a very separable, interruptible kind of sensory feed-in with their host. After all, with tethers routinely broken, that kind of reaction wouldn't be very productive for Polyphemus. But still, the complete deprivation of an important sensory input? My guess is that as long as the sensories are alive and maintain attachment, they transmit a steady flow of 'white noise', random neural firings, to the host. It doesn't experience a disruption of sensation so much as a kind of zero-information state, such as it might experience on a dark night, or very deep down.

"I *am* convinced that as the sensories are killed, Polyphemus will feel a cumulative encroachment of sensory deprivation—a state of 'total blank' as opposed to one of 'no news', and it seems to me this *must* produce a violent reaction of some sort. Now understand that from this point I'm only guessing, but it's often the case that creatures as primitive as Polyphemus is, when you consider it apart from this startling

adaptive turn it has taken—that such creatures can be relatively insensitive to extensive physical disruption. For my
money, Nemo should have a good chance of killing at least a
majority of the sensories before any radical sense of anomaly
begins to dominate the giant's behaviour."

Now Nemo repeated Orson's words in a snarl—"for my
money"—and began firing on the sensories his ploy had ag-
gregated into a desperate snarl no more than twenty-five meters from the titan's mouth. He was prodigal of shot,
perforated the bloody, frantic mass from every angle. When
his magazine emptied he let the rifle drop and grabbed his
last. After a moment—during which the redundant butchery
had him in a kind of vengeful trance—he realized his work
was done. It was then that the giant moved again.

It filled Nemo with awe, as Polyphemus' previous, lurching
movement had not done, for this was an immense, concerted
muscular effort of the biocosmos that held him. The pressure
of the ichor increased upon him as the entire orb tautened
and strained to pull itself offshore, out to deeper waters. The
message of darkness had at last definitely reached the titan's
murk-shrouded ganglia. The giant was alarmed.

And on finding that a quintuple thickness of cable opposed
its withdrawal from shore, alarm became the plainest panic.
Nemo, who had felt so huge and blatant during his soaring
approach of the enemy, now felt he was reduced to a jot of
foam in the raging prow of a tidal wave. His motor's effort
mouthwards, skywards, seemed a ludicrous trivium. Polyphemus had a very powerful—awesome, even—capture-
resistance taxon. It had sought to move, and found that
painful stasis opposed its murky will. It tried again, and a
fang of pain on a scale that it could feel was sunk into its
core. And now Polyphemus was an earthquake. Volcanic
clouds of its black blood roiled up from the roots of the
stalks that its panic was tearing loose. Pain could not vie with
the blind will to escape that it had kindled in this colossus—
unmolested, no doubt, through centuries of easy gluttony.
Polyphemus strove, and an ink-storm arose from its tearing
entrails.

And when they tore free and the boat, trailing broken trees
of nerve-chord, came vomiting, rocketing mouthward, Nemo
knew he would be trapped in the ichor's inertia—would fall
with Polyphemus, and join him in his dark retreat, if he

failed to reach the boat before it erupted free. He gave up vertical striving and fought to intercept it.

As it erupted he saw he was missing it, was a helpless half second too slow, but mindlessly he sustained his drive after the craft had passed him. A trailing nerve-stalk clubbed his belly, and he hugged it with both arms and legs, while all the fluid volume of Polyphemus strove to strip him off and flush him down. The boat, the stalk, and then Nemo, were plucked into the sky.

The sudden surge into freefall tricked Nemo out of his grip on the stalks. He could see he was falling free of the sinking feeder-tentacles, but that he was going to dive into the cilium-field sluggishly following the giant's subsidence. He fought to straighten for a sharp, hands-first entry so that he could pull the dive shallow as soon as he struck. He hit the vipered foam and arched his back strongly as he entered. As he surfaced he felt himself pulled short. A fibril had snarled in the screw of his motor.

The field was retiring laterally before it sank under—Polyphemus was pulling its skirts, so to speak, off of the mid-shallows they had overlain. Nemo threw his feet in the air to flop backwards where he could get a grip on the cilium. He just managed this, but was too awkwardly folded, legs flailing, to get a scythe free from his snarled rack. A red shock of pain ruptured his left foot.

An instant passed before he had the wit to seize hold of his foot, and grab the line of the harpoon that pierced it. He wrapped it round his arm, feeling nothing so much as a vivid embarrassment and indignity in his position as he fought for his scythe with his free hand. He had been dragged past the littoral drop off before he had it out, and went under.

For a brief eternity he expected Polyphemus' full weight to haul against his steel-wound arm, and then he got the scythe-tip under the fibril, and pulled mightily.

Jones lay on the beach the expedition had first set out from. Japhet had brought the medical kit from the sand-hog, and waited at a discreet distance while Sarissa cleaned and bandaged Nemo's foot. She finished the bandage and patted his thigh, smiling absently with an unconscious appraisal and satisfaction in her eyes, such a gaze as a breeder might bend upon his prize beast, knowing it safe after some hazard.

"No artery hit," she said, "a few of the metacarpals bro-

ken, I think. At the worst you'll have a slight limp and that
won't make *you* any the less active."

Nemo nodded gravely, and didn't answer at once. "I love
you all the more for your . . . determination to save me," he
said at last. "No doubt you had an agonizing moment there
as you fired, dreading that the shot might be . . . a little off."

"Not the slightest." She said it fiercely. Her large black
eyes came up and bullseyed his; a distinct frost of impugned
expertise gave them added bite. "I knew it before I even saw
exactly what kind of fix you would get into: there was no
way I was going to miss *you*, Jones."

Nemo nodded. "I see." He looked at the lake, and smiled.

Down in its waters, their enemy still pursued its ponderous
retreat. Deep in the lake's root, the cold and lightless magma-
tic shaft, it sought the realms that were the ancient nursery of
its evolution. Its encounter with the vertebrate bipeds had reft
it of the fruits of five million years' development. It had
found the butcher-work of these midgets far cannier than its
own, and so it stumbled back down to the night of its origin.

ABSENT THEE FROM FELICITY AWHILE . . .

by Somtow Sucharitkul

*Here's a variation on a theme that a few coura-
geous writers have tackled before—with a certain
dread and a shock of horror. Live life over again?
Yes, and then again, no. But this story manages to
turn a new direction. The right to achieve adulthood
in a cosmic community must be learned.*

1

You remember silence, don't you?

There were many silences once: silence for a great speech,
silence before an outburst of thunderous applause, silence after laughter. Silence is gone forever, now. When you listen to
the places where the silence used to be, you hear the soft insidious buzzing, like a swarm of distant flies, that proclaims
the end of man's solitude. . . .

For me, it happened like this: It was opening night, and
Hamlet was just dying, and I was watching from the wings,
being already dead, of course, as Guildenstern. I wanted to
stay for curtain call anyway, even though I knew the audience wouldn't notice. It hadn't been too long since my first
job, and I was new in New York. But here everything
revolved around Sir Francis FitzHenry, brought over from
England at ridiculous expense with his new title clinging to
him like wrapping paper.

Everything else was as low-budget as possible, including me. They did a stark, empty staging, ostensibly as a sop to modernism, but really because the backers were penniless after paying FitzHenry's advance, and so Sir Francis was laid out on a barren proscenium with nothing but an old leather armchair for Claudius's throne and a garish green spot on him. Not that there was any of that Joseph Papp-type avant-garde rubbish. Everything was straight. Me, I didn't know what people saw in Sir Francis FitzHenry till I saw him live—I'd only seen him in that ridiculous Fellini remake of *Ben Hur*—but he was dynamite, just the right thing for the old Jewish ladies.

There he was, then, making his final scene so heartrending I could have drowned in an ocean of molasses; arranging himself into elaborate poses that could have been plucked from the Acropolis; and uttering each iambic pentameter as though he were the New York Philharmonic and the Mormon Tabernacle Choir all rolled into one. And they were lapping it up, what with the swing away from the really modern interpretations. He was a triumph of the old school, there on that stage turning the other actors into ornamental papier-mache all around him.

He had just gotten, you know, to that line:

Absent thee from felicity awhile . . .
To tell my story.

and was just about to fall, with consummate grace, into Horatio's arms. You could feel the collective catch of breath, the palpable silence, and I was thinking, *What could ever top that, my God? . . .* and I had that good feeling you get when you know you're going to be drawing your paycheck for at least another year or so. And maybe Gail would come back, even.

Then—

Buzz, buzz, buzz, buzz. "What's wrong?" I turned to the little stage manager, who was wildly pushing buttons. The buzzing came, louder and louder. You couldn't hear a word Horatio was saying. The buzzing kept coming, from every direction now, hurting my ears. Sir Francis sat up in midtumble and glared balefully at the wings, then the first scream could be heard above the racket, and I finally had the nerve to poke my head out and saw the tumult in the audience. . . .

"For Chrissakes, why doesn't someone turn on the house

lights?" Claudius had risen from where he was sprawled dead and was stomping around the stage. The buzzing became more and more intense, and now there were scattered shrieks of terror and the thunder of an incipient stampede mixed into the buzzing, and I cursed loudly about the one dim spotlight. The screaming came continuously. People were trooping all over the stage and were tripping on swords and shields, a lady-in-waiting hurtled into me and squished makeup onto my cloak, corpses were groping around in the dark, and finally I found the right switch where the stage manager had run away and all the lights came on and the leather armchair went whizzing into the flies.

I caught one word amid all this commotion—

Aliens.

A few minutes later everybody knew everything. Messages were being piped into our minds somehow. At first they just said *don't panic, don't panic* and were hypnotically soothing, but then it all became more bewildering as the enormity of it all sank in. I noticed that the audience were sitting down again, and the buzzing had died down to an insistent whisper. Everything was returning to a surface normal, but stiff, somehow; artificial. They were all sitting, a row of glassy-eyed mannequins in expensive clothes, under the glare of the house lights, and we knew we were all hearing the same thing in our minds.

They were bringing us the gift of immortality, they said. They were some kind of galactic federation. No, we wouldn't really be able to understand what they were, but they would not harm us. In return for their gift, they were exacting one small favor from us. They would try to explain it in our terms. Apparently something like a sort of hyperspatial junior high school was doing a project on uncivilized planets, something like "one day in the life of a barbarian world." The solar system was now in some kind of time loop, and would we be kind enough to repeat the same day over and over again for a while, with two hours off from 6 to 8 every morning, while their kids came over and studied everything in detail. We were very lucky, they added; it was an excellent deal. No, there wasn't anything we could do about it.

I wondered to myself, how long is "over and over again for a while"?

They answered it for me. "Oh, nothing much. About seven

million of your years." I felt rather short-changed, though I realized that it was nothing in comparison with immortality.

And, standing there stock-still and not knowing what to think, I saw the most amazing sight. We all saw the aliens as gossamer veils of light that drifted and danced across the field of vision, almost imperceptible, miniature auroras that sparkled and vanished. . . . I saw Sir Francis's face through a gauze of shimmering blue lights. I wanted to touch them so badly; I reached out and my hand passed right through one without feeling a thing. Then they were gone.

We turned off the house lights—we had until midnight—and went on with the play. The buzzing subsided almost completely, but was very obviously there all the time, so everybody gabbled their lines and tried to cut in quickly between speeches to cover up the noise. The applause was perfunctory, and Sir Francis seemed considerably distressed that he had been so easily upstaged.

I walked home at a few minutes to midnight. I saw peculiar poles with colored metallic knobs on them, all along Broadway every couple of blocks, like giant parking meters. The streets were virtually empty, and there were a couple of overturned Yellow cabs and an old Chevy sticking out of a store window. It had been too much for some, I supposed. But I was so confused about what had happened, I tried to think about nothing but Gail and about the bad thing that had happened that morning.

I climbed up the dirty staircase to my efficiency above an Indian grocery store and jumped into bed with all my clothes on, thinking about the bad thing between me and Gail, and at midnight I suddenly noticed I was in pyjamas and she was lying there beside me, and there was a sudden jerk of dislocation and I knew that it wasn't *today* anymore, it was *yesterday*, it was all true. I squeezed my eyes tightly and wished I was dead.

2

I woke up around 11 o'clock. Gail stirred uneasily. We made love, like machines. I kept trying to pull myself away, knowing what was coming. Whatever the aliens had done, it had turned me into a needle in a groove, following the line of least resistance.

We got up and had breakfast. She wore her ominous dishevelled look, strands of black hair fishnetting her startlingly blue eyes.

"John?"

The dinette table seemed as wide as all space. She seemed incredibly unreachable, like the stars. "Umm?" I found myself saying in a banal voice. I knew what she was going to say; I knew what I was going to do. But whatever it was dealt only with appearances. In my thoughts I was free, as though I were somehow outside the whole thing, experiencing my own past as a recording. I wondered at my own detachment.

"John, I'm leaving you."

Anger rose in me. I got up, knocking over the coffee mug and shouting, "What for, who with?" like an idiot before going off into incoherent cursing.

"Francis FitzHenry has asked me to stay with him—in his suite at the Plaza!"

The anger welled up again. Blindly, I slapped her face. She went white, then red, and then she said quietly, dangerously: "You're too petty, John. That's why you're going to be a Guildenstern for the rest of your life." That hurt.

Then she walked out of my life.

I shaved and walked slowly over to the theater. We played to a full house. The aliens came. Sir Francis seemed considerably distressed that he had been so easily upstaged. I walked home, casually noting the two overturned Yellow cabs and the old Chevy stuck in a store window, past the overgrown parking meters, to my efficiency above an Indian grocery store, and threw myself fully clothed on the bed. I fell asleep.

I woke up around 11 o'clock, Gail stirred uneasily. We made love mechanically, and I knew that the two people who were lying there together had become totally divorced from themselves, and were going through preordained motions that bore no relationship whatsoever to what was in their minds. And there was no way of communicating.

We ate breakfast. She wore her ominous dishevelled look, and I desperately wanted to apologize to her, but when I tried to speak my facial muscles were frozen and the buzzing seemed to get louder, drowning my thoughts. Was the buzzing an external sound, or was it some mental monitor to enforce the status quo?

"I'm leaving you."

Anger rose in me. I quenched it at once, but it made no difference either to my posture or to my words.

"Francis FitzHenry has asked me to stay with him—in his suite at the Plaza!"

I slapped her face. Suddenly the veils of light came, caressing the musty stale air of my apartment, touching the dust and making it sparkle, like a golden snow between the two of us. They faded. We had been watched; we were trapped in a galactic Peyton Place.

"You're too petty, John. That's why you're going to be a Guildenstern for the rest of your life." And walked out of my life. It hurt me more every time. I was doomed to be a Guildenstern in this play too, a Guildenstern for the old ladies and a Guildenstern for the veils of light. It was hell.

I shaved and walked slowly over to the theater. We played to a full house. The aliens came; Sir Francis seemed considerably distressed that he had been so easily upstaged. I walked home, past the overturned cars and the gigantic parking meters that had materialized out of nowhere.

As I fell asleep, just before midnight, a thought surfaced: we were supposed to have two free hours every morning, weren't we? For months now, I had slept through those two hours.

I resolved to force myself to wake up at six.

3

I jerked myself awake at 6:30, snaked into unostentatious jeans and a T-shirt, and came down.

The brilliant summer morning hit me between the eyes. It had been autumn the previous night. Everything was to wonder at: the trash drifting down the sidewalk in the breeze, the briskness of the air, the clarity of the sunlight . . .

Two tramps were leaning against the first of the alien poles. They had their eyes closed and were very peaceful, so I crept away. Portholes exuded smoke, people jostled each other, and everything seemed astonishingly normal, except for the insistent buzzing.

Another of the poles had a man in a scruffy three-piece suit and blatantly orange tie, holding up a sign on which was scrawled VON DANIKEN LIVES! He had acquired a squalid-looking collection of onlookers, whom I joined for a moment.

". . . man, these critters built the *Pyramids!* They built the *Empire State Building!* They're the Gods! Alexander the Great was one! Richard M. Nixon was one! God was one! . . . and you, too, can be saved, if only you'll just throw a quarter on the altar of repentance! Hallelujah! Thank you, ma'am. . . ."

I walked on.

At the next extraterrestrial parking meter a group of Hare Krishna types was dancing round and round like they had a missionary in the pot. In the middle a scrawny, bespectacled shaven man was caressing the shaft, which was glowing a dull crimson. He seemed transfigured, almost beautiful, much more like the real thing than Sir Francis FitzHenry could ever be. I watched for a long time, fascinated, my mind dulled by the hypnotic repetitiveness of their chanting.

They ceased, jolting me from my reverie. The lanky one came up to me and started to whisper confidentially, intensely. "Did you know they're only a few microns thick? Did you know that they're called the *T' tat?* Did you know they have a shared consciousness that works over vast reaches of space-time? Did you know they've reached an incredibly high evolutionary phase, huh?"

"You don't talk like a Hare Krishna person."

"Hey! . . . oh, the clothes, you mean. Actually, I have a Ph.D. from M.I.T. I *talk* to them, you know."

"No kidding!"

"Hey, really! Listen, come here," he pulled me roughly over to the pole, which had stopped glowing. "Just sit down here, relax now, touch the pole. Totem pole, divine antenna, whatever. Can't you hear anything . . . ?"

Hello.

I was shivering. The voice was so close; it was speaking inside me. I drew back quickly.

Hey, did you know they have many doctors, that each color shows their status based on age? Did you know that, huh? Did you know they don't join up with the collective consciousness until they're almost half a billion years old, that they have these learning centers all over the galaxy, that they originally crossed over from the Great Nebula in Andromeda? No kidding, man!"

I didn't know what he was talking about.

"Here, touch it again, it isn't so bad the second time." He was twitching all over, a bundle of nerves. "Sorry I'm acting like this. It's my only chance to act normal, you see, the rest of the day I'm either stoned or asleep, according to the script. I can't wait till we all wake up!"

I reached out. *Hello.*

"Isn't there any way we can *resist* them?"

"What for? Don't you want to live forever? This is just a sort of Purgatory, isn't it? We all get to go to heaven."

"But suppose I wanted to, you know, contradict them, or something."

"Dunno. They can't control *everything.*" He paused for a moment, but then launched himself into a stream of information again, as though I'd fed him another quarter.

"I have the general equations worked out." He flashed a bit of paper in front of my face, then thrust it back into his pocket—"but you obviously have to be in control of unified field theory, and even then there's the power source to worry about. I have a couple of theories—f'rinstance, if they had sort of a portable mini-quasar, like, a miniature white hole worming through space-time into a transdimensional universe, they could tap the energy, you see, and—"

He had lost me. I touched the pole, and his voice faded into nothingness. The buzzing intensified. *Hello.*

"We're just dirt to you, laboratory animals," I said bitterly. "I wish it was back to the way it was."

You can't help being a lower being, you know. There's nothing you or I can do about that.

"Well, will you tell me one thing?" It suddenly occurred to me that everyone had left. The Hare Krishnas, hands linked, had gone dancing off.

Sure.

"Is this thing really worth it, for us? Seven million years is a long, long, time; it's the same as eternity for all practical purposes."

Hah! Fat lot you know.

"You didn't answer my question."

All in good time. But it's almost 8 o'clock. Hold on, you'll be dislocated back to yesterday in a few seconds. You're pretty lucky, you know; in some parts of the world the two hours' grace comes at some ridiculous time and nobody ever gets up.

"Goodbye."

Goodbye.

I woke up around 11 o'clock. Gail stirred uneasily. We made love mechanically, like machines, with living sheets of light, only a few microns thick, darting between us, weaving delicately transient patterns in the air, and I felt hollow, transparent, empty.

4

I met Amy Schechter in Grand Central Station, coming out of the autumn night into a biting blizzard of a winter morning.

We were both standing at a doughnut stand. I looked at her, helpless, frail, as she stared into a cup of cold coffee. I had seen her before, but this morning there were just the two of us. She suddenly looked up at me. Her eyes were brown and lost.

"Hi. Amy."

"John."

A pause, full of noisome buzzing, fell between us.

For a while, I watched the breath-haze form and dissipate about her face, wanting to make conversation, but I couldn't think what to say.

"Will you talk to me? Nobody ever does, they always back off, as if they knew."

"Okay."

"I've been standing here for five years, waiting for my train. Sometimes I come an hour or so before 8 o'clock, you know, just to stand around. There's nothing for me at where I'm staying." Her voice was really small, hard to hear against the buzzing.

"Where are you going?"

"Oh, Havertown, Pennsylvania. You've never heard of it." I hadn't. "It's sort of a suburb of Philadelphia," she added helpfully. "My folks live there."

"Buy you a doughnut?"

"You must be joking!" She laughed quickly and stopped herself, then cast her eyes down as though scrutinizing a hypothetical insect in her styrofoam cup. Then she turned her back on me, hugging her shaggy old coat to her thin body, and crumpled the cup firmly and threw it into the garbage.

"Wait, come back! We've got an hour and a half, you know, before you have to leave—"

"Oh, so it's score and run? Nothing doing, friend."

"Well, I *will* buy you a doughnut then."

"Oh, all right. A romantic memory," she added cynically, "when I'll be dead by dinner anyway."

"Huh?"

She came closer. We were almost touching, both leaning against the grubby counter. "I'm one of the ghosts, you know," she said.

"I don't get it."

"What do *you* do every day?"

"My girlfriend walks out on me, then I play a poor third fiddle to a pretentious British actor in *Hamlet*."

"Lucky. In *my* script, the train crashes into an eighteen-wheeler 25 miles outside of Philadelphia. Smash! Everybody dead. And then every morning I find myself at the station again. I was pretty muddled at first, the aliens never made any announcements to *me* while I was lying in the wreckage. So I do it all over and over again. One day I may even enjoy it."

It didn't sink in. "Chocolate covered?" I asked inanely.

"Yeah."

There was another pause. I realized how much I needed another person, not Gail, how much I needed someone real. . . .

"We should get to know each other, maybe," I ventured. "After it's all over, maybe we could—"

"No, Joke. Nothing doing. I'm a ghost. I'm not immortal, don't you see! The whole deal ignores me completely! I'm dead already, dead, permanently dead! You don't get to be part of the deal if you die sometime during the day, you have to survive through till midnight, don't you see?"

". . . oh God." I saw.

"They've just left me in the show to make everything as accurate as can be. I'm an echo. I'm nothing."

I didn't say a word. I just grabbed her and kissed her, right there in the middle of the doughnut stand. She was quite cold, like marble, like stone.

"Come on," she said. We found a short-time hotel around the block; I paid the eight dollars and we clung together urgently, desperately, for a terribly brief time.

I woke up at around 11 o'clock. Gail stirred uneasily. As I

went through the motions for the thousandth time I was thinking all the time, *this isn't fair, this isn't fair.* Gail was alive, she was going to live forever, and she's just like a machine, she might just as well be dead. Amy, now, she was dead, but so *alive!* Then I realized a terrible truth: *Immortality kills!* I was very bitter and very angry. I felt cheated, and the buzzing sounded louder, like a warning, and I knew then that I was going to try and do something dreadful. ("They can't control *everything*," wasn't that what the Kirshna freak had said?)

I struggled, trying to push myself out of the groove, trying to change a little bit of one little movement, but always falling back to the immutable past. . . .

We got up and had breakfast. She wore her ominous dishevelled look, strands of black hair fishnetting her startling blue eyes.

"John?"

"Umm?"

"John, I'm leaving you."

"What for, who with?"

"Francis FitzHenry has asked me to stay with him—in his suite at the Plaza!"

I lifted my hand, then willed with every ounce of strength I could dredge up from every hidden source.

I didn't slap her face.

A look of utter bewilderment crossed her face, just for one split second, and I looked at her and she looked at me, her emotions unfathomable; and then the whole thing swung grotesquely back to the original track, and she said quietly, dangerously, "You're too petty, John. That's why you're going to be a Guildenstern for the rest of your life." As though nothing were different. That hurt.

Then she walked out of my life.

But I had changed something! And we had communicated; for a split second something had passed between us!

The buzzing became a roar. I walked slowly to the theater, bathed in the glow of a hundred diaphanous wisps of light.

5

It was a couple of minutes before 8 when the phone rang in my apartment. I decided to make a run for it, so I made for the kitchenette in the nude.

"Yeah?"

"This is Michael, John." Michael played Horatio. He was sobbing, all broken up. I didn't know him very well, so I played it cool. "John, I'm going to do something terrible! I can't stand it, you're the first person I could get through to this morning, I'm going to try and—"

I woke up around 11 o'clock. Gail stirred uneasily We had breakfast, and I didn't slap her face.

It seemed too natural. I realized that I had changed the pattern. This is the way it would always be from now on.

I had never slapped her face.

A look of utter bewilderment . . . but it was no longer a communication, it was just a reflex, part of the pattern, and then she said quietly, dangerously, "You're too petty, John. That's why you're going to be a Guildenstern for the rest of your life."

That hurt. Then she walked out of my life.

I went to the theater. There was Sir Francis, making his final scene so heartrending I could have drowned in a sea of molasses; arranging himself into elaborate poses that could have been plucked from the Acropolis; and uttering each iambic pentameter as though he were the New York Philharmonic and the Mormon Tabernacle Choir all rolled into one. He was dying, and he clutched at Horatio, and he said, measuring each phrase for the right mixture of honey and gall—

Absent thee from felicity awhile . . .
To tell my story.

and was just about to fall, with consummate grace, into Horatio's arms, and you could feel the collective catch of breath, the palpable silence except for the quiet buzzing, when Horatio drew a revolver from his doublet and emptied it into Sir Francis's stomach.

After the aliens departed from the theater, the play went on, since Hamlet was dead anyway, and afterwards I walked home. I saw peculiar poles with metallic knobs on them, all along Broadway every couple of blocks, and there were a couple of overturned Yellow cabs, but the old Chevy was gone from the store window. Good for them.

In the morning I met Amy. I told her about what had happened.

"When you get to just before your accident, try to jump

out of the car or something. Keep trying, Amy, just keep trying."

She chewed her doughnut, deliberating. "I don't know."

"Well, we've got another six million, nine hundred thousand, nine hundred and ninety-four years to try in. So keep at
it, okay?"

She seemed unconvinced.

"Just for me, try."

I kissed her quickly on the forehead and she disappeared
into the crowd that was heading towards the platform.

6

The pole was glowing a pale crimson when I touched it.
Hello.

I couldn't contain my rage. "You bastards! Well, we're not
powerless after all, we've got free will, we *can* change things.
We can ruin your high school project completely, rats that we
are!"

*Oh. Well, that too is one of the things under study at the
moment.*

"Well, let me tell you something. I don't want your immortality! Because I'd have to give up being a person. Being a
person means changing all the time, not being indifferent, and
you're changing us into machines."

Oh? And do you deny that you've changed?

It was true. I had changed. I wasn't going to be a Guildenstern for the rest of my life anymore. I was going to fight
them; I was going to learn everything I could about them so I
could try and twist it against them; I was going to be a real
human being.

*There are things you can't do anything about. You're in a
transitional stage, you see. With immortality will come a
change in perspectives. You won't feel the same anymore
about your barbarian ways, Earthling.*

I had to laugh. "Where did you learn to talk like that?"

We monitored your science fiction TV broadcasts.

The picture of these alien schoolkids, clustering around a
television set in some galactic suburbia somewhere in the
sky. . . . I laughed and laughed and laughed.

But then, seriously: "I'm still going to fight you, you know.
For the sake of being human." I had a new fuel to use, after

all, against them. Love. Revenge. Heroism. I was thinking of Amy. The good old-fashioned stuff of drama.

Go ahead.

I woke up around 11 o'clock.

OUT OF THE EVERYWHERE

by James Tiptree, Jr.

It's good to see this author return again after a period of literary abstinence. Tiptree fuses several elements in this story and manages to make everything come off in a grand climax that combines icebergs, split personalities, and a ravening monster. All in the context of today's world.

Enggi was a cold deep-space cub, out on his first lone venture. His co-grex didn't know where he was, nor even that he'd left them. Precocious as Enggi was, he was yet far too young—millennia too young and unprepared—to roam the galaxy alone.

Enggi and his kind resembled nothing of Earth, being nearly immaterial sentiences evolved in the energic vortices of near-vacuum and icy radiations, where life takes root in the complex molecular debris of stellar catastrophes. Yet, as with any earthly cub, the strayer from the pack meets mortal dangers.

At first all was exhilaration.

He was thrilled by riding real astral currents—excited by bombardments of radiations that had been only dull teachings—delighted by clearly perceiving cosmic wonders that had been no more than blurs from within the gas clouds of his grex's nest. The buffetings of an immense explosion shook him with real fright, but lit him with the exultation of

143

unaided mastery. And above all there was no one to direct him! No one to say no!

On certain older star systems he even found fading sign of a foreign grex, and boldly obliterated it with his own. Yes! Perhaps in the future, Enggi might claim this territory for himself, when he had grown enough to contest any of the former owners who might be still about.

Vastly pleased with himself and all he was finding, Enggi wandered up the pressure gradient that was a great galactic arm, now propelling himself athwart the flow, again drifting with it. And after a short while, quite thoroughly lost.

Meanwhile his absence from his grex had been discovered. Alarm, search, confirmation. Two scouts from an experienced subgrex set out to trace Enggi's cold trail.

They were not alone.

Some star clusters back, Enggi had unknowingly picked up a third, much closer follower, who now slunk and circled just out of range, scarcely believing its luck.

Earthly predators do not include beings of such passive rapacity, such sophisticated yet oddly automatonlike evil. Call it the Eater. Eaters are rare, but very long-lived. In their normal form they lie in ambush in any gaseous tangle, waiting the chance to display their attractants to some innocent of space.

This Eater was presently certain that Enggi was not part of a trap, that he was just as he appeared: alone. It stationed itself in the path of the unwary cub.

The two scouts patiently tracking Enggi's spoor were quite aware of this danger. When presently they came on an Eater's deserted lair they knew Enggi *had* to be found, and fast. But this was not from benevolence toward Enggi.

What they expected to find was not a killed or partly eaten cub, but an apparently intact, normal Enggi, their own bright friendly grexling—who nevertheless must be killed, by the scouts themselves.

For an Eater does not attack its victim from outside. Instead, it attracts the prey to contact and is subtly ingested. Here it begins inexorably to eat out its host from within, always taking care, as long as possible, to replace vital structure with its own body matter. Thus an infestation may go undetected for a long time. Finally comes the bout of terminal agony, after which, where the victim was, are three or more strong young Eaters—ready and able to attack any nearby prey. A single unsuspected Eater can thus in time destroy most of a grex.

Enggi's race had learned no defense against the attractant, no signs of early infestation, and no cure or means of expelling or cutting out an ingested Eater. Hence their only solution was the destruction of a known parasite by destroying its host, no matter how beloved in the grex.

Thus when the scouts observed the Eater's empty lair they knew that Enggi was the obvious, indubitable victim-to-be. And Enggi had made himself dear to his grex, with his vitality and promising ways. Sadness came to the scouts. As they followed him to what must be his fate, a strange mourning music drifted from them amid the spectra of the stars.

But before Enggi was reached by any of his pursuers, a quite different disaster intervened.

He was idly investigating a busy little single-sun system, when he found himself gripped in an intense local field configuration too strong for his fledgling powers. Much too late, he recalled a teacher's warning about the anomalous magnetic fluxes which may invest certain types of stars. In the very moment of recall, he realized he was tumbling helplessly, faster and faster, toward the small yellow sun whose heat meant his death. Panic!

Why, oh why, had he not attended more closely? There was something he should do—but what? Was it to do with these planets, perhaps?

The Eater, observing the start of Enggi's trajectory, knew what should happen, and prepared to settle down and wait. It was not dissatisfied; the prey, when it reemerged from defensive stasis, would be confused and highly vulnerable to the taking.

But what should happen did not, because Enggi had not recalled in time. The icy outer gas balls on which he should take refuge were already flashing past. Ahead lay only the small, fatally hot inner satellites. Puzzled, the Eater followed.

Desperately, as Enggi plunged on, he racked his memory. Something—there was something that might still be tried—*if* he could discern the axial topography in time, and *if* the planet bore something called life. Yes—he had it! A frantic emergency measure, his only hope. But the first of the small planets was already too near.

Wild with terror, he deployed his sensors to their utmost, and at the last moment he found it: the magnetic configu-

ration that allowed him to deflect his sunward fall. And
yes—yes! As the next planet's gravity seized him, he found
the polar vortex they had told him of. Cold—life-saving cold
might be here. The cold that might help him for a little
while.

But his crash would be frightful. He would be terribly
damaged, and need much time to heal, if he were not killed.

Again he pounded at his memory. What must he do? If he
recalled right, he must physically encyst, and at the same
time fling loose the vital components of his psyche, in the forlorn hope that they would find living lodgement, to be recalled when his body healed. But where? Which?

He was hurtling toward extinction, no time left. Desperately he cast from him all he could grasp—will, thought,
love, technical knowledge—all but bare identity. In his panic
he almost forgot the most vital of all—*directionality*, that he
might someday reassemble, or be found. There! Already in
atmosphere he hurled the vectors out, sheer will taking the
place of expertise.

And then he could do no more but clamp himself into ago-
nized encystment, bearing the horrible crash of his physical
self among the icy molecules, feeling himself splash and re-
clamp. And then all space and time and stars closed away,
and it was too late for anything but luck.

At that moment in the human world, three small events occurred.

In a corporation office in San Juan, California, a middle-
aged woman felt an abrupt inner jolt: mild but enough to
make her hands drop a sheaf of data printouts and go to the
desk for support. Her gaze was blindly on the windows facing
north.

Migraine, she thought first; and then, *heart?* It was all over
in a second, her secretary hadn't even noticed. But as she
moved to her chair, still absently gazing north, she decided to
accelerate certain private arrangements she was making, for
the good of Marrell Tech.

Simultaneously, in the maternity waiting room of a nearby
hospital, a man clutching a huge sheaf of wilting yellow roses
found himself staring north across the freeways, blinking
away some kind of strange eidetic flash within his eyes . . .
or had someone called his name? He shook himself thinking,
Too much caffeine and stress on too little sleep.

And then a door opened and a nurse really was calling him.

"Mr. Paul Marrell?" Behind her a baby squalled.

The third small happening had just taken place in that delivery room.

As the doctor lifted the newborn by her ankles, the baby girl jerked and twisted with such extraordinary vigor that he had to use both hands to grab the slippery little legs. Still the tiny mite managed to contort herself round so that her large, light-blinded eyes were staring northward as she gave her first cry.

From the hour when his young wife died just after giving birth, Paul Marrell detested the infant and didn't care who knew it.

The blood clot had meandered its lethal way toward his wife's aorta slowly enough to let her gaze into her daughter's enormous violet eyes.

"We'll call her Paula. Hello, Paula!"

The baby twisted its head comically, still seemingly trying to sense something beyond the north wall. His mother laughed adoringly.

And then all laughters stopped.

Two dreadful hours later Paul Marrell was roaring up the San Fernando Freeway alone forever, with a case of Jack Daniel's in the bucket seat beside him. He was thirty-nine, an A-1 aero engineer who had put his heart into building up his own company before meeting the real love of his live. Now he had lost her.

Some days later his long-time executive secretary got the baby Paula home and properly installed, with a real nanny. With the help of Paul's friends, she sobered him up and slowly got his attention, if not his heart, back on his company. Marrell Technologies, which was prospering inordinately.

Little Paula soon began to do the same, although that nanny left soon. The next one Miss Emstead found lasted three months before she had to be replaced. The home was chaotic; Paul would spasmodically fill it with miscellaneous party people—service-station attendants, fading movie stars, dentists—and then forget them all. Miss Emstead would discover them and tactfully cope. When he recovered enough he took to marrying random women, and forgot them too, and

Miss Emstead coped again. Finally one night he proposed to Miss Emstead, on the intercom.

"Miss Emstead—Gloria—darling—you're the only good person in the world. Will you marry me?"

"I'm terribly sorry, Mr. Marrell. Thank you ever so much, but Tim and I have been married for over ten years. I'm truly honored though, and I'm so sorry. But you need someone young and jolly and sweet."

"Why have you turned against me, too? No, cancel that. Who's Tim?"

"Tim Drever, your chief draftsman. I thought you knew, you gave us a lovely present."

"Oh. Fire the bastard first thing Monday. No. Cancel that, too. Give him a raise. Give yourself both raises. And send me up a fifth of Jack Daniel's and get me that red-haired girl for tonight—you know, the one with the cats."

"Yes, Mr. Marrell. But about the raises, you gave us one last month and I think the company's cash flow is getting excessive. If you'd like to do something, we'd love another share of stock. I'll send you up the fifth right away, only it'll be just a little different, maybe with a snack and some black coffee and the Putnam Air Force contract draft. And Miss Fitz is in Honolulu now, I'll try Miss de Borch. You know, the black-haired girl with the boa constrictor. You seemed to enjoy her company last week."

She started to add that little Paula's new nurse was at the airport, but choked herself off. Paul had only looked at the baby twice.

"Okay. Okay. Great. Hey!"

"What, sir?"

"I really meant it, about marrying me. Tim's a fortunate man."

"Thank you with all my heart, Mr. Marrell."

She clicked off, smiling oddly. She had always been a hundred-percent sure that Paul had not the faintest memory of a rather confused evening long ago, when he and a very new young typist had worked till dawn in an office with a couch.

Certainly Gloria Emstead had never mentioned it to a soul, not even Tim, but she had found herself unable entirely to forget. The problem had been handled with her usual discreet efficiency, and the evening's result, a young lady known as Girta Grier, had been lovingly raised by a widowed relative in San Francisco whom she believed to be her mother. Girta was doing exceptionally well in business school. Miss Emstead smiled again, sighed, and turned to the airport problem.

It was strange about Paula's nurses. They wouldn't stay, although the little girl was sweet and well behaved. She was also very pretty, in a tiny, frail, dark-haired way, and the huge violet eyes of her early infancy stayed on. Party women would find her and coo over her. But something about the waif's questioning stare would silently turn the coos off. Apparently it did the same for the nannies and *au pair* girls and RNs Miss Emstead hired, even when Paul briefly married one of them.

That was when he had to see a little more of his daughter.

It was the night of San Juan's first snowfall in twenty years.

He and Frederika, the current Mrs. Marrell, came home late, and she excused herself to go up and check on Paula, leaving Paul to wander in the little-used quarters below. Presently he came to where a French window stood open in a foyer. As he closed it he noticed footprints in the paper-thin snow, leading away. He had been much in the woods as a boy, and automatically paused to look; one set of stub-heeled woman's tracks, one set of small fresh sandal tracks, and a fading set of very tiny child's bare footprints. He recalled that Frederika seemed to have been wearing sandals. She was one of the *au pair* girls who had taken care of Paula before she began taking care of Paul, a tall, shaggy-blond Belgian whom he thought of as tender and fun, with unknown competencies—in which last he was quite right.

It was a gorgeous night now, a half-moon glittering on the crazy whiteness, and the stars blazing through. Paul stepped out to follow the tracks.

They led him across empty gardens and straight up the side of the first big grass-covered berm that protected the house. From above came a burst of high-pitched voices and, in the distance, a growl that meant a guard dog being restrained. Suddenly a child's voice was crying, "I hate you, I hate it here." Then there came the sharp smack of a slap on flesh, and silence.

Paul reached the top to find his wife and the RN standing a little back from a tiny child, who must be Paula; she was crouched down, almost naked in a skimpy nightdress.

"What's going on here?"

"She attacked Miss Trond," his wife exclaimed excitedly.

"She sneaks out in the middle of the nights," Miss Trond smoothed her uniform, her accent regrettably Germanic.

"That's right—she did it with me and the girl before me," Frederika added. "She's had us all scared silly."

But their stories didn't go down too well, especially when Paula raised her head to gaze beseechingly at her father, revealing the dark print of a grown woman's hand, complete with ring scratch, on her small white face. There was also the mark of her supine body behind her, in the snow.

"Why did you have to hit her?" he asked slowly. This didn't seem to be the monster that had killed his beloved. In fact, it didn't seem to be a monster at all.

The women were jabbering something about the danger from the dogs, and not being able to sleep. The child's big eyes never left his.

Uncertainly, he moved toward her and reached down his hand. She gazed up a moment more, and then her own hand went up to his and she grabbed hold, her hand cool and tiny as a baby animal's. He lifted her the short distance to her feet.

"Check with Miss Emstead tomorrow, you two," Paul said. Leading his daughter, he went down and away to his old bachelor suite.

Paula was soaked and shivering, so he took off the filmy shortie, dried her, and wrapped her in his old camel-hair robe, looping the ends up over the cord. It never occurred to him that a six-year-old could dress herself. He hadn't seen a naked girl child before, and the little bare body confused him slightly.

She remained totally silent through his ministrations, until he had picked her up and plunked her down on the dressing-room cot.

"You all right, kid?"

"Yes, sir. Thank you very much," she said politely. Then she suddenly sat up and burst out, "Oh, Daddy, could you help me please?"

"Help you? How?"

"Let me look at your library books! They won't let me read them and they only give me icky stuff. I wouldn't hurt your books, ever."

"What do you want to read?" he asked, purely amazed.

"Arithmetic," she completed his astoundment. "And about the stars. Astro-no-my."

"Why of course you can. You go in there and take any book you want. And stay as long as you want. I'll tell Miss Emstead. She can find you some beginner's things."

Seeing the look of joy turn wary, he had the intuition to add, "If you find you need them."

What had he spawned here? Now that he observed her more carefully he could find little resemblance to her mother, yet she reminded him of someone. Himself, as a boy, perhaps?

"What were you doing out there, anyway?"

"I like to look at the stars. I only know the name of one: Po-laris." She ducked her head down, ashamed. "They say it's un-natural."

Ah! He had it—his young brother Harry, who had been killed in a car crash at eight. She was a mini-edition of Harry. Harry'd liked star-gazing too, come to think. Had the gods sent him back his kid brother, and he all blind to it?

"Well, we can fix that too. Next time you want to go—any time of night—you just ring the guard station and they'll send a man in five minutes for as long as you like."

Again the dismayed look on the so-expressive little flower face.

"What's wrong now?"

"Oh, it's nothing . . . it's just that I like to look *alone*."

So had Harry, he recalled.

"We can fix that. You just tell them when you go out and when you've come back and you won't see a soul. Or he'll be fired in the morning."

"Ohhh . . . *thank* you, Daddy! I mean, sir. Thank you so much."

"Daddy's okay for now. Where did you get that 'sir' anyhow?"

"You said to, sir. I mean, Daddy. And to never let you see me."

He hadn't the dimmest recollection. "Well, I didn't mean it. I was—sort of crazy for a while. That's all over now."

Her face radiated joy. And then suddenly, babylike, the dark furry eyelashes dropped to her cheeks and she was asleep sitting up, slowly toppling into a pillow almost as big as she. He settled her down straight, and went to his bed to think. It had occurred to him that something had to be done about Paula's schooling, and the usual kindergartens were clearly not the answer. But he was too tired—he had only time to tape instructions to Miss Emstead to find a good tutor as well as a new nurse, and to get the divorce lawyers going again, before he was asleep, too.

All these matters were duly attended to, and in the next weeks and months Paul became accustomed to coming across his little daughter curled in a library corner with anything from an astronomy journal to a math text to his old science-fiction comics. Or he would look out and see her walking—more often, running hard—on the berms. She continued to be very undersized, but the doctor said she was in perfect health and very strong for her weight. "Regular gibbon," he said. "But a lot better-looking."

Strange considerations moved him. Paula and her new nurse got used to the erratic arrival of vans from Chez Niçoise bearing huge delicious platters of filet mignon, oysters, lobsters, which they—especially Miss Timms—enjoyed wholeheartedly.

And then there was the ludicrous affair of the Children's Party. It took place, not on her birthday, which was never referred to, but on Paul's; a stiffly rowdy afternoon assembly of strange youngsters of disparate ages, mostly the offspring of Marrell Tech executives, among whom Paula was supposed to find friends. Paul looked in and even he was able to interpret the sight of his little daughter standing frozen with terror amid the tumult, cake knife in her hand like a sword.

Miss Emstead reassured him. "Paula'll find her own friends, Mr. Marrell. Slowly, among children of smiliar interests and abilities. When she goes to a suitable school." And she handed him the brochure of a special school for gifted children.

"Too far away. Find one where she comes home nights."

And the right school was duly found, even though it entailed twice-daily use of Marrell Tech's helicopter.

After a year or so of this, Robby, the helicopter pilot, took occasion to tell Paul that his daughter was no ordinary little girl.

"That kid Paula, she's something else. You better watch out, sir. She knows every chopper model on the market, and she helps me do the tune-ups. Last week I tore the engine down, she came out and worked for me till eleven P.M. Her nurse like to went ape. And she's after George to take her up in the jet, I caught her crawling around the pods. I think she could fly the chopper if I'd let her. And if her feet would reach," he grinned.

"Hmm."

It was about this time that the school notified him that they wanted to run some special tests on Paula. It seemed she had independently found the general solution for a class of differential equations. For a time Paul was afraid that he had an infant Gauss on his hands.

But it turned out that Paula was not of that calibre; only very bright, very motivated, and very, very quick. Next term she was into computers and electronics. He found her trying to measure the piezo-electric output of an old crystal with a beat-up ammeter she had begged off the electrician, and fitted her up with her own little workshop, to which in due course were added a closed-circuit computer system and a photo lab.

Before that, however, had come the telescope, and the pathetic business of Christmas. In her first term at the school the science teacher had suggested to him that he get her for Christmas an equatorial-mount 'scope with maybe a camera attachment. When he asked Paula what she wanted, she looked perplexed. "Daddy—exactly what *is* Christmas?"

"Why, it's—it's—" he began, and suddenly realized that never, in her six or seven years of life, had he given her a Christmas present.

"Haven't people given you things for Christmas?"

She shook her head, still puzzled. "Miss Gibbs had me put some cards around, one year," she remembered slowly. "And Mrs. Finney gave me a hanky and said I should give everybody something. But I didn't have anything. So she showed me how to make some folding cutouts with, I guess, trees and deer on them. And a fat man. They weren't very nice."

He now recalled the strange sticky object that had been among his cards one year. It was, as she said, not very nice. But the whole thing moved him horribly, and he could only mutter, "I'm sorry, kid, I'm sorry." And then, "They said you wanted a telescope."

"Oh! Oh-h-h-h, Daddy! A *real telescope!?*" Her joy was so contagious that he forgot all about the pathos while they plunged into the wonders of Edmund's Scientific Catalogue, and all the delicious temptations and countertemptations of rich-field vs. long focal length. And space was found among the rooftops for a real mini-observatory, and the problem of Paula's night wanderings was solved for a time.

But he still worried about her apparent frailty, until Miss Emstead suggested that he take her on some camping and fishing trips in the nearby air force reservation. That worked out fantastically, with her delight and wonder at the wilderness, and his recognition of her surprising coordination and stamina. In outdoor gear she looked a lot more natural; he took to calling her Pauly and even Paul, and sometimes Harry by mistake. She was only fair at fishing, but he found her reassembling his old twelve-gauge over-and-under, and it wasn't long before she had her own cut-down .475, and presently a real rifle with scope sights.

To no one's surprise she turned out to be an excellent shot, and he was only briefly disturbed when he had to give her a couple of lessons on hunting ethics. After all, at her age he had been fairly bloody-minded too.

It was curious how much they both enjoyed the cold, or rather, the experience of exploring ever farther north.

He took her to see the great Athabascar ice cap near Jasper, and they spent two happy shivering hours prowling the caves beneath the melting glacier's huge tongue. Deep green light struck through here; the glacier's vast icy udders dripped millennial snow water, and a cold foul breath, the melt of life killed a thousand years back, flowed from under the ice and made miniature storms and rainbows in the sunlight out beyond. A Mountie finally routed them out.

Afterward Paula pored over bundles of maps, and they gloated at the fun they would have when time allowed them to visit the real Alaskan ice fields far to the north.

"I bet Miss Emstead would love to go, too," Paula said.

Paul agreed instantly—without either of them noticing the utter insanity of the notion that an older, sedentary lady executive in uncertain health would "love" to leave her husband for the joys of exposing herself to the hazards and rigors of the world of ice.

These camping-trip years with Paula became the happiest of his life; certainly the most innocent.

Around her eighth year a new phase of life with Paula started. On a whim he let her stay through a small dinner party that ended early, and afterward he jokingly asked her what she thought of a man he was considering as division chief of his new aerospace facility.

"He waits to be told what to do. He pretends not to, but he does."

"And how do you know that, Miss Paulie?"

"I watched him with his knife and fork. And the wine. He didn't know if he liked it until he saw your face."

"Hmm. I thought he spoke right up."

"No. He watched you, first."

"Um hmm."

After that he took to letting the child play hostess at small gatherings, both at home and at restaurants, with a few coaching sessions from Miss Emstead. Paula proved a model of precocious tactfulness, silence, and charm. She was, it appeared, very interested in "serious" people; she watched everything, and was a memory machine. This actually proved useful to him; men tended to talk quite freely in her presence, taking her as even younger than she was.

But in his private chats with her, it was impossible to recall how short a time she had been alive. She was so interested in his work, first in the actual technology, and then in the business aspect, the contracts, the problems, the new aerospace venture. When she was ten she asked him for the history of Marrell Technologies, and sopped up all the literature he brought her. He found himself using her for a sounding board, and talking over people and projects with her as if she were an adult.

One weekend afternoon when Paul was in Chicago, his daughter received an unexpected caller. It was Miss Emstead, with a portfolio under her arm. Two pairs of eyes, one huge and violet, the other hazel and old and smiley, met in a wordless mutual examination and appraisal. There had always been an unspoken bond of congeniality and affection between the two. But this meeting was on a different plane.

Miss Emstead didn't bother with the "my dears" or "how you've growns" (Paula had not grown, much). She said directly:

"You have a great deal of influence with your father, on topics in which a quite young girl is not usually interested."

Paula, equally direct, simply nodded.

"We at the plant, we older ones, never thought that Mr. Marrell would have a child to carry on the enterprise after him. But I'm beginning to think your interest is sincere and enduring. Am I right?"

Paula nodded again, very affirmatively.

"Good. That's good. Of course, you might change your mind later, after boys and things come along. What do you think about that?"

"I can't be sure," the child said carefully in her soft voice. "People—grown-up women—seem so strange, some of them. But I don't think I'll change that much."

"There's no reason why you should," Miss Emstead said heartily. "Lots of grown-up women are deeply involved in business and have families, too."

"Like Mrs. Plum."

"Yes. Like a lot of us. Which brings me to the next point. Quite a few of us old-timers have invested our whole lives in Marrell Tech. It's all we have; it's all our security for our old age. Forgive me, but you still are very young, although your mind isn't. I would like you to take just a moment to— well, kind of appreciate that. Try to put yourself in our places. Recall that—forgive me again—Marrell T. isn't in any sense just a hobby for us, or a temporary enthusiasm. It's years and years and years of hard work, and putting everything we have into in bad times and good, so we'll be safe in our old ages. Try, just for a moment, would you?"

Gray eyes bored hard.

The violet eyes were serious in response. They only flickered once, briefly, to the briefcase under Miss Emstead's arm.

"I think I understand," Paula said carefully. "I—I don't feel it's a plaything, Miss Emstead."

"Yes. And it's all you have too, you know. Although you're young enough to start over, Marrell Technologies is your total security, the source of everything for you, now at any rate. To damage or lose it would mess your life up."

Paula's little lips set, she nodded hard.

Miss Emstead gave her one more long look and then smiled, relaxing.

"Good, Paula. And I think you might try calling me Gloria if you like. I've brought something alone, in hopes you were serious. You remember that history of the company we sent you, the one on glossy paper?"

"Oh yes," the child said politely. "Thank you." But her little nose wrinkled slightly.

"Exactly," the older woman smiled. "I thought that if I found what I hoped, that it was time you had a *real* history. So I've put together a short account, just for you personally. I'm sure you won't mind if I stay here while you read it, and take it back to the safe. I'm told you have a phenomenal memory. But anytime you want to see it again, *any*-time at all, you just call me and I'll have it out to you by courier, who'll bring it back again. You do understand that, don't you?"

"Oh yes, Miss—Gloria. I really understand and I really thank you. There isn't much, um, security around here. And people think they should walk right in on me."

"They could even read over your shoulder, or take it away from you. You see, some of this even your father doesn't know. Do you understand what I mean when I say we all decided to try to keep the business end off him? If your father isn't an engineering genius he's the closest thing to it I'm apt to see. We didn't want to make the mistake other companies have—spoiling a fine engineer to make a mediocre business-man."

"I think I understand that. It's like when they made Mr. Endicott school principal and he can't teach us anymore. Because he's an ad-ministrator."

"Perfect. All right, here you are. I think you'll want the next hour free, don't you?"

The little girl reached for the typewritten sheaf as an ordinary child reached for candy.

"Let's go up to my darkroom!" And she bounced out of the big chair, for the first time showing her true age.

"Good."

And so began the strange alliance, by which the now-giant Marrell Technologies was run in the main by an aging woman and a ten-year-old child. And a carefree engineer filled the safes with his best work.

The congeniality or empathy between the three such disparate minds really was quite extraordinary; sometimes it seemed to go beyond speech. Tim Drever, Gloria's husband, with that combination of vagueness and essential acuity so often found in art workers, took a careful look at it. Perceiving that the strange bond did not threaten him, he continued his genial presence rear stage.

But not even he could have guessed that the sharing really was that of the fragments of one mind—still less that the body to which that mind belonged lay frozen in molecular stasis, two thousand miles away in northern ice, knowing nothing of humanity. All that Enggi, or what was left of him there, was aware of was that healing went on—and also that a faint discomfortable disturbance occasionally threatened him from beneath.

Halcyon days, when for a brief time the tempest and conflicts grow calm in the eye of winter, and the birds of halcyon nest together in harmony.

They did not end, at least on the surface, when at the age of eleven Paula sexually seduced her father.

It happened in the most normal way, as such things do, on one of their camping trips.

There had of course been outdoor intimacies before—like father and son, they swan nude. He had nursed her through dysentery, and she had rubbed his twisted ankle and later his strained back, the small hands very quick and strong. Once or twice he had found himself slightly aroused, and pushed the thought from him. She was still as sexless-looking as a minnow.

On this night the open tent was caught in a downpour and her sleeping bag got soaked. (Paula loved to sleep right in the door, where she could gaze at the stars.) As Paul had done long ago, he rubbed her dry, and then took the cold little body in his arms in his bag with him, and they slept so.

But in grey dawn he wakened to find her curiously touching his genitals—so softly, gently, it was like a dream whispering. "Oh Daddy, I love you so." Only after it had become far other than a dream, only after there were muffled yelps and writhings and a confused partial entry bringing his relief, did he begin to know what had happened.

But she was ready for him, strong small arms holding, trying to rock him soothingly. "*It's all right*, Daddy. We love each other so. Daddy, it's *all right*." And telling him how she had read that such things happened a lot, and she was his girl, so how could it be wrong?

And then, very soberly, "Daddy—I have to learn about things, don't I? And I haven't anyone, no one at all. You're my teacher, you always have been."

He had barely time to take it all in before she was up and challenging him to race to the lake. The rain had quit, they had a fine breakfast and a great day's stalk of quail, and he took the subject as closed.

That night she went to her own dried bed. But before dawn she came into his sleeping bag as if by right, and this time she made him actually be merry, touching and asking questions like. "How does this feel?" with giggles and squirmy demonstrations till the day broke on her—so clearly innocent and happy in her newfound sensuality that he lost all but the last shreds of his guilt.

And there was, as she said, always this curious sense of *belongingness* in their joinings, of that which had been split apart again becoming one. He put it down to rationalization; how could he know how right he was?

And after all, it wasn't as if this had never happened before, he told himself. One or two of the new books about the house seemed to make quite a point of this, when he came to look.

And so began a last enchanted time of overt comradeship and covert delights. Paula was growing and rounding out a little now, but with her usual tact she hid it under boy's clothes and childish dress. At home all was as before; her hostessing of his parties became ever more winning and delightful. The parties themselves had long changed too; in place of the miscellany now came hard-working politicians, engineers, and scientists, always with a lovely girl or three for Paul; while Paula, who seemed totally unjealous, attended as zealously upon the wives as she did the men. She became adept at finding and charming people who could be of use, especially in the new aerospace aspect. She also suggested financial contributions to the PACs of certain aspiring politicians, some of whom proved definitely helpful to Marrell Tech.

Paul took to giving her joking rewards for her work, in lieu of allowance. Her simple delight in crisp new thousand-dollar bills amused him, and with money pouring in on all sides he could afford it. Marrell Tech was taking over a few struggling small firms; Paul depended on Paula to keep his memory straight, and indeed she once stopped him, at a party, from informally opening bids against himself.

So passed the last year of halcyon. Their sexual contacts, by tacit consent, were confined to camping trips. For a time that worked well. But Paula had underestimated matters; she had no real concept of the tumult she had unleashed. The poor besotted man developed an unnatural passion for the outdoors, and began dragging Paula out with him in all weathers and on any pretext.

Perhaps by coincidence, it was at that phase that Miss Emstead issued one of her rare warnings.

"Always remember, Paula, there's a lot of smart people out

there, and few of them are friendly. There *are* other people as intelligent as you—I'm not one of them, but they exist. Some may even be smarter. No matter how well things seem to be going, it's always good strategy to run a trifle scared."

And she told Paula the story of the man who sold Stanley Steamers. The Stanley was an excellent early steam car, but it weighed tons and was a bitch to steer. In those days motor roads often consisted only of two deep ruts. So, as he crossed the West selling cars, the salesman told his clients, "When you meet another car, don't bother pulling her out of the ruts to pass. You keep right on going. That thing is a monster; when the other driver sees you aren't pulling out he'll yank his car aside and let you by."

It was good advice and worked well, until the day one Stanley Steamer driver met another.

Paula, in all her short life, never met another Steamer—or rather, when she did she didn't recognize it. For it was in part herself.

Whether it was truly, improbably, inadvertence; or pique at her first failure in a test of her power to charm; or simply a miscalculation due to ignorance—for she *was* still a child, unknowing of the strength of tribal mores, and everything had gone her way for a long time, so she may have actually failed to understand what being legally very much a minor could mean in terms, say, of gaining control of her inheritance; howbeit, whether from hubris or error, there came a party evening when Paula found herself alone with Nicky Benson.

Nicky Benson was a youngish man of great physical and mental charm. Paula may have temporarily forgotten that he was also a devout Mormon and his wife Joan a fanatic one. But it is barely credible that she could have forgotten that Nicky was also an executive with Nippon/Sterling, Marrell Tech's only serious competitor in several fields.

What was visible was that after an unclear twenty minutes alone with Paula, Nicky abruptly left the party, his face flushed angry red under his butter-yellow hair. He told the details only to his wife, which was little better than putting them on CBS News. For two days, while Paul was in Chicago, the phrase "Daddy shows me how" cascaded through that sector of the industrial-social world, gaining new color and specificity with every telling. On the evening of the second day, three of the household staff gave notice en bloc, and

Robby the copter pilot quit. The phone was unnaturally quiet.

Paula spent an increasingly dismayed and horrified night; she was, as mentioned, very quick at extrapolation. She may have done some growing up.

At three in the morning she did one of the incontrovertibly decent acts of her brief life. She phoned Gloria Emstead. Appropriately, there was a wild electrical storm over San Juan.

"This is Paula. Sell all your Marrell stock."

"I know your voice, Paula." Miss Emstead did not sound sleepy. "Would you please repeat what you just said?"

"I said—" the young voice quivered and was under control again. "Sell all your holdings in Marrell Tech. And your husband's. And tell G-George Henry and the others too; you know. Right now, first thing in the morning." The last word trembled away as the storm spewed static.

"Paula. I'll never forget this, my dear. As a matter of fact, we already have sold out; we did it in little dribs and drabs, it never showed. But I'll always remember that you called tonight."

"Oh," Paula said exhaustedly. Then, childlike, she asked, "When did you sell, GI—Miss Emstead?"

"We started over a year ago. Now you better try to get some rest. Draw out all the cash you can in the morning, and hide it. And remember this law-firm name—Armistead, Levy, and South. He's with them, he's—" a lightning bolt crackled the line. "Good-bye now. Keep that chin up, nothing lasts—"

The line went dead.

Paul bounced off the Marrell jet at nine next morning with nothing but plans for a trip to the Great Slave Lake wilderness in his head. He was met by a green-faced George Henry and two very polite senior policemen with a warrant.

For the whole next year everything went bad.

Paul was of course soon free under bail, but forbidden contact with his daughter. This was enforced by an ever-present police matron. Paula tried to charm her, but the catastrophe seemed to have spoiled her touch; it was as if the stress had caused her to revert to the childhood she had never known. Patrolwomen Haggerty, Kelly, or Wyskof munched Paula's liqueur chocolates, casually evading those which tasted a bit odd after a visit to Paula's workshop, and watched sleeplessly over her. Paula improvised a series of visits to museums in which she would stand for three excruciating hours at a stretch, apparently engrossed in the more insipid tableaux of Pueblo Indian life; the patrolwomen stolidly stood by. Paula spent whole days in the planetarium; the policewomen did, too.

The only news she got was bad. Paul had started to drink heavily. And then Gloria Emstead developed a heart condition and came out of the hospital with all business communications forbidden.

The trial was disaster compounded. Pressure seemed to be coming from somewhere; despite all the Marrell side's protests the trial took place in open court.

Nor could Paula prevent old Mr. Northrup, the chief of Marrell Tech's legal staff, from defending Paul in person, armed with little but a metaphysical belief in his clients' innocence. It seemed to be his idea that he had only to let people see his principals, and they would be smitten with a revelation of the wicked absurdity of the charge. He had never heard of *Lolita*, and let the term "nymphet" go past him unchallenged three times in the prosecution's opening remarks.

Worse, he caused Paula to appear in her little navy school dress with white collar and cuffs, in which she looked positively edible. Judge Dyson, who had read *Lolita* with care, took one look at her and began to pity Paul, who was looking abnormally haggard and dissolute in the dreadful executive-type clothes Northrup had clad him in.

At the first break, the prosecutor's female aide took a short stroll, eyes flickering to where Paula tried to sit composedly. When the trial resumed, Prosecutor Baylor unexpectedly changed the order of witnesses. He finished up with some repulsive expert testimony on the composition of stains in Paul's camp sleeping bag (which Paula had been unable to get to on that last night, although she had thought to destroy some of her own garments) and then recalled her governess to the stand. Miss Briggs was one of those who had quit on that final afternoon.

PROSECUTOR BAYLOR: "Miss Briggs, I want to ask you about the dress which your employer's daughter is wearing now. You can see her clearly, can't you?" (*General craning of necks.*) "Is that one of her normal school uniforms?"

MISS BRIGGS: "Yes, sir."

BAYLOR: "And do I see correctly that it has been shortened?"

MISS BRIGGS: "Oh yes, sir. Miss Paula is very small."

BAYLOR: "I see. The skirt was made shorter, and perhaps the hips and bodice were taken in a little, made to fit better?" (*Gestures suggestively.*)

JUDGE DYSON: "Counselor, I fail to see where this questioning is leading."

BAYLOR: "Your Honor, I wish to establish that it was evidently the practice to alter this child's clothing to make it unusually tight and seductive-looking, as Your Honor can see for himself."

JUDGE (*somewhat absently*): "Denied."

At this Paula herself spoke up. Her young voice was so quick and clear and indignant that Dyson stayed his gavel long enough to let her get out: "I'm *not* seductive—I'm embarrassed! I've grown while they made me wait for trial and there's nobody to sew my clothes!"

It might have made points.

But Paul chose that moment to break down, and in three minutes the courtroom was a chaos of strobe flashes, falling chairs, Northrup gibbering and shouting, and Baylor shouting back, the judge's gavel going futilely—and all in perfect time for the afternoon editions and TV, on an otherwise newsless day.

The headlines ran from the comparatively sedate MARRELL TECH HEAD ADMITS INCEST through the colorful MARRELL CONFESSES SEDUCING 10-YR-OLD DAUGHTER to "GOD HELP ME I CAN'T KEEP MY HANDS OFF HER," CRIES POP; "I'M BETTER OFF DEAD!"

And when Paula tried to get to him to quiet him it was a photographer's picnic: PAULA RUNS TO COMFORT DAD WHO DEBAUCHED HER—PAULA MARRELL BATTLES POLICE TO REACH DAD AFTER HIS CONFESSION—PAULA VAULTS TO POP'S ARMS DESPITE POLICE—with a full view of her skimpy little-girl white underdrawers as she all-too-expertly one-handed the defendants' rail.

She had forgotten the damned dress, or the classic courtroom chase would have lasted longer than it did. One photo of Paula sailing flat-out between a fat policeman's legs became a collector's item.

The remainder of the trial was a quick farce.

Poor Northrup withdrew "for reasons of health," and the junior staff was able to inject a medical-psychiatric plea that had the effect of obtaining one of the new and controversial indefinite "psychotherapeutic" sentences for Paul.

As for Paula, her head seemed to clear. The explosive exercise of the courtroom scene may have been cathartic. Also instructive, when she came to notice it, was the fact that Nicky Benson's name had never appeared in the whole scenario. (Only one easily muffed female reporter associated "James N. Benson-Flitch, complainant," with the Nicky Benson who had just made VP at Nippon/Sterling.) Paula resolved that she would never again fight the world alone and in the open.

But when the dust settled, things couldn't have looked worse. Paul was out of contact, being done God knew what to in a minimum-security facility at Tehatchapi. Miss Emstead was recovering, but still allowed only one business conversation a week. Paula herself was a ward of the court under the governance of appointed strangers, attending P.S. 215 in San Juan, plus private tutors. Marrell Tech's common stock was on the ground, and the firm itself was living precariously on Paul's stored-ahead plans, under the wobbly guidance of old George Henry.

Paula dispassionately took stock, and bethought herself, belatedly, of a certain untaken piece of advice. But how to find the unknown?

Her "touch" was coming back. The weekday guardian soon relaxed a bit, helped along by variants of the museum ploy. Paula worked on a driver well enough to establish written communication to and from George Henry, but he was no help in the central matter. So, gaining an hour free for "shopping for girls' things," she went to search head-on.

The secretaries at Armistead, Levy, and South were fairly used to appointments being made for a "Miss Smith." They were not used to having "Miss Smith" turn out to be a girl child whose feet didn't quite reach the waiting-room floor. Nor was Mr. Armistead used to opening notes consisting of a crisp thousand-dollar bill, to which was attached a modest card inscribed with a child's notorious name.

"I want you to get my daddy out. I'm sure he didn't get a fair trial and the business needs him."

Armistead hemmed and pontificated at Paula, who thoughtfully retrieved the $1,000 and retreated to try again. She perceived she had remembered sloppily; Miss Emstead had said he was "with" the firm—thus obviously not one of the senior partners.

She used one of Gloria's permitted visits to get the name, and after two more tries she caught her quarry alone in the elevator.

"You're Ellis Donohue?" Handing him the note.

The short but conventionally handsome, clean-cut young lawyer opened her note slowly, studying her in a way that told her he knew something of her previous calls. She was pleased to note the way he took hold of the bill; not quite the grip of a drowning man, but not far from it. His eyes met hers with an expression combining the gravity of the law with the activism of a man whose mistress has fifteen credit cards.

"I believe something could be done on a mistrial. For example, his lawyer never seems to have considered a change of venue. And there are several other aspects."

They made a coffee-shop date at the museum, and she hurried to swoop up random additions to the "girls' things" she was supposed to be shopping for.

When next they could talk, she had a list of requests, headed by "Free access to my lawyer" and, second, "Acess to my bank."

"I'm pretty sure we can do that one fast," Ellis told her. "But . . . am I your lawyer?"

In answer she took out a frilly pink Kleenex case. Under the top Kleenex lay a wad of crisp new bills. She made a little napkin tent, and in its shelter started tearing the bills in neat halves. Ellis Donohoe caught his handsome eyes starting to pop, and lost count at fifteen.

"I'm sure you'll forgive me, Mr. Donohue. You see, I'm very young, and people have played bad tricks on me. A story I read suggested this." She handed him one wad of halves, wrapped in another intact bill.

"Oh c-certainly."

"There's my guardian!" She waved childishly, and slipped from her chair, putting her halves back in the Kleenex case. "Mr. Meyers, I'd like you to meet Mr. Donohue. He was telling me about poor Mr. Northrup." She extracted a Kleenex from the case (giving Ellis fits) and blew her nose. "Maybe Mr. Donohue will find Daddy a new lawyer."

That night, as often, Paula stayed long in her observatory, scanning the familiar wonders somewhat absently. She had expected to feel more satisfied. Certainly everything hu-

manly possible to her was underway, or being done. Only
there was a pressure, a sense of unease she could not quiet.
Almost as if some unheard voice was calling, calling her
name. Again and again her gaze went to the northward smog,
but nothing, of course, was there.

Paula sighed, putting away the scope.

Then she walked out onto the rooftop, casting off her little
robe, and sat down and stared upward with an expression as
unreadable as it was intense. Puzzlement—longing—a faint
smile—a clenching of the small jaw. Finally her lids dropped,
and she breathed deep and hard, shivering a little, before she
took up her robe and went in. An acute observer might have
noticed that the tile where she had sat was very slightly worn.

The tears that had been shed on that coping had left of
course, no trace.

Events of the next weeks moved right along, spurred on by
the contents of the pink Kleenex case. The Armistead senior
partners gave Donohue his green light, and he began to deliver: appeal, mistrial, change of venue to a backwoods portion of an adjoining state where the alleged offense was
claimed to have occurred, and a quick and private hearing,
with Paul and Paula clad in their normal outdoor clothes.

Nicky Benson proved to have no more appetite for blood,
especially when some of it might be his own, and two more
of the original complainants could somehow not be found. In
four months the whole matter was dismissed from the courts
and Paul was home, a free and technically innocent man.

Meanwhile Marrell Tech had scraped up a respectable PR
budget, and its flacks succeeded in persuading a large section
of the public that some slight incident, more the fantasies of
overwork than real, had been used against Paul by unscrupu-
lous rivals. Paula herself was duly seen about with a squad of
healthy youngAmerican boys fresh from Central Casting.

When Paul came home Paula all but smothered him with
determinedly sexless affection, and this, plus his now-personal
hatred of Nippon/Sterling, put him well on the mend.

Even here fate took a helpful hand: before Paul's detesta-
tion of Nicky Benson could take on unhealthy virulence, the
Mormon couple met with grisly disaster. While passing
through a riot area, their car was caught and rolled. Its defenses weren't breached, but a tank full of a defense-security
compound that Nicky was testing developed leaks as the car
was righted. Nearby a liter of the stuff rained onto Nicky and

Joan. The test worked all too well. It was hoped that the couple would recover some eyesight, but much of the other damage was beyond all plastic surgery's best skills.

Ellis Donohue found Paula reading about it.

"Your lucky day," she told him. "This was a job I was saving for you."

The young lawyer chuckled, and then suddenly peered more closely at his small client. She met his gaze unsmiling, watching him pale as the chuckle died in his throat. It had been the whim of a moment, but she found herself fascinated by the chance to guess at just how much power she might wield—were she to wish to, which she at present did not. Only—the Nicky Bensons of the world would never get their yellow hair through her defenses again.

"I better get this to Daddy right away. He'll probably want to send flowers. Perhaps some kind that can be smelled?"

Ellis tottered off, trying to look worldly.

But when Paula found Paul, they didn't discuss the Benson thing. She found him uncharacteristically moody; pacing, breaking off a sentence to stare out across the freeways, pouring out a Jack Daniel's and pushing it away untouched. This last convinced her he was suffering from more than the effects of Tehatchapi. Perhaps he was worried that irreparable hurt had been done to his beloved Marrell Tech? He had never seemed to care for their public image, but still, they had never had such a problem before. Certainly something more in the PR line could be useful.

But Paula had an odd feeling that this was all beside the point. He was acting the way she herself felt. But what *was* the point? She hadn't a clue.

At this point Paul's new young assistant, Girta Grier, came in to remind Paul that it was his and Paula's afternoon to visit Gloria Emstead.

"Good-oh. We need some air. Some good cold north air."

"Do you feel it too, Daddy?" Paula asked him in the car.

"Feel what?"

"Needing something—some north air, like you said."

Instead of replying verbally, he just looked at her, and they both knew the answers.

"Something's bugging us," Paul muttered at last. "I mean, more than all that crap. That's all over and past now. It's—it's like something we should *do*."

"Yes." And Paula added by one of those peculiar inspirations, that made no logical sense, "Let's ask Gloria. I don't think it would upset her. Maybe she'd know."

"Right-oh. I don't know why but that's a good idea, kid."

They found Gloria Emstead out of her chaise, making a shaky march around the room. She greeted them gasping, laughed apologetically as they helped her back to the couch.

"I'm just not fit for much yet."

"But there's nothing you have to do. Take it easy."

"*Isn't there?*"

"Gloria, do you mean what I think you do?"

It soon turned out she too was suffering the same inexplicable malaise; as of something unknown, needing ever more urgently to be done.

But what? They couldn't define it, only discuss it by half-sentences and shared silences.

In one of the silences Paula remarked abruptly how she and Paul had once found great fascination in a glacier, and how much they'd wanted to experience the real ice-country to the north.

"We even thought you'd like to come with us. Of course that's crazy."

"No," said Gloria quietly. "Not crazy at all. Of course I can't get far right now. But—look." She reached behind her for a much-folded magazine, and handed it to Paula.

It was an account of a series of seismic tremors in the McKinley Range north of Fairbanks, which were causing several local glaciers to be shunted seaward. One photo of an ice-lined bay with a line of great bergs splitting and calving off drew Paula's eyes like a magnet. When she passed it to Paul she noticed her own heart thudding.

"What—what is it with us?" Gloria Emstead asked, only half-humorously, watching their reaction.

They didn't know. Who could?

But an idea suddenly was born in Paula's head, so intensely that she felt as if she were lighting up with a cartoon light bulb.

"Gloria—Daddy—listen! Let's go for broke. Los Angeles is already burning up with drought, the whole coast is, and the summer's barely started. The Colorado River is down to a trickle, people are starting to shoot each other over water. Fresh water! Everybody wants it, everybody has to have it. And Marrell Tech needs some really good publicity. People've talked about towing icebergs here for years—why don't we *do* it? It would supply I forget how much fresh water—years' worth. Suppose we tied into one of those really big bergs and towed it down here and grounded it right off-shore where they could just run a pipe out to it? And suppose we did it free, the first one anyway, with 'Gift from Marrell Tech' all over it?"

"Hmm," said Paul. Gloria Emstead's eyes were shining as she looked from face to face. Paula suspected the idea wasn't new to her.

". . . currents. The California sets in somewhere along Portland, it'd help," Paul was muttering. He had produced one of his battered envelopes and was scribbling on it. "Shelf depths? Those things need channels . . . sea mounts? How to get a grip on it, storm-proof? Not to lose it. Lease dredges, tugs. Could a chopper turn it? Experts—do we need experts! Georgie Warner for a lead-in . . . And probably there's some damn book of regs saying, No Way. Lawyers. Bet that'll be the worst. . ."

There was no more formal discussion. From the moment the idea was voiced, it was settled: Marrell Tech would spend every penny it could muster, employ or invent every device needed, to bring that iceberg south.

Only once did Paul say lightly to Gloria Emstead, "Well, I guess we're going to see our glacier together, after all. If Mohamet can't get to the mountain . . . !"

Her smile was more than radiant.

And yet no one of the three ever really asked why? They only acted.

If questioned, they would have explained that they were helping out a drought-struck state for the good name of Marrell Tech, and seizing the initiative in what could become a new engineering field.

Experts galore were duly called in, and feasibility studies made—not in formal leather-bound presentations, but under forced draft through nights and dawns, recorded on Paul's crumpled envelopes. By this time Marrell Tech had a small work camp on Jackson Promontory, near several likely berg-calving points, and experiments with towage and grappling techniques were underway. Ice presents problems of variable strain tolerance, and of unpredictable slippage under pressure and friction. Paul soon found himself doing what he did and loved best, problem solving, inventing, improvising in a new field. Paula and Gloria managed to pry enough data out of him to secure future patent claims, though somehow even that didn't seem important.

As he had predicted, the legal and governmental obstacles provided the worst hassles of all. By this time, various ecological groups had also gotten into a dozen facets of the project. But as the cruel drought worsened, and crops and toilets dried up, the loudest adversaries did likewise. And Ellis Donohue, now provided with ample staff, had sufficient needs and greeds to keep him tramping the halls of the Maritime Commission, the navy, the coast guard, and half a dozen others almost as fast as his principals demanded.

The final impasse came when they were denied permission to tow a berg into shipping lanes. This too was broken—in private by a few discreet transfers of funds to certain political action committees, and in public by commissioning the iceberg as a ship. When the proper berg was selected, and two special waterjet motors, at least in theory capable of deflecting it, were mounted, the documentation by which it would become the *U.S.S. Marrell Tech* under Panamanian registry, would be ready.

The actual selection of the berg came in two stages. Paul and Paula, on their first overflight of the upper shelving area, saw at the same instant a huge, snowy, crater-topped monster, newly separated and glittering in the morning sun amid a jostle of lesser ice. There was no need for either to point to it; it was almost as if a vector lit in their heads. Photos were taken, and rushed back to Gloria, who reacted exactly as they had.

But the engineers had already fixed on other, smaller bergs farther from the dangerous east-west Alaska flow. Paul overruled them curtly. As if to oblige him, the great berg soon wandered into better, less crowded water. It was also found to have a favorably broad and comparatively shallow underwater configuration. Then, too, its crater shape would facilitate and prolong meltwater collection. The engineers were pacified.

At last came the day when the first towlines tightened. Sirens blared, various fireworks and assorted explosions went up from the Jackson camp, now a small town, and the enormous white presence began imperceptibly to change course and ever so delicately to accelerate on its two-thousand-mile journey south. It was hoped to deliver it to Los Angeles in something under three months, about Labor Day. Dredges were already at work carving a berth for her at a safe distance from the oil drillers off Catalina.

As the voyage of the *U.S.S. Marrell Tech* became a reality, the events and excitements of the trip came more and more into the news, especially when the craft met and mastered her first storm without breakaway. But the most important event escaped all but perfunctory notice.

When the iceberg began its course, the suction wake created by the underwater passage of its huge, irregular volume caused a flotilla of small chunks and berglets to trail after it. These gradually melted or fell away, until only the largest was left—a respectable-sized small berg that seemed determined to accompany them. There was talk of exploding it, but since it too was fresh water, and not endangering anything at the moment, the decision was delayed. A surplus tugboat laid a couple of grapples on it and it gave no trouble.

When Paula was shown it from the air her small brows drew together. "I don't like that thing. It looks ... dirty."

The pilot chuckled.

"I mean it. I wish we'd at least X-ray it or probe it; maybe there something inside."

"Ah, it'll get lost pretty soon."

But it did not get lost. To the presence embedded in stasis deep inside, the stimulus-configuration of receding, escaping prey was acting as a tropism. Human eyes saw only that the harmless small berg seemed to be caught in the currents, maintaining a roughly constant distance from their tow.

While, in the tow itself, all oblivious of danger or of humanity or of the means which moved him or even that he was moving, the helpless cub Enggi continued to beam out his unearthly call for his own reassemblement. He felt only a tiny discomfort from the growing warmth nearby; overriding this was a contenting sense that slowly, slowly, regatherment was taking place. For some time he had felt faint twinges of anticipation as if parts of his missing selfhood were coming close. But the situation was incomplete; an important aspect or aspects was still missing. No less than all of him would serve.

In the human world, another event caused even less notice: one morning the smog-shrouded sunlight of the California coast was briefly dimmed by two tenuosities passing far, far overhead. The apparent passage of some gaseous wisps at orbital heights may have puzzled an astronomer or two. The phenomenon vanished eastward, and no one could have observed them taking up Earth-stationary positions in the 20,-000 mile-out zone to await the moment when an alien cub would emerge and meet his fate.

Meanwhile the Marrell Tech fleet ploughed on, insignificant to astral senses, but becoming ever more stimulating to local humanity. It angled laboriously across the Alaska current, and accelerated as it picked up the southward California flow. Fishermen of Queen Charlotte Island sighted it, a moving mountain of shining snow, trailing fog like steam. Seattle and Portland sent marine excursions out to see it go by. By the time it reached California waters it was an Event, and San Francisco became the leader among cities suddenly demanding an iceberg of their own.

Inland the drought burned on, and jokes about berg-jacking became loud enough to generate watchfulness in the coast guard escort. Obviously, a stolen berg could not be hidden, but the berg might be deflected and irretrievably grounded on a rocky shore, where its use could scarcely be denied. The escort was doubled. And then, as berg fever grew, and the general public began trying to join the flotilla in everything from kayaks to yachts, the escort doubled and redoubled again. A maniac almost crashed it with his helicopter, and an even crazier soul sky-dived into it; a permanent air-safety patrol had to be set up. Marrell Tech was turning out its pockets to pay the security bills; it could not let go of its tiger, and it was becoming a financial disaster to proceed.

Yet the goal was now almost in sight, and just as total chaos threatened, the *Marrell Tech* solved her problems herself. Deceleration, the shedding of its enormous momentum, had to begin far to the north of target, not far from San José. And as the great ice mountain lost way, the fog which it generated, and which had been trailing it like smoke, caught up and closed over it, ever thicker as it slowed. Advantage was taken of this by slowing the berg even more than necessary. Soon, on all but gale-force days, nothing was visible of the whole enterprise but a vast shining slow-moving fog bank, etched here and there with rainbows, above which a glittering ice turret might appear at long intervals and vanish again.

The fog of course created its own problems, but these were manageable with ordinary care, and only a dozen or so idiots required to be rescued in their efforts to reach their invisible goal. The only serious injury came to a lunatic hang glider who broke both legs on the little maverick berg, which was still stuck in the suction wake of the *Marrell Tech*, causing no trouble.

"Two for the price of one," the tow captain grinned.

But Paula turned pale at the news that the small berg was still there.

She and Paul and even Miss Emstead had been causing the tow captain a great deal of trouble by their eagerness to fly out and land on the great berg. He had only just managed to use all his authority, plus Gloria's obvious frailty, and the heaven-sent fog, to keep them off it until it was officially "berthed" and out of his command. This was now a week away.

Meanwhile Gloria had improved enough to make visits to the office, which she spent supervising candidates to replace her. Girta Grier was one of these; the young business school graduate's "mother" had recently died, and slightly against her own better judgment Gloria had invited her down to try out at Marrell Tech. The girl was doing well. Gloria struggled to remain impartial, and to subdue a growing natural affinity between them. Girta didn't resemble her physically, but an artist might have traced out a similarity between Girta and Paula, minus Paula's intensity and diminutive size.

Miss Emstead was somewhat dismayed to note that there seemed also to be a strong natural affinity budding between Girta and Paul, which the senior office staff warmly approved. But she was a philosopher. If society had wrenched a man out of one daughter's bed only to push him into another's, who was she to defy Fate? She contended herself with seeing to it that Girta was as capable as possible in her grasp of Marrell Tech.

Thus it was that when the great day finally came, and the fantastic sight of an enormous iceberg being grounded in its channel near Catalina was before the people of L.A., Girta Grier, with Tim Drever, were part of the small unofficial advance party to copter out and land.

Coming in, they all fell silent with awe. There it sat at last!

Resplendent in its pearly fog and rainbows, with just enough breeze to clear them a landing site on the seaward side, at the nearest approach to the crater.

Deep within that crater, a being so alien as to be incomprehensible to humans, stirred and relaxed its long icy clamped encystment. His stirring did not much disturb the earthly matter about him; the substance of Enggi's body was only loosely intermeshed in the molecular lattices of ice. He was conscious of little but great joy. A desperate hope had won out, his hour of returning life had come.

As the copter came down beside cliffs of ice, Girta and Tim Drever exclaimed in unison, "God, it's huge!" "I thought it'd be just a little hilltop," Girta added, "a big ice cube!"

"It's a landscape," Tim said. The Marrells and Gloria were silent as the pilot helped them all out. The copter had landed them on a big steel-mesh mat laid on a dry place in the shelving shore that ran around the berg. Beyond them farther out, men in wet suits were splashing in the shallows, securing mooring grapples. Out of sight around the blue-white cliffs were the mountings of the two motors, and the official "stern," flying the Marrell Tech flag.

Another copter droned by overhead on its way to deploy a big new Marrell Tech sign of netting, on the shoreward cliffs. There were no permanent structures on the berg, only a faint trail leading to the cratered summit above them. Since this was a potential drinking-water reservoir, all traffic had been kept to the wave-swept shelf around the edge. The melting process so far had done little but slightly widen and raise this water-level ledge; under it all hung the great volume of the ice.

To Tim and Girta's surprise, Paula, Paul, and Gloria had already started up the steep trail to the top. Paul was helping Gloria with an arm around her waist, and she was climbing up quite rapidly.

"Take it easy, honey," Tim called. A cold, damp downdraft blew in his face. He and Girta began to follow more slowly.

"Our iceberg nuts." Girta smiled uncertainly.

Tim grinned briefly. "I'll be glad when she's safe off this thing. Why does she have to climb up there?"

"I know what you mean," Girta said thoughtfully at the first pause. The climb was quite steep. For a moment the fog blew thinner around them, so they could see over the water. "Look, there's that other iceberg, the follower."

The maverick berg was moored a couple of hundred yards off, momentarily sunlit.

"It does look rather dirty, as Paula said."

"Probably just a layer of old volcanic ash," Tim told her. "What are they all shouting about, back there?"

The men on the shelf were hallooing to others who seemed to be out of sight around the cliffs. As Tim and Girta looked, the chopper pilot waded out to join them.

Meanwhile the three above them had reached a point where they could begin to see down into the great shallow irregular crater at the top.

"Look!" Paula cried. "There's a—a cloud coming up!"

Enggi's body did not reflect much visible light or heat, and he was not inordinately large compared, say, with the crater itself. As parts of him came free of its icy matrix, the humans saw only what might have been a whale-sized, peculiarly dense and defined white cumulus cloud beneath them. He did, however, emit and reflect a considerable UV and microwave spectrum; the commotion among the workers was caused by the fact that most of their electronic gear was going into overload or malfunctioning erratically as Enggi came into line.

The emerging cloudlet humped and swayed toward them, a beautiful prismatic white in the sun. As it did, the three humans unconsciously moved toward the brink to meet it.

They felt only a generalized glad rightness; warmth, welcome, perhaps. And for two of them there might have been a brief mild jolt of joining, as if something intangible had met or been passed. No words exist to express what is felt when a fragment of aspect of personality—a fragment of what had been the person—leaves. There is no "emptiness" because that which could have felt empty is simply gone. The only "feeling" left here was a kind of joy, as Enggi's own joy in his recovery of himself leaped the momentary link and overflowed into the abandoned matrices that had housed him. Neither Paul nor Gloria were harmed, or left mutilated; they had, after all, been fully functioning adults when they received Enggi's last desperate transmission.

But Paula—Paula who had been newborn . . .

Blinking away a brief sense of disorientation, the other two turned and saw that the girl had gone a little to one side and closer out, on the crater's lip, so that the strange snowy apparition seemed almost to touch her and light her up. She gave a strange wordless cry, and then seemed as if fighting to retain or maintain herself; her small arms hugged her own body. Then she flung back her head and screamed, or shouted, almost commandingly, "Take me, too! Take me with you!"

At that Paul found voice, though it was little more than a croak of "No! No, Paulie!"

But that moment something new happened. As if jerked by an invisible bond, the beautiful apparition towering above the girl visibly turned from her, and bent or curved its energies so directionally away that they all turned to look.

And they saw it.

Atop the nearby maverick berg, a smoky gray presence was exhaling, or writhing out. A gray tentacle extended toward them, and then *bloomed*, at its tip, into something half visible and wholly fascinating—a great smoke flower, set with stars of piercing, luminous, summer-sky blue.

It was that which Enggi had sensed, and toward which he was now drawn, his innocent cub's curiosity pulling him in every fiber. What—what was this wondrous new thing? All incomplete and unwary as he was, he must—he must draw closer!

But Paula, who had held—and still held—so much of his being, was neither unwary nor naive. With her whole human/unhuman soul she distrusted and dreaded this glowing lure. She had even seen such blue before, in Nicky Benson's eyes. With all her might she willed the white presence, which was somehow half herself, to reject it, to beware and turn away.

"No! No! No!" she cried to it, sending at Enggi all the force of her will.

And indeed she felt his fascination waver, his attention start back to her.

But the Eater brightened and enlarged its attractant, with mesmeric smoky involutions of the "petals," and ever brighter, bluer stars. To half-seeing human eyes it was a fantastically alluring sight, like looking into infinity itself. To Enggi's senses it was all but overpowering. He was yielding, turning fatally back toward it and away.

"No!" Paula shouted. She had no weapon but her naked will, yet that will was half his own, and she strove somehow to connect, to compel. "Come back here! Turn away!"

At this moment Tim and Girta, who had begun to run stumbling up the ice when they heard Paula's cries, burst panting onto the summit. They saw the girl poised straining on the utmost lip of the crater, half enveloped in a great alien whiteness that was pulsingly alive.

As they stared, Paula's head snapped back, and for an instant she stared sightlessly straight up, as if seeking or receiving some signal from the empty sky.

Then she screamed, with more power than seemed possible in her small body, "Get us away from it! Go!"

—And something like a bolt or umbilicus of diamond fire poured between her and the alien thing. The whiteness straightened itself skyward around her. And both Girta and Tim said afterward that for an instant they had seemed to see the outline of a naked girl, unbearably bright, curled within the glittering white cloud.

Then it was going, accelerating impossibly, bolting, streaking for the open sky above, dwindling to a pinpoint star—and vanished before they could draw a breath.

And behind it, from the adjacent berg, a smoky thing with all jewels gone, shot up like a great squid in pursuit.

An Eater was no match for Enggi's speed in open chase, but this one's hunger and frustration were so fierce that it tried. It strove so hard that it did not sense until too late Enggi's two protectors awaiting it with their adult energies at ready.

The resultant flash at 21,000 miles set the astronomers of several nations searching to see whose stationary satellite had exploded.

But on the iceberg top off California, all human eyes were on what had been a living girl, lying like an empty glove at the empty crater's lip. Long before Paul and the others reached her they could sense that, all life was gone. Paul could only hold her, stunned and disbelieving, and yelling for futile ambulance planes.

When the copter pilot finally screwed up his courage to respond to his employer's howls—there had been some fairly unnerving phenomena experienced below—he found Paul and Girta embraced in grief around Paula's limp form, while Tim Drever comforted his exhausted Gloria.

And thereafter matters on Earth took their purely human course.

The events of the Marrell visit, and the sad loss of Paula, were officially ascribed to accident and the premature malfunction of fireworks prepared for the evening. The electronic disturbances ceased and did not return. And the entire enterprise redounded to the eventual great profit of Marrell Technologies, the happy old age of Gloria and Tim, the satisfying if somewhat irregularly joyful conjugation of Girta and Paul, and a notable, if temporary, improvement in the coastal California water supply.

Elsewhere in space and time, Enggi and the two scouts were on their journey home, in travel mode.

For some time Enggi journeyed in silence, until he judged that he could be considered to have digested the angry and sobering lectures he had received. The next time they broke mode to navigate an eruptive complex, he offered respectfully, "I have learned another thing."

"Be silent, worthless young one," returned one scout. "You have caused enough trouble."

"Wait," objected the other. "This cub, reprehensible as it is, has yet faced an Eater at close range, all untaught, and survived. It is possible that something has been found. What is it, Enggi?"

"It is the—the life on these strange little satellites. My essence lived in their minds and thought their thoughts. I'm not sure even now that I'm wholly myself. There's a part of me that had never known of an Eater, yet knew at once it was evil and forced me to escape."

"So!" retorted the first scout. "Undoubtedly it felt no lure."

"It felt it," Enggi persisted. "It felt it strongly. I know. But that isn't it. It's that their lives are so different from ours. I believe," he signed formally, "that I have found my life's work. When I have completed my duties to the grex, of course," he added hastily.

"What do you mean, your life's work? What could you do?" asked the first scout.

"And all that matter is so short-lived," the other remarked thoughtfully. "A mere passing fritha-gust."

Enggi was silent for a long distance. In him lived one aspect of a human mind that had been tormented by a hopeless

longing for the stars. Now he had the stars; their glories and
infinite spectacles were around him as pebbles had been underfoot for the beings on that far-off Earth. And now, para-
doxically, in this same part of him another longing was being
born, a shadowy nostalgia for the soft-colored organic intrica-
cies, the growing things and tactile breezes and blue skies and
racing waters—all the micro-life he had loved as a human
mind, or minds. Even for their strange mutual fevers and
complexities, so intense, so meaningless to Enggi's kind, yet
now not meaningless to him.

"I don't know," he admitted honestly. "But I believe there
is something of value there. Perhaps on other satellites as
well. If we could somehow manage to interchange, for short
times, without all that terror and desperation, if we could
know and experience different kinds, and learn which are
most promising. It might be that some of their knowledge applies to us, as did the one who recognized the Eater without
teaching. Yes, they are brief, but their minds are rich. Maybe
their short lives force them to learn quickly, and then push
beyond what they have been taught. This could be of use to
us. And there is something strange about Time itself—it did
not seem short while I was in their bodies. Could it possibly
be that Time is not the same everywhere?"

"Youngling, your experience has unbalanced you."

"Perhaps so," Enggi persisted stubbornly. "But I am now
not content to go on as before. I believe I will study these
things."

"There was one who had some such idea," the first scout
remembered.

"Where is he? I would seek him and learn!"

"You can't. A neutron sink got him. You haven't learned
of *those* yet," the first scout made a sign of grim amusement.

But Enggi said, "What a loss. But see you, why do we
learn so slow? The mind I shared could have absorbed that
and the Eater and much else in a morn—in a very short
cycle."

"It is our only, our right way."

"Nevertheless I am sure I shall do this thing. Perhaps some
cycle I shall start by returning to the world I left, and trying
to offer to exchange some parts of being for a time. If I
could communicate with one of the star-longers, I'm sure
something would be possibe. I *felt* its need. And they
might help me choose others."

The scouts were returning to travel mode; but the first scout, who had been most scornful, suddenly made an archaic sign, as if Enggi's thoughts had moved him.

"Fair faring . . . And now we must journey on."

SLAC//

by Michael P. Kube-McDowell

The double slash which is part of the title of this story is merely a means of indicating a sound which cannot be transliterated in the standard alphabet. It's part of a name—an alien name to be sure—and a problem in identifying intelligence.

Against regulations, Terence Calder spent two hours of his last sleepmode aboard *Cimara* in the language lab, worrying over the troublesome Semu verbs. He knew his language skills were marginal for a Contactor; and the Semu verbs, marked by sounds more suited to an oboe than vocal cords (Quon, the linguist, called them pipe-sounds*), were to him unpronounceable. And what he could not pronounce, he could not remember for long.

Marisa, his partner, slept soundly in her compartment three bulkheads aft. With her superb language aptitude, she had picked up the Semu tongue as quickly as the crackers had been able to break it down. She had even removed three words from the "In Question" list of undeciphered terms.

*/, / /, and / / / are the graphemes adopted for the three Semu pipe-sounds. The pipe-sounds, which are made with the breathing tube rather than the vocal chamber, are polytonal; however, a workable approximation can be made by whistling the first harmonic ($/=270$ cps, $/ /=461$, $/ / /=908$). It has become common for non-linguistic personnel to say "slac-whistle" (or equivalent).

Calder glanced up at the list hanging on the language lab wall. Removing the remaining fifty-one terms from it was just one of his and Marisa's tasks, beginning with planetfall tomorrow.

The next morning the ship's gig took them down to 10,000 meters, safely above prying Semu eyes. From there they were on their own; the tiny gravwarp generators in their leg pouches would permit a controlled freefall to the uninhabited region below. Marisa went first, clad as Calder was in the orange-red hue of the Semu sun. By the time Calder wriggled out of the embrace of the gig pilot, Marisa was a mere dot far below.

Then he, too, was out of the chute. In the exhilaration of the first moments of freefall, he took his eye off Marisa, and then was unable to spot her. No matter; the gravwarp guidance system would bring them to a side-by-side landing.

Even after three months over Semu, the bluish surface rushing up at him seemed unreal; Calder was from a planet dominated by green chlorophylls. No amount of observation had been able to remove that sense of strangeness. Calder shook off the feeling and concentrated on the fall itself—the easy, peaceful glide down.

Then, as the ground grew near, Calder's arms and legs became inexplicably limp and unresponsive. He began to tumble slowly, and was unable to halt the motion. The gliding turned to falling, and his peace to distress. His ears heard a shouting his mind did not understand. But there was no time for puzzlement; the ground was too close. As the blue Semu countryside rushed up to embrace him, Calder tried and failed to remember the Semu verb for dying.

The tech looked uncomfortable, like a dog expecting to be struck. "Captain?"

"Yes, Nixon."

"I'm not getting any biotelemetry from Terry and Marisa."

"Lost signal or flat trace?" Captain Lanton half-rose from his chair.

"Lost, sir."

Lanton sat back. "I was afraid you were telling me they're dead."

"I think I am, sir. They don't answer my signals."

Lanton frowned. "Let's take a look at the recordings. And hold off on the landing on the far side."

"I already took that liberty."

By the time the recording ended, most of *Cimara's* small complement had formed a solemn half-circle at the perimeter of the tech room.

"High fever and then nothing," Lanton said to no one in particular. "EEG normal, even calm."

"Yes, sir," Nixon said, stepping forward. "If it had just cut off I'd say it was an equipment problem, or interference."

"Did you track them?"

"They made planetfall on the beam exactly."

"Time of LOS?"

"Five minutes after landing, perhaps a little more."

"And they didn't signal us."

"No, sir. Not a peep."

Lanton drummed his fingers on the console.

"Nephei and Quon will follow them down, if you'd like," Nixon offered tentatively. The Lyraen couple nodded.

"No. No second team."

"Yes, sir. What, then?"

"Put us in synch orbit over the site the next pass. Send the gig down now to search from 5,000 meters." He stood. "Let me know the moment they have anything. And check out a mobicom."

"Yes, sir." Surprise showed on several faces, including Nixon's. The mobicom, a powerful communications unit wedded to a gravwarp, was ordinarily used only after a team had set up relations with the planet's inhabitants.

"One more thing," Lanton said, pausing at the door and jabbing at them with a finger. "When you update your logs, they're missing. Not dead. Missing."

Lanton sought the privacy of his compartment during the fifty-minute wait until they were over the landing site again. "I should have had us in sync already," he started on himself when he was alone. "Followed them down with a sight-sound peeper or have them carry one—"

He stopped berating himself when he realized he was merely forecasting the conclusions of the inquiry board. Point was, no ship had ever lost a team on planetfall before—later, certainly, but not in the first five minutes. If there had ever been any special precautions, they had long fallen out of use. Getting on the planet had always turned out to be the easy part.

The details of contact with underdeveloped planets—no other kind having yet been found—had been worked out in theory by the exopsychologists and in practice by the Service. The crucial step was to monitor the communications of the inhabitants from orbit, and let a team like Nephei and Quon use a linguacomp to crack the language. Or if, like Semu, the planet had no advanced communications, plant a selection of sight-sound peepers. That took longer, since conversational language was invariably harder to decode than broadcast formal.

Then, language in hand, simply go meet the inhabitants. When a new animal approaches you speaking your language, it gives you pause—pause enough for the Service to establish contact with twenty-two intelligent, thriving species. There were some curious similarities among them—each was top predator on its planet, entering or facing the crisis that comes when evolutionary programming becomes outdated. The knowledge that they were not alone had helped two or three species totter back from the brink, and only one species ended up worshipping man—a good scorecard.

The rest of the procedure was mere detail. Wear the color of the planet's primary sun: the safest color, given the nearly universal sun-worship of surface dwellers. Display as little technology as possible—the only devices carried were the gravwarp generators, and even those were integral with the jumpsuits. The biotelemeters and microradios were implants—the former in the chest and the latter in the left pinky. Planetfall was made in an uninhabited region, to avoid mass reactions and let the Contactors choose first contact. Finally, teams of two gave an accurate picture of human biology, allowed for complementary abilities, and were small enough not to constitute an invasion. An unvarying, reliable formula.

Except for this time. And he, Aldis Lanton, was faced with answering the question that no one had ever had to answer before: *what next?*

It was not a question for long. The Service's contact captains were a special sort. Typically, they had the lowest I-score on their ships, in part because it was undesirable that they be bright enough to be erratic. What was desirable was a certain firmness of mind, a decisiveness in the face of both too little and too much detail. With a mission by its nature unpredictable, and a crew of talented, occasionally temperamental specialists, the ship's captain had to be a locus of calmness.

And Lanton was one of the best, because he understood his role. Twelve years ago he had faced the realities of a shrinking military and his own personality, and transferred to the Advance Exploration Service. Though he committed himself to becoming conversant in all the contact skills, and pioneered the now-common practice of requiring the entire ship's complement to learn the new languages, he would have been respected and successful without those acts. And when Nixon finally knocked and stepped into the cabin, Lanton had things clear in his mind.

"No sign from 5,000, Captain. Shall I send them lower?"

"No point—if the team were still on site, the sensors would pick up their telemetry. Correct?"

"Yes. It seems the next step is to put a team on the ground."

"Yes. But differently this time. Is the mobicom checked out?"

"Yes. I don't—"

"It's their planet," Lanton said, standing. "We were ready to contact them. There's apparently something critical we don't know about the planet. Let's get their help."

Semu—the planet. Geologically unremarkable. Smaller than Earth and more dense—net effect, a slightly higher surface gravity. A day of 29.2 standard hours. Two continents, the smaller northern one permanently ice-encrusted. The larger, dubbed Drumstick by Quon because of its shape, wrapped two-thirds of the way around the southern hemisphere. Almost 60 percent of it was rugged highland, including a range of inner mountains which were low but forbiddingly severe. A semi-circular plain of rolling lowlands on Drumstick's larger western end, almost enclosed by two fingers of highlands, contained nearly all the fertile land. Biologically, Semu was marked by short food chains. And, like most planets with a variety of life, Semu had large plants that were not trees but would be called such, and small plants that were not grass but would suffer the misnomer. Blessedly, it did not seem to have insects.

Semu—the people. Cell-based and humanoid, but clearly not human. Aside from the usual variations in sense organs, musculature, and so on, two features clearly set them as a species apart. The Semu head was articulated much like a Terran owl's, capable with its loose-skinned neck of rotating through nearly 400°. Moreover, the Semu were ambidirectional—that is, their arms seemed to function as well in back of their bodies as in front. They were also extremely pair-oriented; in nearly five months of observation, only twice had a Semu been seen more than twenty meters from his *otati*, or mate. Total population: perhaps 100,000, in over 2,000 villages scattered over the coastal plain and fertile lowlands. They were gatherers rather than farmers, and the villages were separated by the invisible, mutually respected lines demarking their food territories.

Lanton studied the reaction of the Semu villagers to the suitcase-sized mobicom descending toward them. Nixon, brought it in on one side of the village, so only a dozen Semu paused to note its approach. They watched dispassionately, neither drawing near nor fleeing, and then most turned away. It was not what Lanton had expected.

Only two pairs remained interested long enough to see Lanton's face appear and hear his greeting: *"Bantroi."*

"Bantroi," echoed the nearest Semu, his head twisting toward his *otati*. The second Semu repeated the greeting.

"I am Aldis Lanton," said the captain. "What you see is not my body but a *kisemu* I have sent you so that we may talk." He used the Semu word for statue or portrait—literally, "not-self."

"Yes," said the second Semu, moving forward and nudging the first aside. To Lanton's ear, both voices were male.

"I am a visitor—*kiranchi*. Two of my companions are missing near your village. We will come and meet with you and search for them. Is it to be so?" A Semu request was a statement of the future, then a request for confirmation.

"It is to be."

Lanton waited, expecting a question, but none came. "Before nightfall," Lanton said finally. *"Bantroi."*

Switching off, Lanton shivered. There seemed to be nothing behind the yellow Semu eyes—a vacant look, as though the owner were out to lunch. He chided himself for anthropocentricity and turned to the others in the room.

"Mandy, you and I will make up the team."

Mandy Wells looked up, startled. The exobiologist was *Cimara's* newest and youngest specialist, and had kept to herself enough that she was more like a passenger than part of the team. She had come to them in the usual way—basic training in a top Earth school, advanced work on the Jovian moons, research on a "safe" planet (in her case, Kruger 60-E), and two intern missions at the elbow of an experienced XB. Semu was her first solo mission, which Lanton saw as the reason for her reticence. Whatever the reason, Wells did not give much of herself away. Her small smile at being selected was comparatively revealing.

"Thank you, sir. Captain—" she began hesitantly.

"Yes?"

"I know it's difficult to tell with ET's, but they didn't seem very surprised."

Lanton's expression was sober. "I know."

The gig pilot set the tiny ship down gently within sight of the village walls, then lifted off again as the humans walked side-by-side down the knoll to the gate in the low village wall. A pair of Semu waited there; they seemed agitated, heads turning repeatedly through full circles. As the humans drew closer, other pairs appeared in the yard just inside the wall.

"*Bantroi*," Lanton called as soon as he thought they would hear a normal speaking voice.

"*Bantroi*," said one of the newly arrived Semu. "I am Gision Ah, Protector of the village of White-hill. We celebrate your safe arrival."

"We celebrate your continued health," responded Wells.

"Have those who are missing been found?" Gision Ah asked matter-of-factly.

"No. They are still missing."

Those Semu who stood watching muttered at this. "Slac//," one said clearly.

"Where did you last know of them?"

Lanton pointed east. "Three hills—two *kai* walk-time."

"And the missing are like you?"

"They are."

Gision Ah made a sweeping downward motion with his hand, the fingers coming together to touch at the tips—the Semu gesture for "gone," equivalent to a shrug of hopelessness.

"Have you heard anything of strangers in that area?"

"We know nothing of the world there."

"Your travelers—hunters—"

"Nothing."

Wells stepped forward. "We are *kiranchi*. We ask your help."

Gision Ah's *otati* spoke, a harsh, incomprehensible outburst. Looking back, Gision Ah answered with equal intensity, then said to Lanton: "You will wait for us. It will be so?"

"It will be so," Lanton said. Immediately a pair of the large Semu ushered the humans away from the gate and deeper into the village. Surprised, the humans let themselves be steered into a small, sturdy building. It was dark inside; the windows were mere slits in the wooden wall. "Prison?" Lanton wondered aloud.

Wells moved to the doorway and looked out. "Three pair of them standing close by, including our escorts. And this door is lockable—there are holes and loops for vertical crossbars."

"Come have a seat." As she joined him, he continued. "Some of those pairs are homosexual, correct?"

"Oh, yes. They seem to place no stigma on it—male-male and female-female pairs are as common as mixed ones. It was part of the report I submitted on the Semu social organization."

"Ah. Remind me of your conclusions." Lanton remembered the report clearly; he was trying to draw her out.

Wells nodded. "Generally, there is a strong correlation between the formal social acceptance of homosex and crowded niches. But that doesn't seem to be the case here—the food supply appears adequate for five times the population."

Lanton was mildly disappointed; her tone was professional and deferential, not personal. "So?"

"So the pairing patterns are just variation, not adaptation. Unless this *is* overpopulated for Semu sensitivities."

"Or their diet is more specialized than we realize." Lanton grasped the pinky of his left hand and pulled, as if he were unjamming a finger. "Nixon?" he said experimentally.

"Here."

"We're a bit isolated just now. Try to find out what's happening with the group that greeted us."

"Call when I have something," the tech promised. "Nixon out."

Gision Ah sounded the three pipe-sounds, and the room fell silent. "Nepion Tu has asked for a sharing-time concerning the *kiranchi*."

"I wish to know what Protector Ah sees," Nepion explained.

"Protector Ah does not see clearly, and would accept the sharing of others on this question."

"Clarify."

"What is done? They are not slac//; they are not lessers. Are they Semu? They are two, and yet not *otati*."

"They are insane," spoke up one of those who had watched the humans at the gate. "They wood-walk with eyes down and ahead." He made the 'gone' gesture. "They are insane."

"They are strangers," offered another.

"They speak language—"

"Like a poorly trained child."

"But still they speak."

Gision Nu rose. "Our ways permit only one response. They have demanded *kiranchi* with us. *Kiranchi* must be given."

"They are not Semu," protested Nepion Tu. "Would you grant *kiranchi* to a slac// if it demanded it?"

"It seems to be a meeting over your status, sir. I don't dare move the mobicom for fear of alarming them, so I've got the long mike on them—but the gain isn't too strong. Here, Quon wants you."

"I'd say we misread *kiranchi*," said the linguist. "It's not 'visitor', it's more to a temporary communal membership—a reciprocal relation between villages, apparently."

"How are we doing?"

"Hard to say. Several 'In Question' terms have shown up already—brings an element of uncertainty into any analysis."

"Keep listening. I don't like uncertainty. And give Mandy a signal feed so she can help."

"Yes, sir."

"Where is their village, where we may claim *kiranchi?*"

"If they are from it, it must exist."

The argument went on, the alignment of delegates shifting on nearly every new point that was raised. "I could make more progress with a committee of snakes," grumbled Nixon, eavesdropping from *Cimara*. But Gision Ah seemed content, sitting back and staying out of the discussion.

Three hours later, the vigor of the debate undiminished, the door to the building opened and a young Semu poked his head in. *"Ginu,"* he called, and without a further word the delegates hurried from the building in the ubiquitous Semu pairs.

It was about that time that the signal from the mobicom died.

"What do you want me to do?" Nixon asked plaintively. "If I recall it for maintenance or send down another, they may not take it well. We've shown them a lot of technology for this point in the contact."

Lanton decided quickly. "Do nothing. The information hasn't been that valuable. We have to make things happen from here, and we've just been sitting."

"Good luck, sir."

"I'm a believer in making your own luck."

"Yes, sir. Uh—Captain? Think the Semu tampered with the 'com?"

Lanton exhaled heavily. "I don't know."

"Check in in three hours?"

"Yes. Lanton out." He looked expectantly across the room at Wells. "Ready to go?"

"More than," she said eagerly.

But this time, the door would not open.

Without benefit of clock or crier, as sunlight began to reach the village of White-hill, the delegates migrated back to the meeting house.

This time, however, Gision Ah reined in the wandering thoughts. "We know of only one thing that may be done. *Kiranchi* has been claimed, and will be granted. But there is more. They seek their missing in the open lands. If we permit them to search freely—"

Several of those in the front circle made the sign for 'gone'.

"Yes. More is called for from us."

"There must be a *tiranon*," said Nepion Tu.

"There must be a *tiranon*," Gision Ah agreed. "But because they are strangers, it is required of no one. Return to your homes and seek out those who will serve. Send them to me. When a *tiranon* has been found, we will proceed."

Aldis Lanton had taken a long time to fall asleep. He and Mandy had found out at the cost of bruised hands and shoulders that the door was strong enough to hold them, and at the cost of their voices that no Semu could be persuaded to release them. Nixon's offer to intervene tempted him briefly, but in the end he decided to wait until the situation was clearer. Still, he could not seem to close his eyes, his hopes for finding the Contact Team alive having reached a new low.

In the morning, the posts were noisily removed and the door thrown open by a young Semu. "*Ginu* ends," he said, then disappeared from the doorway.

When Lanton tried to follow and get an explanation, however, he found himself quickly surrounded by Semu—not threateningly, but purposefully.

"I will talk with Gision Ah. It will be so?"

"It will not," was the answer. "He is occupied."

Lanton frowned. "We must begin looking for our missing companions. Too much time passes."

"It will not be," said the Semu who barred his path. "*Kiranchi* has been granted, the *tiranon* forms. Wait."

His frown deepened, and Wells touched his arm. "We're not in danger," she said in English, "and it sounds like we've been granted a protected status. Perhaps we should give them more time."

"Time is the problem," Lanton said simply.

"I think it would be a mistake to force the issue now. There's no indication they don't intend to help us."

The forcefulness in Wells's voice was a welcome surprise. Perhaps, Lanton thought, she's starting to find her professional backbone. But he was not as convinced of their safety as she was.

"We will wait—two *kai*," he said to the Semu. "Come on," he said to Wells, and ducked back inside the hut. Sitting down, he signaled the ship, aware that the Semu way of doing things was wearing on his patience.

"Put Quon on."

There was a short silence before they heard the Lyraen's voice. "Yes, Captain?"

"A translation on *tiranon*, please."

"Repeat?"

"*Tiranon.*"

"Must be a new word. Any contextual clues?"

"I was thinking it might be 'search party', Captain," offered Wells.

"Um. Translation on *ginu*."

"Still on the 'In Question' list," said Quon. "Best guess would be 'sunset', except we already have a word for it and they're very economical in their vocabulary—"

"I don't want might be, I want to *know*," Lanton said heatedly. "Start doing your job." He looked up to see Wells considering him curiously. "What do you want?"

The look vanished. "Nothing."

Near noon, the Protector came for them.

"We are ready," he said simply, and they followed him out into the sun. Standing there were a dozen Semu, each carrying a sort of rigid sling that the humans had seen used in play—it was one of the three Semu tools they had identified. But the short five-pointed arrows that they were also carrying were new. It was clear that the arrow was intended to fit in the groove along the upper side of the sling.

The band moved off to the nearest village gate, where they paused while Gision Ah moved among them, rubbing a yellow-white cake across the arrow points. The Semu gabbed animatedly as they waited, then fell silent when Gision had finished. Offering the humans no explanations, the Semu leader moved to the front of the group and set the pace with long, smooth strides. His *otati* followed close behind him, stepping into his footprints with a precision that seemed practiced, her head facing back and sweeping slowly from side to side.

The other pairs arranged themselves similarly, spaced at regular intervals across the open meadow. After an exchange of glances, Lanton and Wells fell in behind them.

"We haven't seen that sling used as a weapon before," said Lanton.

"No. But I have seen them walk this way—the young have a kind of game they play," she said, watching them intently.

"That cake must be some sort of poison."

"Or it could have ritual significance—the Semu are big on ritual. I think this is what we wanted, though—a search party. Look at the way each one of them only scans a small part of the surroundings—but between them not a bit is missed. Remarkable example of social coordination, don't you think?"

"I think Gision is going too fast."

The countryside was gentle in slope, but the long-legged Semu were not dawdlers—they proceeded without pause at a rate awkwardly between human walking and running. For the first hour, the *kiranchi* kept up, breathless. But as they drew nearer to the landing site, legs tired and spirit flagged.

It happened then, in one terrible moment. A shadow flashed across the ground unnoticed. At a noise, no more than a breathless rush of air, Lanton's eyes flicked upward. There was not enough time to sort out the impressions—he smelled something pungent, saw claws, sensed *close*, and threw up an arm in self-protection. Something hard and sharp struck his arm with surprising force, glanced off, and raked his head.

Wells spun at the sound and saw Lanton spin slowly into a jumbled pile of limbs. "Slac//," cried a shrill Semu voice as the creature glided overhead on its sail-like wings.

A flurry of five-pointed arrows filled the air, and three came to rest in the flesh of the attacker. The slac//'s grasp on the heavy stick it carried in its lower claws weakened, and the stick fell to the ground; a moment later the creature folded its sails and followed it, thudding against the ground fifteen meters from where Wells crouched. With an effort she released the air in her lungs and hurried to Lanton's side.

Lanton's eyes were closed and his temple bloody; his left forearm made an angle of 40° where the designer had not intended one to be. But he seemed to be breathing regularly, and Wells took time out to signal the ship. "Lanton's been hurt—get the gig down here ASAP."

"Hold on." After a pause, Quon's voice returned. "Nephei's boarding now. Six minutes or so—will that do it?"

"Yes." She looked yearningly in the direction of the slac//. "You can cross slac// off the 'In Question' list—it's what the Semu call the flying species that attacked Lanton. About a meter long, wingspan about the same—ruddy orange color."

"With a pipe-sound, it should be a verb."

"For attack, maybe." Looking down, she saw that there was considerable blood on Lanton's face. "Nephei coming?"

"On the way," Quon reassured.

"Wells out." Kneeling, she wiped away the blood and found, to her relief, that there were no deep gouges—the blood was from capillaries torn open by the stick scraping across his face. Reassured, she checked his pulse and breathing again, then crossed the meadow to the circle of Semu. Shouldering her way to the inside, she stood beside Gision Ah and stared at the creature.

The slac//'s wings were simply loose flaps of skin connecting its upper limbs to its body, though in flight they had the shape of a parasail. Its legs had enormous extensor muscles, and ended in powerful claws that were not at all birdlike. Similar but smaller claws were at the end of each sailstrut.

"The stick it carried—" she said to Gision.

Gision Ah struck himself in the throat with his forearm. "The slac// neck-break."

Wells suddenly felt exposed. "No one is on lookout now," she said. "Couldn't there be another nearby? Are they never found in groups?"

"The slac// dislike each other's company."

"A *kiranchi* from Low-tree told once of a *tiranon* that slew two slac// in a single day," said Gision Nu.

"The people of Low-tree are known braggarts and liars," said Gision Ah. *"Beyta,"* he barked suddenly, and the Semu began to scatter in all directions. Two headed for Lanton, and Wells hastened protectively back to his side. But the pair continued on with barely a glance at Lanton, and disappeared into the woods as the others all had. Before Wells could wonder about it, the gig swept down and settled with a muffled roar a hundred meters away.

Nephei examined Lanton quickly and sniffed, "Nothing serious." Producing an airsplint, she worked to immobilize Lanton's arm. "Help me get him to the gig."

The Lyraen woman was strong, and Wells felt unneeded in the four-hand carry. The feeling was confirmed when Nephei changed her grip and carried him up the ladder and into the gig herself. Arranging him on a flight couch, she turned and poked her head back out the hatch.

"Coming?"

"I think not."

"Standard prac says not to be groundside solo."

"I'm not. I'm with them," Wells said with a jerk of the head.

Nephei glanced up. "Speaking of whom—what the hell are they doing?"

"My specimen!" cried Mandy, running toward the gathering. But she was too late; flames were already leaping up through the mound of brush the Semu had collected. Atop the mound was the slac//.

"Gision Ah," she called across the circle. "I need to—" She stopped, frustrated. They had learned no Semu word for 'study'. "To look at it."

"The fire will put the smell of death in the air—no slac// will come for days. It will be safe to feed here." The flames leaped up and hid Gision Ah's face from her.

Horrified, Wells watched the slac// writhe until its flesh turned black. Once she had seen a boy torment a Terran worm with a hand lens; the feeling of mixed fascination and disgust was the same then and now.

Though Wells pleaded with Gision Ah to go on to the landing site, he would not hear of it. "The *tiranon* has known fire, and darkness comes. At *ginu*, the world belongs to the slac//."

He strode off, and Wells hastened to fall in beside him. "The door to our sleeping-place would not open once." Semu was sparing with time words; anything past was *esu*—once.

"Yes," acknowledged Gision Ah. "A Semu forgets—the madness comes. He must be helped to remember."

"The slac// see well in the dark," Wells suggested.

"For slac//, there is no dark."

An odd speculation came into Wells's mind, but she dismissed it quickly. "We will look for the missing again tomorrow. It will be so?"

Gision Nu clucked reprovingly—an unnerving cross-species parallel—and said, "It will not." She looked to Ah.

"It will not," he agreed. "You must find a new *otati*, now that yours is lost."

"He's not lost. He was taken back to have his injuries attended to."

Gision Ah said nothing but exchanged a glance with his *otati*.

"We must look again tomorrow," Wells pressed. "It will be so?"

"It will not," Ah repeated. "You must find a new *otati*, now that yours is lost."

Wells took the Protector by the arm and stopped him. He looked at her blankly.

"Gision Ah, what am I?"

The blank look continued.

"Am I a Semu?" She held their forearms up side-by-side before him. Behind them, the rest of the *tiranon* had come to a stop.

"No—you are not Semu." Ah seemed disturbed.

"Then what am I? Where do I come from? What took Lanton away?"

Again the blank expression. "You are not Semu," he said slowly. "You are not slac//. You are not lessers." Then, as though he had solved a great puzzle, he pronounced, "You are *kiranchi*." Satisfied, he resumed walking.

Wells stood and watched him go, astonished. The Semu had not asked them a single question about humans, had never reacted in the least to the coming and going of the gig or the mobicom. She had noted it, of course, and attributed it to caution.

Now she began to wonder—could it be that they simply weren't curious?

Mandy Wells squirmed uncomfortably on the sleep-bench and stared up toward the ceiling, somewhere above her in the darkness. The last few hours had been the best since they had left port—finally there was no one looking over her shoulder, ready to judge and find her wanting. When the gig had left, Wells had felt a wave of relief. For a while, at least, the pressure to prove herself was gone.

But she still could have been happier. She hated the guessing—pretending that it was possible to somehow make human sense out of alien strangeness. She hated guessing wrong still more—and she had a deep suspicion that she had been very badly wrong about the Semu.

On top of that, there was something troubling about the attack on the captain. The use of the neck-break stick could be overlooked; many more animals used tools than made them. But why had the attack taken place at all?

At first, Wells had dismissed it easily. Just as the Semu are sensitive to "mad" behavior, so too must be the slac//. She and Lanton had walked as a human couple, not a Semu *otati*—and they had been singled out just as any predator singles out the cripple in the herd. But now, under closer examination, that explanation fell apart. What would the slac// have done with Lanton had it been successful? It wasn't a flier, merely a glider; and couldn't have carried him away.

Nor could it have fed, with a band of arrow-slinging Semu forty meters away. The attack defied survival instinct.

Then the scratching began.

It was above her in the dark, on the roof outside the shelter. Wells sat up and clutched the edge of the sleep-bench tightly in both hands. The scratching circled the roof twice, then stopped. A moment later another sound began at the door—the sound of the lock-posts turning in their holes in the ground. Finally the door itself came alive, shaking back and forth against the lock-posts and the frame. The shaking was almost frantic, and Wells had little doubt about what was outside the door.

At last, to her relief, the noises stopped, But it took a long time for her to relax enough for sleep to come.

In the light of her second dawn on Semu, with the visitation more tantalizing than frightening, Wells was determined to find a slac// to observe. But Gision Ah refused to help, and when she tried to leave the village alone a small crowd of Semu converged on her at the gate, lovingly but firmly turning her back. When a second effort was just as fruitless, Wells retreated to the center of the village and contacted *Cimara*.

"Morning, Mandy," Nixon said cheerfully. "I wasn't five minutes from checking on you. Night pass uneventfully?"

"More or less. How's the Captain?"

"Out cold right now—Nephei's warming up the microknitter to fix that broken wing. As soon as she's done, she and Quon are coming groundside to start formal contact procedures."

"What about me?"

"You'll be staying—to concentrate on the slac//. The captain wants us to give the Semu something to help them with that problem."

"Isn't that a bit premature?"

"He doesn't seem to think so—and you can't exactly discuss it with him now. Oh, and another thing—that mobicom that went out. Chip failure. Not tampering."

"What about Terry and Marisa?"

Nixon hesitated. "We've come to the conclusion that there won't be much to find."

"You're writing them off."

"Not exacly. But it's pretty unlikely they're going to show

up alive, wouldn't you say? After all, without a little help
from the Semu, you wouldn't be in much of a talking mood
yourself."

"I'd be dead, you're saying."

"And the Captain. You disagree?"

Wells frowned. "No. That's probably right. Wells out."

Gision was playing *tiranon* with five young Semu when
Wells found him. "I have to talk to you."

"I knew the need once—Nu is my third," Ah said, waving
the young ones away. "Share."

"Protector Ah, I know what you're trying to do. You're
convinced I'm insane because I don't fear the slac// every
waking moment—and because I've lost my 'otati'. You're trying to save me from my madness. But it isn't necessary!"

The protector waited patiently, and Wells continued. "It's
become a problem—I can't do my work. I can care for myself. I'm an experienced—*kiranchi*." It wasn't the word she
wanted, but the maddening Semu language straitjacketed her.
It had no word for exobiologist, of course, but it did not even
have a word for explorer. "Please tell your people to leave
me be."

"When I lost my first *otati*, the madness stayed for fifty
days," Gision said gently. "I did not gather food—I longed to
kill slac// singlehanded. But my friends were good to me,
and locked me in a sleeping-place, and I became well again.
How can I tell your friends not to help? You ask me to take
your madness and spread it among them."

"I'm not a Semu," Wells said heatedly. "Forget *otati*, forget
madness. Look at me—if I'm not the same as you on the outside, why should I be the same on the inside?"

"The madness runs deep in you, *kiranchi*," said Ah, ever
gentle. "But we will help you, do not fear."

Wells stared at him, then turned and stalked away. Behind
her, Gision Ah called loudly to the nearby adults, and Wells's
steps became running strides. She headed unerringly for the
nearest gate, meaning to test at last the strength of the slender Semu arms that barred it.

Though there were five of them, the struggle was brief.
Wells broke free and ran for the forest, leaving the Semu dismayed and largely prone behind her.

Heading toward the nearest portion of the Wishbone, Wells
ran herself to near-collapse through the wood. When she felt

she had won enough time from the Semu's doubtlessly concerned pursuit, she slowed to a walk. Though finding a slac// would be, on the face of it, difficult, she had the idea that given a chance to they would locate her.

Protecting her back by resting against a trunk at the edge of a large clearing, Wells sat down to wait. The slac// would have to approach head-on, and an attack would be difficult.

A new vision of the Semu took form in her mind as she waited. *Tiranon* was not search party, but hunting party. *Otati*, the strongest relationship in their society, was not reproductive-mate, but partner, or buddy as in buddy-system. The slac// seemed to thoroughly dictate the Semu way of life.

As she mulled over the new observations, a graceful orange-red creature glided down to settle in the middle of the clearing. Its lower claws were empty.

"Now we'll find out what sort of creature you are," she murmured, leaning forward. "I prefer my specimens live, anyway." The slac// and the woman considered each other across the expanse of blue meadow. The gaze of the slac// made Wells uncomfortable in a way the Semu never had.

"Do you speak? Do you have language?" she said loudly, hoping not for understanding but to encourage the slac// to display similar ability. But there was no response.

"Are you the one that came last night?" she asked, standing. "Or is there a nest of you somewhere near?"

The slac// took two awkward steps toward her.

"A little test, then. It's easy, you can do it. Give me something I can show the Captain." She extended a closed fist, then uncurled a single finger from it.

With what to Wells was painful slowness, the slac// unfolded its right sailstrut and flexed one, then two of the diminutive claws at the end.

Resisting a premature smile, Wells raised one, then two, then three fingers. She watched eagerly as the slac// uncurled its last two claws, then shifted its weight from foot to foot.

"Beautiful!" she said, applauding. "There *is* something behind those eyes. You gave me sequence, not simple imitation. Use of symbols and number sense. It's a start. God, if you could only talk to me." She tugged on her radio. "Maybe this is enough."

"Enough for what?" crackled a voice.

"Wells here. Is the Captain available yet?"

"Didn't know you wanted to talk to him," said Nixon. "He's a bit groggy—can it wait? Or can I handle it?"

"Not really."

Nixon sighed. "All right. A word of warning—he's been rather humorless since we picked him up."

"Noted."

"Problem, Mandy?" Lanton sounded tired.

"How are you, sir?"

"Skip the pleasantries, please. What's your difficulty?"

"I've been looking into the slac//—"

"Good. I presume Nixon told you what I want done."

"He did, sir. I'd like you to reconsider. There are some questions that should be answered first."

"Such as?"

"Such as why they're on the flatlands at all—they did *not* evolve there. Their exact relationship to the Semu—"

"*Cimara* is here to find and contact intelligent life, not write the final text on this planet's ecology," Lanton reminded her. "You can leave some things for those who follow."

"I know. But there are indications that they're intelligent."

"What indications?"

"Number concept, for one thing. And I believe they're trying to contact me—"

"The way they contacted me? Come now, Mandy, you're dragging your feet. Don't you want to give the Semu a chance to devote their energies to growth and development? We gave the k't'p'ch a selective pesticide, and the Mau vaccination. You did excellent work with the killflies on Kranh—how is this different?"

"We missed the slac// completely—what else might we have missed? Our planetary survey is suspect—I want to go back and review our procedures. In the meantime, we should hold off on any other contact."

"Contact's already begun, and we don't have the kind of time you seem to be implying. Mandy—don't lose confidence in your work because I don't know how to duck. *I* haven't lost confidence. Just think of the slac// as a natural enemy of an intelligent species, and figure out what to do about them. In nine or ten days we'll be on our way home."

"Nine days," she echoed hollowly.

"Yes—sounds attractive, doesn't it? Quon says they're progressing well. Report in at the regular time."

"Captain, I'm standing here looking at a slac// who—"

"Good. Find out how to kill it. Lanton out."

Wells looked unhappily at the slac//. "We have a problem," she said softly. She stepped toward the creature, and it turned and waddled away. Then with a boost from its powerful legs, the slac// launched itself into the air. As it rose, it filled its sails with air and glided downhill, holding an altitude near two meters. Dismayed, Wells watched it go.

At the bottom of the slope, however, it banked and landed, looking expectantly back at Wells. Opening its mouth, it filled the clearing with a modulated trill that said to Wells as clearly as if it had been in English, "Aren't you coming?"

Jubilant, she set off after it. The slac// waited until she caught up, then pushed off again to glide alongside her. As it lost momentum, it would near the ground and the powerful legs would lash out again. It was a strange feeling to run within arm's reach of the living glider.

But it was a good strangeness. Her legs were tireless, her breath came easily. She found that she did not even care where they were headed—to share this moment, this place, with it was enough.

Before long, it became clear they were headed for the isolated outcrop of bedrock known to the *Cimara* as the Boil. As they neared it, her escort sent excited cries on ahead. Answers came back in many voices, and when she was finally led into the rock-encircled nest at the base of the Boil, there were fifteen slac// waiting. At the sight of her the air became thick with trilling.

Wells walked to the center and sat, to bring her eye level down to theirs. A fuss was being made over her escort, but most were studying her and jostling for a clear view.

Finally one waddled a few steps closer to her.

" *'antroi, kiranchi,*" trilled the slac//. The voice was high-pitched and slurred, but intelligible.

Wells was stunned. "*Bantroi,*" she managed to say. "I am Mandy Wells."

"I am (double-whistle, click)," said the slac//. " *'andy 'ells—what are you?*"

"Captain, there's something down here you should see."

"I'm not planning on coming back down. Can't you handle it?"

"It has to do with the slac//."

"Pass it to Quon then. I don't need to be involved in the details."

"I'm afraid you do. There isn't going to be any slac// control program."

There was a pause. "I think perhaps you'd better come on back up to *Cimara* and explain that."

'I can explain part from here. The rest you have to see. The slac// *are* intelligent, Captain—there's no question now."

"That's a conclusion. Give me the data."

"Well—they have language—"

"Many species communicate with sound."

"Captain, some of these creatures speak Semu."

"Mimicry is not unknown, is it?"

Gritting her teeth, Wells continued. "They're socially organized—"

"So are bees. Are they tool-makers? Do they have writing?"

"No. Not that I've seen so far. But—"

"Aren't those the prime determiners? It seems to me as though you're losing both your objectivity and sight of your goal."

"It seems to me that your mind is closed on the subject of slac//. Is it guilt over Marisa and Terry, or self-pity?"

"Don't try home psychotherapy on me," Lanton said ominously.

"I'll use anything I can to break through to you. Captain, I'm sorry you were hurt—but so are the slac//."

That took Lanton aback. "How do you know?"

"Come down and I'll show you."

"That's out."

"Then you're going to have to deal with me helping the slac// while you help the Semu."

"What are you saying?"

"I thought I said it quite plainly."

Lanton's voice was cold. "I don't like threats, especially from my own people. Come up here and present your case. That's all you have to do."

"Captain, remember that we said the Semu weren't surprised by us. We expected them to react to our alienness, to our display of technology—and they didn't. They *couldn't*. Does a cat wonder about electric lights? Is a shark impressed by a submarine? Is a baby awed by sleight-of-hand? The Semu lack the capacity for true intellectual disequilibrium.

They didn't and don't understand who we are. But the slac//
do!"

Lanton frowned. "Meaning what?"

"That we contacted the wrong species."

"That's nonsense."

"No—an educated opinion. And one you can't fairly contest until you see what I've seen—down here."

"Why do you insist I come down?"

Wells's face and sigh showed that she was perturbed. "Captain, I've always said that the true sign of an intelligent
species is that when you point, it doesn't look at your finger
but at the place to which you're pointing. *You* keep looking
at my finger."

There was a pause. "You may be right, at that. All
right—I'll come down."

Wells met the gig a kilometer from the nest.

"Stay inside," she said sharply when Nixon started to follow Lanton out of the gig.

"Why?" asked Lanton.

"It makes me uncomfortable to be one against your two."

"*You* make *me* uncomfortable," Lanton said shortly, but
waved Nixon back. "Where are they?"

As though cued, three slac// burst out of the trees and
glided down to settle beside Wells. Lanton shied back at their
approach.

"Face of the enemy," he said. "How many times did you
practice that entrance?"

Wells ignored the gibe. "The Semu's enemy, yes. But not
necessarily ours."

"I realize now why I don't like them. They remind me of
the witch's monkeymen from *The Wizard of Oz*. Know it?"

"Science fiction?"

"Old-time flat movie—saw it as a child. Not important. I'm
here. You had something to show me?"

"I want to explain about the attack on you first. The one
that went after us had lost a vote in conclave and acted on its
own. It was one of the first to spot us, and urged we be killed
to eliminate the threat."

"What threat?"

"What's my current assignment?" she asked pointedly.

"Um. But he lost the vote."

"The majority voted to 'wait and see'."

Lanton's hand went slowly to the heal-seal on the side of his face. (Double-whistle, click) advanced toward him.

"You are Protector Lanton," it said in Semu.

Startled, Lanton nodded.

"Why do you help your enemy against us?"

"*Our* enemy? The Semu?"

"Do they find your missing?"

"Can *you*?"

"I can take you to the place." (Double-whistle, click) launched himself, and the other slac// followed. Wells took a step, but Lanton grasped her arm firmly.

"How do they know?"

"They have the whole flatland under surveillance."

"Or because a predator can find old kills?"

"We'll see," said Wells, pulling free and starting after the slac//.

Lanton caught up to her in a few steps. "I don't know what to amke of you, you know."

"What about the slac//? That's more important."

"I can see they have some intelligence," he said. "But so do most species."

"Not like this," she protested.

"But it's a sliding scale—there's no line that separates intelligent from merely instinctive. One graduates into the other."

"Admitted."

They ran in silence for a moment, then Lanton asked, "So what else have you found out?"

"They originally were highland creatures, capable of something approaching true flight using the updrafts. They're moving here not because they have to, but because they want to. In the highlands almost all their labor is devoted to feeding. In this richer habitat, that won't be true."

"They're conducting a war, then—they don't feed on the Semu."

"Yes. They have scout-soldiers everywhere, working alone but part of an organized web. The Semu are a race in garrison."

"My sympathies are still with the Semu—perhaps even more so now."

"I don't doubt that the Home Worlds would consider them our closest kin. But that's not the point, is it?"

Ahead, the slac// had come to a stop and were waiting. "You admit the Semu are intelligent," said Lanton.

"Yes—though I think it's of a lower order."

They reached the slac//, and (double-whistle, click) extended a sailstrut toward the ground. "Here."

There were two blackened circles, each a meter across. A few stalks of fast-growing grass poked up through the low mound of ash.

"I don't understand," said Lanton.

"The Semu have a ritual when they kill a slac//," Wells explained. "They immolate it."

"So two slac// were killed here."

"No." Kneeling, Wells raked her fingers through the ashes and came up with a slender bone. She handed it up to Lanton and continued sifting.

"This looks like a human radius."

"It is." From the ashes she plucked the blackened cylinder of an implant radio. "This is Marisa—or Terry."

"But the rest of the bones—"

"The Semu take souvenirs—trophies."

Lanton stared at her. "The Semu killed them? They thought they were slac//?"

"Not thought. They reacted to a particular set of stimuli—the color, diving—and ignored the anomalies."

"They ignored a lot, in that case."

"We've seen the Semu aren't very flexible conceptually."

Lanton turned the bone over in his hands. "But the biotelemetry—we should have seen they were dead. The EEG was normal—only the high temperature—"

Wells shook her head. "The substance Gision Ah used on the arrows was a tranquilizer. I don't think Terry and Marisa were dead until the Semu burned them. Your slac// wasn't."

Lanton drew a deep breath, then exhaled. "So little to take back," he said, staring at the ashes. "And now I have a problem, don't I?"

"I hope so, sir."

Lanton toed the ash and said nothing.

"There are *two* intelligent species on Semu, and they're competing for essentially the same niche. The slac// have the individual physical and mental advantages, and the Semu are countering with social adaptation."

"And whichever side we come in on, wins," Lanton thought aloud.

"Yes. With all respect, I suggest it's not a choice we have the right to make."

"Is there any chance the slac// can be persuaded to return to the highlands?"

"None. They feel as though they have finally discovered a food heaven."

"To leave the Semu alone, then."

"That calls for a moral development neither side has come close to achieving."

"Working with both, then. Your opinion."

"The slac// are in a better position to take advantage of the contact. And is creating and juggling a balance of power our role—like we were lords of the planet?"

Lanton did not answer immediately. Instead, he signaled Nixon, instructing him to ferry the gig to them. Switching off, he gazed at the circle of ashes with a troubled expression.

"Captain?" Wells said softly.

Lanton rubbed at his right eye, turning half away. Wells knew he was not thinking of slac// and Semu but of his two dead crewmen. Finally he turned back.

"You enjoy complicating my command, don't you?"

"In this case, yes."

"You flirted with insubordination."

"I'm a naturalist first. I thought it worth the risk. Or am I being premature—what are we going to do? Do I need to keep on flirting?"

Lanton smiled ruefully. "Please, stop. There is only one option that makes sense to me. We'll do what any polite human would do when he accidentally comes upon an arguing couple—quietly leave and come back later." The slac// scattered suddenly at the approach of the gig. "Would you say they'll have this worked out in, oh, a hundred years?"

Wells smiled back, relieved. "A hundred years ought to be just about right."

THE CYPHERTONE

by S. C. Sykes

Anyone who has noticed the kind of electronic toys that are all the rage among the young will find this story both logical and perhaps even prophetic.

They were all the rage that Christmas. The computer game bombarded TV ads and left children clamoring and nagging parents for the new-age toy. Dan Morgan, remembering how hoola hoops had swept his neighborhood like a colorful tidal wave when he was a kid, gave in and bought a Cyphertone game for his nine-year-old son. It was a deceptively simple game, Dan mused, as he watched Jarrod shred the wrapping from the box. Designed like a pie-sized black flying saucer, the computer game challenged one to repeat an increasingly complex pattern of flashing lights and sounds. Four colors—red, blue, yellow, and green—flashed in ever-changing random sequences, accompanied by four electronic audible pitches.

"Wow! Cyphertone!" Jarrod whooped, placing his hands Ouija-board fashion on the colored panels, already expert in theory from watching the commericals inserted between slices of Saturday morning cartoons since early October. Cass paused in her admiration of the silk gown Dan had selected for her, to watch her son's enthrallment with the toy.

"I'm glad you remembered to get batteries for it," she said later as they cleaned up the Christmas-morning leavings of bows and boxes and exuberantly rainbowed wrappings.

"It was damned expensive for a game," Dan grumbled. "It'd better last longer than last year's air-hockey game."

"You broke it, Sweets, not Jarrod."

"That's beside the point. Are you going to save all this paper again? You never use it."

"Just the big pieces. And the bows. You never know."

While Jarrod was down the block showing off his new bike to his friends, Dan paused in the clean-up to try out the computer game. When he placed his fingers on the pie-wedge colors nothing lit up. He pressed the panels gently as he'd seen his son do, but still the toy remained silent.

"Damn, it's broken already."

Cass looked up from her paper folding. "Already? Are you sure? Did you read the directions?"

"Where's the box?"

Cass rooted through the piles of paper. "I think you already burned it in the fireplace."

"I'm so efficient," Dan sighed, replacing the game on top of Jarrod's spoils. "The kid didn't read any directions. How come he knew how to work it right off?"

"The miracle of television. If you got up every Saturday morning at dawn you, too, could become a computer-game expert and be able to sing every cereal jingle on the air as well."

"I think I'll pass. You know what they say about old dogs."

"Let old sleeping dogs lie. Lay?"

"Old dogs, new tricks. You're mixing clichés."

Cass stood and held her new filmy negligee up to her. "If you've heard one cliché you've heard them all. Is this me? Is it really the real me?"

Dan waded through the Christmas paper. "Let's go upstairs and find out," he grinned, nuzzling her neck.

"Ouch, you're sandpapery," Cass giggled, pulling away as Jarrod bounded in.

"Where's the Cyphertone?" the child asked. "Are you guys gonna do mushy stuff all day?"

"Only if your father consents to shave. The Cyphertone is on your pile. Take your plunder up to your room and wash your hands. Dinner's almost ready."

"I wanna show my Cyphertone to Mike and Kevin."

"Later," Cass said.

"But it'll only take a minute!"

Dan cleared his throat. "You heard your mother." How much he sounded like his own father, he thought. Patterns of response learned in childhood. Some day Jarrod would probably say those exact words to his own son. Other classic parental responses were: "We'll see. Ask your mother. That's the last time I'm going to tell you. Do it now! When we get home . . . by the time I count to ten . . . how many times do I have to tell you? Apparently enough times until the patterns were transmitted unbidden to the next generation.

Dan lay down his newspaper to watch his son sitting cross-legged on the floor playing the Cyphertone game. It had been two weeks now and the child showed no boredom with the game, unlike his other toys. In fact he seemed increasingly preoccupied with the flashing lights and oddly harmonious sounds. He actually opted to play the game in lieu of watching television at times, a miracle unto itself, Dan thought.

"Let me try it," he said finally, dropping the newspaper. Jarrod seemed not to hear him, continuing to repeat the pattern flashing before him. Each time he made a mistake the computer made a harsh dissonant sound and a new pattern was begun, one light and sound at a time. A green light flashed. Jarrod pushed the green panel and repeated the pattern. A green and yellow light flashed, accompanied by the soft pleasant sounds. Jarrod pressed the green and yellow panels and was rewarded with a third color and sound. When the pattern built to twelve color combinations and sounds Jarrod made a mistake and had to start over from scratch.

"Hey," Dan said, getting down on the floor with his son. "Let me try it."

Jarrod was oblivious.

Dan touched him, amazed at the child's deep concentration. "Jarrod?" Only then was the trance-like focus broken. Jarrod looked up at his father and for an instant Dan caught a look in his son's eyes that shocked him. It was as though a stranger was looking at him, someone much older and far wiser than a nine-year-old boy. Then the gaze faded and the child was there again.

"What's the matter, Dad?"

"What? Oh, un . . . can I try your Cyphertone game? It looks like fun."

"Sure. Here." The boy handed over the toy. "Know how to do it?"

"Of course. Just repeat the pattern, right?"

"Right. And if you goof, it gives you a raspberry sound. Better start with the easy level. You gotta get eleven in the right order to win at the easy level. I'm working on level two. I have to be able to do twenty in a row. So far I can only get to thirteen before I blow it. My unlucky number."

Dan sat cross-legged like his son and placed his hands on the four plastic panels. "Nothing's happening."

Jarrod giggled. "You gotta turn it on." He pointed to the small switch Dan hadn't noticed.

"Oh. Right. Okay Cyphertone, let'er rip." Dan got to five before he messed up, much to his son's glee. Cass came into the living room and stood watching.

"Time for supper, children," she said.

"Damn! You made me miss," Dan said, starting over.

"I did not," Cass argued. "All I said was . . ."

"Hush, I can't talk and . . ." The Cyphertone raspberried him again. Jarrod rolled onto his back, laughing.

"Dinner is on the table," Cass said.

"Inna minute," Dan said. "Let me get to eleven first."

Cass watched in bemused silence as her husband hunched over the game. Each time he got to seven before he pushed the wrong sequence and had to start over. "It'll be leftovers before you win," Cass sighed.

"Shhh . . . It goes faster after you get to five. Did you notice?" Dan said. "If you pause for more than a second you're out."

"Wait till you try level two," Jarrod said. "I know a kid at school who broke through level three. But he's a super whiz at math. Also he takes piano. I think it helps. Dad, can I take piano?"

"What's piano got to do with playing the Cyphertone?" Cass asked.

"I don't know. It's sorta muscial. Bobby Avery can do it with his eyes shut, up to ten sometimes. He says it makes a song in his head."

"Will you two be quiet?" Dan grumbled. "I can't concentrate."

Cass looked heavenward. "Why can't you watch the 6-o'clock news on TV like other husbands? I only need one nine-year-old and the position is already filled. Chow is on, gentlemen. Wash up."

"You heard your mother," Dan said to Jarrod.

"You too, Dad."

"Be right there."

Cass and Jarrod were at the table eating when Dan sat down, triumphant. "It beeps when you win," he announced. "Got eleven in a row. Not so hard, once you learn to concentrate."

"Only took you thirty-five minutes," Cass agreed.

"You exaggerate. It was only . . ." he glanced at his watch and blinked. "Well, it *seemed* like it was only a couple of minutes. How 'bout that?" The meatloaf was cold but Dan thought it best not to remark on its condition.

"You going after level two, Dad?"

"Sure. Why not? Twenty should be a snap."

Twenty was not a snap. To Dan's chagrin, Jarrod accomplished the feat first and went on to level three which built to a pattern of thirty-two lights and sounds. The last level, level four, was fifty-six flashes, so it was rumored, but no one Jarrod knew had managed that impossibility yet.

"It's all a matter of concentration," Dan explained to Larry Hayes, as they commuted into the city to Vossman Associates, where they worked in the electrical engineering department. "A fascinating game, really. It sort of hooks you. You can't stop once you get started. You just keep wanting to work it, over and over. It's been three months now and Jarrod still hasn't tired of it. He's working on level four now, the highest level. I'm putting in level three. I don't know if I'll ever retain thirty-two moves at a time in a sequential series."

Hayes chuckled. "My kid wants that game for his birthday. I think it would drive me crazy."

"I'll say this," Dan smiled, "I credit that game for improving Jarrod's grades. I'm not sure how, but the kid is making straight A's for the first time ever. And he begged us, *begged* us, to let him start piano lessons. Said it would help him with the Cyphertone. Can you imagine it? I had to beg *my* parents to let me *quit* violin when I was his age. Strangest game I ever saw."

"Well, our children belong to the computer age, that's for sure," Hayes nodded. "My boy is eleven and he's got four

. . . no, five different computer toys and games. Half of 'em
I don't know how to work. Makes you feel obsolete, you
know? God, whatever happened to baseball and kite-flying,
and tag? All that physical stuff? Now all they do is sit around
pushing buttons. I'm not sure I like it."

"Dan?" Cass poked her husband in the darkness. "Dan,
wake up."

"Wha . . . ?"

"Wake up."

Dan yawned and rolled over. "What's wrong?"

"Listen. Don't you hear it?"

"Hear what?"

"He's at it again."

Dan listened. Faintly he heard the slightly melodious
sounds of the Cyphertone, coming from Jarrod's bedroom.
Fumbling for the clock in the darkness, he frowned at the
luminous dial. "It's after three, for chrissake. What the hell's
he doing playing the Cyphertone at three A.M.?"

"I told you I thought I heard it last night, but you said I
was nuts. Dan, go take it away from him. This is getting ridiculous. It's all he ever does anymore. I'm sick of hearing it.
I think it's affecting him."

"How?"

"I don't know. It just . . . he's changing. Haven't you noticed?"

"He's making top marks in school. Maybe we have a budding Einstein on our hands. What's so bad about that?"

"It's not his grades, Dan. It's . . . something else. Have
you seen the way he looks after playing that damned game?"

Dan had seen the look in Jarrod's eyes more and more often. It was the same stranger's gaze, but now it lasted longer
and faded more slowly after the child surfaced from his intense concentration. He had not mentioned his observation to
Cass, thinking it was possibly a figment of his own imagination.

"It's like he's mesmerized," Cass went on. "I can't seem to
reach him for a few minutes afterward. I think the game hyp-
notizes him. I almost have to call him back from somewhere.
It's eerie. Surely you've noticed it?"

Dan hadn't had time to bother with the game in months,
but he knew vague wisps of that feeling of distance after
playing with the flashing lights. He had compared the sensa-

tion to that of deep meditation, or at least what he suspected deep meditation must be like, since he had never had the time or inclination to explore yoga or TM or any of the other esoteric mind exercises so popular when he was younger.

"Well, are you going in there, or do I have to?" Cass yawned.

Dan groped for his slippers under the bed, then decided to hell with them. Without bothering to turn on any lights which would leave his pupils screaming for darkness, he padded down the hall to Jarrod's room. The gentle beeps continued. Dan counted them silently at the door until the raspberry sounded after fifty-one.

He opened the door, prepared to congratulate his son for coming close, then reprimand him for his late hours, but the scene before him let all words dissolve unspoken. There in the darkness a small, shadowed figure sat cross-legged in the center of the bed, spine ram-rod straight. As the lights flashed yellow and red and green and blue, they lit up Jarrod's face in a garish way. His eyes stared, unblinking, unseeing, as his hands moved to the colors and sounds. Dan felt a slight chill creep down his neck as he watched the child, a stranger, work the computer at a dizzying speed. Something whispered a warning in the back of his mind. It told him not to disturb the boy under any circumstances. He was to stand quietly and wait until Jarrod . . . returned. To jar him now would interfere with . . . with what? With the transfer . . . He did not question the term, nor why he thought it. What he was positive of was the delicate stage of his son's corporal state. He stood and watched in silence, counting the pattern of lights and notes. Fifty-one, fifty-two, fifty-three and then the soft, chiding series of dissonant beeps scolded the child for his mistake. Jarrod took a deep breath and set the game aside.

"How long have you been watching?" the boy asked, turning on his bedside lamp.

"A few minutes," Dan said, feeling somehow guilty, as though he had intruded upon someone in deep prayer. Jarrod looked up at him and Dan felt slightly awed by the intensity of the wise and benevolent gaze. His child was not there, in those eyes, but the being who watched him now was somehow silently reassuring him that all was as it should be.

"Do you know what time it is?" Dan asked at last.

"I don't need much sleep anymore. Very little in fact," Jarrod replied, somber. "I feel quite rested. Does the sound of the game bother you?"

"No . . . Jarrod . . . don't . . . play the game anymore."

"But I'm almost there."

"I know that. I just think . . . you should put it away for a while, that's all."

"If you could reach level four, you could come with me," the boy said quietly.

Dan felt a damp fear settle on his skin. He moved to his son's bed and sat down. "Come with you where, Jarrod?"

"There."

"I don't understand. Where . . . do you go?"

"It's . . ." The child blinked, and the stranger within him faded softly away. "It's . . . somewhere else. . . . They . . . teach us."

"They teach you what?"

"What we have to know."

"Who are *They?*" Dan wasn't sure whether Jarrod was asleep or awake. He was too old for fantasies, having left behind his last invisible playmate when he set out for nursery school five years ago. He must be asleep—sleep-talking instead of sleep-walking, he thought.

"I'm not asleep," Jarrod said, reading his thoughts. "You don't need to be afraid for me. They won't hurt any of us. They're trying to help."

Dan picked up the computer game. "I think you've had enough of Cyphertone for a while."

Jarrod reached out for the object. "No! Please! You can't take it away. I need it. Dad, I'm almost there!"

"The hell you are. Now go to sleep."

"I've gotta have it!" The child who was his son was totally back now.

"Maybe later. Not tonight. Now go to sleep!" With that Dan reached over and turned off the light. "We'll talk about it tomorrow." His father's voice. Exactly the same. How many cliff hanging emergencies in his own childhood had been shelved "until tomorrow?"

"So that's Cyphertone," Hayes said, as Dan held the game in his lap, on the train.

"This is it. Caught Jarrod playing with it at three this morning. Wide awake. I think. He's up to fifty-three flashes in a sequence. I've got a funny feeling that if he hits the jackpot he'll be carted off to the loony bin. He really had me scared last night."

Hayes reached over and took the game. "How come?"

"I'm not sure. He was rambling on about how 'they' were teaching him something, and that he 'went' some place. He really had me worried, Larry. The damned game is hypnotic, almost like an addictive drug. I took it away from him."

"Sure you're not just jealous that you can't crack level three or whatever? How do you play it?" Hayes punched the panels with no results.

"I'm not sure I should show you. Imagine the whole country walking around with zombie eyes after breaking through level four."

"Your kid gets zombie eyes?"

Dan reached over and switched on the game. A red light lit up and beeped. Hayes followed the pattern. "I wouldn't say zombie eyes exactly. But . . . they change. I get the feeling somebody else is looking at me—somebody much older and far more intelligent than I am. It's pretty creepy."

"Hush, I'm concentrating," Hayes said.

The ticket conductor came by. "Hey, Cyphertone," he grinned. "My kid has one of those things. Damnedest game I ever saw. He's working on level four and he's just seven years old. So smart he scares me sometimes."

Dan felt the flash of sweat through his clothes. Somewhere in the back of his mind he remembered part of a poem, about music and children and . . . colors and . . .

"I did it" Hayes crowed. "I got eleven. On to level two."

"The Pied Piper of Hamelin!" Dan said aloud.

"What?"

"A computerized Pied Piper. Cyphertone is . . ." he stopped. Crazy. Absolutely inarguably insane. "Larry, I'm going to be late to work. Tell Wilson. I have to go to the library about something."

There it was:
"His queer long coat, from heel to head
Was half of yellow and half of red . . .
. . . And green and blue his sharp eyes twinkled,
Like a candle flame where salt is sprinkled . . .
. . . And ere he blew three notes (such sweet

Soft notes as yet musician's cunning
Never gave the enraptured air)
There was a rustling that seemed like a bustling
Of merry crowds justling at pitching and hustling,
Small feet were pattering, wooden shoes clattering,
Little hands clapping and little tongues chattering.
And, like fowls in a farmyard when barley is scattering,
Out came the children running.
And all the little boys and girls,
With rosy cheeks and flaxen curls,
And sparkling eyes and teeth like pearls,
Tripping and skipping, ran merrily after
The wonderful music with shouting and laughter."

Dan sat back and ran his fingers over the toy. Was it a toy
at all? Or was it something much more? Were children playing a simple child's game, or were they . . . being trained?
And if so, by whom, and for what? Were the lights and
sounds innocent, random patterns, or were they some kind of
code that progressed steadily from Dick and Jane simplicity
to infinitely more complex information? Dan pulled from the
shelves several books on meditation and hypnosis and
checked them out.

"Meditation And Your Karma," Hayes read, sorting
through the stack of books on Dan's desk. *"States of Consciousness, Programming And Meta-programming In the Human Biocomputer.* You giving up gothics for some lighter
reading, Morgan?"

"Maybe I should be looking into science fiction," Dan muttered, looking up from *Hypnosis And Alpha Waves.* "Better
yet, full-fledged fantasy. I think it's loony-tune time."

Hayes pushed the books over and perched on the edge of
the desk. The Cyphertone game lay belly-side up in the center of the desk, disemboweled, its batteries piled in a heap.
"What did you take it apart for?" Hayes asked. "You can't
pirate a copy. It's patented."

"I can't get into it."

"Into what?"

"That . . . thing." Dan poked at the game with a screw-
driver. "There is no visible means of prying the thing apart to

look at its innards without destroying it. I can remove its batteries. That's it. I'm about ready to take a hammer to it."

Hayes *tsked* and shook his head. "Makes you feel that inferior, huh?"

Dan sat back and placed his hands behind his head. "Larry, I called the toy company that makes those things. I wanted to talk to whoever invented the damned thing. You know what they told me? They said nobody invented it. A *computer* invented it."

"A computer gave birth to little baby computers?" Hayes nodded solemnly. "Well, it had to happen some day. Let 'em start thinking for themselves, the next thing you know, all they think about is sex."

"But nobody knows who fed the information into the computer, so it could come up with the . . . game. Nobody seems to be directly responsible for it."

"So what? It's a helluva toy. Stores can't keep 'em in stock, they sell so fast. I went to five different toy stores looking for a Cyphertone for my kid and they were all sold out. I was put on a waiting list, for crying out loud. They'll call me, they said. For a toy!"

Dan leaned forward and slowly replaced the batteries in the game. "If it *is* a toy," he said.

"What's that mean?"

"Larry . . . let's suppose you were a . . . oh, say a 'missionary', and your job was to go into the jungle, search out the most primitive, savage, superstitious, distrustful, and nasty heathens on the face of the earth. Your mission would be to bring those stone-age minds into the 20th century. You have to educate them, teach them, introduce them to technology so far beyond their undertsanding that you scare them to death with your every appearance. But it's your job. You have to do it. Because they're going to kill themselves off very shortly in their ignorance. They don't know how to . . . survive in their own backward little culture. They live in their own filth and garbage. They're unbelievably cruel to each other. Their tribal customs are so barbarous that they attack and kill others out of fear and superstition. You get the picture?"

Hayes got up and moved over to a leather chair. "Sounds like a fun weekend."

"Be serious. This is just hypothetical. A supposition. How would you go about accomplishing your assignment?"

"Well . . . frankly I'd be opposed to it," Hayes shrugged.

"I think they should be left alone. I support the law of natural selection. Maybe they're supposed to kill one another off. Maybe they weren't meant to survive."

Dan slowly rubbed the Cyphertone in his lap, as though it was a magic lamp. "No, your personal philosophy can't apply in this situation. You're supposed to save them from themselves. How do you start? Remember, they run away at the sight of you. You can't get near them."

"Do I know their language?"

Dan frowned. "Well, you know *some*thing about them because you've studied them surreptitiously for, oh . . . years, let's say. So you know something of their . . . patterns of communication. But their vocabulary is crude, very limited. It's more advantageous for all involved that they learn *your* language. How would you teach them when you can't even approach them openly?"

Hayes examined a hangnail and then rummaged in a pocket for nail clippers. "Dan, why are you asking me these things? Are you trying to tell me you want to join the Peace Corps?"

"Humor me. I'll explain later . . . maybe."

"Well . . . let's see. I'd have to communicate with them in some way that wouldn't frighten them."

Dan nodded. "Good idea. How?"

"I'd . . . see what made them curious. What things they liked. Like, say they really dug trinkets or mirrors, or tools or . . ."

"Toys?"

"Yeah. Stuff like that. I'd maybe . . . leave stuff in a certain place under a tree till they got to know the spot and came to take away the gifts. Maybe I'd leave food. Things like that."

"But you'd stay out of sight?"

"At first. Then maybe . . . I'd leave a picture of myself tacked to the tree." Hayes beamed at his sudden inspiration. "That's what I'd do. Then later on, I'd show myself . . . just a little, at a distance. Then closer. And so on."

Dan continued to stroke the computer game. "Remember, these are savages. They could kill you out of sheer terror. You've got to lead them into the modern world and you don't have a lot of time in which to do it. They're slaughtering each other daily, and fouling their villages. They're disease-ridden."

"I can't imagine who would want to bother with them," Hayes sniffed. "Oh my God. You're trying to brace me for something. I can tell. Wilson's moving us to a branch office in South America, right?"

"No. Please. Just bear with me. This is important to me like you wouldn't believe."

"Probably not. Okay. Let's see. Not much time . . . then I'd have to reach the ones who'd be least afraid, the ones easiest to teach, the most trusting, the . . ."

"Children?" Dan's knuckles were white as he grasped the Cyphertone.

"Yeah, the kids. I mean, that's what the missionaries do in all those foreign countries, isn't it? Get the kids into missionary schools, teach them Bible songs . . ."

"Good way to teach a language, wouldn't you say?" Dan asked. "Remember your first French phrases in school? Everybody learned Frère Jacques, right?"

"Yeah. And then the kids can teach the parents. Before you know it, voilà, technology; i.e., TV antennas in the jungle. And everybody's saved. The end. Do I get a prize? A commendation? Something?"

Dan got up, moved across the room and placed the Cyphertone in the man's lap. "Suppose I told you that I don't think this thing is a toy at all . . . that I think it's a . . . tool. A teaching tool. Designed specifically for children. Its purpose is to train the mind so efficiently that a child can learn deep meditation techniques in a very short time. He can accomplish in weeks skills and techniques that take a yoga master years to achieve. What would you say to that?"

Hayes looked down at the colorful object in his lap. "This? Are you serious?"

Reaching for one of the books on his desk, Dan nodded. "Listen: 'At the highest stage of meditation, one loses sense of self and identity, joining in a oneness with God. . . .' Jarrod is just this side of Nirvana. About three beeps away to be exact. When his ability to concentrate is adequately . . . trained . . ."

Hayes stared at the toy as though fearful that it would give him an electrical shock if he moved. "What? What happens?"

"I don't know. I'll lose him. In some way . . . he'll be lost to me forever. I know that much. Larry, I know this sounds as crazy as they come, but I think these 'toys' were dropped on us from . . . some place else."

"Russia?"

"Farther away than that."

Hayes lifted the Cyphertone gingerly and placed it back on Dan's desk. "Just . . . how far away did you have in mind?"

"Oh, a few light years, maybe."

"Uh huh."

"You think I've snapped, right?"

"Absolutely. Listen, Dan. . . ."

"I don't care! I think it's crazy, too. But dammit, it makes sense. They're using these things like . . . tuning devices. When a kid's brain is emanating alpha waves or whatever, long enough—*strong* enough—it's like a hot line to . . . God only knows where. Maybe it's a way for them to travel here, for all I know. They get inside the kids' heads, set up housekeeping, train them for . . . what's coming."

"Close encounters of the weird kind," Hayes agreed, rubbing his temples. "You're out of your gourd, buddy. You know that, don't you? You think they're sending their 'missionaries' here to educate the savages?"

"Something like that, yes."

"Dan, go home. Take a week off. I'll explain to Wilson. It's the Bowers contract. It'll work out. . . ."

"I'm not crazy, Larry."

"I didn't say you were. You're tired."

Dan sighed and rubbed his eyes. "Yes. I am tired. But I'm not crazy."

"Go home."

When Dan entered the house, he could hear Cass in the kitchen, humming, as she chopped celery for a salad. The TV was on in the living room, an afternoon game show in progress.

"Where's Jarrod?" he asked, entering the kitchen.

"Oh! You scared me half to death! What are you doing home so early?"

"Headache. Where's the kid?"

"In the living room, I thought. You want beets with the chops or green beans?"

"It doesn't matter."

"Okay, beans. Jarrod hates beets." Cass felt Dan's forehead. "Hon, you want an aspirin? You don't look good. You really don't."

"I'm all right." He went back into the living room and turned off the TV. Faintly, from somewhere upstairs, he heard the soft beeps of a Cyphertone.

"He borrowed one from a kid down the block," Cass said as Dan took the stairs two at a time. "Said something about breaking through level four. . . . Dan, don't be angry with him. . . ."

As he reached the bedroom door the melodious beeps ceased. Dizzy from the rush of adrenalin, he pushed against the door. It would not open. "Jarrod! Jarrod!" he yelled, heaving his weight against the barrier. Suddenly, with a rush of wind that smelled of clover and ozone, the door banged open. In the center of the bed and somewhat above it, a pale blue shimmer was fading even as Dan stumbled across the room. He lurched toward the Cyphertone which had, moments ago, rested in his son's lap. A small indentation in the bed was still warm. But the child was gone.

Gingerly, Dan sat on the edge of the bed and took the candy-bright toy onto his lap. He sat quietly until his fingers stopped shaking, then whispered, "Hang on, son. Wait for me, Jarrod. I'm coming. Daddy's coming."

Slowly, he began to play the game.

THROUGH ALL YOUR HOUSES WANDERING

by Ted Reynolds

Here's a wonderful romp through many alien worlds and many very alien minds. But there is a system to these visits which will become apparent in time. John W. Campbell delighted in speculation of this sort. And Isaac Asimov published this one, although the denouement runs directly counter to some of his most vigorous campaigning.

Quiet brooded over the cold-darkened land eastward. Low over the horizon stretched a bar of heat, dimly visible. The air was utterly still.

Thomas Simmons's roots gripped the uplands soil tightly. Restlessly the tree opened and closed his umbrella, testing its operation. As, minute by minute, the far border widened, lightened to the ultraviolet, pressed upwards relentlessly into the dark sky, Simmons began to sense the objects in his nearer environment, and strained to make out more.

The growing warmth broadened across the land, and the eastward slopes began to draw out of the night chill. Simmons stood at the crest of the low pass through the hills to which the tree had sped his course the day before. Downslope to the east lay a free blow of several kilometers, hindered only by a scattering of gray snappers. Sensing his presence, they had drawn a loose cordon across the lower pass during

222

the night. Simmons could see the dull sheen of their back-plates as they waited for him below, among the brittle stalks of night-growth.

Still the mounting light spread. The first warning puff of breeze eddied about him, fluffed his leaves, caught fretfully at his half unfolded umbrella. Simmons prepared himself for the sunrise.

Further off down the slope past the crouching snappers, well beyond where the pass opened onto the plain, a huge dome raised a wide arc, shining vermilion in the opening dawn. It would cover most of the slice of land Simmons could hope to pass. The tree observed it, seeking the best way around it. He would have to angle left as sharply as possible.

Topping the farthest horizon, the rim of the sun cut a vast swath across the borders of his perception. Round and violent it arose, its boiling surface too hot for him to observe directly. From the horizon rose long lines of glazed vapor, drawn explosively upwards towards its irresistible thermal summons.

And with an abrupt explosion, the dawn wind struck like a stone. It hummed and shrilled through his branches. Feeling his roots give, Simmons planned his course once more and then, as the hurricane reached crescendo, retracted roots and spread umbrella to the storm. On the instant he was swept downslope toward the waiting snappers. Gauging his feint precisely, the tree sideslipped gradually, tacking towards the snapper on the farthest left of the pass; when only a few hundred meters away, he spilled air from the leading edge of his umbrella, spun rapidly to the right, collapsing all branches and drawing them in close to his trunk, and was whipped on the gale past the snatching pincers with centimeters to spare.

Safe, Simmons extended the umbrella again and drove on before the dawn wind. Behind him he perceived, amused, that the snapper that had missed him had, in its eagerness, over-reached its center of gravity; the dawn wind had caught it and was hurling it down the slope from ledge to ledge, fragments splintering off into the air at each rebound. *Stupid snappers,* Simmons thought, and forgot them, looking forward to the next obstacle.

The ground fifty meters beneath him had vanished in a seething broth of dust, small stones, bits of night-growth swept up before the shattering dawn wind. The sun had not yet cleared the horizon; but the storm would drop shortly, he knew, as abruptly as it had begun. The dome extended too extensively across his line of flight to tack by completely, Simmons realized, thinking rapidly. He should, to be safe, try to clear the dropping arc of the dome at as low a point as he could manage, so that less harm would result from a drop if the wind broke before he was past it.

But on the other hand, the thought came to him unexpectedly, *if I aim for the very highest point of the dome itself* . . . The tree began to flex the corded muscles that controlled the umbrella.

Wait a moment, thought Simmons, *that's crazy. That's two hundred meters up. A fall from there would kill me.*

He tried to jockey the umbrella back where he wanted it, but his limbs wouldn't respond.

I know what I'm doing, said the tree. *Be quiet and enjoy the ride.*

Who are you? asked Simmons. *I thought this was me.*

I don't know who you are, said the tree, *but you're certainly not me. You're some sort of free-riding passenger. I noticed you in me for the first time this morning.*

The umbrella pitched to hold the tree on a direct course for the peak of the dome. It was rising higher and higher above the plain, which now skimmed by far beneath its roots. Scattered boulders loomed through the haze spun up below, and the flung matchwood of night-growth smashed by the dawn wind. Closer and closer drew the purple dome.

I really thought this was me, Simmons repeated tentatively.

No way, thought the tree. *I've always been me. Look, I don't mind your being along, but this is going to be cutting it pretty close; would you mind keeping quiet for a bit?*

Simmons quieted and watched the approaching mass of the dome speed towards them. He was extremely perplexed, and more than a little nervous. As far as he knew, this was the only body he had, and the only senses he was familiar with; if *they* weren't his, where *were* his? The only memories he seemed to have were umbrella tree memories; for example, that a dome such as this, perhaps to be met with only once in a dozen times around the world, was set up by non-tree creatures from some other world, beings so incurious about their adopted surroundings that they never emerged from their shells. How could he remember things if they weren't his own memories? It didn't seem quite right, somehow.

Just because I share my memories with you, the umbrella

tree was saying to him off-handedly, *doesn't mean they're* yours. *Now keep your thoughts quiet, or we're both of us in trouble. Or have you forgotten what will happen if I make a mistake up here?*

Simmons thought about that, as quietly as he could. If the dawn wind broke before they reached the dome, or on the other side before they could drop to a lower altitude, they would end up as kindling. He followed the expert maneuvers of his pilot with a certain amount of personal concern, feeling the subtle play of guiding muscles up through every branch and twig, as the tree played the wind for their lives.

It was timed perfectly; just as the skimming roots passed over the rounded apex, the cyclone shattered, and the tree plummeted a mere score of meters, striking the far curve and sweeping down the side, plunge broken, to land upright on the soil a few meters from the dome.

Beautifully done, Simmons said in relief after a moment. *Really lovely work. I don't think I could have done that.*

You're telling me? thought the tree, a bit smugly. It was already striking its roots down through the loam. *I've been looking for a break like this. Now I'm planted to the leeward of the best windbreak I've seen in my life. With any luck I'm protected from the dawn wind. I've wondered what it would be like to stay in the same spot a few days. Now maybe I'll find out.*

The air beneath the now warmly tinted sky was fragrant with useful tastes. A rivulet of delightful effluvium ran out from the nearby dome. Simmons could already feel the tree's taproot begin to imbibe healthful material from the undersoil.

Can I stay here with you? asked Simmons. *At least till I find out who I am? If you're really sure I'm not you.*

It's not really up to me, said the tree with a certain lack of concern, being quite taken up with its new surroundings and prospects. *It seems to me like you're already leaving, though.*

Simmons felt it then, a certain rarefication of his senses, an unravelling around the edges of his perception. His presence here in the umbrella tree was indeed beginning to appear highly problematic.

But then, thought Simmons desperately, *if I'm not you, who am I?*

I don't know, thought the tree. *But I suggest you find out. You can't really get down to anything till you know who you are. Good luck.*

Simmons tried to hold on; but he felt himself slipping out, the feel of the delicately woven leaves fading first, then the finely articulated branches; and then, drawn from the close awareness he had shared with the tree, he was split off from the complex central nexus of the only being he knew. He passed, grieving, out from the body he had thought his, and the cold took him. If this was not death, it was very like it.

The man in bed stirred slightly. The figure beside him leaned forward intently.

"Can you hear me, Tom? Are you all right?"

The eyes of the man in the bed did not open. Faint words emerged from his mouth.

"But who am I? Who am *I*?"

"You are Thomas Simmons." The auditor spoke quickly, clearly. "Can you hear me?"

The man's head tossed very slightly from side to side. "I know *that*," he said with a touch of asperity. "But who *am* I?"

And abruptly his body froze, all motion stopped; and wherever Thomas Simmons was, he was not in that body on the bed any more.

He was somewhere else.

One thing seemed clear. He was no longer a guest of the umbrella tree. Whose guest he might be he did not yet know. Or, hopefully, perhaps this time he was himself. That would be a relief.

Through his senses of vision, touch, and pressure came conflicting messages which confused him. He tried to sort them out. He was pressed heavily upon some solid medium, while a more viscous one flowed past him. There was, however, an obliqueness to his position. Colors swelled, merged, and broke, fleeing in one general direction. He tossed these elements back and forth, trying to let them cohere in a comprehensible pattern.

There was here none of that immediate and effortless identification with body, environment, and memories, that had led him to believe he was himself the umbrella tree. His host's inner mind, assuming there was one, was still opaque to him.

Curved limbs extended before his vision, cupped with octopoid discs. These were methodically clamping to surfaces and slowly pulling forward the body in which he had found himself. Yet he himself had no connection with the volition which moved them.

Hello, thought Simmons carefully. *Is anyone there?*

No response from his presumed host. The extremities continued their slow weave, found a surface to their pleasure, adhered to it strongly, and propelled the sprawled body forward a few centimeters more.

The movement was crosswise and upward over a flattened metallic surface. The skatelike torso was being pulled up after the clinging tentacles like an overloaded gunny sack. About ten centimeters of liquid with a strangely heavy heave to it was lapping the body, washing on down the slope. Again the limbs reached out, and pulled once more.

Can you hear me? asked Simmons. *Hello, there.*

No response; although somewhere Simmons sensed an odd susurration, a rising and falling pitch, slowly pacing the movement of this body. The creature, it seemed, was humming at its work.

It was moving up a meter-deep groove in the slope, testing and touching the walls as it ascended. It reached a spot where the side of the trench was wet with beaded droplets, an incipient metal melt. The tentacular limbs lingered on the spot for a moment. Then one reached back to a pouch between humped shoulders to extract some pinches of powder. Several layers of this were rubbed carefully over the weakened layers. Then, with the same slow persistence, the ascent continued.

There was a slight shuddering felt through the surface up which they were crawling, and the host drew itself together momentarily, huddling. A rushing from above, a sudden build of pressure, and abruptly they were bathed completely with a drench of warm liquid, draining from above. This new fluid preserved its level, refusing to mix with the earlier liquid.

The humming stopped, and at last the slow thoughts of Simmons's host came ponderously up. *As expected. The Flelt has melted. Soon will come the melting of the Rayl metal. The final test of my channels. So far, so well.*

It heaved itself up another short distance, and came to an abrupt halt, quivering with a new thought.

But the Flelt metal is not flowing straight down the slope as it should. It flows in part from the western quarter. That is not expected.

It huddled into itself again, considering.

If the mass of Rayl also slants down from the west, it may breach the walls of my channel. That would prevent the proper downflow of melt. But I have often checked the westward rise. What can be diverting the flow?

Don't ask me, said Simmons. *I seem to be just along for the ride.*

The host, absorbed in its own meticulous thoughts, was oblivious to him.

The upper portion of this channel is almost certainly in fair order. I checked it the day before. But this new divergence can spoil my whole plan. It must be sought out. Yes, I must examine the westward rise.

It turned weightily to the side of the trench and lifted its grasping limbs to the top of the bank. With one strong pull it raised its whole body to the top of the channel bank. Here it sprawled, again half out of the flowing metal, scanning the upward slope for anomalies of vision or pressure.

There is something up there that should not be, it thought. *It is a wall, an unwanted embankment.*

It paused to consider a moment.

The melt pushed aside by that barrier will breach my channel banks. I shall have to destroy it rapidly.

It inched up the slope, observing the barrier as it neared.

Yes, it is all Gurjek and Krohn rock. It will not melt. This is not natural. It is a thing that has been done, and I must undo it.

Reaching the barrier, the host began to grip portions of the wall with its powerful limbs, and exerted pressure backwards and forwards, dislodging the material and rolling fragments downslope.

A wide enough breach here, it thought to itself, *and the melt will flow through, and not pile up against my channel.*

There was a sudden surge of pressure through the atmosphere and, an instant later, through the surrounding fluid; although not detectable in auditory terms, it was indisputably an angry roar. Thought from another source followed immediately, cold, heavy, and directed.

You will not destroy my wall. You will desist at once.

Simmons's host methodically dislodged another large chunk of rock and flung it downslope before turning lumberingly to its left. Approaching from that direction was another creature; and, assuming similarity of species, Simmons saw that there was far more complexity and heft to his own hindquarters than he had been able to see yet. Behind the flattened head and the grasping forelimbs rose humps and hollows of hardened armor, each with its own array of tiny manipulative limbs and organs. It was a landscape in miniature. It had the appearance of inertia embodied. And it was very angry.

You will not touch my wall again, its thoughts boomed around them. *You will be cast in small pieces down this slope yourself.*

This wall cannot stand, said Simmons's host, unmoved by the approaching menace. *It destroys my downslope preparations.*

It makes mine possible, said the other. *Move from here, that I may rebuild your desecration.*

I shall not move nor desist, said the host. Simmons could feel the strain of muscles in its hindquarters as subsidiary feet braced its body more firmly to dodge or charge at need. *My needs are essential. I have a plan that must be fulfilled.*

Your plan is of no consequence, stated the newcomer flatly. *In the unlikely event that you are not impervious to reason, I shall shortly, and only once, explain. This wall protects an area of this slope from the coming melt; within the shelter of this wall lie structures, completed by myself over the past season, which must be protected from the incipient melt and refreeze. No one has had such a plan before; I have had it, and shall fulfill it. Now go.*

Retracting his shoulder blades, Simmons's host projected a long spike from his upper anatomy. It thrust outward toward the other like a standard.

Trivial, it thought. *Such petty protected domains, I hear, are common in the luxury lands. Now I, in the improbable hope that it may sway you to retreat and preserve your unnecessary existence, will explain to you that I have a plan which is one indeed. One which your trifling wall is endangering. Downeast from this point I have, with care and forethought unexampled, prepared a series of channels and sluices, fully constructed of the unmelting materials, leading to a complex of formed molds. The melt shall follow these channels, enter these molds, and refreeze to their forms. From them I shall retrieve implements, tools and apparatus to cut and dig and build through the whole cold season, to form larger structures and molds for next melt. No one but I could have formed such a mighty plan, and no mere cretin like you shall disrupt it.*

Enough cant, cried the other. *Prepare a rapid plan for meeting your demise, for it approaches.*

Boys, boys, cried Simmons, or something like that; but he was just not on their wavelength. The two began warily circling each other in a slow dirgelike tread. From far above on the slope there came another, far stronger shuddering, and the feel of something terribly heavy and totally massive plunging downwards towards the warriors. Their stomping shuffle was not interrupted, but Simmons imagined that the fight was going to be broken up pretty soon. He was awfully afraid the Rayl had melted.

Simmons was not displeased to find himself parting, being withdrawn from this scene. Parting he certainly was; he was being pulled from his temporary lodging by unimaginable forces, and tossed carelessly out again into the lonely wastes of non-identity.

Simmons's eyelids fluttered open; and the auditor was beside him instantly, smoothing the hair on his forehead. "Take it easy, Tom," she said. "You've had some kind of an accident, but you're in good hands. Don't talk unless you feel up to it."

Simmons's eyes stared at her awhile, and then moved on to examine the rest of the visible room in slow wonder. Finally, after seeking other forms of communication which seemed to be unavailable in his present state, he stumbled into speech.

"I don't suppose this is me either," he said. He fell silent.

His auditor was uncertain of his meaning. "I think you'll be all right now," she said carefully. "Just don't strain yourself. We've been worried about you for hours."

Thomas looked up at her again, wondering how long he would be able to stay in this world. "I don't know the purpose either," he said slowly.

"The purpose of what, Tom?"

"That is what I do not know," he said.

And with a rush, he was drawn inexorably away by the wash of the tide that held him, leaving a tenantless body on the bed.

There was no need or chance for choice of destination for Simmons. He was not sure if he was being reeled in by one or a many, but whichever, it was united in taking him over. It/they seemed pleased to have him. He was being maneuvered into position, set up, plugged in, turned on. He could sense nothing but the fact of the manipulations until, like the snap of a switch, there he was. Not that *there* had much placeness to it; there was no sensory data that he could isolate, no body, no environment. There was only the knowledge that he was in proximate juxtaposition to a very volatile them/it which was quite aware of him, and very eager to communicate.

Hi there. Well, if those weren't words, or if there weren't words at all, that was the very idea. *Glad you could make it. Someone new in town. How've things been going for you?*

Simmons felt himself surrounded by cheerful back-slapping joviality.

Casting about for some form of organ for communication, he found none; but his response came through anyway, and seemed understood. *Not too hot, I guess.*

A shame. Well, he's right now, he got here, didn't he? Mind telling us who you are?

This was not the perfectly tactful question at this point. *Well, I'm not sure,* managed Simmons. *I seem, to have been more than one . . . person, recently.*

Don't worry about it, the friendly presence(s) said reassuringly. *Isn't it obvious he's got a memory leak? No harm in asking, is there? Just give us a quick rundown on what you know.*

That wouldn't take long, said Simmons wryly. *I'm not sure I know anything at all.*

A mercurial laugh ran about him. *Then he's certainly come to the right place. We know a bit of something about everything. Just ask it, you've got it. Hey, pal, what are friends for?*

Simmons gave up searching for body or senses that obviously were not available to him. *Then you could probably be a great help,* he started. *If you could give me an idea . . .*

Say, are you Fendrain? Crastite? Floxine? I'll bet he's a Chrondoseer; look how mixed up he is!

I haven't the slightest idea what I am, said Simmons. *Really.*

That's simply fantastic, said his auditor(s). *Someone check it out. Can we get a fix on this one? Take a few circuits off the Grondel border. Can we spare them? Sure, this is a real find. Tell us what your gig is.*

It took him a moment to realize the last was directed at him again.

I don't know who I'm supposed to be, he said again. *Or what I'm supposed to be doing. Or anything. I'm hoping you can help me. Who are you?*

Just us, tossed off the voice glibly, a single intonation through all the plural repartee. *He's not from anywhere around here. Not within a gross of parsecs, at the least. Boy, but he must be a wide-open TP pickup for sure. Can we get a directional reading on his source? Not yet, give us time, will you?*

Simmons roused himself to break into the steady, self-interrupting stream of words. *Hey, look, you seem to know a lot more about this than I do. Can't you give me some basic background or something? It sure could help me out, the way I am now.*

Why, sure, pal. You look like you need it. Ask questions, that's the only way you'll ever find out anything. Wherever he's from, it's pretty nearly dead in towards the galactic core from us. Could he be from the Shaft civilizations? Hey, buddy, are you from anywhere near the Shaft?

I don't think so. I don't know what that is.

Hey, you are in a bad way. Someone with your pickup, anywhere in that way, should have been able to tap into the Shaft like crazy. Look, we already told you his memory's leaked. Wait, did we check for deceit? Of course, first thing, do you think we're asleep? He's sincere then. Just ignorant. Chances are he won't stay long; he's on a swing cycle not under his control.

Simmons's temper reached snapping point, and he surprised himself by the rage of his scream. **Will you shut up a minute!**

There was a sudden silence in his mind.

Simmons collected himself. *Look, if I don't have much time, let's use it. You tell me something, then I'll tell you something, as long as I'm here. Okay?*

A short pause. *That makes sense. Well, that's what we've been doing, isn't it? Of course it is. He didn't have to interrupt. We forgive you, you don't have the education; not your fault. Look at this readout, he's not from the Omphalos. Hell, we knew that, he's from in towards the core. Look, friend, where were you just recently?*

If you'll listen, I'll tell you. Just a little while ago I was a couple of hours on a planet so hot that metals melt and freeze like ice.

Get that? Right, sounds like Menkar inner-planet stuff. That would make sense, if he's cycling counter-clockwise. He may make the Omphalos yet. Did you notice his thought of freezing ice—that pins down his home world type pretty narrowly . . .

Simmons raised a mental shout. *That's right! Ice is natural to me, and melting metals aren't. I must be from . . . No, wait, the dawn storm seemed quite natural to me too, at the time.*

Dawn storm? The voice mingled with excitement. *We don't know that one. Tell us . . . Oh-oh, we've got trouble along Grondel. Full force to the border, and step on it.* The voice cut off abruptly.

Simmons waited awhile, surrounded by silence and nothing else. At last he thought cautiously, *Hello? Are you there?*

The voice answered, more subdued than before. *Partly,* it said. Then, *You're that involuntary mind-switcher, aren't you?*

Wasn't it you I was talking with before? asked Simmons.

Probably, said the voice. *Almost certainly. But I wanted to ask you a question.*

That figures, sighed Simmons.

It's like this, said the voice. *We gather you've been in the position of having perceptual senses, right? Could you maybe tell us what that's like? We've never been able to get it straight.*

Senses? You want me to describe what they're like?

If you could.

Simmons considered briefly. *My experience is short, but it seems to depend on the body one is in. Maybe you are aware of differences in thermal distribution, or optical wave length, or pressure gradients . . . whatever. And whatever it is, it's translated into a spectrum of qualitative differences with a . . . with a special feel to them.* He was pretty pleased with himself. It was the first time, in several hours of remembered existence, that he had thought something out and explained it, and it felt all right.

But the feel, the voice persisted. *That's the part we don't get. What's it like?*

Tell me what you're like, first, asked Simmons, adding, *I think it's your turn for answering.*

I'm . . . just us, said the voice. *Most everybody else we come across seems to have senses, but they can't get the feel across to us.*

Do you have . . . bodies? asked Simmons.

How should we know? inquired the voice. *I'm not aware of any, but, if you're right about senses, we might have them and not know it, check? There was a visitor a very long time back who claimed, while he was talking to us, to be standing in the center of a plain filled with millions of crystals, sparkling and shining, he called it; and he thought they were us. But we're not sure; I think it may have been his idea of a joke. Anyway . . . wait, you're beginning to slip away! Can we hold him? Against the Omphalos? No way, you've got to be kidding. Hey, fellow, come back any time, we've a lot to ask you; we never did get where you're from. Look, there's a new thought construction at Malerithon, hurry . . .*

Simmons found himself deserted and disconnected even before he was drawn away.

Simmons's eyes opened again. A look of bewildered surprise came over his face.

"I've been here before, haven't I?" he asked. "Where is this?"

The same woman was still beside the bed. "You're at home, Tom. We brought you right here from the lab. Do you know what . . . ?"

"What's happening to me? What's going on?" asked Simmons in a rush. "Tell me everything, what it all means."

She brushed the hair back from his face gently. "We're still trying to figure it out, Tom. You've been slipping into a series of strange comas all evening. The main thing . . ."

"Why am I? What's the reason for this nonsense? Tell me everything you know."

"There's plenty of time, Tom. The main thing is to keep quiet. You seem to be getting better every time you come out of your comas. Do you think you could eat . . ."

Simmons pushed himself up in bed with arms he had not realized he had until that moment. "Do I belong here? Is this my body? Can I stay . . ." He froze a long moment, head tilted up towards the other, and then slowly his gaze fastened on a corner of the ceiling, but an infinite distance beyond it. His lips parted.

"The Omphalos?" he asked in surprise, and his elbows gave way.

The woman leaned over and felt his pulse. Turning, she beckoned to the doctor across the room. "He's gone off again," she said.

"The cycle remains constant," said the doctor. "Just about two hours."

The woman looked down at the figure molded by the bed linen. "Call me in just under two hours, then," she said.

She took three steps, collapsed in an armchair, and in seconds she too, in her own way, was gone.

Simmons's first panicky reaction was to hold his breath, which was patently ridiculous. If his new body hadn't been adapted to its environment, it wouldn't have been alive to receive him. Still, he filed the incident under his growing collection of possibly important clues; it could be that *he* did not come from a totally water-breathing organism.

The muddy bottom upon which he wallowed stretched away in every direction until it vanished in the murk. Sight was soon swallowed up by that gloom. To compensate, he appeared to possess a very useful ability to pinpoint the location and texture of objects at fairly great distances from the patterns of flow in the currents about him. He allowed his body to observe his surroundings, and in turn observed those observations.

Uncouth plants trailed quiet fronds through the slowly stirring water. They did not show great complexity, and he felt they were not as intelligent as the other plant he had known, the umbrella tree; but he kept an eye on them. With the other eyes he noted squat structures in the middle distance, slime-coated and blunt-edged, which might have been constructed or perhaps just came that way. Here and there over the flat bottom rested unmoving dark rocks of all sizes. These he regarded curiously, feeling that he himself now resembled a rock, but they preserved their immobility.

Simmons tried to move, but found it impossible. There seemed no musclar response to anything he requested of this body, which seemed a hell of an unlikely survival setup for any creature. He was confined to his senses, which included neither mouth nor ears that he could locate. There was only the heavily concentrated feel of his own body, the limited sight, and the detailed picture built up by every nuance of direction, pressure, temperature, and salinity of the passing currents.

He focussed again on the scene before him, and wondered. Surely that nearer rock, downslope from him, had moved some distance. Not directly towards him, but it was certainly nearer than it had been. He watched it a while, but it didn't stir.

There was something familiar about some of this, far down beneath that part of his mind which he could read at all; the gentle sway of the water-plants, the drift of the murky water, the squelch of the mud along his sides. On the other hand he was certainly not familiar with this body itself. He could dredge up no image of what he might look like.

He was sure now that the rock had moved again while he hadn't paid attention to it, angling obliquely towards his nearer left. He centered his perceptions on it, determined not to let it evade him again.

Nothing happened for a long time. Then, far off to his right, he perceived the abrupt eruption of a large bubble, rising rapidly up through the water. His eyes would not move, but he sensed it soaring upwards, trailing long tendrils, from several of which dangled heavy objects resembling mud-encrusted boulders. It rose and vanished in the distance above.

Simmons twitched at the realization that the nearby "rock" had arrived, unobserved, at a position only a few meters from him, and was observing him stonily. From this distance it appeared like a mere rock; Simmons supposed that he could now guess what he himself looked like.

The body appeared clumsy. The upper portion bulged outwards like a guzzler's abdomen over a too-tight belt. The face, as marked out simply by the three eyes, was wide and full; the eyes were, incongruously, a vivid and penetrating blue. The full length of the creature's sides and back was lined with numerous fringes or cilia which swayed delicately in the currents.

Simmons, in the absence of any known speaking apparatus, pondered how to communicate. He tried to blink significantly, then to ripple his own presumed cilia, both without success. What a useless body this was. He could do nothing with it.

A thought entered his mind. *Go home. You don't belong here.*

Simmons mentally cuffed himself for forgetting that telepathy was possible. He left it to his bodily reflexes to speak, while he provided the concepts.

I was just wondering whether I do belong here or not. Are you quite sure I don't?

The creature shuffled nervously through the ooze, a few centimeters this way and that.

Not here, not here! You're some sort of thing from outside. Now get out. You're bothering the family.

I can't go home, protested Simmons. *I don't know if I've even got one, much less where it is if I do. I don't know how I got here, or how to leave, either.*

Likely story, said the other grumpily. *That's what they all say.* It settled itself into the ooze. *If you refuse to leave, then just shut up. I'm not in the mood.* It shut its eyes, and the feelers along its sides subsided into stillness.

There was a long pause. Simmons wasn't sure what he could gain from further conversation anyway. Presumably he would eventually switch bodies again. If it turned out he had to stay here, he could reopen discussion at that time.

But he couldn't hold to that resolve. He needed information. He remembered *ask questions, that's the only way you'll ever find out anything,* and before that, *you can't get down to anything till you know who you are.* He hoped it was good advice; it was all he had.

He awakened thought channels. *I'm really sorry to trouble you,* he thought, *but you see, this is my situation,* and in one burst of recollection he poured out his remembered life of the last few hours, a torrent of images and feeling without words. He noted a thread of self-pity in the flood which he had neglected to perceive in himself until it had been objectified. Am I as unstrung as all that?, he wondered.

The creature's eyes snapped open, and it solemnly regarded him for a long moment. Then it sent out a cry.

Hey, Mama. Mama!

From nowhere, a large rock loomed up downcurrent from Simmons.

Don't shout so, Zeef. Your daddy's working.

But there's another invader in Corrlee. A very peculiar one.

So? That happens often enough. That's what Corrlee's for, isn't it, Zeeferry?

But this one's in trouble, said Zeeferry. *Listen, Mama,* and the whole content of Simmons's experience was spilled in an instant into yet another mind.

Simmons waited while the new arrival digested the information. Then she turned her bright blue eyes towards him.

Well, sir, you do have troubles, don't you?

I have been thinking that, admitted Simmons.

I wish we could help you, said Mama, *but I don't really see how. It's about all we can do to keep the Omphalos in order, without worrying about all you odd creatures out there somewhere. But I do hope you find your way home all right.*

So do I, chimed in Zeeferry. *Imagine, not even knowing where you belong. I'd go stark wild!*

Would you like a bite of something? asked Mama. *That, at least, we can give you. None of your previous hosts have even thought of that, more shame to them.*

He can't eat, Mama, said Zeef, sniffling in sympathy. *He's a botch-baby.*

Simmons wondered that he didn't feel more surprise to be squatting here on a sea bottom being offered chicken soup by a couple of boulders. Chicken soup! Where had that swum up from? He added it to his file.

The most help you could give me is information, he suggested.

Mama was silent a moment. *I really shouldn't tell you much about the Omphalos,* she said at last. *We like what we've got here, and don't care to spread it all over. We've had quite a few invaders in Corrlee's body, though most of them knew where they were from, and what they were after. You wouldn't believe the odd and often quite unpleasant things that have sat right where you are now, sir. Things that want to take us over, or steal our heirlooms, or make us build stupid things for them, or devour us for food, or change our opinions . . . it's terrible.*

She sounded frightfully depressed.

It must be hard on Corrlee, thought Simmons, feeling about without success for any traces of prior occupancy.

Mama laughed, a mental trill that produced a contagious mental grin from Simmons. *Oh, there isn't really any Corrlee any more,* she explained. *She was a botch-baby, who would have died anyway. We just keep her life-functions working, boost her TP glands, and remove the rest of the brain. That way, any of you space-hopping monsters will turn up in one of them, you see, instead of one of us. And of course, sir, as*

*they are quite immobilized, sooner or later they get bored
and go back where they belong. No successful invasions of
the Omphalos, no sirree.* She laughed right up the scale again.
Like a lightning rod, thought Simmons, and then, thoughtfully, added *that* to his file.

It's quite kind of you to tell me all this, ma'am, said Simmons. *If you have such reason to distrust all outsiders.*

Oh, but you shared, said Mama. *You gave us all your
thoughts and feelings, Mr. Simmons; how can we distrust you
now? Not that we understand you very well, but now that
we've read you, we have to respect you.*

There's not very much to read, is there, Mama? said Zeef.
He's only about seven hours old. That's even less than me!

He's certainly far older than you, Zeeferry, said Mama patiently. *But something catastrophic happened to him a short
time ago, and he lost himself. Now he has to start all over
again. It's a real shame. Well, I'll do what I can. Here's
something to take with you, sir, a small token of our good
wishes for your eventual homecoming.*

And suddenly a flood of comprehension plunged into Simmons's mind. It was the totality of the Omphalos, the great
bubble filled as completely with love and caring as with
water; all gathered into a single wrapped image of comfort
and home, of family and security, and fastened at the end
with a neat little mental twist that would prevent him from
ever letting it out to anybody else.

And in the moment of receiving that image in all its poi-
gnant beauty, Simmons was drawn away from the Omphalos
on stronger currents, as irresistible as unseen.

Simmons came up weeping and the women was right there
holding him tightly.

"It's all right, Tom. It's all right. I'm here."

He reached out his own arms and held her, gasping uncon-
trollably.

"What is it, Tom? Are you all right?"

He released her and dropped back on the pillows, his hands
drying his eyes as naturally as if they were his own. He
caught his breath.

"It was the Omphalos," he said at last. "It hurt."

She leaned over him, soft hand stroking the wetness from
his cheek. "Talk about it if you want," she said. "Only if you

want. We don't understand what's happening to you yet. But we're trying."

He looked at her and his eyes moved across her face as if at last he really was seeing her for the first time. "I've just been shown the Omphalos," he repeated. "An amazingly tight nexus . . . somewhere. A place to belong. A home." He tightened. "God, I want a place to belong. But not the Omphalos. That could never be mine; that's for someone else. There must be a place for me somewhere." He looked about, at the room, the draperies, the lamp, the fishtank, the clock.

"This is your place, Tom," she said with a quiet certainty. "You belong here. And soon we'll be able to keep you here. Each time you come back you stay longer. Eventually we'll have you back for good. Don't worry."

He was fingering the white sheets with wonder. "I wish I could believe it," he said, and then, looking at her again. "And you are . . . who?"

The quick twist of pain across her face was erased in an instant. "I'm an old friend, Tom," she said calmly. "You'll remember when you're well."

"So this is supposed to be my place, my world," he asked, flexing his fingers curiously. "This is presumably my own body?"

"How could you doubt it?"

"I've had so many worlds and bodies lately," he said slowly. "I'm not quite ready to trust this one yet. But . . . I do seem to keep coming back here. And I can't contact any prior occupant of this body . . . I'd like to believe it," he said again.

There was an odd look on her face. "Other worlds," she said. "Other bodies? Tom, just where do you *go* when you . . . leave here?"

He might have answered her, if he had still been around.

Simmons found himself in surroundings which eased him with their familiarity. The fact that he still could not remember his own proper environment, to which the sense of familiarity must refer, bowed before the relief of feeling he was in a world more like his own than he had seen in all the hours he could recall.

He was standing (standing! it seemed so natural) on stumpy legs upon what could only be termed a balcony overlooking what was almost certainly a city, and over him was a sky packed with what might very well be clouds. The slight difference (the bases of the buildings were more constricted than the apices, the predominant hue of the atmosphere was a redundant orange, and his body seemed to be thoroughly encased in bark) seemed relatively inconsequential in comparison to what he had been through lately.

The body in which he found himself, even if it did call to mind an overgrown tree stump, seemed one he could get used to. At least it was an individual.

His host was immediately aware of his presence.

"Well, isn't this a surprise? I do believe I have a guest. Welcome, sir. Can you read me?"

"Quite well," said Simmons. "Excuse me for intruding."

"Not at all, not at all. A pleasure, indeed. Allow me to introduce myself, alf-Quatr let-Mimas, court artiste of Phlange. Would you like to see some of my recent productions?"

Without waiting for the other half of the introduction, Alf-Quatr turned from the balustrade and strode on rootlike peds through an oval doorway into the inner rooms. Here were shelves, tables and mantels cluttered with intricate objects of unclear import. Alf-Quatr paused a moment and then, reaching out an arm Simmons couldn't help thinking half a meter too long, removed an item from a wall niche.

"You like this, I hope? It's a throwaway, of course, but I think it has a certain charm. You see what I'm getting at, I suppose."

Simmons found it hard to focus on the wrought object, as his host, to whose visual apparatus he was confined, was not looking directly at it. It was composed of twisted filaments of some plasticine substance, filigreed into a climbing structure of uncertain significance.

"I don't get it," Simmons admitted. "I don't know what it's supposed to be." There were really other subjects he'd rather discuss while he was here.

Alf-Quatr let-Mimas snorted. "Supposed to be! You *are* an idiot, aren't you? See here, if you're a total ignoramus, you might as well go back where you came from. Nobody asked you here, you know."

Simmons found himself mentally backtracking from the force of the other's scorn. "Hey, I'm sorry," he said. "I just meant this is so different from anything I'm used to. I don't know how to judge it. I can certainly see that it's beautiful."

"It is, isn't it," said his host, mollified. "It won't take you long to get used to appreciating this. You're really quite for-

tunate to have chosen me for a patron. Some of these soi-dis-
ant artistes are content with quite shoddy work. Here, let me
show you something a trifle more avant-garde." He picked his
way across the crowded atelier. "This is a little thing I've
been playing with off and on. I know you'll . . ."

Alf-Quatr was interrupted by what was obviously the mental equivalent of a knock.

"Not now," Alf-Quatr thought in irritation. "I have a
guest."

"I am aware of that," came another thought petulantly.
"And it is most ungracious of you to keep him to yourself.
You know I wish to be informed of all visitants. Now pass
him over."

"I protest, your highness," Alf-Quatr was hissing furiously.
"This gentleman is a connoisseur of the arts, and has no interest in your political trivialities . . ." Somehow during this
exchange, Simmons found his viewpoint switching. Alf-
Quatr's atelier faded, and he was looking out from a stumpy
body seated upon what, with all allowances for variations in
culture, was a recognizable throne. From being his primary
host, the court artiste had become a mere distant voice
mouthing threats.

"Well, now," said his new host, severing the connection
with the still sputtering Alf-Quatr with an airy mental wave,
"now that you have been saved from that unparalleled bore,
allow me to introduce myself. I am Khar-Naste let-Ragel, Imperiarch of Phlange, which, if you will allow me to say so, I
feel I have built into one of the finest states, if not *the* finest,
in all outer Ghornest. I trust you will permit me to give you
a small tour of my domain . . ."

"Dearest," came a mental whisper from a new source, "do
let me have a moment with the guest first. You know you
promised."

The Imperiarch of Phlange stamped his peds on the dais in
anger. "Will you lay off, woman," he lashed out. "Can I
never have the pleasure of a state visit without the distaff side
sticking in its superfluous oar?"

"How dare you speak to me like that, Naste, and in company? I've got a good mind . . ."

Khar-Naste cut communication abruptly, and slumped
sulkily back into his throne. "She doesn't, you know. Have a
good mind. Never did. But what a body; built like a glurch.
We'd better be scarce for a bit till she cools off . . ."

At that moment the double doors to the chamber burst open and an infuriated Alf-Quatr let-Mimas appeared. He flung himself forwards towards the throne, waving a sharp and elongated implement of vaguely fatal appearance. The Imperiarch shot to his peds, grasping for a projectile on the wall behind him. Simmons found himself tossed helplessly aside, and hung a confused moment unmoored between hosts, before another mind grasped him and stealthily drew him away . . .

He was crouched in the sunlit corner of a courtyard, under the overhanging sweep of one of the inverted cone structures. Small agile limbs, the bark hardly formed, lifted an object before his new eyes. It was a small carved image of . . . well, it looked like a treetrunk.

"Isn't dolly the most wonderful dolly in the whole universe? I just bet you like her a lot, because if you don't . . ."

Simmons sat up abruptly in bed.

"Tom. You're back, aren't you?"

He nodded, peering at her concerned features carefully. "I remember you."

Her face glazed with relief. "Thank God."

"Yes, you're here every time I pass through this damned place. If you can't do anything about my condition, I guess I'll have to. Get out of the way, please; I'm going to get up."

"Maybe you'd better stay put a little longer, Tom. It might not be safe . . ."

"Good lord, woman. Whatever is happening to me, it isn't sickness. Don't do me any favors." Then, looking at her stricken face, "It's not that I don't appreciate your trying to take care of me, but it isn't necessary."

He swung his feet out of bed and, with the precarious caution of a beginner, rose and took two steps. With a mild smile he stopped before her and made a slight bow.

"Allow me to introduce myself," he said regally. "Thomas Simmons, of many forms and many places, briefly here and at your service. I have been surveying the myriad lands of my realm and shall, for your pleasure, report to you upon their condition. As far as I am aware, none other has ever had the dubious honor of performing such progresses."

"Please, Tom, I'd rather . . ."

"But first, if you will, a bit of something would be appreciated. I presume, even in this forsaken corner of the universe, you creatures consume esculents."

She nodded, and reached for the phone. Picking it up, she spoke into the mouthpiece without dialing, "Send up some food. He's hungry," and replaced the receiver.

"Very good," said Thomas Simmons. "And now let me explain to you what the situation is. You see, I hop from world to world. I suppose it's not the usual thing to do, but I'm doing it. It's just a matter of time before I learn to control the procedure, and then, well, it will become a virtue rather than a liability. So don't worry about me, okay?"

"You believe you actually go to other worlds?" she asked in amazement.

"I'd rather you didn't even look like you're doubting me."

"But . . . could you be going telepathically?"

He looked at her in surprise. "What do you know about telepathy?"

"Well, that's what the experiment was for, Tom. You really don't remember? We were trying, for the dozenth time, to induce a telepathic state in you!"

He stared at her, considering. "Then," he said at last, "the experiment worked with a vengeance. I am now in telepathic communication with creatures light years off, on some random basis. Is this induction, by the way, something you know how to turn off?"

She shook her head at that. "But, Tom, if you are telepathic, you must know what I'm thinking. You couldn't get into the minds of creatures way out there, and not into human minds here on Earth, could you?"

There was a long pause as he looked at her, weighing her point, and then she just managed to catch him as he fell.

Simmons was paying closer attention to what was happening to him now. The new pull entered his mind with a definite jolt, far-off but unmistakable when one was attuned to it. For a few instants the new element was simply *there*, without content, and then it began to permeate his thoughts with a sense of authenticity which his human environment could not counter. *There* became more real, more vital, than *here;* and then here and there changed place. There was an instant in which the single pull enlarged, became multiplicated into a large number of smaller component attractions; and then his own mind, at some level he could not control, selected one, seemingly at random, and the others faded. The chosen attraction loomed and became *the* world. Multiplicity faded, and he was in a new *here*.

If any of that made the least sense.

He rested, and tried to survey his situation. His surroundings were confusing, but he had come to expect that; he would have been perplexed had they not been. But the amorphousness of everything, the ambiguity of these shifting flashes and glooms, did seem oddly familiar in its very surrealism. He didn't seem to have a body at all. He searched for a host mind.

When he located it, he understood. His host was asleep; the fragments which passed before him were scraps of dreams.

That was all very well for his host, but Simmons didn't have much time here, and didn't care to fritter it away in sleep. He strained for wakefulness, and felt his host stirring and struggling against him in protest. Simmons proved the stronger. He opened their eye.

An inner voice, still drowsy with interrupted sleep, was wondering what had woken him. Simmons ignored it, and explored his new senses and surroundings.

Sight: dim lighting, falling through translucent over-head panels into a domed and circular chamber. He was immersed up to his long jawbone in some cool liquid in ceaseless bubbling motion. Sound: a continuing susurrus of fluid flowing and falling; a gentle wind brushing the outside of the chamber. He sensed his own body, the long, easily bending coils resting in the liquid like a many-limbed salamander. The coils seemed so multifarious that he suddenly doubted they were all his own, and belatedly remembered to seek out his telepathic sense. There was someone else in the chamber with him, he realized, another sleeper, coils intertwined with his own.

The voice of his host, outraged and terrified, had been screaming silently inside him. He now listened to it.

What's happened to me? Am I mad or ill? Why am I awake when I should be asleep?

"It's all right," said Simmons soothingly, in control of things. "I won't hurt your body in the least. I'm sorry if I've disturbed you, but I shall be gone soon."

Currents, I AM mad, said the interior voice, and then, after a brief pause, broke out again. *You get out of me right now, you understand? Right now! I'm a decent glowl, I keep*

*healthy, I work hard, you've no call to get into me like this.
Now clear out.* There was a strong undercurrent of panic.

"I'll be out when I'm out," said Simmons, as consolingly as
he could. "Just relax and stop distracting me. Or tell me
about your world and people; I need all the information I
can get." He flexed himself, ascertaining how his stubby
limbs-cum-fins could be used to propel him; it involved
muscles lining the entire lengthy hose of a body.

Stop wiggling me! cried the other. *Have you no sense! No
shame! You'll WAKE THE WIFE!*

Simmons shrugged, a more impressive gesture in this body
than in his previous one, and glided out of the wife's coils.
He made an investigatory circuit of the room. It was a
pleasant change to be in control for once.

The chamber was ringed with louvered window slots.
Through them he could make out, through night gloom, an
extensive sea. The chamber seemed a capping turret atop a
high tower in the midst of the waters (or acids, or whatever).
He could dimly glimpse islets in the distance, as well as what
might be two other far-spaced towers, and thin dark lines
running towards them, perhaps low causeways.

Pushing his host's head out the window slot, Simmons
looked back at his tower. Water was being pumped up to this
height, where it bubbled in the turret and then flowed down
the sides of the tower into the ocean again.

There was a stirring in the pool behind him, and an increasing sense of wakefulness from his sleeping partner. He
drew in his head again. *Oh, newts,* came from his host. *I
warned you. Now I'm in for it. Will you please, please get
out and let me try to handle this!*

Across the chamber, the other creature opened its large
scarlet eye and gazed reproachfully at him. A tightly directed
communication, revealing no more than necessary, came to
him.

*Why are you wakeful in sleeptime, Tideraker; are you ill
or mad?*

The interior ego tried to assume control and failed. It whispered desperately. *Demon, tell her . . . tell her a change in
the sound of the osmotic pumps woke me.*

Simmons managed to produce a rather ragged directed
beam of thought. "Esteemed wife of my host, I am a random
visitor to your charming world, and find myself for a brief
period encapsulated inescapably within the mind of your

worthy spouse. Pray forgive any temporary inconvenience this visitation may cause to eventuate." It seemed impossible for him to produce less effluent conversation with this mental communication apparatus.

The wife eyed him steadily for a long moment, and then oscillated her upper torso in what he identified as a knowing nod.

Mad, she said. *I thought so.*

"Your husband is not insane," said Simmons, "merely temporarily incommunicado. You deal at present with a creature who, though alien to this place, bears no intention of ill to you or yours."

I must inform the authorities, she mused abstractedly. *The sooner the better, for all concerned. Oh, Tideraker, how could you?*

Deep within, Tideraker's thoughts were raising a mournful chant, all about how could this have happened to *him,* who had always kept his mind alert and his scales polished and his morals scrupulous. No help there.

"I am of the hope that you do not in precipitation bring woe upon your husband, who is totally without responsibility for my present occupation of his august person," suggested Simmons wryly. "By the time the authorities have arrived, I myself shall long since have departed."

The wife gave him a sullen stare and then slithered to a cluster of paraphernalia along the far wall, where she occupied herself with the local equivalent of making coffee. *If there were truth in that mad contention,* she tossed off indifferently, *it would hardly absolve my husband. To allow himself to be possessed by some monster freak from outer space hardly smacks of a proper guarding of his own mental state, now does it?* She hesitated, neck fin poised with a small scoop over a metal vessel. *Are you having coffee?* She didn't think "coffee," but that was what she meant.

"Why not?" said Simmons. The wife flipped the scoop over, and stirred the resultant mixture.

Now, she said, returning towards him, her upper torso protruding sternly from the pool, gazing at him eye to eye, *Tideraker, it is not too late for me to retract the call to the authorities. But you know in that case I must have assurances from you, as to your future conduct. I must think of our status and our nestlings. For myself, I do not fear, of course, any possible behavior of yours.*

"What kind of assurances?" asked Simmons. "Out of curiosity merely."

Inner shout. *Holy currents, she'll want the cash and the keys!*

I want the keys and the cash, said the wife.

Give them to . . . no, don't. Oh, how did I let myself get into this? moaned Tideraker.

You must realize, said the wife, *that if this does get out, I will be severely blamed by association. You know I had hoped for more rapid advancement from you. Now that you are mad . . .* she shrugged, *you realize I will have to be given full power to keep it quiet, and handle the nest in my own way; or else have you turned over, so I can reestablish. It is hard, because I really do love you. Tideraker, but . . .* she sighed, *what else could any decent wife do?*

Simmons's first words on his return to Earth were, "I'm sorry."

There were others in the room, moving quietly about him; one handed him a sandwich. But his eyes were on the woman.

"I behaved rather unpleasantly to you the last time, I believe. I only hope you understand the strains that I'm under."

"That's all right, Tom. I do understand."

"No, but it was inexcusable. It won't happen again. Now, what are we going to do about me?"

A broad-faced man appeared beside him. "Hopefully, you're coming out of it yourself gradually. Six hours ago, you were hardly rational."

Simmons glowered. "You should be rational under what I've been through? Do you understand that I've actually been in six alien bodies, seven if you count this one, in just . . . how long?"

"About twelve hours," said the woman.

"We're beginning to believe you have," said the man. "And we'll want to hear all about them, eventually. It's just a surprise to be working on telepathy, and stumble on space travel. Well, astral projection."

The woman laid a hand upon his arm. "We hope that's right. It's such a relief to find it isn't a matter of physiological . . . or mental . . . breakdown."

Simmons looked from one to the other, and suddenly realized that he had accepted them as his kind. For better or worse, and until shown otherwise, this was his world. At least it was something he came back to. They have to take you in.

"We figure that if you really are picking up telepathic races out in the stars somewhere," the other man was saying, "and no human thoughts at all, it can only mean that humans just are null telepathic senders. It takes both senders and receivers for contact, and humans aren't either. We seem to have made you a super-sensitive receiver, and you still can't pick up human thoughts."

Simmons took a meditative bite of the sandwich in his hand, and discovered a yet unnoticed sensory capacity of this body. He liked the taste.

He spoke to the woman. "I'm afraid I've had to think of you as merely 'the woman' up till now. You do have a name, I suppose."

She bit her lip. "I'm Debbie. Deborah Simmons."

"Oh." He thought. "Not a sibling or something?"

She shook her head.

"Oh," said Simmons again. And then, "Say, look, Debbie, I am sorry. It will all come back to me, it's got to."

"Better get back to bed," said the other man. "Judging from past experience . . ."

"Oh, no," groaned Simmons, "I was just getting to like this place! You mean I'm about to go off again?" He let himself be led back to bed, still protesting. "What did I do to deserve this kind of treatment? I didn't ask for it, I don't want it. Someone else go world-hopping for awhile, huh? Why can't I just stay home decently, and get to know my home and Debbie again and . . ."

The complaints sputtered out somewhere in the void.

Once again Simmons found himself in an unformed void prepared for yet another alien birth. Ages passed, while he strained for senses.

Is anyone here? he thought, and the thought receded from him in all directions, passing on without echo into the distances. There was nothing to sense with, nothing to move.

At the worst, he decided, he'd be here in nowhere for somewhat over an hour, and then returned to his own body . . . if that human one was his own. No, no more doubting; he had accepted the human role as proper to him.

There was an abrupt sense of shining motion, as of a streak of light running past him, and then flicking off as rapidly as it had appeared. "Yo!" said Simmons. "Someone here?"

There was a pause, and then another flash of light, slicing from one side of a newly perceived field of vision to the other with extreme rapidity. Then another.

"Wait," said Simmons. "I can't catch it."

The light reappeared, chastened to a lower rate; it turned and returned, like an array of marquee bulbs flashing on and off in fractional seconds, tracing out words before him in the blackness. "YO. CATCH IT. SOMEONE HERE. CATCH IT. YO."

"I can see words," said Simmons. "But I don't think we're getting very far."

The light reformed. "DON'T THINK, DON'T SEE. THINK WORDS, SEE WORDS. CATCH IT. GET FAR. THINK WORDS."

"You can only see the vocabulary I've used," guessed Simmons, and the lights leaped in triumphant agreement.

"YOU USE VOCABULARY, I USE VOCABULARY. WE GET VERY FAR. USE VOCABULARY."

Simmons settled down to vocabulary. His communicant learned rapidly. Soon Simmons felt ready to broach his problem.

"YOU THINK PROBLEM, I THINK . . ."

"Answer, maybe?" suggested Simmons.

"I THINK MAYBE ANSWER, MAYBE I DON'T THINK ANSWER. YOU THINK."

This looked to be a useful discussion. Aware of his time limitations, Simmons ran through the main points of his predicament quickly, and was rewarded with a full three-second cessation of the lights.

Then: "SEVENTEEN POSSIBILITIES NOTED. ONLY PROBABLE TWO, IN SHORT TIME WE TALK TO YOU. ON ONE HAND, YOU MOVE, BEYOND SELFWILL, IN JUMPS OF MIND TO MANY MINDTHINK PEOPLES."

"How does that work? And how can I stop it?"

"WHY STOP. CAN CONTROL, VERY MORE GOOD. WORK WAY MAYBE LIKE PROBABLE THIS."

The light went utterly wild, and produced a vivid rendering of a galaxy, spinning before him in silent glitter. Since each of those million unblinking stars seemed to be based on a stroboscopic flashing effect from a single moving light source, the motion of the point must have been rapid indeed.

Text appeared beneath the image. "OUR GALAXY," and then, with sublime understatement, "THERE ARE OTHERS."

"Uh-huh."

"IN LIGHT OF SORT YOU SEE. NOW, YOU SEE NOT MIND-THINK. IF SEE MINDTHINK, SEE GALAXY LIKE THIS WAY."

The Galaxy wavered and clamped into a new appearance. Most of the individual stars had winked out, but many sources shone more brightly, and the core glowed in close-packed splendor.

"SEE MINDTHINK AS LIGHT," blinked out his mentor. "ARE NATURAL PEOPLES MAYBE, PEOPLES' MAKE-AND-USE THINGS MAYBE . . . OTHERS. THIS MINDTHINK," a red pointer of lights darted about the stars, "VERY LARGE, LARGE CLOUD, PROBABLE NOT ALIVE THING, BUT THINK, VERY LARGE INTERESTING THINKS. HERE, HERE, MANY PLACE, NOT ONE PEOPLES, MANY PEOPLES, ALL NOT LIKE ALL; BUT ALL ONE MINDTHINK. OTHERS, HERE, HERE, HERE, HERE, ONLY ONE PEOPLES. BRIGHT IS LARGE THINK, NOT BRIGHT SMALL THINK."

Simmons was awed. He was trying to memorize as much of the Galaxy's layout as he could, but the complexity overwhelmed him. "Where are we now?" he asked. "And where is Earth?"

"MAYBE NOT CATCH," came the response. "YOU AS BODY NOW ON EARTH. WE MIND AND MIND MEET NOT IN ANY PLACE. BUT WE HAVE HOME PLACE HERE, SEE HERE, .67003% OUT FROM CENTRAL GALAXY. YOU ARE OF NOT-MINDTALK PEOPLES, NOT SEE HERE. NO MINDTALK LIGHT. BUT MAYBE PROBABLE CATCH WHERE. YOU GO TO OMPHALOS. WE KNOW OMPHALOS PEOPLES. HERE. SOME PEOPLES YOU MINDTALK TO, THINK YOU SOON GO TO SHAFT, MEAN CENTRAL GALAXY PEOPLES. SO PROBABLE MAYBE YOU PEOPLE ARE HERE." The marker slewed about a huge sector of the galaxy. "ON OTHER HAND, PROBABLE MAYBE NOT."

The Galaxy vanished, replaced by the schematic view of a planet rotating slowly upwards against a constellation-specked background. A red cross appeared on the planetary surface, and the view moved with it.

"YOU HAVE BODY AND MIND ON PLACE MARKED RED. YOU NOT CATCH MINDTALK. ON SUDDEN, YOU CATCH MINDTALK, AND . . ."

Above the horizon of the turning planet, the starry background suddenly exploded into new glows and sparks and clusters of red light.

"YOU SUDDEN SEE MINDTALK, LARGE, SMALL, FAR, NEAR. LARGE MINDBLOW. YOU FORGET SELF, GO FROM SELF TO . . .

YES, THANK YOU, TO AMNESIA. SAME TIME, MIND EMPTY AND
SEEK SELF." From above the horizon rose a bright point
source of light, eclipsing all others in that part of the sky,
"VERY VERY LARGE MINDTALK COME. LARGE STRONG SELF,
LIKE YOU SEEK. MAYBE TRUE FAR AND STRONG, BUT I THINK
SMALL AND VERY CLOSE TO YOU. WE SELVES NOT NEVER
MINDTALK UMBRELLA TREE PEOPLES."

Simmons watched in fascination as the planet before him
continued to roll, and new stars inched their way into the
sky. Suddenly a new point pierced from the horizon.

"YOU STILL SEEK SELF, FIND SELF NOT UMBRELLA TREE.
BUT NEW MAYBE-SELF APPEAR TO YOU. YOU LEAVE UMBRELLA
TREE, GO TO NEW MINDTALK."

Simmons watched the new explosion of telepathic light
climb the sky. "And so I've been tossed like a frisbee from
mind to mind," he said slowly, "as each new broadcast captured me. And after twenty-four hours I'll start to repeat, I
suppose." He noticed something startling. "Where did you get
that star pattern?" he asked quickly. "I recognize it." A part
of his mind wondered at the kind of amnesia that could forget both self and species, but remembered constellations and
frisbees.

"FROM YOUR MIND. PROBABLE STAR PATTERN AT TIME OF
YOUR FIRST SEE MINDTALK. EXACT STARS WITH MINDTALK NOT
KNOW, NATURAL. THIS PROBABLE MAYBE SUPPOSE COULD BE
PATTERN OF MINDTALK PLACES, SEE FROM YOUR EARTH."

"That red star's Alderbaran," said Simmons. "That constellation is Taurus."

"SO IN YOUR MIND," said the lights. "YOUR MIND CALL
PEOPLES YOU HAVE MINDTALK WITH IN SUCH VOCABULARY AS
SERIES YOU KNOW."

"What series?"

"AS ARIES, TAURUS, GEMINI, CANCER, LEO, VIRGO. IN MIND
YOU CALL WE LIBRA."

"No!" said Simmons. "No, it can't be as neat as that!"

"NO PROBABLE MAYBE EXACT RELATE ONE TO ONE. PROBA-
BLE MINDTALK PEOPLES EACH ONE SAME . . . YES, THANK
YOU, SAME GENERAL LONGITUDE AS IN SERIES. NOW, ON OTHER
HAND, NUMBER TWO PROBABLE POSSIBILITY YOUR CONDITION."

Simmons had forgotten there was supposed to be another.
"What's that?"

"YOURSELF IS NOTSANE. VERY STRONG PROBABLE. YOU
THINK YOU GO STARS IN SERIES. AS IN . . . NO . . . NO . . .

YES, THANK YOU, ASTROLOGY. YOUR MIND SEE NOT-THINGS, BELIEVE NOT-THINGS . . . YES, THANK YOU, HALLUCINATIONS. NO SUCH THING ASTROLOGY, YOUR MIND FIND FROM NOTHING."

"You can't think I'm hallucinating *you!*"

"VERY PROBABLE POSSIBLE MAYBE YES. POSSIBLE MAYBE NO. ON OTHER HAND . . ."

The lights all went off, very abruptly.

"Libra? Libra, are you there?"

Simmons was alone again in the nothing.

"I think we've got it now," said Simmons suddenly, and every head in the room snapped about. A minute before, he'd been quite out of the world. Now he paced the floor rapidly.

"First, let's assume that my telepathic planet-hopping is an actual fact. The alternative is that I'm crazy, and I'm not about to buy that. Those places are as real as this one is. Anybody who'd prefer to think I'm hallucinating is welcome to work along that line, but don't tell me about it; I'm not interested. Next, the modus operandi makes sense. There are hordes of telepathic broadcasting stations out there; and I'm picking them up, as the world turns, one after the other, click, click, click . . . what's the matter, Debbie?"

She was looking at him in awe. "We're just off balance," she said. "One minute you're deep in coma, and the next you're spinning off points faster than we can keep up."

"I haven't been in coma," Simmons said shortly. "My body has been resting, while *I've* been getting a quick cram course in telepathic galactography. The situation is complicated, but we can handle it if we just think it through. The benefits are enormous. We have to, first, perfect this telepathy induction business, and just as important, find a way to turn it off. Eventually, we'll want to find a way to control it, pick up the stations we want. Meanwhile, we'll be getting information on the state of the Galaxy. Listen, there are arts and philosophies and sciences out there just waiting for us. This isn't a disaster, it's a vast opportunity. We're in a position now to listen in on the universe, from our safe little cubbyhole here on Earth."

"Sounds great," said the round-faced man, whose name Tom still didn't know. "But if all this stuff's going to flow in through you, we've got to take good care of our receiving station. We still aren't quite sure how we created it."

Simmons swung towards him. "What kind of experiment was it?" he asked. "Can we replicate it?"

"Brain surgery, drugs, hypnosis, all in a particular mix you worked out yourself, Tom," said the other. "We could do the same thing again, if we had another volunteer. So far, you've been the only person nuts enough . . . sorry, figure of speech . . . to try out your own concoction." He paused. "I don't know if what's happening to you will make another volunteer more or less likely."

"Okay. Look, everyone, think it out, think it all out. Brainstorm . . . on the experiment, on possible dangers, on those points I mentioned earlier. By the next time I come back here, I wish you'd have a list of recommendations about what we need to know. I may well come across minds out there which can answer them. Cancer, war, energy . . . space travel, if we still need it . . . all the answers are out there, and in a little time we'll have them."

"Tom," Debbie asked, "what's it like out there? You haven't given us a clue yet."

He smiled at her. "It's like all the mad science fiction ever written. Have a recorder ready when I get back, and I'll start setting down my travelogue. Okay, I'd better get on my back."

He lay back on the bed and smiled up at Debbie. "See you in a couple of hours," he said, and closed his eyes.

"I don't know what the hell to think," admitted Dr. Berkson. "Medically, there's nothing I can find wrong with his body. It's all in the mind . . . and you can take that either way you want. What's with this business of telepathic journeying, Art? Could that be possible? It's not my field at all."

"It makes a weird kind of sense," admitted Art Hover, pushing his spectacles up on his forehead. "It's absolutely impossible, of course; but that might not keep it from being the truth, I suppose."

"But what do you really think, Art? This is no time for your paradoxes."

"I'm afraid he's gone off the deep end," said Jim Lindland. "We've got to fish him back."

Deborah Simmons looked at the three men from where she sat by the deserted body of her husband. "He's not crazy," she said firmly. "I think he's telling the truth about what's happening to him."

The three men looked at her, and then spoke together more quietly.

Deborah looked back at Simmons. His eyes were open. There was a long pause. Then he spoke.

"Move off. I've got to get up."

"But you just left five minutes ago," she said, as if it were the most natural thing in the world. But she got up from the bed.

Simmons stood up. Dr. Berkson started to say something and stopped.

"There is very little time to act," said Thomas Simmons in a flat voice, "and none to explain. Listen carefully. It is absolutely necessary to move me rapidly, in the direction countering the Earth's rotation, so that I will be above to preserve my present vector angle to the sidereal sphere. How do we do it?"

There was a stunned silence. Then Art Hover cleared his throat nervously.

"I don't think we quite get you, Tom. What are you after?"

Simmons frowned. "I thought I was very clear. I must travel . . . westward, at the rate of the planetary rotation. And at once. I'm counting on you to arrange the details."

"We can't do that," said Jim Lindland, and Dr. Berkson said, "Get back in bed, Tom," and then they both fell silent, as he looked at them.

Deborah spoke up. "They can't do anything unless you tell them why you need it, Tom. They haven't quite decided whether you're rational yet."

There was suppressed fury beneath his even tones. "I said there's no time to explain, and I don't like to repeat. Let's move!"

"We'll move faster if you give us a quick 'why,' Tom," said Art nervously, licking his lips.

Simmons's hands lay straight at his sides, but the fingers were flexing spasmodically. "Quickly, then. There'd be no chance for us at all, but for one extremely fortuitous fact; that there *is* no telepathically powerful civilization broadcasting from within this particular thirty degrees of longitude. That means that during this two-hour period, and only then, I am in control of my own mind. If we can *keep* me at this angle to the constellations, I'll be safe. And, more importantly, humanity will be safe. Now can we please get the hell on our way!"

"Humanity safe? From what?" asked Lindland.

"From the most insidious and total alien invasion you can imagine. Do you want to keep me talking here until it's too late?"

Art looked at Jim. "I don't believe it, I don't think we could possibly get anything in time, but I'll call the field and see." He left the room.

"If we can't manage it this time," said Thomas Simmons, "I want you to promise me this. Keep my body here, locked in at all times. Do *not* pay attention to whatever I may say at other times; it will not be Thomas Simmons speaking, but something so alien you couldn't believe it. Only during the empty vector can I operate freely, at this season between eight and ten in the evening."

"You can't be serious," said Lindland. "You can't expect us to believe . . ."

"The universe is a very ruthless place," said Simmons, "and it cares little what you or any man may believe. It *acts* while you are posturing and trying to make up your mind. Now, next, I want you to arrange for others to replicate my experiment. We need as many telepathic receivers as possible for human defense."

"It's not my decision, Mr. Simmons," said Dr. Berkson, "but I don't think you're likely to get many volunteers to follow you until it's clear what's happened to you."

Simmons crossed to face the doctor and looked directly into his eyes.

"It is immaterial whether they are volunteers or not," he said coldly, "as long as we get them." He stared till Dr. Berkson looked away, and then crossed to the window, and drew the curtain. He stood there stiffly, looking out at the night sky to the east. "Until we have at least one telepathic receiver placed within each thirty degrees of longitude, we are wide open to invasion, now that we have broadcast our presence to the Galaxy. We can't wait on niceties."

Deborah Simmons, standing behind him, looked out to where Antares brooded in the far depths of the night. "Would you guys leave us for a bit?" she asked. "I want to talk to Tom alone."

When they were alone, Simmons turned to her with a frustrated gesture. "*You* understand," he said. "I know you'll help me." He placed his hands gently on her shoulders, and looked at her with tender pleading. "You're the only one I can really count on to help me when it gets tough. You will, won't you?" Very slowly, he pulled her to him and kissed her for a long time, then held her to his chest. "You don't know how much I need you."

She held him a long moment, and then slowly pushed herself to arm's length and looked up at him. "I certainly don't want an alien invasion of Earth," she said.

"Then help me persuade them. I know what I'm doing, it's the only way."

"Kiss me again," she said.

He did.

She finally pushed away from him. "I'm sorry," she said. "I'd do a lot for that sort of thing, but I told you. I don't want an alien invasion of Earth. I won't help you."

"But I told you . . ."

"I don't believe you. You're lying. And I've got to tell them that."

She turned from him and was stopped by his hand gripping her shoulder.

"You are not going to make a fool of me. You will not say a thing to them!"

"I've got to. You know that. You've changed too much. I don't think it's you any more. You're a . . . an 'it,' aren't you?"

His hand squeezed and twisted, and suddenly she was on her knees. His other hand darted out and lifted the telephone from the bedside stand. He stood there above her, as she squirmed to release herself, the phone raised above her head, and his voice falling heavily upon her.

"But I told you, honey, you're not going to tell anybody anything!" . . .

and then he spoke again, grasping. ". . . believe it. Don't believe it. Don't . . ." He stood swaying for a moment, and then collapsed on the edge of the bed. There was a long silence as he revolved the telephone in his hand. Finally he looked at Debbie.

"It wasn't me," he said.

She nodded silently, white-faced.

He gulped. "I've been trapped in here all this time, trying to shout out to you, to stop him. But his control was too great. I hadn't a chance." His eyes were pleading. "You do know it wasn't me?"

She was on her knees beside him, holding him tight. "Oh, God, yes. I know, Tom! Don't you think I can tell the difference? Thank God you're back!"

His look was still haunted. "The one thing he lied about was that so-called unoccupied vector. It's occupied, all right . . . by *them.*"

"Who are they?"

"Who knows? Minds powerful enough to snap me up the moment I touched them, and ride back here. Ruthless enough to determine to take the world over. Competent enough to almost do it."

She sat there on the bed, arm around him, and he couldn't stop shaking.

"You're going to have to knock me out with drugs or something at eight o'clock every evening, Debbie. I can't go through that again. We can't take the chance."

She ran her hand along his thigh and squeezed. "Remember what you said before . . . while you were still you. You'll find someone out there who knows the answer to . . . to *them* too."

"I better. But, Debbie, I'm scared. I don't want to go out again. I thought it was all worked out; there were friends out there, with knowledge and benevolence. Well, there are other things too, you see?"

"You'll make it, Tom. We're all with you."

He grinned wryly at that. "I'll travel a long way from your moral support. But I appreciate the thought." He subsided into a silence so withdrawn that she suddenly looked at him to see if he'd gone off sitting up this time. But he was still there. What he finally said should have surprised her.

"He was getting to you, wasn't he?"

"I knew it wasn't you, Tom. Almost right away."

"And he almost got to you anyway, right?"

She rose and paced, uncomfortable. "Tom, this is terribly confusing for all of us. Not like it is for you, but . . . you understand?"

"I understood how you looked at him when he was coming on strong. I was trapped in here, there was nothing I could do but look, and scream without you being able to hear. He almost had you, Debbie, you can't deny it." He paused, and then said quietly, "I gather it's been a long time since you got what you really wanted from me. Or have you ever?"

She ran to him with a sob, and caught his face between her

hands. "Tom, Tom," she said tightly, "for heaven's sake, not jealousy! Listen, dearest. He was there, he was coming on like a girl's dream, he was *in your body*, for Christ's sake . . . and he *didn't* get to me. Because he was *not* you! Okay?"

Simmons put his arms around her, and pressed his cheek against her breast. "Okay, Debbie," he said at last. "Thank you. That's a nice thought to take with me. Because I'm afraid I've got to go to Sagittarius now."

And where the hell'd you come from, Buster? was the gist of the first communication. *Don't answer right now, this is pretty ticklish right in here. I'll be with you in a minute.*

It would be hard to be more *with* someone than he already was, thought Simmons. Talk about togetherness! He strove for a feel of his latest temporary lodging.

Hey, don't do that, came the cry of his host. *Leave those damn muscles alone. The last thing I need at this point is any extra twitches.*

Simmons subsided, and contented himself with passively observing his fresh environment through his new senses. The first entry into a new body in a new world was still a time of utter bafflement, and not being able to initiate motor activity made it almost impossible to differentiate between his body and the rest of his surroundings. He started shuffling his senses into some kind of order, trying to fit them together into a coherent situation. It was fairly complicated, since he had only his habitual subjective senses to fit quite other objective imputs into; what he decided to interpret in visual terms might be direct sensation of magnetic fields, and his aural readings might spring from a kind of sonar. And then it all would get too weird and inconsistent, and he would have to try again, feeling the magnetism and smelling the echoes. This kept him occupied for some time. Meanwhile his host remained busily engaged in affairs of his own.

Partway through this procedure, Simmons became inescapably aware of some*thing* which was making itself increasingly evident in all sensory modes. It was either growing, or nearing, or intensifying, in a manner he found unnerving, whether he took it as a steadily rising sound, a growing light, or an increasing stench. A quick extrapolation suggested that whatever it was, in a few instants it would be all there was. Its existence in that mode seemed incompatible with his own.

And then, in a Doppler switch, it had passed, and was again shrinking, or departing, or diminishing. Simmons would have slumped his new body in relief if he'd known how.

Then his host remembered him at last. *Touch and go for a moment there, wouldn't you say? Well, we're on the straightaway for a little while. Who did you say you were?*

"What was **that?**" Simmons managed to get out.

That? What? Oh . . . we just flashed a solar chromosphere. Fastest way out of the system, but sort of tricky getting it just right. That's why I didn't care to have you squirming.

Playing chicken with solar prominences? For sport? Simmons didn't ask. Belatedly he answered the other's question.

"I'm just a temporary visitor," he said. "I'm not totally in control of where I show up, but I'll try to keep out of your way, if you like. I won't be around long."

Oh, no need to stand on ceremony, said the other. *You're here, let's share experiences, that's what minds are for. It's a way to the next system.*

"Would you mind giving me a bit of orientation," said Simmons. "I'm having trouble figuring out just what is you and what is your . . . ship? Like, is that oscillating bar one of your appendages, or an external bit of apparatus?"

His host achieved the equivalent of a belly laugh; everything flexed and shook. *It's all me,* he chortled. He gave a shake, and motion ran along his whole length, extensors raised, panels contracted, tubes pulsed, circuits flashed. *Just me. Whatever I couldn't move was stars.*

He was about thirty kilometers through his longer axis. He was his own spaceship. Simmons was impressed.

"I never imagined anything like you before," he admitted.

So how does it feel being so ignorant? said the ship, and then, sensing Simmons had taken offense, *Hey, I just meant it's been so long since we got out into the Universe, I'm just sort of curious about what it's like for you baby species, just sticking your snout out of the shell and all.*

Simmons let it pass. After all, the observation was just.

What's your effective range? the ship was asking. *You can't be from that system we just passed, I'd say. There were null life-readings, and anyway, your strength of presence isn't fading. Do you know if this is a first contact?*

"My first with your type," said Simmons. "Though I've contacted others."

Whee-oo, thought the other. *You must be from out of the cluster entirely. Hold it, another system coming up. Just hold still and don't wiggle anything.*

Another sun loomed up, at first gradually and then with that rush that would have stopped Simmons's heart if he'd been in charge of one at the moment. As it swept away behind them, their shared mind was occupied for an instant with a babbling confusion of incoherent images, feelings, and passions, which vanished as abruptly.

"What was that?" asked Simmons bewilderedly.

Oh, there was rather primitive life on the second planet. I picked up one mind from each species and flipped them all over to Central Process for assessment. Standard Operating Procedure. Of course, in your case, I mean, from out of the Cluster entirely, what's the need? You're a lot of fun, I admit, but the Cluster's our main concern, wouldn't you agree? Besides, you can be more help with me just now. If you don't mind pulling your weight, okay?

"Not at all, though I doubt I'll be with you long enough to really help much."

Oh, you're doing great, considering the sort of thing you are, admitted the ship airily. *Just make an entry in the log, will you?*

"Log?"

Oh, yeah, look. Feel what I'm doing here. This muscle (got it?) actuates the assessor mech. While it's open, flow in heat patterns like this; in this case, we want to mark that star, second planet, for recheck in about a megayear for further evolutionary progress.

"You do a lot of this?"

Got to. You know how many stars there are in the Cluster? By the time we get a look at all of them, it's past time to start over again. Don't know how the Core Shaft guys ever manage their area. Here we go again. Oh, great, this one's a trinary.

If Simmons had had eyes, he would have shut them the next five minutes.

When it was over, and the ship had straightened onto its next course, Simmons remembered to bring up an important subject. It was all very well to have fun out in galaxy-land, but his own little world was under threat; one he reluctantly had to admit he himself had brought upon it.

"I wonder," he asked his host diffidently, "if you could help me with a bit of a problem."

Fire away.

"Well, I come from a species of non-telepaths on some little planet out there, I really don't know where the hell actually, and we've just gotten in contact with some pretty tough customers." He sketched out the Scorpio menace. The ship was indignant.

Hey, look, I know that kind. They just get a pod in the door and take over entirely. Real pests. Look, there's only one way to handle that type, you know what I mean?

"How's that?"

Well, first, you let 'em start coming in. Meanwhile, you arrange for a mind transfer of your own people to some off-planet source ...

"How are we expected to manage that!"

And then when they're all in your bodies on home-planet, and you're all out ...

"Yeah?"

You blow up the planet. Whap! And they don't bother anybody again. That kind, it's the only way.

Simmons sighed mentally. "I don't think we could arrange that."

Your funeral, buster. Another star. Quiet, now.

The new star swelled and shot towards them. Simmons was almost getting used to the thrill of close passage. This time, however, things went a little differently.

Excrement, the ship projected suddenly. *Left! I meant, right, right, right!* They plunged directly into the maelstrom and, as far as Simmons could tell, were evaporated instantly.

It would have been astounding, had not his capacity for such emotions been overloaded some way back, when he found himself squatting to his neck in a mud-filled box, looking out over rows of similar cubicles. Judging from their occupants, he was in a body somewhat between that of a toad and a lobster.

I meant "right," his host said again, in a sadder tone.

Simmons thought a minute. "I have to assume that you are not *exactly* the ship, but the mental *manipulator* of the ship," he surmised at last.

What, old buddy, you still with me? Yeah, prime klutz that I am, I bunged up another ship, and it'll be days before they get me a new one. You don't think we'd risk intelligence it-self out there, do you? That's hardly necessary.

The erstwhile ship waited for a response, but the temporary guest had departed for parts unknown.

Easy come, easy go, it thought. *My, that was a queer one.* And crawling out of its tank, it set off to look for an unemployed ship.

"Oh, Tom. I'm glad you're out of it. You're just in time to tell these idiots why they can't just take you away. They want to incarcerate you or something."

Simmons sat up wearily. "For the love of heaven, can't a guy even enjoy his ten-minute break without asinine interruptions? What is it this time?"

Mutt and Jeff stood beside his bed. Mutt opened a wallet and flashed something inside it, just like he'd seen it in the movies. It could have been anything.

"Government," said Mutt. "For your own security."

"Get out of here, please," Simmons said, trying to stay polite. "Like I've seen governments you wouldn't believe."

"Sorry," said Mutt indifferently. "You'll have to come with us. Orders from the top." He got his dialogue from the movies too.

"I prefer not to," said Simmons. Eyes flicking towards Jeff in the background, he added, "And you can leave that in the holster. You won't be needing it. What's this all about?"

Debbie broke in. "Oh, Washington is about twelve hours behind on all this. They still think that you can read *human* minds!"

Simmons thought about that. "Oh. Of course. So that makes me a secret weapon, of course, and military security. And probably a political threat as well, right?"

Mutt's face didn't change. "We don't wish to use force, Dr. Simmons, but our orders . . ."

Debbie: "I've tried to explain to them that you can't pick up human thoughts at all, but they . . ."

"Please, leave this to us, Mrs. Simmons," said Mutt.

"No, leave this to me," said Simmons. He looked at Mutt directly. "Tell me, sir, who sent you?" He paused for no reply. "I see. Well, then what do you *really* think of your boss? . . . Okay. Then I'll tell him when I see him just what you do think of him."

There was a short silence. Then Mutt said slowly, "You're bluffing."

"Oh? Then kindly think of your opinion of the average American voter . . . I see. Would you like *that* to hit the press? Now get out!"

Mutt stood uncertain for a moment, then turned to Jeff. "Maybe we'd better . . ."

"Hey," Jeff spoke for the first time. "You letting this creep get to you? Our orders . . ."

Simmons looked at him. "Hey, you, think of a woman you've been with recently . . . Now think of someone you wouldn't like to know about her . . . Got it! You try to lock me up, a lot of people are going to be getting mental messages about things you sure wouldn't want them to know about."

A minute later Simmons was alone with Debbie.

"My lord," she said in awe, looking at him as if he were again somebody else, "How did you get away with that?"

"Dumb fool luck, I guess," he chuckled. "The kind of luck that only works on dumb fools like those. Actually, I suppose I learned a few things from Scorpio."

"Scorpio?"

"My tag name for the monsters that tried to invade Earth two episodes back," he explained. "If nothing else, they have chutzpah, and that's what I needed just now. That won't keep the machine out of our hair long, though. Now I have to add a new item to my list; how to keep governments off. Well, someone out there . . ."

". . . will have the answers to that one. Right," said Debbie. "You know, now that I know you're not crazy, you're really going out there to those worlds, I almost envy you the experience."

"Don't," said Simmons. "Trail-blazing's no fun. You wait till I've scouted out the territory." He held out his hand and drew her to him. "Debbie, you'll be here next time I come back, you hear."

"Of course," she said, smiling down at him. "Aren't I always?"

"You, and no one else, either," he specified. "Let's have two AM privacy."

"I really think some of your memory is beginning to sneak back," Debbie decided. "I thought you had enough other stuff on your mind."

"Because of those Washington goons," Simmons pointed out, "I haven't even gotten out of bed this time back. And I don't intend to next time either."

YOU ARE ABOUT TO EXPERIENCE THE MOST PROFOUND TOUR IN THE UNIVERSE. WE ASK THAT YOU ALL REMAIN QUIET FOR THE NEXT HALF OCCAD, SO THAT EVERYONE MAY EXPERIENCE IT PROPERLY. The mental feeling was of cramped crowding in a nonsensory anteroom.

"Excuse me," said Simmons, "I will only be here for a short . . ."

NO TALKING PLEASE, he was overridden. IT IS UNFAIR TO THE OTHERS. NOW LET ME WELCOME YOU TO THE CORE, THE GREATEST CIVILIZATION IN THE GALAXY, WHERE OVER THREE MILLION SEPARATE SPECIES LIVE IN HARMONIC INTERRELATIONSHIP. YOU SHOULD KNOW THAT WITHIN THESE BOUNDARIES ARE INCLUDED MORE STELLAR SYSTEMS THAN IN ALL THE REST OF THE GALAXY COMBINED. EACH OCCAD AT LEAST 50,000 NEW SPECIES ACHIEVE TELEPATHIC COMMUNICATION WITH US, AND THIS OCCAD YOU YOURSELVES ARE SUCH FORTUNATE REPRESENTATIVES.

"Will this take very long?" asked Simmons. "I've got less than two hours. I don't know how many occads that is, but . . ." He felt an enfolding pressure, soft but irresistible, and found himself incapable of further communication.

PLEASE, said the tour guide sternly, PLEASE BEAR WITH US. OUR PROGRAMMED TOUR HAS BEEN CAREFULLY PLANNED TO PRESENT ALL THE MOST IMPORTANT INFORMATION IN THE MOST EFFECTIVE MANNER POSSIBLE. IF THERE ARE QUESTIONS, PLEASE HOLD THEM UNTIL THE END. YOU WILL FIND MOST OF THEM ANSWERED BEFORE THEN.

A delicate line of thought spun up in Simmons's immediate mental vicinity. "But my species is in great peril. We urgently seek help . . ." Reluctantly, the thought died away, muffled to stillness.

YOU MUST NOT DEMAND PERSONAL ATTENTION, chided the guide. THERE ARE 10,000 SEPARATE SPECIES REPRESENTED IN THIS TOUR GROUP. EACH OCCAD UPWARDS OF 29,000 SPECIES REQUEST APPLICATION FOR CORE MEMBERSHIP, AND WHEN YOU SEE THE ADVANTAGES CORE CITIZENSHIP OFFERS, WE TRUST YOU ALSO WILL BE EAGER TO APPLY. SO, WITHOUT FURTHER ADO, LET US VIEW THE GALACTIC CORE.

And space erupted into view. The Galaxy spun in silent majesty beneath, or possibly above them. It was all the more awesome to Simmons in that he was viewing it through six separate senses, four of which he had never possessed before. They were gazing at it through dark skies, through the eyes and other sensory equipment of the archetype of sphinxes, crouching, head on paws, upon warm violet sands.

THIS IS OUR GALAXY, continued the peroration, VIEWED FROM A WORLD CONSTRUCTED SOME 30,000 LIGHT YEARS ABOVE THE PLANE OF THE GALAXY. OUR HOST IS TILENGH THE MMCIITH OF THE FURINI RACE. SHE, AND HER IMMEDIATE ANCESTORS, WHOSE FULL MEMORIES SHE POSSESSES, HAVE VIEWED THE GALAXY FROM THIS LOCATION FOR THE PAST EIGHT MILLION YEARS. TILENGH, WOULD YOU MIND TELLING OUR GUESTS WHAT THE MAJOR CHANGES YOU HAVE NOTICED IN THAT TIME MAY BE.

Tilengh flexed her mighty talons, and a properly deep and solemn thought rolled through the packed minds. *Well, Clauf, I suppose the biggest changes visible from here have been the core explosion four and a half million years back, and its containment and utilization during the next million years; and then the dimming of the core in the longer wavelengths, with the concommittant increase in infrared output as more and more inner stars are capped in spheres.*

THEN YOU'D SAY THAT MOST SIGNS OF INTELLIGENCE WITHIN THE GALAXY AS SEEN FROM OUT HERE ARE . . . WHERE, TILENGH?

Oh, the Core, most definitely, Clauf. From out here, it is fairly rarely that we see true signs of intelligent manipulations outside the galatic center. The Core, however, has made tremendous strides, quite apparent even from this distance.

THANK YOU VERY MUCH, TILENGH. FELLOW SAPIENTS, THAT IS THE OPINION OF TILENGH THE MMCIITH, POSSESSOR OF A LONGER UNBROKEN VIEW OF OUR GALAXY THAN ANY OTHER KNOWN BEING, AND I THINK YOU'LL AGREE THAT SHE SHOULD KNOW, IF ANYONE DOES. NOW, FRIENDS, WE HAVE A REAL TREAT IN STORE FOR YOU. WE TRUST YOU WILL TREASURE EVERY DETAIL OF THE NEXT SYCCAD, SO YOU CAN SHARE IT PRECISELY WITH YOUR HOME WORLDS.

The small voice was piping again, in a melancholy mode. "My home planet has a life expectancy of *less* than a syccad, unless you folks can get aid . . ." It was muffled.

PLEASE BE MORE CONSIDERATE. A pained tone was apparent beneath the crisp exterior of the guide's thought. IF **EVERYBODY** INSISTS ON SPEAKING, WE'LL NEVER GET ANYWHERE. LET ME REMIND YOU THAT IN JUST FIVE SYCCADS, ANOTHER GROUP OF AT LEAST TEN THOUSAND SENTIENTS WILL BE EAGERLY FOLLOWING YOU ON THIS MAGNIFICENT AND INFORMATIVE TOUR ON WHICH YOU ARE NOW EMBARKED. WE MUST KEEP MOVING. NOW, WE HAVE ARRANGED WITH A TOTAL OF ONE HUNDRED SIXTY NINE SPECIES, DOMICILED BETWEEN THIS WORLD AND THE CORE'S CENTRAL SHAFT, WHO WILL MINDSHARE WITH YOU IN SEQUENCE DURING THE NEXT SYCCAD. KEEP ALL YOUR SENSES WIDE OPEN FOR AN UNFORGETTABLE EXPERIENCE: BECAUSE NOW, FELLOW SENTIENTS AND, MAY WE HOPE, FELLOW COLLABORATORS IN THE GREAT CORE CULTURE, WE GIVE YOU THE GREATEST TREK IN THE KNOWN UNIVERSE . . . THE PLUNGE TO THE CORE OF THE GALAXY. NOW!

And the desert vanished, to be replaced by a somewhat closer view. The Galaxy sprawled wider in a night sky, over the tapering fronds of a boggy marsh in which another creature received the mental passengers for a moment, and then passed them on. Step by step the star swarms neared, breaking up into separate patches and swelling to cover the field of view. The Galaxy, as the trek overran the outspeeding light, appeared to rotate backwards.

Closer and closer, and right into the star fields, the packed center looming up before them, flick, flick, flick; until all the heavens were one blaze of light. There were peripheral screams, quickly stifled, from the more impressionable members of the tour. Through the omnipresent glare slowly appeared an utter blackness, growing at each leap, until the whole sky was dominated by a vast black cylinder driving towards them.

THE SHAFT AT THE CENTER OF THE GALAXY, intoned the guide in solemn mode. THE REFERENCE POINT FROM WHICH ALL DISTANCES ARE MEASURED, INCORPORATING IN ITS STRUCTURE ALL OTHER STANDARD MEASUREMENTS AS WELL. HERE THE CORE COUNCIL, ELECTED MILLENNIALLY, MEETS IN PERPETUAL CONCLAVE; HERE ARE FOUND THE GREATEST LIBRARY, MUSEUM, STABLUTCH, ZOO, PHRENATEUM, AND QUAW OF THE WHOLE CORE CULTURE. FELLOW SENTIENTS, LET ME CONGRATULATE YOU AS, FIRST OF YOUR SPECIES, YOU COME TO

THE VERY CENTER OF THE GALAXY. I GIVE YOU . . . THE SHAFT!

The final words were perfectly timed, as the kaleidoscopic images came to an abrupt and dizzying halt. The ultimate host lay motionless in space, a large blob of protoplasm studded with every form of sensory apparatus known to sentience. There was a psychic shoving, as ten thousand individual minds struggled to appropriate organs of sense with which they were familiar.

NO NEED TO PUSH. WE SHALL REMAIN HERE A FULL 1.4286 SYCCADS, PLENTY OF TIME FOR EACH AND EVERY ONE OF YOU TO OBSERVE THE SHAFT TO YOUR COMPLETE CONTENT.

Simmons slipped his way through the mental pack, and located some optics for himself, a bit further into the ultra-violet than he was used to, but with this view it hardly mattered.

The fellow-passenger Simmons had noted before was speaking to him. "Pardon me, but I had the definite impression that you were sympathetic to my attempts to get attention."

"I think it's a shame they didn't listen to you," said Simmons, turning from the view. "Is your world in really grave danger?"

"Done for," said the other. "Too late for us. What I wanted to say was . . . well, I really think things ought to be better run somehow. Maybe sometime you can do something about it. We'd like to think so."

"All this place makes me want to do is run away," said Simmons. "But, look, about your people not getting any help and all . . . I mean, I'm *sorry*."

"Well . . ." said the other. "I guess that's better than noth—"

THE SHAFT IS FULLY CONSTRUCTED IN BLACK HOLE MODE, AS AN OPEN CYLINDER RATHER THAN A SPHERE. THE RESULTANT RELATIVITY PHENOMENA, BY THE WAY, ARE MOST SPECTACULAR. NOW, WE ARE FORTUNATE ENOUGH TO HAVE BEEN ABLE TO ARRANGE AN INTERVIEW WITH THE FIFTEENTH UNDERSECRETARY IN CHARGE OF CORE CENSUS, WHO WILL . . .

"It's too much," said Simmons tiredly. "Much too much too much. My mind can't encompass it. No man's could. No, nor woman's."

"I wasn't smiling at that, dear."

"You're not smiling at my technique, I hope. You must make allowances, Debbie. I really don't remember how it's done."

"Your body remembers very well indeed. I think maybe it works better when your mind has to let it alone. Don't think about it, just do it."

"Well, if you realize that this is practically an alien body doing alien things, as far as my memory goes, I don't think I'm doing so badly."

"Oh, no, dear Tom, not at all badly . . . Tom?"

"Hmm?"

"If you fall asleep before you go off again, what would happen?"

"I'd spend my two hours in an alien dream. I caught the tail end of that when I entered Virgo."

"I see . . . Mmmmm . . . Tom, that reminds me . . . the wife of the Virgoan . . ."

"What about her?"

"Was she prettier than I am?"

"Look, you don't get on my case about her, and I'll shut up about Scorpio."

"It's a deal. Now snuggle."

"Wish I could, but it's that time again. Bye."

It had to happen sometime, thought Simmons, and really he was a bit surprised it hadn't happened before. He supposed it took a little bit of preparation before the mind could handle mind-sharing at this level of complexity.

He knew exactly where he was. He was crawling through low mud-walled tunnels on flat flippers, and standing on firm tripods on a pitching deck beneath yellow clouds. He was gazing on a baked-ceramic city from a high scalloped tower, and wallowing his bulky form in the mud of a wide-spreading estuary. He looked out, with varied senses, from a myriad different forms, touched as many different minds, and held them all separate. And among them, he kept hold of who he was.

Now this, thought Simmons, *is more like what telepathy was meant to be.*

We're glad you approve.

His contact, Simmons realized, was a kind of quorum, composed of those entities within his scope who chose to become involved with his presence. Many ignored him, or simply filed him as present, and continued their own concerns, all of which he was aware of: fighting wars, building, moving, loving, thinking. But many turned towards him in their thoughts, wholly or partly, and moved together to form a now temporary entity for the particularized purpose of welcoming Thomas Simmons. He was aware of each sentient in his individuality and of the whole as if it were a combined personality. And yet this newly born whole was constantly gaining new adherents, and shedding previous elements as they became bored, or were called away on more immediate business. And throughout the scope of his perception he could sense other such entities, forming, dissolving, modifying, in groups of from two to millions, for every purpose under the suns.

Hi, said Simmons. *I like the feel of this.*

We sort of like the feel of you, said the newcomer. *You seem to need a name for us. Call us Charley.*

A thought emerged, born in the mind of an amphibian lazing on the shore of a warm tidal beach, modified tactfully by a cook on an interplanetary liner crewed by hydrogen gasbag beings, translated into more human terms by a professor in an anthill warren, and presented as the observation to the collective—all in the fraction of a second.

What you need is a way to turn off your telepathy, that's all. Would you like that?

Simmons took what, had he had a body, must have come out as a deep breath. *You better believe it,* he said.

A mini-instant team of experts congealed, examined him, and pointed with a delicate probe of thought to parts of his id. *Think* **thus,** said the others, so, *and then do . . . like* **that,** *Got it?*

As easy as that? asked Simmons.

Once you know how, said Charley. *It's finding it the first time that needs help.*

Thank you, said Simmons. *I think that is going to be a great assistance.*

He noted that the components of "Charley" had changed greatly, even in this short time. Members had dropped out, without comment, some, he was chagrined to note, from boredom with his relatively simple situation. And yet, glimpsing some of the new things they were turning to, he realized that, objectively speaking, he did present a relatively common and uninspiring problem. Others, however, had merged to enhance and modify "Charley," as the mental grapevine brought in those with a particular interest in such as he.

I gather, said Simmons, *you understand my situation as clearly as I understand yours. Have you any advice for me and my race?*

You're doing just fine, said Charley. *As an individual, in less than a day of your time, you've reconstructed yourself from next to nothing to a socially conscious being again. And your species shows every sign of being able to cope with the new environment with which you will, of course, be presenting them. Just take it easy, feel it out, and remember, don't get too close to any one of the major thought-casters—except of course us.*

Some seem to be more dangerous than others, observed Simmons.

They're all deadly, close up, said Charley. *Deadly to your racial freedom and individuality, which is, of course, what is most important. No species can evolve in the neighborhood of one of those high-power stations without becoming a mini-version of their way of thought. Your people are just lucky you're fairly balanced in position between a number of them. It gives you a certain variety and flexibility in place of slavery. Better keep it that way.*

But you're safe? asked Simmons.

Because we don't want you to change to be like us, came the answer. *Be what you are, or what you want to be. Join any of us you care to, as long as you want, and drop out when you're through with us. That's what life's all about, isn't it?*

You might be right, said Simmons. *I'll think about it. Right now, I'm going home. I'm pretty sure I'll be in contact with you again before long.*

Any time, said Charley, already breaking up and reforming in a thousand other combinations far off. *Drop in any time.*

Simmons reached into his own thoughts, did *thus* and *so,* and then like *that,* and opened his eyes.

He swung his feet out of bed and stood up. He looked at the other people in the room and smiled gaily.

"I want to thank you all for your care of me," he said,

"I'm afraid the lot of you are missing your sleep." He moved around the room, shaking hands. "Jim, Art, Dr. Berkson, isn't it? Glad to see you all well. Debbie . . ." He held her close and kissed her with great attention. "Someone get me some coffee, and a BLT on rye. But don't worry. I won't be going anywhere now till I choose."

"You found it?" asked Debbie, looking up at him with half-closed eyes.

"I found it." He gestured expansively to the whole room and beyond it, to the Galaxy. "I've got my memory, I've got control. I can go or not as I like. I can teach others. Man can join the . . . web of thought out there."

"If you're still here in thirty minutes," said Art Hover, the round-faced man, and Simmons's long-time fellow researcher at the college, "I'll begin to believe you've got it licked. But the way you've been turning on and off like a stoplight, I'll wait till then," he added gruffly, and then flung an arm around Simmons's shoulders and squeezed hard.

"If you're back from the dead," said Jim Lindland, "work a miracle for us." He grinned.

"There will be miracles a-plenty," said Simmons. "Soon enough."

Such slow communication, Simmons was thinking. One painful word at a time, one laborious phrase after another. He had certainly been spoiled for oral dialogue. He could have given it all to them by now, if they'd been receivers. No, for humans weren't senders; the Aquarians or Librans would have to catalysts to allow one human mind to meet another. Well, that could be worked out too.

He walked to the window and drew aside the curtains. Behind him the small cluster of friends were looking at him in uncertain wonder. They didn't yet know for sure whether he was Marco Polo or a run-of-the-mill madman. They'd learn soon.

Outside, over the campus elms, the first glow of dawn was beginning to rim the horizon. The last dawn he'd seen had been the Arian one; this would be less violent, but not less beautiful. It was a good world, and in the last day a chance for making it even better had come up. He'd have to be very careful it was used right.

A bright star blazed in the southeast, fighting the dawn. He traced angles with other stars to identify it. Fomalhaut. Pisces rising. So easily and naturally that it seemed inevitable, the last piece fell into place, and the pattern was done.

The signs were not arbitrary. It was not just a graceful mnemonic. It was real.

He wouldn't try to tell them just yet. They had enough and more to grasp, as man prepared to join the largest stage imaginable. People weren't quite ready to feel happy at the thought that they were at the mercy of alien forces, that formed them at birth. That, at least, was how they would view it.

And yet Simmons now was certain of it. The mechanics of it would have to be worked out, the influence of source and distance, stellar angle and movement, terrestrial position and birthdate. But in a rough and ready way, the groundwork had been laid for thousands of years.

These hard scientists would get their backs up at the very suggestion. But Simmons knew. It was too neat to be mere coincidence. The idea of "astrological influence" was anathema to science. And, until a modus operandi could be demonstrated, rightly so.

But Simmons had been there.

He had drifted before the dawn wind with his Arian host, the umbrella tree, and carved purpose from the stubborn rocks with a Taurean. He had had an interview with the volatile Gemini, and gone home for a while with Cancer. He had been hosted in the realm of Leo, and disturbed the tidy world of Virgo, seen Libra struggling for balance, and Scorpio determined to take over the world single-handed. He had stumbled through the suns with Sagittarius, seen the incredible result of the Capricornian organization of the Core, and glimpsed the Aquarian individualism at play.

Even if man's ability to receive was minute and vestigial, he could not utterly avoid the effect of those massive mindwaves sweeping over his little world from without. Each man would be somehow molded by them, starting with the first alien culture under the influence of which he came.

Our salvation, thought Thomas Simmons, comes from our effective equidistance from all those cultures. If we'd been too close to one of them, we'd have been taken over by a single pattern. At least we've got variety, and in that a chance for freedom.

He turned from the window. "Call a full news conference

for a couple of hours from now," he said, "and I'll give the world a preliminary sketch of contemporary Galatic civilization. But for now, I've got a little trip to make. I still lack one house."

Debbie moved to him quickly. "Tom, must you? Can't it wait?"

He turned up her face and kissed her gently. "I'll be back, Deb; nothing would keep me away from you. But I've come this far around the wheel; I'll be damned if I'm going to stop while there's still one more house to go." And he opened channels to the universe.

And was washed on the currents of alien thought, swept away 86 parsecs, to that small world out towards Fomalhaut where God awaited him.

He merges with God, hovering in the immensities, containing the universe. God moves over just enough to let him in. *Welcome, lost one, welcome home.*

Simmons melts into the oneness, the sharing, and joins in the chorus, the chanting of the message, to all beings, all life, everywhere and anywhere.

Come, come, come join us in the whole. God is truth, God is beauty, God is love. God waits for you. Come join us, come.

Through a vast quadrant of the galaxy the merging voices pass and penetrate. On a thousand worlds beings of a myriad alien forms, grazing, hunting, swimming, flying, pause, as through their minds strange music flows, haunting half-felt thoughts spin just beyond their grasp.

God is truth. Come join us, come.

Some distant epoch, evolved to full powers, they will not fail to come. The message spreads out to farther worlds, where it touches other flowering minds; slowly fading, no longer overpowering in its intensity, it leaves the chance of choice.

God is beauty. Join us, come.

On into the distant reaches of space the fringes of the song flee on, wisps and fragments, to where the message will add but the barest touch of lost possibilities and ungrasped beauties, to a still unmolded race.

God is Love, and waits for you. Will you not come?

Simmons knows, as he merges for his two hours of shared divinity, that he is concentered with the denizens of Pisces σ

3, a race of mystic spiders that, wrapped in their cocoons hanging from the plentoon trees, thus send their thoughts soaring into the infinities, and lure ten trillion miles to harmony and peace. Just the strong-minded Piscean spiders. But once you're in with it, it might as well be God. Who knows? It just might really be.

THE LAST DAY OF CHRISTMAS

by David J. Lake

*Welcome to the wonderful world of romance.
For a small fee, you, too, can be the lover of the
century, the kind of person sensualists admire and
seldom reach. But there's a price, as there usually
is. And the author, a professor at a Queensland university, spells it out. In its own way, this final story
is a counterpoint to the editor's opening remarks.*

Big things often have the most modest beginnings. The
Wright brothers started with a small bicycle shop, Henry
Ford with a tiny factory, and penicillin was at first nothing
more than one spoiled culture on one glass plate.

And that was exactly the story of Irresistible (et cetera).
To this day, no one is quite sure where Quentin Dyer started
operations. But certainly it was on the smallest scale. The
best evidence points to Queensland, Australia. Almost on my
doorstep, in fact; because Brisbane, Queensland, Australia, is
where I happen to live.

The thing first registered on me when my wife came back
from the St Lucia supermarket one Friday afternoon with the
weekend groceries. My working hours at the University were
flexible, but they don't usually include Friday afternoons so,
when I heard the familiar dying wuffle of the family Toyota,
I dropped the book I was reading and went out front.

She was out of the car already, and struggling with the
usual bulky paper bag.

'Here,' I said, 'give me that.' And as I grappled with the bag, we got close, and I kissed her.

I almost dropped the bag.

'What—what—' I spluttered.

Marguerite was something of a health-and-nature freak. She did not usually wear perfume at all; she smelt perfectly nice without that.

Well, she smelt nice now, too. *But.* . . .

'Oh, I couldn't resist it, David,' she said. 'There was this man at the Cut Price Stores, doing a Special. He wasn't one of their usual staff. Anyway, he was giving away free samples, and spraying people, and—well, it smelt so nice, I took one.'

'What the hell is it?' I said, as she went in at the front door, and I stumbled after. 'Smells like musk, or—or—I don't know what.'

And our front room also was now beginning to smell of that I-don't-know-what. Faintly, but enough. Little pictures were floating through my mind: pictures of harem girls, belly dancers, that sort of thing. I am no prude, and I have as much imagination for that-sort-of-thing as the average guy . . . but not usually in the middle of a hot bright Friday afternoon.

'What—what is this stuff called?' I asked.

She held up the little plastic bottle. It had a simple hand-puffer spray attachment—none of your ozone-layer-damaging pressure packs. The liquid inside was a dreamy mist-blue, and there was a little paper label with oriental-type logo and Moorish-arch artwork in pink and green.

'It's called Irresistible,' she said. She laughed. 'Damn silly name. . . .'

'Not entirely, silly, this time,' I said. My mouth was dry.

'Do you know,' she said, innocently, 'the chap in the store said it was his own invention. He's an amateur biochemist, or something. He's already applied for a patent.' She laughed again. 'Lot of nonsense, I bet. All these perfumes are just a mixture of the usual old ingredients. But I hope this Mr Dyer does well. He seemed such a nice man. Handsome, too.'

'Oh, really?' I said. My mouth was growing drier.

'Yes. . . .' She was looking almost dreamy. 'Well, he'd sprayed some on himself, just to show it was quite safe. And the women in the store—you should have seen them! They were all over him.'

"I am glad you came straight home,' I said.

After that—no, I'm not going to tell you what happened after that.

There is no need. Similar things began happening all over the suburb of St Lucia that afternoon.

The next thing we knew, there were ads for IRRESISTIBLE on all the local commerical television channels. And the next thing after that, Mr Quentin Dyer was in America.

He had got his Australian patent for the 'new blue, BLUE Perfume', as the ads called it. And armed with that patent, he was applying for a US patent. And (did we but know it), for a French patent, and a British patent, and a. . . . Well, never mind.

At this stage, almost no one did mind. So what, if one toilet preparation was booming in all the states of Australia, and attracting some rather risque TV testimonials? There were a couple of letters to the British Brisbane *Courier-Mail* protesting the vulgarity of the TV ads; one of them denounced the decadence of our civilisation, and the other mentioned the Fall of Rome; but since both emanated from the same well-known wowser organisation, hardly anyone gave them a second glance.

There were too many other things to worry about.

It was a bad year for the economy: the Arabs had raised the price of oil again.

It was a bad year for Chile and China, for Lebanon and Laos, for Namibia and Northern Ireland, for Syria and Somalia, for Zaire and Zimbabwe. In all of these countries, and in parts of several others, people were killing other people by the hundred or the thousand, and for the highest motives, all of which ended in the morpheme *-ism*. The killings, however, did not end in anything but more killings.

It was a bad year for the environment. According to a UN survey team, two more species of whales, three species of rare land mammals, and ten species of birds must now be considered extinct. Twelve more countries announced that they were building nuclear power stations for purely peaceful purposes, including Ghana and Guinea, North Korea and South Korea, Free Yemen and People's Yemen; and Israel, Egypt, and Eire finally admitted that yes, they did have the Bomb, like almost everybody else. Oil spills occurred in the English Channel, the Bay of Biscay, the North Sea, the Gulf of Mexico, the Black Sea, the White Sea, the Yellow Sea, and the Red Sea. Brazil announced another major clearance of the remaining Amazon forest.

The prophets of doom prophesied irreversible damage to the biosphere, if this sort of thing went on, by at latest the year 2000.

So, as I say, we were not worrying much about some slightly naughty TV ads. As for the product itself, IRRESISTIBLE was—well, irresistible! It was refreshing to find a commercial product which seemed to do just what it promised to do. Those of us who were using it—by now, an awful lot of people—sniggered or whispered about it to each other. We felt it wasn't safe to talk about it too loud, or They might find out, and take away this one innocent item of good cheer.

Certain sorts of parties began to be held more often in the suburbs of Brisbane, Sidney, Melbourne, Adelaide, Perth . . . and they were spreading to the smaller Australian towns, too. They were not noisy parties: the hubbub of conversation tended to die away rather early, in fact, and the lights to go out well before midnight. Only, the cars of the guests did not then leave the unlit houses. Mostly, they took off only in the grey light of dawn.

I don't really think that morality was undermined. The swingers just swung a bit more. The staid, not-so-young family men, like myself, merely found they loved their wives even more dearly. Aging spouses suddenly acquired new glamour in the eyes of their partners. It was a fine thing, no question about it.

Especially, perhaps, for those couples where the wife was past child-bearing, or otherwise infertile. For the others . . . well, by that year's end the birth rate in Australia (which had been declining) showed a sudden upswing. For users of IRRESISTIBLE tended to be careless. . . . Merchants and manufacturerers cheered: in spite of the fuel crisis, the economy might recover yet. The horrors of ZPG seemed to have been averted. The new year came in with new hope. . . .

And that was when Quentin Dyer really hit the news.

My work had taken me to America that spring, and Marguerite came with me. We missed our favorite toilet preparation in the stores, for no one in the US seemed to have heard of IRRESISTIBLE; but no matter, we had brought an adequate supply of little blue bottles with us. By now we had learnt to use the stuff with moderation: it was a fixed family rule that we only sprayed it on ourselves after supper. That way, I had some energy left in the mornings, to walk the streets of Champaign, Illinois and go to work on those MSS and first editions in the University library. . . . Ah, those early mornings in bed in our hotel room, dozy and content and peaceful (the stuff was volatile, and quite worn off by 7 a.m.); and the coffee was brewing, and we were watching, through half-open eyes, the *Today* show. . . .

And then, one of those times, Marguerite sat up abruptly.

'Oh, David, look! That man!'

I struggled up a bit higher on the pillows.

'The one they're interviewing,' she said. 'I do believe—it's that *Mr Dyer*. You know, the one who. . . .'

He was tall, slim, dark-haired, elegant, and damned handsome. His features were so faultless, so regular, that they seemed to have been generalised and copied from a dozen ideal Greek sculptures. Alexander the Great, Alcibiades . . . it was only a certain lift to his dark eyebrows that added a touch of irony and saved him from sheer cliche. That, and the odd charm of his accent, which was Australian. Not very broad, but definitely Aussie, with a hint of something else underneath.

The amiable lady of the *Today* team leant forward, smiling broadly. 'And you're the man with the Mana, Mr Dyer? No, I mean the man behind MANA . . . ?"

Nod and tiny grin from Dyer, and a twitch of those eyebrows.

'You're not wearing it yourself, right at this moment, are you?'

'No way, ma'am,' said Dyer, flashing her a charming smile. 'Not that I dislike my product, but—I find I don't need it.'

Merry laughter from the Team.

'I believe you,' said the lady. Then she switched to looking serious. 'But tell me now, Mr Dyer, what are your reactions to this sensational story in the *Washington Post*?'

Dyer spread his elegantly manicured hands. In body-language, he was obviously baring his heart to us. 'There's no mystery at all, ma'am, no dirty little secret. All I did was invent a perfume. I thought it would smell nice, and it does smell nice. If it turns some people on, so what? That's been a function of perfumes since the days of the Queen of Sheba. And in this day and age, is that a crime?' He frowned slightly now, and those chestnut-brown eyes and black brows emanated sincere concern. 'I am all for enhancing the quality of life. I believe in *love*. I would like to make people happy, to the very end of their days. . . . You'd be surprised, the people who've given us testimonials. There was one old lady of ninety, and another old gentleman. . . .' He broke off, with a little laugh.

'Yes, Mr Dyer, maybe so, but what about this medical claim—that your stuff is actually a dangerous aphrodisiac?'

Dyer laughed more heartily. 'Dangerous? Rubbish! Let my opponents produce one creature that's been harmed by it. So it turns on rats also? Very well, it turns on rats. That could be good news for rats. . . . But the stuff evaporates quickly so, unless you go around deliberately spraying rats, there's no danger of a vermin explosion. I'm not scared of these muckrakers. For that matter, it was I who sent in the samples to the FDA, I myself. I have every confidence they'll give my product a clean bill of health.'

'Let's hear a little more about yourself, now,' said the lady.

In the next three minutes we learnt the main facts about Dyer's background. He was a New Australian, more or less—mother Czech, father Irish, but born in Melbourne: which put together might explain his accent. No, he wasn't a college boy: he'd come of a cultured family, but money had been tight. He went to a little private school in the suburbs of Sydney (that school had since folded). He'd always loved chemistry but, for the last ten years, since leaving school, he'd had to work on it in his spare time, while he took casual labouring jobs, mining, bricklaying. . . .

He was, you might say, a self-made man.

The spot came to an end. I leapt out of bed, and switched off. Then we looked at each other.

'What've we been missing?' I said.

But maybe you know how it is when you're abroad—you don't bother to read the newspapers, at least I don't, and our family hates TV ads, and dislikes most American television; so till that day we'd been rather out of touch.

After that day, we bought the papers, and watched the ads.

MANA was pink, and came in little glass bottles, and was somewhat more expensive, but otherwise it was nothing but our old Aussie friend IRRESISTIBLE 'with added coloring,' as it said in the fine print on the label. It had taken America already by storm, thanks to a superb campaign mounted by the firm of Ogilvy & Mather. Their ads, in spite of the nature of the product, were not vulgar. In all the best newspapers, and the glossy magazines, we found a portrait of Quentin Dyer. Dyer, in the ads, was half flinching from a mob of pretty girls. This in spite of apparent handicaps, for he was made up to look older—at least forty—and he had one arm in a sling, and a black eyepatch over one eye.

The caption read: THE MAN WITH THE MANA.

One week later, the FDA announced that MANA was certainly not a health risk. It had now been exhaustively tested on rats and rhesus monkeys, and a survey had been carried out on human users, and the results were all very similar. The active ingredient was an organic compound not known to exist in nature, with a technical name I won't attempt to transcribe; Dyer had nicknamed it *charitin*. Its formula was similar to certain pheromones, those subtle scents which attract the males of many animals to the females at the right season. . . . *Charitin* did definitely turn on most of the mammals and birds of the earth, and it was not sexist, as both the males and the females were equally affected. It had many other endearing qualities. It was non-toxic even when taken in massive doses, either into the lungs or the stomach. If swallowed, though, the stomach acids neutralised it, and its aphrodisiac effects were lost. If sniffed, its effect rose with concentration, but only a little way, and then a heavier dose made no difference at all.

In other words, it could not be 'abused'—unless the use of it at all could be called an abuse. . . .

There was just one noticeable side-effect. Users who suffered from many kinds of asthma reported that their symptoms had disappeared. (I can add my own testimony here. The Brisbane climate gives—gave—me asthma regularly every May and October. Medical science was baffled to cure me. That is, until irresistible *charitin* came along.)

The week after the FDA ruling, all kinds of hell broke loose. There were bills brought in to ban the use of charitin preparations, both in Congress and in many states. Law suits and counter law suits burgeoned from Alaska to Puerto Rico. . . . And meanwhile, a smiling Mr Dyer announced that he was launching another perfume with the same basic ingredient. This one was christened 4321.

4321 came in plastic bottles, its price was ridiculously low, its colour was blood red. The ads for 4321 were not handled by Ogilvy & Mather. They were soon infesting the TV screens on all channels.

The ad punchline went like this:

'4-3-2-1—BANG!'

Or, '4-3-2-1—the countdown that really gets you to Zero In!'

Or, '4-3-2-1—and UP like a rocket!'

Some stations—just a few—tried banning the ads. The Dyer organisation (he really did have an organisation now, a big one) slapped back at them with court orders. Meanwhile, the anti-charitin bill was killed in Congress: too many Reps and Senators were using the stuff themselves. . . .

The TV newscasts began to show amusing pictures of the new charitin factories. The operatives all wore special nose-masks. They had to, or else. . . .

4321 and MANA got banned in Alabama and Arkansas. The bans, of course, had absolutely no effect—except to increase the bootleg use of 4321 and MANA in Alabama and Arkansas.

Oh yes. About this time I had finished my research on the Wells MSS, I had written my article on *The War of the Worlds*, and Marguerite and I flew home to Queensland.

At Brisbane Airport, we found a strange atmosphere. Literally . . . because *that stuff* was in the air. People were tense, jittery. One disembarking passenger had to be arrested for trying to rape an air hostess in the middle of the Arrivals lounge. The customs men were tearing open people's baggage, and nearly gibbering. They were having to restrain themselves in one way, and it was coming out in aggression.

If only the silly buggers hadn't thought to test all suspicious-looking spray-on cosmetics by actually spraying them. . . .

When it came to our turn, the blue-uniformed gorilla snarled, and made a hand-signal with an erect thumb. He was temporarily past words.

'We have nothing to declare,' I said politely.

'MANA,' he croaked, '4321. IRRESISSSS. . . .' He hissed into renewed aphasia.

That was when we learnt it: all charitin preparations were now banned in Queensland.

Queensland is what we call, in Australia, the Deep North.

But we soon found, when we got home, that the effects of the ban were exactly the same here as in the US Deep South.

The Australian birth rate was soaring. And Queensland's rate was topping that of all the other states.

Australia, America . . . and after that the whole world. CHATTERLY and 4321 hit Britain, EROTIQUE and 4321 drove France frantic, CUPIDO and 4321 captivated Italy. Dyer might have been a greater name in Europe than Dior, and all the established perfume houses trembled . . . but quickly their fears were dispelled. Dyer granted licenses on his patents generously, in every country: it seemed his success had been so sudden and overwhelming that he couldn't capitalise on it directly. The result of this policy of his was to spread charitin all over the world as fast as it could be manufactured. For that matter, some countries didn't wait for Dyer's licence. The stuff was not too difficult to synthesise once the formula was published, and of course it had been published as early as the first Australian patent.

Dyer was promptly ripped off, without benefit of royalties, in the USSR, in Mali, Malaysia, Mozambique, Outer Mongolia, and just about every state of the Middle East. The Arab countries especially, with their traditional love of prayer, perfume, and pretty girls (Mohammed's authentic trinity), had soon started up enormous industries. Prayer began to be somewhat neglected in the tents of the Bedouin, but the other two items were flourishing as never before. . . . Dyer made some mild protests: he was rich enough already, of course, but legally he was entitled to be still richer.

In Libya he was promptly denounced as a Western infidel capitalist bourgeois hyena. The USSR stated tersely that Russia did not recognise absolute patent rights anyway. The oil sheiks made apologetic noises, and token payments: unfortunately, they said, it was not easy to police illegal manufacture. . . .

They were right, at that. Once Dyer had shown the world the trick, charitin was as easy to make as LSD. The word 'proliferation' soon took on a new meaning: a more amiable and hilarious one.

But that stage did not last long. About three years after IR-RESISTIBLE hit Australia, people were sniffing, spraying, turning on from Patagonia to the North Pole. No elaborate equipment was needed: nothing more than a cupful of liquid in a gourd, a coconut shell, or the open palm of a hand. The Eskimos had it now, and the last wretched Indians in what remained of the Amazon jungle. And the volatile stuff was now in the air everywhere in tiny but detectable amounts. We were all, all the time, just a little bit in love. . . .

It might have been magnificent. For the first year or two, it looked that way.

The New Hippies, permanently in rut, were shouting louder than in the 'sixties: MAKE LOVE, NOT WAR! And Dyer, who was now just about the most famous (and the richest) man in the world, was preaching the same message on all the media. He was handing out loads of money through his new Charitin Charity Foundation, and all to the nicest causes: Amnesty, Civil Rights, Friends of the Earth, Men of the Trees, Greenpeace—the econuts, the commune dwellers. He had established a bird sanctuary in one corner of his California estate, and when he came on TV he usually came with his pet red cardinal bird on his shoulder. 'Fit-fit-fit-fit-fit you!' said the cardinal bird to the cameras and the world; and Dyer would grin and wiggle those eyebrows of his, and tell us how well his birds were breeding (thanks to charitin) and taking off from his sanctuary to replenish the Earth. . .

Dammit, Dyer was a hero, period. If he had wanted to, he could have founded a new religion, with himself as its Prophet, its Anointed One, its Messiah. If only he had wanted.

But—*dis aliter visum*. That was not how things worked out.

I saw him once more, in the flesh this time, in Brisbane in the fourth year (which some people were now calling blasphemously, 4 A.Dy.).

By then, things had changed.

When he was working in Australia originally, no one had thought him anything more than another ratbag inventor, of which in this country we have plenty. He had never even had a personal appearance on television. But now. . . . This is the typical Australian way. Local boy has to make good Abroad before he can impress anyone here. So now, dozens of people claimed to have been his drinking pals, his backers, and at least two girls implied. . . . But nosy reporters, who ferreted out such folk to get their stories, were distressed to find that their accounts would not stand up under the least bit of cross-checking.

Dyer had been a loner. If he had ever had any close friends, they had not surfaced; he had no brothers or sisters; and both his parents were dead.

And strangest of all, in spite of his fabulous success, he was a loner still. He had flunkeys, but no friends; guards aplenty, but no girls. No girls! When thousands, maybe millions would have given themselves gladly to him, without benefit of any chemical spray. . . . On his Marin County estate, within breakers' roar of the Pacific Ocean, he lived like a hermit behind his barbed-wire fences and his German Shepherd guard dogs.

And now, this time, when he gave his lecture in that Brisbane public hall, he had a ring of bodyguards under the podium, between him and the crowds. The bodyguards were all Americans, apparently, tough silent young men who somehow reminded me of their master himself. These guards were necessary, for the spirit of the audience was not exactly what it might have been one or two years before.

For one thing, there were no women in the hall. Marguerite had to watch our conference on TV from our home. There were now extra locks on every door of our home, and bars on every window.

Rape had become so frequent that now the newspapers had ceased to report it. Male unemployment had been wiped out, as few women dared to go out to work. But industrial relations had never been worse. The workers were so easily distracted . . . to such pastimes as, for instance, sodomy.

Dyer spoke for about half an hour, his eyebrows drawn, his mood grim. He had no pet bird perched on his shoulder now. You would have said, he seemed older. But that must have been just his manner: his forehead, when he did not actively wrinkle it, was as unlined as ever. Alexander the Great, ever young, though conqueror of the world. A young, angry god.

'I thought I would give you a chance,' he ended. 'I *did* give you a chance. Make peace, not love, not war! With just a bit more of native good will, it would have worked. But when a race is fundamentally evil, chemicals will not cure it. Well, the thing is done now. The experiment is over. The attempt has failed. I will now have to try something else.'

As he resumed his seat, a Babel began. There was some

clapping—not much—and rather more booing and catcalls. The wowsers of Queensland had taken over one section of the hall, the reporters another. The Mayor, who was acting as chairman, at last re-established order and the questions began.

Some were purely rhetorical, but he answered even those. No, he did not think he was the Antichrist. A Christian? Not exactly . . . (he paused for the howls of laughter to die down) . . . but the Christian gospel was extremely interesting, He read it every day now. It looked as if Someone had tried before. . . .

A reporter: 'Why do you say you have failed, Mr Dyer? With all your wealth. . . .'

'I don't give a stuff for wealth,' said Dyer. 'I would sell all I have and give to the poor, if that would do any good. But it wouldn't. I have given millions . . . and still it goes on! The massacres, in Cambodia, in Canada. . . .'

'Canada?'

Dyer looked surprised at the reporter's surprise. Then he raised those dark eyebrows of his, and gave a short laugh. 'Oh, yes, I forgot. You don't call it a *massacre* if the victims aren't of your own species. I was referring to the slaughter of the seal pups. The Massacre of the Innocents, which you don't count. As you don't count the whales, in the Pacific.' He was on his feet again, gripping the podium; now he was looking over the heads of the crowd, as if into infinite distance, as if looking, or listening, for far-off unhappy things invisible or inaudible to everyone else.

Another newsman tried to break the tension. He giggled. 'Is it true, Mr Dyer, what we read in *Time* magazine, that your favorite piece of music is the Song of the Humpbacked Whale?'

Dyer looked down at that wretched reporter with a look so terrible that the poor fellow actually staggered, and fell back into his seat.

'Piece? *The* song?' said Dyer. 'You pitiful anthropoid, the Humpbacks are the greatest symphonists this planet has ever known. Thirty minutes they take to get through one theme, and their choirs span a thousand by a thousand miles. I mean, they *did*. They have sung to me Eroicas and Choral Symphonies, as I stood on the shore of San Marin, a music to rival earthquakes and seaquakes and the birthpangs of typhoons. . . . Till last season, that is. This year, there are too few of those mighty musicians left to form a full choir.'

Now we had a yelp from one of our University men, a marine biologist. 'You must be joking, Mr Dyer. Or don't you mean the Grey Whale? Because the Humpbacks don't "sing" that far north. They "sing", as you put it, only in the breeding season, around the Equator. And you surely can't hear them from out of the water and across thirty degrees of latitude. . . .'

'Jesus wept,' said Dyer. 'And I—laugh.'

That was the beginning of Quentin Dyer's Australian tour. And a strange tour it proved to be. . . . Starting in Brisbane was eccentric enough—the great and famous *never* start in Brisbane, they often miss it out altogether; but in Dyer's case this could be explained as sentimentalism: a Brisbane backyard shed was where he had made his great invention. Everyone assumed he would now head for Sydney, the place of his schooldays, and then Melbourne, the place of his birth.

He went neither to Sydney nor to Melbourne. Instead, he and his pack of guards piled into a fleet of hired cars and trucks, and headed west. Into the Outback, the bush, the desert.

Dyer told the press and media that he was going out into the desert, to pray.

Well, the media tried to track him there, and they succeeded for a while; but just about a thousand kilometers inland, in country nearly as dry and red and terrible as the surface of Mars, they finally gave up. Dyer's guards had strict orders: no interviews now. Several reporters got slightly roughed up before the camera crews admitted defeat and headed home to civilisation.

For forty days we heard nothing more. Even scouting planes—Flying Doctors and flying busybodies—could find no trace. And then the convoy suddenly appeared, dusty but otherwise in perfect order, rolling calmly through the suburbs back into Brisbane itself.

Opinion, meanwhile, had been strangely veering in our fair town.

To the solid citizens, before his desert journey Quentin had been Dirty Dyer, the corrupter of the world, the super-porn-peddler. To us liberals, on the other hand, he'd been the hero of our dreams, a sort of cross between Nader and Joan of

Arc and Timothy Leary. But now . . . there were odd winds
of change blowing hot and cold from that silent desert
through all conversations and newspaper columns. One pious
State-government minister actually called on the Lord, in
public, to guide our errant more-or-less native son to repentance; and we liberals didn't know what to think at all. Pray-
ing was not much in our line. . . .

One of my closest friends in Brisbane was Harry Birken-
head, a young historian (of whom more hereafter). Harry
said to me, as we came out of that famous first lecture together, 'Dave, I don't like the sound of all this. There's something damn strange about Dyer, and some time I'd like to find
out what. But right now—I bet you a gallon of gas, he's going
to do a Malcolm Muggeridge on us!'

And, by God, Harry was proved right. When Dyer gave
his parting Press conference at the airport, our worst fears
were realised. He'd ditched us, gone over to the enemy!

'I am renouncing all my patents on this accursed thing,' he
said sorrowfully. 'And I praise and honour this State and its
courageous leaders for banning it. Would to God the whole
world would ban it! This is no time for us to be abandoning
ourselves to the lusts of the flesh. On the contrary, we must
watch, and pray. . . .'

After the sensation had slightly subsided, one of the reporters took him up. 'This *time*, Mr. Dyer? Do you see this time
as a critical period for the world?'

He looked up then at the cameras, and a flash of his old
fire returned. His eyebrows were tremendous. 'It is the time
of the End,' He said; and after that he would say no more.

Well, but it wasn't quite the Time of the End, apparently,
or at least nor near enough to the End to prevent some more
smart business dealings—and some smart chemistry. Back in
California, Quentin for a while became a bit of a joke, a
worldwide amusement. He went around more, especially in
the San Francisco Bay area, but always in a nose-mask—that
same sort of mask which was worn by the workers in his
charitin factories. Quentin was wearing it, he said, to filter
out the filthy traces of aphrodisiac which now wafted on every wind. He wished to keep himself pure for the Day of the
Lord. . . . He went about mostly with the Billy Grahamites
and the Seventh Day Adventists and the Jehovah's Witnesses.
It wasn't quite clear which Christian sect he was converted
to, but he certainly was converted.

And then we found he was still in the perfume business. He flew to Europe to consult with the great fashion-houses which were his subsidiaries, and then—

—Just a couple of weeks later, we learnt that he'd filed a patent in France. The essential chemical was called *puritin*, and the commercial product would be named *Dyer 2100*...

It was a personal deodorant, bland and cleanly sweet-smelling as a cologne. In some countries, it was also sold under the name IMPECCABLE.

It was really the biggest joke of a rather grim year. Women were now going about veiled and chaperoned in all Western countries, when they went about at all. They used charitin, unless they were suicidal, only behind locked doors and barred windows; yet in the open, even without it, they were at risk—because lone men would spray it on *themselves*, with equal effectiveness, and then prowl the streets in priapic condition. The charitin products were being officially banned in country after country, and were being bootlegged in all of those. Crime rates (not just rape rates) were soaring all across the world—and, most terrible of all, so were birth rates. The annual increase of *all* countries was now averaging 5.7 per cent, with rates of nearly 9 per cent in some Third World countries. Death rates were rising too (from murder, mostly), but not nearly fast enough to keep pace.

Even some animal populations which had been dwindling had stopped dwindling. The chimpanzee and the white rhino would clearly not become extinct now, after all. *That stuff* was indeed *in the air*. Gibbons in South-East Asia were becoming a bit of a pest. . . .

And the man responsible for all this, Quentin Dyer, could think of nothing better than to market a nice new *cologne*. . . .

The sheer, smug hypocrisy of the man! In launching *2100* in Paris he stated: 'If worldlings will have their vanities, so be it. Let them try this. It will at least make the Earth a *cleaner* place.'

And in the next breath he announced he would keep his new ingredient secret for as long as possible. The formula wouldn't be published for quite a while, not till the French patent was actually granted, and meanwhile he'd supply the puritin to his factories strictly through his most trusted henchmen. He was determined not to be ripped off again. He needed all the money he could get for Good Causes—like the Bible Societies . . .

A few months later, a sort of hope shot up for about one week, when one researcher claimed that puritin was an *anti*-aphrodisiac. But this hope was soon squashed by the US Food and Drug Authority. They had fallen upon puritin like hawks, to see what new devilry Dyer might be up to—but there was absolutely nothing to it. The stuff was safe, non-toxic, non-everything, and it had no effect on sexuality whatever. Nor (the last gleam of hope) on fertility. They had sprayed it and fed it and injected it into laboratory rats, and the said rats had produced just as many little rats as the untreated control group. . . .

IMPECCABLE, 2100, was nothing but a placebo. It was so silly, so blatant a piece of showy symbolic atonement that it was damn near an insult to the human race. . . .

There were three assassination attempts on Dyer's life, one in Paris, one in New York, and one in San Francisco airport. But each time, those silent young bodyguards reacted with almost supernatural swiftness, and the hero-villain of all our troubles emerged unhurt. I mean, he survived unhurt: after that, he didn't *emerge* at all. He retired into his Marin County fastness, permanently, presumably to listen for the songs of the Humpback whales passing the Equator.

Meanwhile, thanks to mass advertising, sheer curiosity, fashion, and what-have-you, that absurd 2100 began to sell quite well. By Year Six of the Dyer Era, it was the top-selling personal deodorant in most of the developed world.

One little puzzle remained unexplained. Why was the stuff called 2100? It was not quite as obvious as that other product, 4321. 4321 had happened to be the last four figures of charitin's US patent number. But puritin didn't have a patent number as yet; the US patent was still only 'pending'. A *New York Times* reporter put this question to a high executive of the main Dyer company.

'Ah—I'm afraid Mr Dyer hasn't told us,' said the VP. 'It—it has some religious significance, I believe. . . .'

One of Dyer's former sectarian buddies suggested a nice idea. Or at least a more explicit one. The Year 2100 was when Quentin expected the End of the World. . . .

'As a rough estimate. But he's *wrong*,' said the Freak from Berkeley earnestly. 'The Day of the Lord is coming much sooner, you can work it out from the Bible exactly, it's gonna

be in 1997. Quentin—he's a nice guy, he'll be one of the
Saved, but he's too *conservative*. . . .

Marguerite and I were never ones to celebrate the New
Year: we see nothing rational to rejoice at in the mere passing
of time. But last January 1st—when it was still December 31st
over much of the Earth's surface—quite fortuitously we did
give a very small party. We had long owed the Birkenheads a
dinner, and New Year's Day was the first day they could
manage; because Harry and Ginny had been down to Sydney
for Christmas. Ginny had parents there—she is a nice young
girl, the family-loving type; but as for Harry the historian, I
knew he was up to something else.

They came round to our place in their new electric car
(gas was now $9.99 a gallon). They came while it was still
light, with the windows rolled up (the only safe way to
travel). And they brought their baby, little Eva, in a carry-
cot (baby-sitters were an extinct species). And yet, with all
these little inconveniences, they seemed cheerful. Harry especially seemed bubbling over with suppressed excitement.

'Hey, what's up with you?' I asked him, while Marguerite
and Ginny were stowing the baby away in our bedroom.

'Oh, nothing much,' he lied, helping himself to my best
Australian-imitation Scotch. 'Just—things are going well, in
general. Cheers. . . .'

'You must be nuts,' I said. 'What's going well? You don't
mean the SALT talks, by any chance? Or isn't that in your
field of history? SALT III was just then staggering towards obvious breakdown in Geneva. The Russians were suddenly taking an unexpected hard line. No, they would *not* agree to any
limitation on the number of warheads a missile might
carry. . . .

Harry's face saddened perfunctorily, like a man who's
heard of an earthquake in Chile half an hour after winning a
million-dollar sweepstake.

'Yeah, that's bad, Dave.' Then he warmed to the subject;
after all, he'd given a seminar on it last semester. 'You see,
it's like this. The Kremlin are cock-a-hoop over their recent
success in suppressing the sex perfumes in their own territory.
Of course, if you shoot people who smell of the stuff. . . .
Anyway, it's obvious from the whole tone of *Pravda* these
days that they're back on the We-Will-Bury-You syndrome.

The decadent West is decaying fast, while holier-than-thou unholy Russia has got its industries back on their feet—'

'Then why the hell should they want to clobber us with rockets? If we're dying anyway?'

He shrugged. 'Russian logic. . . . Well, maybe they think we'll get desperate and try a first strike while we've got some strength left. . . . Oh, hell, the talks are a load of rubbish anyway. Spy satellites can't check on the composition of warheads, so any treaty they may sign will be just so much toilet paper. Both sides are sure to cheat. . . .'

'*All* sides, you mean,' I said. The Chinese also had a delegation at Geneva; and the Egyptians, and the Iraelis, and . . . I gulped down my whisky. 'My God, what a world we're facing for this next century. I guess I won't be around much after 2000, and I can't say I'm sorry. But our poor kids! Weapons always tend to get used, Harry. And when you mix H-bombs with the sex-spray population explosion. . . .'

He was looking cheerful again. 'We've lived with the Bomb for forty years now. And, you know something? People seem to be getting sensible at last, taking their Pills. *The population explosion is slowing down.*'

'Come on, it's too early for this year's figures. . . .'

'We're getting figures much more often than yearly now,' he said with a touch of professional pride. 'Maybe you guys in Literature haven't been keeping up with telefax and instant census methods? Well, Dave, the trend is definite, and not just in Russia. Things were still bad in the first half of this year, but in the third quarter world average annual growth dropped to 3 per cent. In October it was down to 2, in November to 1. How about that, eh?'

I was staggered. 'What, everywhere?'

'Everywhere we can get data from. Nothing from China, of course, but to judge from the Russian figures. . . . And it's most definite in the developed countries. Dave, in November the US birthrate fell to *just about replacement level!*'

'Whew!' I said. Then I smiled. Then I laughed outright—a thing I had not done for quite a time. 'Well I'll be damned. Harry, bless you—this does call for a celebration, after all!'

Then the ladies joined us, and we all got cheerful together over the wine and the meal. And as we were finishing the dessert, Ginny looked at Harry, with a little laugh.

'And haven't you told them yet—your big news?' she said.

'I thought we already—' I began.

Harry grinned broadly. 'No, Dave. I've been saving this one. . . .' He glanced from me to Marguerite and back again. 'What would you two say if I told you that *Quentin Dyer was dead*?'

The sudden silence was shattered by our timer-alarm. I had placed that on the TV as a five-minute warning before the 7 o'clock news. The thing went on ringing for several more seconds; then Marguerite got up and turned it off, and the TV picture on.

I found my voice. 'You're joking, aren't you?'

'No,' he said.

'Then we'll be hearing all about it in five minutes—'

'No, *no*, Dave.' Harry was triumphant. 'I don't mean that guy in his California castle. Whoever he is! But whoever he is, he's not Quentin Dyer, the Irish-Czech boy who went to that school in Sydney. He—he looks like him, sure, I dug up an old photograph. *But that boy died way back in 1971, at the age of twenty-two!*'

I cross-questioned him, of course; but he had all the facts, and they checked out. Quentin Dyer had perished in a mine accident in Queensland. Harry dug into his wallet, and produced the two pictures: of the schoolboy, of the dead miner. He had been a handsome boy, a handsome young man—and definitely, rather like Him. The miner especially—the resemblance was harrowing.

But it was not perfect. The eyebrows. . . . No.

'Then *who* . . . ?' I whispered.

'God knows,' said Harry. 'These New Australians . . . maybe he was on the run from somebody. Maybe he is a spy. . . .'

Out of the corner of my eye I saw the televised clock jerking its second hand toward the hour. Marguerite went over, and turned up the sound.

After the fanfare, our familiar news-reader looked grave.

'South Africa has placed its nuclear missile system on full alert, following the African Popular Front's capture of Salisbury, Zimbabwe. Massacres of fleeing civilians are reported. In Geneva, the SALT conference has broken up without coming to any decisions. The British Patent Office has announced rejection of the patent application for Mr Quentin Dyer's famous cosmetic 2100. Here now are the details. . . .'

The details which followed were appalling, sickening—and oh, so familiar in this glorious twentieth century. We saw the bodies of raped women and bayonetted children on a roadside in what had once been the land of Rhodesia. Some were black bodies, some were white. But the colour of the blood was always the same.

After that, the rowdy scenes from Geneva were almost comic relief.

The announcer paused. '—and here is a news flash. US Federal agents have attempted to interview Mr Quentin Dyer at his mansion in California, in connection with some technical problems concerning his toilet perparations. They were unable to meet Mr Dyer, however, because. . . .'

—Well, this was the way it happened . . . as the world found out somewhat later.

The convoy of police electrics purred over the Golden Gate bridge, their blazing headlights making fairy silver of the fog ceiling barely ten feet above. Apart from car lights and their cloud-deck reflections, it was black night. There were still cars coming the other way, all through Sausalito—electrics and luxury gas-guzzlers packed with revellers, rich alcohol-drunks and sex-drunks heading for the bright lights of San Fran, even this late. For New Year is a time to celebrate. The world being the way it was, if you didn't celebrate New Year this year, hell, you might never celebrate it again. . . .

The police convoy ignored the speeding drunks, and passed on into the night and fog. In the leading car, the Police Chief was swearing.

'Fuckin' fog cover. The helicopters won't make it. Fuckin' stupid mission altogether. Why'n hell couldn't ya wait till tomorrow? On New Year's Eve, of all nights!'

The FBI man said softly: '*Because* it's New Year's Eve. We know he's holding a party in there for his goons. And if there's fog cover, it works both ways. He won't try to make a bolt for it in that Cessna. If we play it right, we'll be inside before they suspect anything. Our version of the Russkies' 3 a.m. knock, you know.'

'I know it's hard on you, Chief,' said Hildesheimer, the physicist. 'But believe me, this is *urgent*, this is scary. Our Patent Office called me in when they couldn't duplicate the stuff.' He looked quickly at the FBI man and, receiving his nod, continued. 'The British Secret Service was on to us, simultaneously. And a CIA report from Germany has us frightened, too.'

'Of a goddamn cologne? A shaving lotion?' growled the Chief. 'I thought the FDA found it harmless. . . .'

'Oh, it's harmless all right,' said Hildesheimer. 'At least, we think so. It's just the main compound in it—this puritin—it shouldn't exist at all. Dyer's specifications are a fraud—he could only get away with it in a place like France, their patent people aren't like ours. . . . No one can make it, no one can destroy it. The chemists gave up, and called on *me*. They thought it might be something to do with bombs. . . . Well, it doesn't seem to be that. It may be something worse.'

'Worse than bombs? What—'

'I mean the stuff violates known physio-chemical laws. If Dyer can do *that*, we want him. Under wraps. Before anyone else gets to him, you see.'

'I only hope,' said the FBI man, 'that this Dyer isn't Anyone Else himself. We've been checking the ID of those goons he keeps. They're supposed to be good old, I mean good young American citizens. But one or two of them, ah, seem to have *died* already. . . .'

The convoy swung off Highway 101, heading west toward the sea. On the right, somewhere, were those great sequoias which had stood, silent and unmolested, before Columbus, before Leif Ericson, before Christ. But the humans in the cars did not see those trees. They saw very nearly nothing, and heard very nearly nothing, because of the fog and silence of that dark night. The electric cars themselves made very little sound. It was as though the humans, the invaders of the woods, were driving smoothly, peacefully into nonentity.

And then suddenly they topped a rise, and like the parting of a giant veil the fog vanished. By some quirk of meteorology, the sea fog was absent from the sea. A waning moon was rising: in the distance they caught a glint of moonlight on the calm black face of the Pacific. And in the foreground, very close, loomed the wire fences and the main metal gate of Dyer's stronghold.

It was a great relief, to come out of that deathlike silence. Now all would be bright lights and action. Maybe violent action . . . a little of that, too, would be a relief. The cops tumbled out of their warm cars, guns drawn, into the near-freezing moonlight. One in their vanguard hailed the black-walled gate-box. 'Open up there! Open up! Police . . . !'

But there was no answer at all. Not a dog barked, no private guard showed himself. There was no chink of light from that gate-box, no artificial ray anywhere along the fence or beyond it. A hundred, two hundred yards beyond, the wide low bone-white mansion lay inert as a dead whale, half hidden by the eucalyptus of the driveway.

The mansion, too, was lightless.

The Police Chief and the FBI man stared at each other with a wild surmise.

'We'll blast our way in—' began the Police Chief.

Hildesheimer had sidled up to the gate, and touched it with a little instrument. No spark. . . . Now he put his gloved hand to the cold metal, and pushed.

'No need to blast, fellers,' he said. 'It's *open*.'

Within seconds the police cars were whining up the drive; within a few more seconds they were under the porch, and the men were rushing for the front door of the mansion. That too swung open when Hildesheimer pushed.

The interior was as dark and as still as death.

And then, as they paused in the doorway, they heard a full-throated rumbling growl from somewhere outside and beyond the house.

'My God, the plane!' shouted the FBI man.

They scrambled back into their vehicles, and this time the cars did not purr or whine. Their auxiliary motors roared, for this was a dire emergency and they used the hot-pursuit rocket boosters. They left all driveways behind and bounced, half airborne, over rutted dirt trails and open grassland. It was all open grassland now. . . .

'Shit, where's the goddamn copters?' screamed the Police Chief.

He was answered immediately. Two choppers came chopping out of the inland fog-bank, and circled the tiny airfield. Oh, glory! They were not too late, for there in the midst sat the little plane yet, after all. No executive jet, it could hardly be big enough for Dyer and all his henchmen. But it had its lights on, its motor apparently humming. . . .

The helicopters opened fire.

'Fools, *fools*!' yelled Hildesheimer. 'Chief, get 'em on your radio, stop them! We've got to get him alive!'

As he was yet speaking, the little Cessna exploded into flames and fragments. The police, deployed now around half the perimeter of the field, leapt from their cars, ready to attempt a rescue as soon as it was safe to do so. That would be *now*, for the copters had ceased fire, they were moving off. . . .

And then from beyond the flaming ruin of the Cessna, a great squat shape rose seemingly out of the ground. It rose on a tail of blue fire, and accelerated vertically—accelerated incredibly. As Hildesheimer watched open-mouthed, it was a thousand feet up, far higher than the copters, and still rising, inclining now away from the vertical toward the north-west.

'A VTOL,' said the FBI man bitterly. 'The goddamn bastards, a vertical jet hidden in a pit. The Cessna was just a decoy. . . . They were tipped off, of course, they had us beat from the start. And now I guess they're on their way to Moscow.'

'I'm not so sure they're going to Moscow,' said Hildesheimer.

On the way back to the mansion, the others heard him muttering, '20g, 30g. . . .'

When they entered the mansion and turned on the lights, they found the place neat and clean—and as empty as a mausoleum. It was all very tidy. There was just one loose scrap of paper—a typed note on the big bare desk in Dyer's study.

WE TOOK THE DOGS, said the note. WE ARE FOND OF ANIMALS.

The first week of January in that Year Seven of the 'Dyer' era was a strange, tense, uneasy time in Brisbane, as elsewhere. The reports from California were not nearly so clear yet as I have just set them down. We only 'knew' that He had decamped, or defected, in some sort of private jet plane for a destination unknown.

The world was buzzing with peculiar but unsubstantiated rumours. There was a sort of hysteria everywhere. . . . In downtown Brisbane I saw cultists parading with placards: BEHOLD, HE COMETH, and AND EVERY EYE SHALL SEE HIM. I don't think the cultists were referring to 'Dyer,' though. I think they meant someone else.

The nuclear war in South Africa had not broken out, not yet, after all. The blacks and the whites were facing each other across their frontier; but they were not moving. There were lulls also, apparently, in the guerrilla wars in Ireland, the Middle East, and Central America. There was a curious dearth of real news in the newspapers.

It was as if the whole world was holding its breath.

Oh, there were small things. One British biologist claimed to have found a useful fertility-inhibitor by working with rhesus monkeys. If you gave them massive inhalations of *both* charitin and puritin, they acted very randy, but they produced 5 per cent fewer offspring than the control group. This Dr Ramsbotham suggested that the effect might work with humans too, and might even be of use in combating the population explosion. The cartoonists seized on this idea with glee. The *Courier-Mail* editorial commented drily that a more effective, and cheaper, treatment would be to employ the standard contraceptives such as the Pills, male or female, or even the simple old sheath. . . .

Flying saucer reports were booming. Australia had a specially grand crop. A huge 'mother ship' was reported rising up-and-away near Alice Springs, in the dead centre of the Dead Centre. . . . But people always see more flying saucers in times of stress. NASA and the other space agencies issued a few weary denials; but the saucerites riposted that, nowadays, since the economic crisis of the 'seventies, we had so little hardware in space that we couldn't hope to detect the saucers once they were well out. . . .

And so it went.

Harry and Ginny invited us round for drinks at their place for Twelfth Night. Then we found we weren't certain when Twelfth Night was. I thought it was the 6th, Harry said the 5th, and then he proved he was technically right, the 6th was the day beyond Christmas, the feast of the Epiphany; but the 6th was more convenient, and would do, since it would still be Twelfth Night, the last day of Christmas, round half the world.

'And by then,' said Harry on the phone, 'I may have some *real* news for you, Dave. I know a chap or two in Government, and I've sent in *my* little report on Dyer to very high circles indeed, so. . . . Well, you may be surprised.'

That evening of the 6th I was bloody restless, looking at my watch, waiting for it to be time to go. It was a long, hot summer afternoon. . . . Marguerite was taking things much more calmly, sitting in our front room, working away at a crossword.

'Come on,' I said, 'they asked us for 6, and you know it takes longer in this new damned electric—'

'I've just got one more to do,' she said, smiling and looking up. ''s blank N blank RGY. the clue is, "When two get together, this is often the startling result".'

'SEX ORGY,' I said impatiently. 'Now, will you—'

'It's an N, not an X. And it's all one word. But all right, I can leave that till after. . . .'

When we reached the Birkenheads', I was a little surprised that Harry didn't come rushing to greet us, as was his usual habit. Nor was there any mood-creating music floating out of the front windows. We had to ring the bell. And then, after about a minute, Ginny opened the door to us.

Marguerite uttered a cry. 'Oh, my dear, what's the matter?'

Ginny was deadly pale, but her eyes were red. 'H-Harry. . . .' she stammered. Then she gulped, and took control of herself. 'No, he's not ill, and—and little Eva's all right, too. But—'

Then Harry staggered into the living room himself. From the depths of the house, we heard the baby's wail.

'Come in, come righ' in,' said Harry, flourishing a half-empty whisky bottle. 'Join the party, you two. . . .'

I tried to get things onto a more comfortable level. I laughed. 'I see you've started without us, Harry. OK, I'll have a whisky, and Marguerite would like a weak one of the same. . . . And now, Harry, what's the news of the world?'

He put down the whisky bottle. 'Do you really want to know?' He sounded suddenly a lot more sober.

'Of course I want to know,' I said.

'I've got the world birth-rate figures for December,' he said.

'Well? What are they? Terrible? Right up again . . . ?'

'There were no births in December,' he said.

'No what—where?' I laughed, and shook my head. 'Sorry, I didn't quite get you.'

'I said there *were no births in December*,' he repeated, very clear, very loud and getting louder. 'No births nowhere, *nada, nichts, niente*, fuck-bloody-all, anywhere in the fucking—but not procreating—*world*!"

'Darling,' said Ginny, reaching out her arms, clasping him, 'don't, don't. There must be some silly mistake. It's just not possible.'

'You must be joking,' I said; but already I knew he was not. Harry never used bad language before women.

'If you think I'm joking,' he said, 'try ringing up the Queensland Census. No, don't bother, because they won't tell you. All round the world, the census guys are sitting on this secret, keeping it from the average man. Because they don't trust the average man not to go berserk. But still, it's leaking out. The census workers themselves. . . . Have you wondered why there's a sort of madness in the air? It's leaking out, I tell you. I give it one day more, or two at most, before it breaks, and then—God help us—'

Harry was right in a way, but it took less time than even he had reckoned. Because the next moment his big TV set in the living room came on.

It came on, I mean, nice and bright and clear, without having been switched on. More than that: the lead was lying loose on the floor, the set was unplugged.

And on the big, twenty-five-inch screen, we saw the face of—

—But I needn't tell you. For that matter, a good half of you saw him too. At the beginning of that broadcast he was dressed, you might say, normally, in an elegant dark suit which matched those dark eyebrows of his, and his dark hair. He was as young and handsome as when Marguerite and I first saw him. Alexander the Great, Augustus . . . with a plain background of sky-blue radiance.

But his expression, his eyes, his brows held no radiance. Not menace either, nor anger, nor threatenings. Just—finality.

'This is my last message to you, people of the planet Earth,' he said. 'You are all hearing me, every one of you, in your own language, for we have skill enough for that. Our skills are not what you call magic, but they are so far in advance of anything you can do, I am glad to say, that they may seem to you magical.

'Where we come from matters not greatly. It is a far world, whose sun you can barely see in your sky on a clear night. Some of you have had inklings before that we were among you. Until recently, those inklings were false guesses, provoked mainly by your own guilt and fear and longing for peace. But at last we came, we saw, and indeed we decided to give your world peace.

'We are not a cruel people. We think it most terrible to

take the life of any living soul—any fish, any bird, any beast, any anthropoid. We know that *you* think otherwise, and do otherwise; and we have heard the cries of your victims on the land, in the air, in the sea. Those creatures, great and small, which are dumb to you their torturers, are eloquent enough to us. The noble giants of your deeps, especially, have cried out to us to save them: and we have answered their prayer.

'We have indeed, in our wanderings among the stars, sometimes met races with a little of your temperament. And we treated those races—as we tried to treat you—and in all cases, we cured them. Only in this one case have we failed. But then, we never before met with quite such a degree of egotism, speciesism, and general rooted evil.

'This evil we have decided to end. *You* must end. But we are not cruel; it is abhorrent to us to kill, and we shall not kill. We even wish you well, we wish you peace in the time that is left to you.'

(—'He's mad—it's all a fake—a joke—!' cried Ginny.)

'Now to be blunt,' said the young and dreadful god in the business suit. 'The mechanism is this, which you will soon verify. The two compounds *charitin* and *puritin* are separately harmless, but they combine readily even in the greatest dilution: they seek each other out, and then their combined molecule is indestructible by any process you can discover in a million years. The combined molecule, *puri-chartin*, will permeate any and all of your barriers, even those of rock or metal a thousand feet thick. It has already permeated all your nuclear warheads—and rendered them inactive. It has rendered inactive all your other most horrible devices of death: napalm, nerve gases. . . . I need not give you a list, you will find out. We have given you indeed peace. Peace in your time.'

Ginny began to laugh hysterically with half-incredulous relief. Marguerite clutched my arm and whispered: 'Oh David, if only that's true!'

'I said, in your time,' that calm voice resumed. 'But that time will not be over-long, as the times of a planet go. Another effect of *puri-chartin* is that it sterilises, permanently, both sexes and all ages of the genus *Homo*. It has no such effect on any other genus on your planet, except for very mild depressions of fertility in your nearest relatives, the anthropoid primates. We are confident that all the ape and monkey species which you have not already killed off will survive. But you, you humans, will not. The effects are irresistible, and irreversible already: if by any stroke of ingenuity you could seal off some of you in a pure oxygen vehicle, and depart for your Moon or Mars, those colonies would still be sterile. And on Earth—no human babies have been born since the 28th day of November last year. And none will be born ever again.

'You are sterile, but that does not mean you are impotent. On the contrary, you may now have sex to your heart's content, with no fear of one kind of consequence. Your population peaked at a disgustingly high figure in November of last year; but that trouble will soon cure itself.

'It remains for us to say, without malice, farewell. But before we end this manifestation, to clear any doubts in your minds that this may be merely some kind of hoax, we will show you one thing more. Up to now, I and my followers have worn always a disguise—we have appeared, for obvious reasons, as humans. Not it is time to remove the mask.'

The TV picture dissolved, changed. And then, we all four screamed. Ginny and Harry went on screaming for some time, but Marguerite and I checked ourselves more quickly. After all, we two had read certain works of science fiction; and for several minutes now we had been expecting something like this.

'Dyer' was no longer handsome in any human way. He had small curly horns, his huge eyes were fiery red, and he wore a long red robe. The background was obiously some sort of fantastic spaceship; before the back wall of that cabin stood a line of henchmen, or rather hench-devils, in long robes of many colours. There was just one homely (and very incongruous) touch: two or three of the background devils were petting a couple of German Shepherd dogs. The dogs were wagging their tails, bounding about, trying to lick the horned figures. They were obviously very happy.

And then a little red bird flew into the picture and alighted on His red-robed shoulder. It looked straight at us.

'Fit-fit-fit-fit-*fit* you,' said the bird.

'Goobye,' said Lucifer-Dyer softly. 'And may there be peace on earth to all men of the slightest good will. We are sorry about such ones, but believe me, there was no other remedy. At least, you will not suffer."

And then the miraculous broadcast was over, and the screen went dead.

We four sat very quiet for a while. Then litle Eva, the Birkenheads' baby cried softly from the bedroom.

'Oh Christ,' said Harry suddenly. 'Now I know why He called that stuff *2100*. Approximately—oh Christ. . . .'

I had got it too, in the same second that he did. Little Eva was six months old now—she had been conceived just in time, just before IMPECCABLE/2100 had begun to flood the markets, and the atmosphere.

With the greatest possible luck, a human being does not live beyond the age of about 115.

With the greatest of luck, little Eva could live to be the last woman on Earth.

Marguerite and I looked at each other. I knew what she was thinking.

Thank God, we were already a good deal too old for that sort of luck.